# The Entitlement

By
**Petra Croft**

# About the Author

Petra Croft writes extensively in other genres and is the pen name for this saga of period literature. She has an interest and knowledge of this circa of British life – the 1800s. **The Preference** was inspired by private family diaries. She lives and works in the U.K.


**'The Entitlement,"** is a follow up to the first book **'The Preference'** – available now.

The next in the series, **'Briar Lodge'** by Petra Croft, is due to be out soon.

# About the Book

Melissa and Anthony have a highly quirky relationship, maybe erotic, maybe just dysfunctional. Perhaps because he taught her languages at a younger age... Perhaps not! Perhaps simply because it is in their natures to be that way.

Melanie is her closest friend. And her historic acrimony towards Melissa's husband doesn't lessen with time. It's a source of fascination as well as a source of irritation to her that Melissa ever married him.

**The Entitlement** follows on from the first novel – **The Preference –** where it all began.

Witty, funny, erotically charged, timeless in its emotional by-play, the book is written with irony and insight, and is a delightful journey into an era of double standards, sexual tension and changing values.

* * *

It's the 1850's attitudes were very different towards love, sex, marriage, what is to be resisted, and what is not. The Victorians were renowned for many things: philanthropy, parks, museums, industry, social reform... and also for being 'uptight,' 'upright,' and for 'stringent moral values,' and at the same time 'double standards.'

The fascination for me as an author was to explore, from chronicled journals, some of those values and bring the memories of real people to life. Using the 'author's license' and imagination around dialogue and narrative, but keeping to the main details and story.

The attitudes of most people nowadays have changed considerably, in most places, but the dilemmas and concerns have not. The quest for security, power, validation of feelings, and sincerity of intent remains at the heart of nearly all relationships and close bonds.

Beyond that, readers, like others, are free to make of things what they will. But to most of enjoy.

# Contents

# Prior to Christmas – 1852

# Land with No Name

"What are you looking at?" Melissa Fairchild sipped the last of her tea and looked at Melanie Gillis, who was staring over the tea shop at someone on another table. "There is a woman over there staring over at you, I think... not me." Melanie gazed purposely in the opposite direction. "See, with the three other women, all with those turban things that are so à la mode... inappropriate for a tea room at this hour."

Melissa turned sharply.

"Don't look right now," said Melanie. "'Tis most vulgar!"

Melissa moved her vision to a far wall, away from the table in question, and then slowly swivelled it to where Melanie was indicating subtly with her teaspoon below the table.

Melissa gasped and exhaled with annoyance.

"Do you know her?"

"Caroline Wentworth, I believe..." She barely moved her lips as she imparted the information and looked again fastidiously at the far wall, which held nothing of any interest.

"What? The mistress of your brother-in-law?" queried Melanie, now herself unable to resist gazing over at the infamous Caroline Wentworth.

"The very same... don't stare at her, Mel... she will come over and it may get back to Anthony."

"Oh phooey!" said Melanie. "I have heard so much of her... I would adore the opportunity to meet her."

"So might I," replied Melissa, through a mouthful of marble cake. "But if he finds out he will be mortified and accuse me of encouraging her... He has forbidden me to have contact with her."

"Good God!" expostulated her closest friend. "As if you care tuppence for that!"

"Well, I do," said Melissa. "At least when he may find out."

"Too late... I do believe she is coming our way."

Lady Caroline Wentworth (so called) sallied forth across the tea room in her blue silk day dress, her fan and reticule dangling from either wrist. She looked, Melanie perceived, like a character from a French farce. Melanie met her gaze first and smiled. Lady Caroline smiled and nodded, and turned at once to the other girl. "'Tis Mrs Fairchild, is it not?... Melissa? Richard's sister-in-law!"

Melissa smiled upwards at Caroline. "It is, yes..." She raised her brows as if she were at a loss.

"You must remember me..." said Lady Caroline, seating herself in the third chair without invitation, arranging her voluminous skirts about her with scarcely a hesitation in movement. "We met briefly at your wedding... Richard brought me, though Anthony had not invited us, if you recall."

"I do," said Melissa, and was taken aback by this direct admission of a snub, as if it were not at all unusual or highly awkward.

"He could not say anything about our appearance, of course... t'would have looked churlish and indelicate... their mother was present... as were most of their relatives..."

"Yes, yes..." said Melissa with some brusqueness. "I was actually in attendance myself... as the bride."

Caroline trilled a light laugh, so falsetto in tone it threatened to crack the mirror on the wall behind. "Of course you were, my dear... and how delightful you looked on the day..."

Melissa gave no comment, frozen with uncertainty as to what to say.

"Did she not!" agreed Melanie, and she smiled unctuously at Lady Caroline. Melissa kicked her under the table. She was courting trouble before Melissa had decided whether she actually wanted it, or what to do about it if she did not.

"I felt I had to come and say good afternoon..." Caroline continued in her artful way, "It would have been rude of me not to..."

"But I would not have known," said Melissa coolly, and Melanie kicked *her* this time. The remark was almost rude, in keeping with some of Melissa's worst remarks when unnerved.

"Well, I am here now..." said Lady Wentworth, somewhat offended at not being recognised from a short distance, and her smile faded on her painted features – which left to their natural state were dour and uninviting. She was fifty five, and admitted only to thirty five. Unrealistic unless in very low lighting. "I expect that husband of yours does not wish you to speak to me... as well as his poor brother?"

Melisssa cleared her throat. "That is somewhat true..." she said. Though how it could be only *'somewhat'* true was beyond understanding. The requisite smile had returned to Caroline's face. "I hear you are an accomplished artist..."

"She is," said Melanie, who felt that self-praise was not called for in this situation. "She is simply superb..."

"I wouldn't go that far..." said Melissa.

"No but others might..." persevered Melanie, "on your behalf."

Lady Caroline smiled at them both, her eyes betraying her underlying contempt should anyone bother to look closely into them. "'Tis about that I wish to speak... your art!... I wonder could I come and call on you? I wish to have a painting... a particular painting made... to be done in just a certain style..."

"No, no..." said Melissa, and thought of her husband's fury if he found Lady Wentworth in their drawing room. Not just his mild anger or irritation but his fury. "What I mean is... I think..."

"What you mean is you do not think your husband would allow it!" The woman's smile feigned ingenuousness, with a little remorse mixed into it, as if she had long since adjusted to this cruel rebuff from Richard's relative.

"Yes..." Melanie said, again on Melissa's behalf." That is what she means."

Caroline paused for a second and watched Melissa, whom she believed was not yet brave enough – or clever enough – to try outwitting Anthony Fairchild; he of strong principles and even stronger inclinations to being the man of the house, no doubt. "Then perhaps you might call on me instead?..." said Caroline lightly with the kind of outrageous presumption that had carried her through life to date.

Melissa gaped at her disbelievingly and opened and closed her lips. "We could then arrange for the said painting to be commissioned... I would pay you handsomely..." cajoled Caroline. "And he does not have to know... Tony Fairchild... your husband!..."

"Yes, yes... I do know my husband's name," said Melissa, with the ironic tone she felt was needed when forced into society and the pressure extant within these occasions.

"Would Wednesday next suit?" pursued Lady Wentworth.

"Well, I do not know," said Melissa, "I have not agreed to it yet..."

"I could bring her..." offered Melanie and received the inevitable kick beneath the table.

"I expect you could," said Melissa with an arch abhorrence that most people would find off-putting. But Lady Wentworth was not most people. She looked winningly at Melanie Gillis, whom she surmised often spoke for Melissa Fairchild as her unofficial woman of affairs or mentor... or some such. "Thursday is also a likely day... either day would suit," said the lady next

"I am sure it would," said Melissa, regaining her composure. "But it would not suit me..."

"I would pay you whatever you asked..." Lady Wentworth leaned across the table slightly and lowered her voice and spoke directly into Melissa's averted face, "and other people I know would want your services, having seen the finished work, I am sure..."

"Services!" echoed Melissa, diminished, she thought, to the level of a laundry maid.

"Talents..." amended Caroline swiftly. "They would all want your artwork in their houses... at least a good many would. Richard and I have considerable influence in places! Amongst people who can afford to pay you generously."

"I do not need money..." Melissa asserted, because it was true, whilst all the while the thought of earning money from her expertise was pulling her.

"Perhaps not at present... but one never knows when one might need it... every lady should have a little put away... and not be totally reliant upon their husband." Caroline rose, with the same swift tidying of self and attire as when she first sat. "And think of how much more renown you would become as an artist..."

Melissa took in an exasperated breath and then sighed. "You are appealing to my vanity now, Lady Wentworth..."

"Caroline, please!... and not so much your vanity, my dear, as the pride you have in your work... your gift."

Melissa felt as if a great rush of air – like from a cave beside a waterfall – was drawing her backward to a place she longed to see. As if a force of some kind was holding her even as it moved her. She was speechless. She regarded the older woman and thought about her expertise as an artist – it was the main thing in her life that compelled her, apart from her desire for Anthony Fairchild.

"I shall bring her on Thursday..." affirmed Melanie into the chasm of rushing wind and waterfalls which assailed her best friend, and thinking that the interchange may go around in circles forever. "I shall bring her in my carriage..."

Melissa looked at Melanie and opened her lips to object, but then found her tongue would not obey her intent. Meanwhile, Caroline took her card from her reticule and handed it to Melanie whom she felt would sort things out efficiently. "It is settled then... I shall see you on Thursday. between two and four?... " Within a minute she was back at her own table, discoursing again with her companions.

"What did you say that for?" demanded Melissa. "I never encountered anything so audacious in my life.... why did you agree to it?"

"Because it will be diverting..." said Melanie, "and we need to always have some fun... we agreed that before we both wed."

"It will not be fun if Anthony finds out... which he will, I am sure."

"Phooey..." declared Melanie. "It will then be more fun... you surely don't deny that!"

"Well, I do deny it..." said Melissa indignantly, aware of not being entirely honest with either herself or Melanie. And she called for the bill.

* * *

Their new home was small, next to her family home at 'High Lawns,' but she enjoyed it immensely. She would enjoy living anywhere with him.

She went immediately and sat in the drawing room and bit her thumbnail nail and thought of what she had done. If he discovered what they had planned, she would need to be in the mood for running. He would pursue her, but she would run. He might catch her, but really the odds were even. She sipped a cup of hot chocolate and thought of him and herself in close proximity, in intimate and sensual positions, in the large bed they shared. The dangers of the afternoon were as nothing next to the thoughts of he and she making love. Of sharing erotic games. Of never-to-be-agreed-upon reasons underlying those games. The level beneath. A foreign land with no name. A haven with no defined entrance or exit. Very few people were so fortunate. Perhaps very few were so inclined or so tenacious. Although perhaps those who were did not speak of it openly, like themselves. So the exact numbers remained unknown.

* * *

In Caroline's abode - the one she sometimes shared with Richard Fairchild - she reclined on the chaise longue, her feet resting on its curved elevated high end. She watched Richard enter, his shoulders and upper back rather stooped and becoming more so with each year, as a result of all his leaning over money ledgers and vital documents, with very little exercise elsewhere. So unlike his youngest brother in face and form as to be positively unrelated.

She watched his face to gauge his mood. Then he crossed to the decanter of whisky and poured a glass of it, and looked at her. "Well, did you see her?"

"I did... her friend is bringing her here on Thursday... she won't allow me to go there."

"Of course!" said Richard and exhaled enthusiastically, having swallowed the first mouthful of the liquor.

"He is not to find out... he is still forbidding her your proximity."

"Of course," said Richard again and smiled widely. "How very satisfying... and of course, he will find out. I shall see to it."

"You are such a troublemaker Dickie..." said Caroline with indifference. "And she is a good little wife... one can see that..."

"Of course..." Richard agreed.

"Stop saying 'of course' to everything," Caroline snapped. "You are sounding like a clockwork budgerigar..."

Richard snuffed laughter as he lit a cigar - not the kind his younger brother smoked, but a longer and more expensive variety. "You have done well... I doubted you could do it."

"'Tis not done yet... so do not congratulate me now. She may well change her mind."

"Have you offered her enough remuneration?"

"I have not set a fee... but I have intimated that a generous fee is to be had..." Caroline stretched herself out more on the chaise longue. "And be assured, 'tis the only thing I am coercing her to... I will not corrupt her into any other of your ruses. You know I like your brother... and therefore his little wife too."

"Of course." Richard said despite himself, consumed by his own envy. "Though why you like him, defies my understanding."

"You have just said it again..." she raised her head and glared at him. "Are you doing it on purpose to vex me?"

Not receiving a reply, she extended her left leg. "And when you have done quaffing that, massage my feet for me... they are aching with all the walking today."

"Anything else you would have me do?" asked Richard. "Besides altering my mode of speech and rubbing your feet!" He took hold of her left foot and perched on the end of the chaise longue to oblige her. She put back her head and closed her eyes and luxuriated for a few moments, until he raised her foot and sank his teeth into her big toe.

"Bastard!" said Caroline, lamenting the ceasing of the foot massage.

* * *

"So what are we to do about Honoria?" Melissa said to Anthony at dinner. Honoria was her only female cousin, amid a plentiful number of male cousins, and therefore she cherished her somewhat, even at a distance.

Anthony Fairchild raised his face from papers he was scanning, both of them prone to reading at the dining table when alone, both engrossed in their separate pursuits. Though it had surprised her, this deviation from his usual code of manners once they were wed.

She was flicking through an art journal and he was scrutinising a German dictionary for suitable translation to a word he could not rightly interpret. He was a linguist and had a thriving enterprise nowadays with his close friend and associate, Timothy Trimingham. A far cry from when she first encountered him – as a lowly schoolmaster.

"Honoria?" he repeated. "Honoria who?"

"My cousin," she replied with asperity. "We discussed her only yesterday at breakfast..."

"Oh yes." He recalled the vagaries until they became clearer. "Well, we leave her be."

"What?... I thought we had agreed to rescue her..."

"We had agreed no such thing, Melissa. You suggested it and enthused... and I rejected the idea... "

"You poo-pooed it... which is not quite the same."

"Then I am doing so now." He closed his dictionary with a snap and looked at her. They adored each other's looks, their physical attributes, their sensual excursions. "We cannot go about interfering in other people's lives and domestic arrangements."

"She is my cousin."

"I am aware... you have told me five times at least."

"She needs rescuing... she needs our help... she needs -"

"Has she said this to you?" he interjected. "Has she actually appealed to you for rescue or help?"

"No... but she laments her cruel fate..."

"Do not begin speaking like someone from a novel," he said. "It irritates me beyond measure."

She opened her journal again and thought how next to proceed. It was preferable to thinking how to broach the subject of Caroline Wentworth's offer, or whether to broach it at all. Or if it might just be something she blurted out under the tension of keeping it secret.

Her cousin Honoria was a better subject matter. She lived with her parents – her mother being her own mother's younger sister – as an only child, and was virtually forbidden the outside world.

It took little to keep someone like Honoria captive, it was done simply by depriving her of lack of accessible opportunity or alternative, or money. She was virtually a prisoner. Her parents no doubt assuring themselves of having her to look after them in their increasing old age. Honoria was now twenty four and had never had a beau or a suitor... or, God forbid, a lover.

"I think we should interfere..." she persisted. "We should call on her... then invite her to stay with us..."

He looked at his young wife and composed his face as he thought of words. He was disposed to grin, but tightened his jaw to prevent it. Amusement shown now would change the mood, but would not see the subject dispensed with. "Invite her to stay here? What on earth for?"

"So she can acquire some freedom of course... and I can take her to various places... afternoon tea and art galleries and for lunch with Melanie and I and to visit friends... and she can become accustomed to life in the world. How would you like to be caged like an animal?"

"I doubt she is caged like an animal, Melissa... I doubt it greatly."

"No, but you know what I mean!"

He picked up his cigars and selected one – another of his strict personal conduct rules relinquished when dining alone with her. He regarded her with his light and opaque green eyes. His blonde hair was longer again in style, with side locks which fronted his ears, in keeping with the current fad for male facial hair. Though he had so far resisted the urge to grow a moustache or beard.

She reached over and curled a tendril of his hair around her finger.

"You will not persuade me with that," he told her, even while he knew that she might.

A visit from Honoria was not the most inconvenient thing in life. But he was not, *definitely not,* agreeing to some kind of invasion into the home of her aunt and uncle. He was not going there with her on some bombastic and foolhardy mission. He had only met them once – at his wedding – and it was to be said that they were indeed strange people. And that Honoria could not benefit from being their child. But he was not interfering, and he was not allowing her to do so in any unconventional or shocking way, beyond an invite for a night or two.

"Let us go upstairs..." suggested Melissa next, her fingers in his hair and his fingers on the softness of her throat. Her solution to most dilemmas and conflict was to take the matter into the bedroom. He was aware of it and knew how to negotiate the territory.

# Tentative Steps and Tight Corners

Melanie's small phaeton struggled around tight bends and ruggedly untended roads in some nether region they were unfamiliar with. Melanie was driving – she loved driving, and riding – but even she was beginning to show concern. "Where the hell is the place?" she opined, and Melissa scanned the map once more. It was handwritten by Melanie and therefore not that reliable; a good driver she may have been, but a cartographer she was not.

"It should be a left turn just ahead... but your scale is dreadful."

"At this rate one of the horses may shed a shoe..." said Melanie. If her own husband found out she was attempting this hazardous venture he would be very displeased. She had refused the groom, who could not be trusted to remain discreet about where they had been.

Melissa held the map this way and the other, close to her face, then said. "I need not remind you, I am sure, that this was your idea... this foolhardy venture."

"Oh look..." cried Melanie in a childish gleeful way. "There is the sign... just ahead... 'Golden Oaks'... is that not it?..."

"From Caroline's card it looks to be..." agreed Melissa.

"What a very pretentious title the house has..."

"According to Anthony, they are very pretentious people..."

They drove along a short driveway which was scarcely better tended than the lanes leading to it.

A shoddy looking boy emerged from the side of the building and awaited them alighting from the conveyance. He was some kind of groom, no doubt, but he looked more like a farm hand. He tugged at his frontal hair, which badly needed a wash and brush. "Take your carriage, ladies?" he volunteered.

"Take it where?" enquired Melanie, uncertainly. He chose to ignore the question, thinking it a witticism, and indicated the dilapidated stone steps to the left and then drove the trap at an unnecessarily high speed to somewhere behind the house.

The two young women stared at each other and Melissa sighed in exasperation. "Now what have we done?"

"We have merely accepted a gracious invite from people who most likely are not as affluent as our own families."

Melissa was disposed to giggling, but she strode to the steps and mounted them and looked about for the bell. Melanie ran exuberantly to catch her up and then slowed and acquired the right poise for the occasion.

The bell was positioned in the centre of the door's overhang which in turn was beneath the peeling plasterwork of the upper section of the porch. Melanie pulled on it and it rang out with a metallic clanging sound, emulating a blacksmith's anvil rather than a bell. Rusty and desperate and altogether jarring on the nerves.

Presently a maid opened the door and peered at them. She was ancient and ill clad, like the groom. "Yes?" she said in an unwelcoming manner.

"We are here to see Lady Caroline." announced Melissa. "We are expected..."

The servant said nothing but turned away and shuffled in badly fitting shoes towards the inner hall which was dark and poorly lit and unappealing, eventually turning again and beckoning them in. As if words were in short supply and not to be wasted.

They followed and looked about them. "What an odd sort of maid," opined Melanie. "And an even more depressing abode..."

Melissa felt herself again inclined to merriment. She retrieved her kerchief from the sleeve of her pelisse and made a taught mouth and raised her brows. "Do not make me giggle, Mel!..."

"I have said nothing to do so..." replied Melanie, her own amusement not far away.

And then Carolone appeared from a door at the far end of the hallway. Dressed in a dark purple day dress with a faded ermine wrap about her upper body. She had on her head a gaudy piece of taffeta in the same colour as her dress, with gold threads woven into it. Her neck jewels sparked in the dim lights, all manner of stones and gems of differing hues strewn from golden chains. She was like someone seen in depictions of Vienna in its heyday. "Ah... the young ladies... how good of you to come."

"We had some difficulty finding you," said Melissa. "So out of the way is your home..."

"Yes... 'tis rather..." agreed Caroline. "But very secluded and private... and with beautiful scenery... which is what Richard and I both like."

They followed her to the large drawing room – agreeably more well set up and decorated than the hall. Ostentatious and lavishly furnished with cushions and rugs and furs and paintings in garish colours from artists Melissa did not recognise; the room also looked as if it had emerged from Vienna in the last century. The place boasted faded grandeur as though it were all the rage.

They exchanged glances and immediately looked away from each other – the comedy of where they had landed was about to overtake them. Tea was brought by the aged maid, who scowled at them as interlopers and not guests.

"You have forgotten the dainties, Miriam..." scolded Lady Wentworth and the maid scowled more deeply. "I am so sorry..." Caroline said to the girls as Miriam hobbled out. "She is very old now... but Richard and I feel we must allow her to stay... for where else would she go?"

Melissa took a breath. "My father makes provision for all our aged staff..." she said proudly. "He upkeeps a house where they retire to and support each other, with some younger help if they so wish..."

"I am sure he does!" replied Caroline in a tone which could be read many ways; the wealth of the Shaw family should not be under-estimated.

Caroline poured the tea, and Miriam returned with a plate of fancies on a silver tiered stand.

"We must not tarry long..." said Melanie.

"No indeed..." echoed Melissa. "Perhaps you should begin outlining your art needs?"

Caroline looked at them both in turn, her grave expression concealing an intelligent amusement, but not quite well enough, so that smug self satisfaction lurked around her face. Her mouth was pushed into a perusing expression, surrounded by the etched fine lines which powder could not conceal. Her exact age was the most closely guarded secret of Richard Fairchild's portfolio. "Let us at least take a few sips of tea..." she admonished. "Lars!... you have only just arrived."

"I know, Lady Caroline, but we have been an age in getting here... and Melanie must return to attend to Robert!" said Melissa.

"Caroline, please!... call me Caroline... or Caro if you prefer..." said Lady Wentworth. "And who is Robert?"

"My son," said Melanie. "He is eleven months old."

"Aaah..." mewed Caroline in a softening and false way whilst pouring the tea – she took less interest in children than in Miriam's plight of old age. "How adorable." Replacing the tea pot on its holder she indicated the silver cake stand and said. "I will fetch the sketch I have of the painting I require..."

They sipped their tea and did not exchange glances for fear of renewed hilarity, and then Melanie took two fancy shortbreads and stuffed one into her mouth whole and chewed it swiftly. Melissa giggled. "Anthony once told me they were both caricatures..." she whispered into Melanie's ear. "And he was right... judging by Lady Vulture..."

"Lady who?" Melanie coughed as pieces of the biscuit refused to leave her throat.

"That is what he calls them... Lord and Lady Vulture!... they prey on people, apparently..."

"In what way?" queried Melanie.

"Of that I am unsure... their money or something... 'tis why he does not want me associating with them... because of the family wealth, he does not—" She broke off as Caroline entered again, her ermine wrap cast over one arm so that she might more easily clutch a sheaf of papers in the other hand.

"Here we are..." she seated herself next to Melissa on the sofa and Melissa placed her cup and saucer onto the low table to look at whatever was being shown. Melanie stared at *Lady Vulture* in a new way, as if she may suddenly reveal ugly black wings from beneath her fur wrap and begin that terrible cry that vultures emit. It made her smirk and then want to giggle. Sensing this, Melissa nudged her sharply with an elbow.

"This is the rough drawing made of the residence of my aunt... the one she would love to have painted for posterity..."

Melissa scrutinised the charcoal line drawing of a large imposing property, which was perhaps the size of the royal palace, but prettier. It had turrets and balustrades and barley sugar pillars situated in various places along the frontal lower terrace, which was of the Spanish style. It was indeed an impressive property.

"Why does she not have an artist to visit her?... instead of your intervention?" said Melanie astutely. "Surely she wants to have a say in how this is interpreted?"

Caroline looked sharply at Melanie, and for a moment her heavily painted face became mutinous. She hesitated for mere seconds, long enough to rouse suspicion. "Well... to be truthful, she does not know I am commissioning this... 'tis to be a surprise... for her birthday in four months... if that gives enough time..." She stared at Melissa.

Melissa was between wanting to say no and wishing to say yes. The building was something she would love to get her brushes into.

Before she could speak, Melanie said. "What fee did you say you were offering?"

Caroline was taken aback, a woman with a head for business to rival her own. But before she could reply, the door opened and Richard Fairchild came in. "Caro I wondered..." he began as he entered, stopping just inside the door to pretend amazement. "Oh I do beg your pardon... I did not realise you were entertaining." He stepped forward some few feet and pretended more surprise. "If it isn't the young Mrs Fairchild..." he claimed. "And her friend Mrs Gillis..."

Melissa began sating her curiosity over this detested brother-in-law, who was nothing like Anthony. His posture was poor, and he was much stouter and bore all the signs of indulgent living. His light brown hair was thinning and his jawline weak.

"There are several Mrs Fairchilds, it must be said... your cousins' wives also bear the name, do they not! So who is the older Mrs Fairchild to whom you refer?" enquired Melissa, cleverly, extending her hand to meet his.

Richard Fairchild disguised his surprise at this wisdom and digressed. "I almost said my mother... but she is now Mrs Wyevale..."

"Indeed she is... my mother-in-law... whom I quite adore!" said Melissa. He took her hand and kissed it, and then repeated the process with Melanie, assessing their faces in the penetrating manner of someone obliged to read faces for his very survival.

"What a delightful surprise..." said the sanguine Richard Fairchild, and Caroline cast him a warning glance not to overdo things – these two young women were perhaps as astute as himself, and he would overlook the fact in his overwhelming self importance.

"Perhaps you could come back later, Dicke." She told him. "We are talking now of Aunt Rosalind's painting... and they are short of time... Mrs Gillis has a small child to return to."

"How delightful," said Richard, his smile wide, though he was perhaps even less interested in other peoples' infants than Caroline. "I suppose you will be doing the same before long..." he said to Melissa and Melissa recoiled under this impertinent suggestion.

"*Dickie!*" said his paramour sharply. "We do not need your suppositions at this precise moment..."

"I shall leave you ladies to discourse..." said the unctuous Richard and swept an obsequious and complicated bow – seen mostly in plays about Elizabethan England.

"Now..." said Caroline. "Let us talk money."

* * *

The carriage ride back was more fraught than the journey in. One of the horses partially shed a shoe and they travelled at a very reduced speed and lost their way twice. But the picking over of the details of Caroline and Richard was therefore done at greater leisure.

"She is lying..." Melissa said. "I do not believe her aunt wants that painting... or even knows of it."

"But why?" said Melanie

"Well that's the question... and he is just as Anthony described... he's a vulture."

"He's odious." declared Melanie.

"Perfectly... but he is more than a little colourful and quite interesting..."

"Interesting!" exclaimed her closest friend. "Like certain insects in glass cases in science museums!"

"From an artistic perspective he is interesting..." Melissa explained, "... but how on earth can he and Anthony be related?"

"That is one of the mysteries of the world, my love, how siblings can be so different... like the mysteries of male-female coupling..."

"It would be marvellous to capture his qualities on canvas." enthused Melissa. "Her's too... they are both like to something from a Holgarth."

"Shall you undertake the work for Caroline?"

"I shall have to think about it" said Melissa, not displeased with the position of sought-after-artist.

* * *

"I refuse to believe it..." declared Anthony Fairchild of Timothy Trimingham, his close friend and business associate. "You are expecting me to believe that you are actually marrying her in two weeks?"

"I am," said Trim and raised his glass in a salute. He had been betrothed to Susan Darnley for at least seven years now. They led a life of relative freedom not granted to many couples of their class in provincial Britain. "And obviously you will be my best man!"

"Obviously!" agreed Fairchild. "But I shall not set aside the actual date until three days before... in case it does not happen." He laughed briefly and then caught sight of the barmaid, Clara Anstey, now Clara Jones since her marriage. His erstwhile and clandestine lover, daughter of the landlady at his town lodgings before her marriage and his. She raised her hand to him and he raised his glass to her. He had not seen her in a good while and he had heard it was because she had birthed her second child.

"I swear, Tony, 'tis going to happen... it has to happen this time..." Trimingham was asserting.

Fairchild brought his mind from memories of Clara and himself in carefree abandon in the bedroom, and realised what Trim had just inferred. "What?... do you mean?... is this what I think it is?"

"Depends what it is you think." replied Trim, becoming somewhat diffident and reddening.

"She is with child!" muttered Fairchild in a barely audible voice.

Trimingham nodded and studied the counter top on which they leaned, intending only to have two drinks at most. He lifted his head eventually and studied his friend's face.

"You might knock me down with a father, Timothy.!" Fairchild remarked, and then thumped him on the shoulder. "It was bound to happen... you could not keep on forever beating the odds... She is a woman and you are a man... and nature sometimes prevails..."

The tone was jocular and skittish, and Trim nodded while trying not to look pleased with himself.

"You are glad!..." observed Fairchild. "In fact, you are delighted... own it!"

"I am... I am pleased... it has brought her to the point of commitment she could not reach before..."

"And damn well overdue... it calls for another drink!" He summoned Clara, and she came. "Mr Fairchild, how do you go?" she enquired formally.

"Very well, Mrs Jones... and how are you now?... have you recovered and is all well?"

"We have another daughter!" she said and took on a similar coy look to the one Trimingham had worn moments before. "Nathaniel is pleased... though he was hoping for a son..."

"Time aplenty before you..." said Fairchild and smiled at her warmly. Clara smiled warmly in return and for a few seconds they bonded in shared memories. "So, Trim here has just announced his forthcoming nuptials... and we will have two glasses of your finest brandy, if you please... large ones."

Clara grinned at Trimingham and then winked. "T'aint so bad, once you get the hang of it... wedlock that is!"

They laughed heartily, as if it were the funniest thing ever.

"You see, Clara, these two...Trim here and his fiancée... they are married these past few years in all but name, so they have the hang of it already!" said Fairchild as she poured the brandy.

"Does Darnley know?" Fairchild enquired after a couple of swigs of the brandy.

"Not about the expectancy... though I think he may guess... and she will tell him soon, and it will not be a shock to him."

"The devil it will not... he's been anticipating it... he'll be elated. You and Susan making him a grandfather yet again... You once tried to lay a wager..." Fairchild continued. "When I was very ill, before my own wedding... about me cradling my first born before you did yours."

"I do not recall..." said Trim.

"Liar... you are just loath to admit how much you may have lost had I accepted..."

Trimingham took a large mouthful of the brandy. "You know..." he dropped his voice. "I somehow think that this wasn't an accident... I somehow think she may have planned it to happen. I think she did it to bring herself over her own reluctance to wedding me..."

"God's Teeth!... you are not so unappealing!..." jested Fairchild.

"I mean her reluctance in general to being married at all... She had to give herself the best reason to make the leap."

Fairchild slapped Trimingahm on the back a second time. "'Tis as Clara just said... once you get used to it, t'aint that bad. Look how loathe I was... and now I am tolerably happy."

Trimingham made a face and finished the rest of the liquor. "Tolerably happy?"

"Well you know what a realist I am, Timothy..." He called Clara over again to pour another couple of brandies. "There are parts of it I find difficult... and parts which are quite beyond my wildest expectation..."

"We must not have much more to drink..." Trim sanctioned. "We were only supposed to be taking a couple while we talk of the staffing agenda for next week..."

"I know... but now we have extenuating circumstances!" declared Fairchild, whose capacity for liquor was healthy from a young age, and not much diminished with time. "We will have another one... and then leave!"

"Agreed!" said Trim heartily and Clara produced the bottle again and poured.

They had several more, and he went with Trim to Trim's private rooms in his family's mansion. Keeping to the vow he had made when he wed that he would never be around her when intoxicated. He had made the promise to himself and knew that she did not demand it of him; he demanded it of himself, his upbringing as the son of a clergyman was entirely against inebriation in the company of females.

* * *

"What have you decided?" Melanie asked of Melissa in the drawing room at Melanie's home the day following. "She wants an answer by Friday..."

Melissa wrinkled her nose to denote uncertainty. They were playing with baby Robert on his blanket, taking turns to jiggle and wiggle toys for his distraction. Melissa was his Godmother.

"Overall, I think I am against it," she declared. "I do not think I wish to run the risk... he may find out."

"That is what Geoffrey said too..."

"What?" Melissa rose from her knees and stared. "You have surely not told him?"

"I had to... he would not accept the excuse I gave for being two hours later than I promised... besides, he will not tell anyone."

Melissa let out a long breath. "'Tis to be hoped not!"

"Of course he won't... why would he!"

She could think of no answer and sat back on the sofa. "They are quite odious... both of them... and I am satisfied now I have met them for myself."

"Geoffrey thinks Richard a scoundrel." Melanie said.

"And I have never met a scoundrel before!" laughed Melissa.

"Not that you know of..." said Melanie sagely. "Did he ask you where you had been all that time we were gone?"

"No... he was not home... he did not come home at all yesterday!"

Melanie looked at her sharply. "It will be nothing..." said Melissa, "t'will be because he was inebriated with Trim, I expect... he always sleeps on Trim's sofa when that happens... his excellent breeding does not permit him to show himself to me when foxed."

"I should think not!" Melanie said, and it would be hard for anyone to tell how serious she was. She rang for the maid to fetch the nursemaid to give back the baby. "Of course, she may want her drawing..."

"I imagine she will... anyway, I shall send it with the letter declining the commission."

And then Geoffrey Gillis entered and greeted Melissa effusively. He was an effusive man of strong character. A successful lawyer. "I hope you are not thinking of accepting the commission from Richard Fairchild's lady friend..." he said straight off, not a believer in bush-beating.

Melissa was taken aback by this forthright query on top of their conversation. Perhaps he had been listening. "I am thinking to decline."

"Good..." He picked up his son and bounced him up and down to delight him.

"You will make him sick, Geoffrey." Melanie chided. "Then you will need to change your clothes..."

Geoffrey ignored this admonishment but ceased bouncing his first born. "It is not a good idea to go against your husband in that way," he told Melissa and Melanie sniggered. "And don't be coerced into it by this one here!" he pointed to his wife.

"I don't see what it has to do with him." Melissa replied.

Geoffrey looked at her sidelong and placed the baby into Melanie's lap. "It has everything to do with him... this painting is simply a way of getting to you."

"To what end?"

"That I do not know... but why risk your husband's wrath?... and there are other people to paint for!"

"She has a morbid interest in scoundrels," quipped Melanie.

"She can come and work for me then!" Geoffrey replied.

"Not those dreary sort of scoundrels..." Melanie said. "We are talking of the mealy-mouthed sort with artful veneers and credulous disguises..."

"The ones who fawn over people while contriving plans..." said Melissa, "twirling their moustaches and making overtures to upper class ladies."

"Yes, yes..." Geoffrey concurred with enthusiasm. "They are the only ones who can afford our fees, my dear."

# Back Lane House

Two mornings later, she lay in bed next to her husband, staring at the window curtains where the sun was creeping in between cracks. The room was small – Back Lane House was small, when compared to her family home, 'High Lawns.' A mansion with twenty odd rooms plus servants' quarters. But this house was temporary, a first home, until his business was thriving more.

She put her hand on his thigh and turned towards him, and he awoke. He sat up quickly and looked at the clock on the dresser, squinting for lack of light. "Good Teeth! I am late!"

"Well then, tarry a little longer," she said and rubbed his thigh tenderly. He moved to kiss her, lingeringly, but holding himself away from her to avoid being detained by arousal. "I cannot."

Despite the claim of lateness, he flopped onto his back and stretched. "What detained you the day before last?" he enquired.

She froze. "Detained me?" she echoed.

"Yes... Mrs Harrington said you—"

"It's Harrison!" she interjected.

"What?"

"Her name is Harrison... not Harrington... you always say it wrongly."

"She could not pay the butcher's lad when he came with their monthly bill as you were not home..."

"Nor were you. at all... you were foxed with Trim, if you recall and did not return."

"Yes... too true. But I am sober now."

She tutted. "This quaffing you do... the two of you!" She thought of Mrs Harrison, the cook they employed, who did a little housekeeping as well. They could only afford three servants, and one to come in from the village once a week to clean.

"What detained you?" he persisted, in the way she knew of old he could do most doggedly. She thought rapidly.

"Well?..."

Another long pause. He waited, as she had expected.

"Perhaps I was foxed too..."

He groaned but still waited.

"Why do you wish to know?" she said. "Is it a crime to be detained?"

He sat up in the bed in preparation for rising. "I am your husband and need to know these things." He moved her hands away from his sensitive regions. "And I am curious."

"I do not know if I shall tell you..." She had not thought of a credible reason. Mrs Harrison was a talker who loved to reprise small details, even to her employer, as if gossiping in the market square. She would have given him the precise time of the butcher's lad's call, and her consternation at being without the funds. She would say it was embarrassing, and he would agree with her, being fond of his reputation and respect for the commerce of others. "I shall not tell you," she claimed. It was the best she could think of.

"Oh, I think you shall..." he rolled on top of her and pinned her wrists to the bed, and she closed her eyes. She adored morning union.

"Tell me!" he said in a semi-threatening voice.

"All I shall tell you is this..." she squirmed about and he released her.

"What?" His ardour was fading as he thought of the time.

"I shall run down the back stairs to the garden..." She leapt out of the bed and dived for her slippers, "... and if you catch me I shall tell you."

"Melissa, 'tis too early for these ludicrous games... I want an answer now."

She yanked her robe from the bedpost and ran to the door. "As Granny often says... *them as wants don't get!...* "

"Melissa..." he called wearily. "Come back here."

"No... I have laid the odds now."

She laughed as she descended the stairs in a reckless fashion. Moments later, he had pulled on his own robe and was hard on her heels. She flung open the door to the garden, which the tradesman and staff used, and mercifully was unlocked. But she had to remove someone's boots from the step before she could venture out - the boots were heavy and she failed to kick them away. He was in the passage now, and she tore into the depths of the small trees bordering the back of the house. "You heedless girl..." he called, and paused to listen for sounds of her direction.

She considered her next move. She crept and crawled and clawed her way into the depths of the undergrowth, fighting with the tangled low bushes. She was twenty one and he thirty one, and the difference was not so considerable. An older husband might never catch her... but he could!

She thought she could stay hidden while he counted the time and remembered his responsibilities. It was December and very chilly, the ground cold. The dampness seeping through her dressing robe. Then she heard him move along the path and retreat. "We will continue this conversation later..." he called. "Do not think we won't"

She waited about fifteen minutes – or maybe it was less. Then she crept in again. Quite frozen. She was moving silently along the passage to the stairs when he came into the hallway, turned and saw her. She made to run and he caught her by the arm. "This does not count!" she squealed. "You did not catch me first time."

He released her and closed his eyes; he had married a veritable child still. "Go and dry yourself... 'tis not the weather for this... and besides, I have not agreed to the wager..."

"Too late... the wager was laid." she said and turned her face and kissed him. "Anyway, t'was only an excursion with Melanie."

"Yes but an excursion where?" he said. "The very fact that she is involved is enough..."

"Into the countryside... you know how she loves to drive about... and I accompanied her."

"For four hours!"

"Let me get dried and dressed," she said in a loftier manner. "Anyone would think you were my jailer, not my husband..." she skipped up a few steps and then paused. "Although there are some people who would say there isn't much difference." Her laughter petered out as she rounded the bend of the stairs, and he called after her. "We will talk of it tonight..."

She summoned the maid to bring hot water, which would take an age; they did not have the same modern water facilities her father had installed at their family mansion. She wrapped herself in a cochineal blanket and was not displeased. She had until this evening now to fabricate the tale of the day before yesterday

* * *

Later that morning she sent a letter to the home of Caroline Wentworth from the dispatch office in the town to the address she had visited with Melanie.

The letter was returned three days later, in an envelope marked *'Undelivered - address not known.'*

The maid, a cheerful and dozy girl whom he had employed from one of his mother's orphanages, brought it in over breakfast with the rest of the post. He saw it first. He looked at her name on the envelope. "What the devil is this?" he muttered.

She dropped the fork she was holding and guessed rather than read the addressee name on the envelope. "'Tis mine..." She snatched it from him easily - he was not expecting to be so intercepted. "'Tis my name."

He watched her put it into her skirt pocket and was calm. He expected she would give an explanation after she had swallowed a mouthful of food.

She did not.

"What is it?"

"Nothing to concern you..." she said and blushed a little.

He raised his brows, not looking directly at her. "I think I should like to know."

"Of course you would... but I do not ask you every little detail of your morning correspondence..."

"Because 'tis usually not of interest... undeliverable mail naturally arouses one's curiosity.

"Well yours anyway." She was between the need to leave and escape and the need to sit it out with impunity.

"Why are you not telling me?" he demanded. "It must have something to do with your long unexplained absence last week!" He had suddenly remembered and he cast aside his own correspondence and watched her shrewdly. His green eyes a mix of feelings. "Melissa!... tell me!"

She rose and went with haste from the dining room, doing a circle of the hall and changing her mind as to direction three times. He came after her as she headed to the small room where her art was kept - her larger art room still remained in her parents home. "I shall not tell you..." she declared, a sudden flaring of resentment making her unwise in her words. and she went into the room.

Accustomed to this flaring of her worst moods he stood back and regarded the door and deliberated. Often the old resentments rekindled in her and he knew the signs and felt the temperature drop like the outdoor weather.

Had this been her art room at High Lawns the fire would already be underway and she could have dropped the envelope onto it and seen it burn beyond his reach. But this was her small make-do art room and fires were not lit unless she specifically ordered them – today she did not require one to be made.

She had but moments before he thought of how to proceed. They knew each other well. She pulled a wooden chair and jammed it under the door knob to forestall his entry. A massive overreaction to alert anyone's suspicion. He pushed the door which moved fractionally. "Let me in!" he said in a patient tone laced with ire.

"No... you are altogether too nosey..." She ran to the empty fire grate and pushed the envelope up to the ledge of the cold chimney. Kneeling in the hearth and arching her back painfully to accomplish the task. Her hands were then filthy so she wiped them on a paint rag. And now they were full of dark blue oil paint. But better than coal dust to give away the hiding place. She pulled the chair from the door and opened it, frowning at him as he stood there.

His own darker memories surfaced. He was reminded of her and Melanie and the rest of them in his classroom years ago, passing notes between themselves and fooling and foiling him. "What is going on?" he demanded.

She pushed him a little to one side.

Catching hold of her arm he prevented her from moving quickly, but they proceeded together in the direction of the dining room so that breakfast may be concluded. "What?" he said loudly.

"My privacy!" she retorted.

He stopped inside the door before moving to the table where the remains of his hot breakfast stood cooling. "'Tis a surprise!" she invented.

He sat down and sipped cold coffee. "It has to be a good one."

She drank her own coffee and was silent.

"If that letter is from the Braithwaite fellow..." he said at length. Roger Braithwaite was her erstwhile friend from childhood, her some-time sweetheart in his own estimation, who refused to give her up entirely.

"It is not." she said.

He decided to believe her. He was in the middle of translating a book from German into English and it required the utmost concentration. He was already behind and it was easier to just believe her. He almost forgot the letter existed – but not quite – and he relapsed into an early morning mood, looking from the window and taking his mind to the book. It was raining again and he watched her rise from the table. "I shall see you later." She leaned over and kissed him, tasting of orange marmalade and butter.

"The letter?" he repeated.

"What of it?" she threw over her shoulder as she headed from the room.

"I shall find it... or you shall tell me!"

She laughed the tell-tale sign of her sainted secrecy.

Her quest for secrecy and his quest for dominance.

Minutes passed rapidly as he conjectured. He compared his timepiece to the grandmother clock. He must make the next town by ten thirty – it was Monday morning and he had a meeting with the author of the German/English translation. If this translation was successful more would follow. It was lucrative. He left the house hurriedly and made for the stables.

An hour later she ordered a fire to be made in her art room and watched as Mr Harrison, husband of the cook, laid the fire and lit it. All evidence of her letter to Caroline Wentworth going up in smoke.

* * *

"But why did you not invent something?" enquired Melanie, handing baby Robert to Melissa as they seated themselves in the drawing room of Back Lane House.

"I cannot invent things as quickly as you..." she said. "I can only act on impulse... words always escape me."

"More likely you saw a good chance to play your game... and were allowing him time to join in..." Melanie assumed her scornful expression and closed her eyes.

He had taught them languages at school and Melanie had never forgiven him. She did not actually believe that Melissa had either. She believed that her marriage to him might be some kind of protracted revenge, a long played out vengeance to an unknown climax. She could not tell if she was right, and the more Melissa talked of her complicated feelings the more confused things became. Melissa herself admitted to enjoying her own confusion. Her *state of two hearts* as she referred to it.

"But the more important question..." Melissa said next, to detract Melanie from her angry memories, "... is why the letter was not delivered? We definitely went to that address, did we not!"

"Perhaps because 'tis not registered at the dispatch office..." Melanie's eyes opened again, construing the situation. Her wits were razor sharp on matters like these: razor sharp on all matters needing penetration of thought and comfortable survival. "It will be a place Caroline Wentworth likes not to be found... unless she chooses to be... It must obviously not be registered."

"But she chose us to find it."

"Indeed... it says a lot!" agreed Melanie. "And she knows clearly that you would not accept an invite from Richard Fairchild."

"How annoying!" said her best friend.

"How cunning!" corrected Melanie.

"But how did she think I would communicate with her to accept her offer?... if I had decided to do so?"

"Perhaps she does not care whether you accept or not..."

Melissa became rueful – hating anything where people proved themselves more inscrutable than herself. Melanie watched her. "I think you are best out of the whole business. 'tis too convoluted altogether."

"But what else does one expect from scoundrels?" Melissa said, prone suddenly to laughter: the finer points of the dilemma had not yet occurred to her.

Then Peggy came in and said that Miss Darnley had arrived.

Susan Darnley, Trimnngham's intended and the daughter of Doctor Darnley, entered with her genial smile and confident air and stopped on seeing Melanie whom she had met only briefly at Melissa's wedding. "I hope I am not intruding."

"Not at all, Susan..." Melissa passed little Robert back to his mother. "I think you met my dear friend Melanie, Mrs Gillis, at our wedding?..."

"I did indeed." Susan inclined her head to Melanie and then looked immediately at Robert, recalling that Melanie was expecting at the wedding party. "You have your baby now..." she said with great warmth and moved over to look at him.

"How do you do, Miss Darnley..." Melanie said. "And yes... this is our first born... Robert!"

"Please call me Susan..."

Susan Darnley said nothing of her own impending motherhood and wondered if Anthony Fairchild had informed Melissa. "He is a darling..." she told Melanie. "May I hold him for a moment?"

"By all means!" agreed Melanie, who in the past had referred to Susan Darnley as a *parochial busybody* due to her renowned good works at the alms schools and among the poor. Now she saw first hand that she was a woman of strength and character like themselves. Not one to be dismissed lightly. Baby Robert gurgled and smiled and allowed himself to be taken by Susan who sat with him on her lap – accustomed as he was to being passed about and admired.

Melissa rose and shook out her skirts, then remembered. "Susan, let me say how glad I am of your news!... She is to wed Timothy Trimingham just after Christmas." she told Melanie as she stooped to kiss Susan's cheek. "How wonderful!"

Susan flushed delicately. Embarrassed by displays of affection and such attention, she found them intimidating. "And how necessary!" she replied ambiguously, then hastily covered her words. "I mean it has been so long in coming that everyone has written us off as heathens."

The three women laughed together comfortably, but having heard Susan's sotto voce comment and knowing of her and Trimgham's long betrothal Melanie's eyes roamed to Susan's stomach to see if she could spot tell-tale signs of expectancy. She could not but felt she was right in her assumption. Robert laughed merrily with them, his blue eyes turning to first one then the other, his open countenance and broad little features radiating trusting pleasure for things he could not understand. "What a cheerful, engaging little soul he is!" enthused Susan.

"He has his father's temperament..." said Melissa and then giggled as Melanie made an exaggeratedly outraged face. "You have to admit, Mel!... he is Geoffrey all over in his ways."

"Yes he is!" concurred Melanie. "Let us hope he doesn't inherit the tendency for random bursts of raucous laughter which startle the wits out of people..."

Susan smiled and Melissa giggled and Robert gurgled and all was good humour. "That is sometimes what Geoffrey does... 'tis true!!" Melissa told Susan in a serious voice.

They watched the baby for several moments - as if he might decide to see the funnier side of life and emulate his father to entertain them - and then Susan ventured: "I called, Melissa, to ask you if you will perhaps be my Matron of Honour?... 'tis to be a civil wedding at the house, so we require an adult female... and as Tony is to be best man I thought you—"

"Of course I will." Melissa interjected. "I shall be delighted... tell me what you would like me to wear."""

"Excellent!" Susan looked at the baby, and became both coy and exultant all at once. "Wear whatever you like, that doesn't matter to me."

Melanie looked at her askance, not understanding a woman who cared little about what was worn at her own wedding. Then they both gazed at her fondly, not wishing to break the spell of her sheer gladnes.

Meanwhile Anthony Fairchild had entered the house and paused outside the drawing room door to eavesdrop. Female voices were chattering and It was obviously a conclave of feminine topics in full session. He had thought to catch his wife off guard; she would talk more honestly when surprised by him. Now he had little choice but to enter. Or creep away as if he had never been - but the maid had spotted him, quite evidently listening outside the door. It was embarrassing, so he coughed and pretended to dive into his inside pocket for things which were not actually there, and then he entered the room. They turned to him of one accord, and he bowed to them formally. "Ladies! how are you?" He noted Susan holding the baby and thought of her pregnancy and allowed his gaze to move fleetingly over her middle body - as Melanie had done - to see if in fact she showed yet. "Susan..." he began and crossed to her and took her hand, the one she freed from Robert's tiny arm, and kissed her fingers. "Let me congratulate you on the good news!"

Susan looked at him whimsically. "Lars, Tony!... 'tis not as if Timothy and I are twenty and have only recently been introduced..." she laughed, overwhelmed once more.. "It has been on the cards for years... more of a formality than anything..."

Melanie was gratified at being proved right and glanced at Melissa who was not looking at her husband, whose visage she never tired of beholding.

"Well, 'tis certainly overdue..." Fairchild told her with the audacity allowed of those who have been friends since childhood. "But nonetheless pleasing for that..."

Susan blushed and was struck dumb – an eventuality which Fairchild found novel in the extreme.

"We have Robert with us today!" said Melissa, so that he would be obliged to acknowledge Melanie's child, her own godson.

"I can see that!" He ruffled the baby's hair with his fingers. "How are you, young man?" he asked Robert obligingly, and Robert gurgled and stuck his fist into his mouth.

"He is teething!" explained Melanie.

"Of course." he replied, as if he knew anything about these matters. And he attempted a smile which went someway past her head; they loathed each other.

"Join us..." said his wife, "while we have tea..."

"I cannot, I am afraid. I called in briefly for some papers I forgot... but I must be gone again."

"What a pity!" said Melanie in her ambiguously whimsical voice, causing Susan to look at her and sensing something she could not yet name.

"Is not Robert splendid now?" Melissa said to him, determined to make sociability of the situation.

"He is indeed!" enthused Susan before he could comment.

He nodded and smiled at no one in particular, and watched Robert bounce on Susan's lap. *Women and infants! It was almost a closed world.* He resorted to wit. "Yes... he is splendid!... he already has horsemanship, by the look of him... what a pity he isn't more popular with the ladies..." He bowed to them a final time and left.

It took a few moments before they extracted the irony from his wit as they gazed as one at little Robert with further doting expressions.

Then Susan rose and handed the baby to his mother. "I must go too..." she said politely

"Of course..." said Melissa. "You are always so busy."

"Aren't we all!" added Melanie omnisciently, not to be sidelined by the esteemed Susan Darnley and her pledge to societal reform. *Though it was untrue that they were always busy; unless Melissa's artwork were to be included, and her own pursuit of horse riding and driving the phaeton for the love of it: they had oodles of time in which to enjoy themselves and engage in pastimes of their choosing. But then did not Susan choose to do what she did? – admirable though it was! Life was full of choices. Full of choices that were really conflicts of desire.*

Melanie rose and walked to the door with them, to show that she did not mean her remark to be churlish. Susan Darnley was a nice enough woman it seemed.

In the drawing room after her departure, Melanie was at once curious. "Has he discovered anything?... about the letter... or the reason for your lateness that day?"

"No... not as far as I am aware... I burned the letter... though there is something amiss, he never usually calls in at this time in the afternoon..."

"Perhaps he actually did forget the papers he mentioned."

"'Tis doubtful... and if he does call he never looks in to see who is present." Melissa took the baby and rocked him and watched him become inert and drowsy. "He is not so pressured these days and less on his mind... he seldom forgets important things..."

The afternoon drew longer and the light faded in the room – the run up to Christmas bringing more dismal weather. They watched the embers and small flames of the fire, constantly changing shape and hue. Melanie was the first to speak. "We must hope that she forgets about her painting... the Wentworth person!"

Melissa made a long murmur of doubtful consideration. "Yes... but I doubt she will... she has been to such trouble to bring it to my attention."

"She is certainly a woman not to be trusted... or second guessed."

"I see now why Anthony is at pains to stay away from them... they are too wiley for words."

Melanie rose and lifted little Robert from her friend's lap and began pulling a woollen blanket around him in readiness for the journey home. The groom would call for them at any minute. "You need something to divert you from the worry of it... or you will call in a calamity with your thoughts of her."

Melissa brightened and said. "As you know, I do not fear any calamities with him... I fear only his tiring of me."

"That is not going to happen..." Melanie said. "'Tis more likely to be the other way around..."

"Of course it is not!" objected Melissa. "But I insist on being free to paint for people of my choosing."

"You would not choose to paint for that odious woman though, surely."

"Well... maybe not," said Melissa grudgingly. "But I do not wish to be told who I may and may not speak to."

"That is yet another matter..." Melanie walked about with the baby to lull him to sleep. "Sometimes, we still need another diverting pursuit... to keep us lively and engaged... aside from Christmas preparations, which can be tiresome..."

Hearing the porch bell ring out, Melissa became brusque. The groom was outside. "The only diversion I have to offer is cousin Honoria and her plight... "

They went into the hall, and Melanie gave Robert to Melissa while putting on her cloak. "Oh yes... the liberation of Honoria... that should be a more straightforward mission..."

"Straightforward?... Do you imagine so?"

"Certainly... at least we know what we are dealing with!" Melanie's confidence in worldly matters knew no bounds. "We can talk more of it on Thursday."

"Splendid!" agreed Melissa. One project appearing as another sank into oblivion, to illuminate the winter horizon. She kissed Robert and held him to allow Melanie to board.

"By the way..." she said through the rolled down carriage window, "I think I may be increasing again... me and Miss Darnley together, it seems.

Melissa thought she may have misheard and watched Melanie wave as the carriage rolled away along the drive.

* * *

Before she could commence work on her latest canvass some minutes after Melanie's departure, she had a lightning change of heart and went to retrieve the sketch Caroline Wenworth had given her of the residence she wished her to paint. She put it on the easel next to a large sheet of paper and began to sketch a rough outline for size and perspective in pencil. She would paint it anyway, and keep it for her collection without Caroline and Richard knowing.

She was enjoying the initial feeling of opening up into the world of this stately and ancient building – a feeling known perhaps to many artists, and one which was rivalled by little else – except perhaps sexual arousal.

She was several lines away from the full scale and outline when it struck her that the thing she was copying from did not belong to her. This was succeeded by the alarming thought that Caroline would obviously want it back. She stood away from the easel and contemplated rapidly with no solution in sight on how she could return this. It was the fly in the ointment, the proverbial sting in the tail.

Perhaps she could burn it. Place it in the chimney like the letter and pretend she had lost it! It would have to be done at once, so she flung open the door and called for the maid to light a fire, Mr Harrison being elsewhere in the garden mending broken fencing. She was met almost head-on by Peggy, the maid, who told her that her mother-in-law was in the drawing room. "What?" she said in a stupid fashion.

"The lady what's the Ma of your husband, Madam…" said the maid innocently and carefully. "That's what a mother-in-law is."

Melissa became flustered. "I know what a mother–in–law is, Peggy!" she snapped. "I meant, why is she here now?…"

Peggy gaped at her and wondered if she'd been drinking. "She b'aint telling me them things…" Peggy replied helplessly.

She moved Peggy a little briskly to one side – the silly girl had no notion of the nature of a rhetorical question and was adding to her stress.

In the drawing room, Hildegarde Wyevale was looking out of the window at the front garden, resplendent as usual in her plain but expensive garments, her plentiful silver hair arranged immaculately beneath a tiny bonnet. She turned and came to her daughter-in-law, her movements as majestic as always. Only her smile was missing. Melissa greeted her warmly. She was so like Anthony; her bone structure and facial contours the feminine version of his own. "Mama!" enthused Melissa, preferring her by far to her own mother. "To what do I owe this pleasure?... I shall ring for tea... Anthony has been and gone this afternoon... he—"

"I cannot stay long!" cut in Hildegarde. "Do not bother with tea... Let us sit for a few moments... I am glad he is not home."

Melissa sat in a chair and Hildegarde opposite her. She was alerted to her mother-in-law's air of concern as something quite out of the ordinary. "Whatever is it, Mama?"

Mrs Wyevale – whose second and current husband was a bishop like her first, the father to her three sons – was familiar with difficult situations, both as a vicar's wife years earlier and now the wife of high clergy. She breathed deeply and made herself smile to put Melissa at her ease before commencing. She needed the truth, which was always best gained from others when they were at ease, she had found. "Melissa is it true you visited Caroline Wentworth at her home?"

Melissa's mouth opened and shut rapidly several times, like a landed carp. She was utterly wrong-footed. "Well I... I think I may have done..."

Mrs Wyevale assumed a more upright position in her seat and became earnest. "You may have done?  You either did or you did not!... and you may tell me."

Melissa watched her without speech, aghast at this turn of events. She could not lie... she could not prevaricate without arousing further suspicion. She was without defence.

"Richard tells me you did," said her mother-in-law with the sort of composed disdain so redolent of her youngest son. "He says you and Melanie Gillis visited her last week... and he happened to walk in."

"'Tis true... we did," she said at length and looked at her hands in her lap. Of course, Richard would tell their mother; he was duplicity itself, the very epitome of someone who played everyone against everyone else. Mrs Wyevale closed her eyes and made a sound of agonised confusion, "You must know that Anthony wishes you to have nothing to do with them?"

"I do know that, yes," she replied simply.

"Then why did you call on her?"

"She invited us... she invited me to call and discuss a painting, and I thought there would be no harm in it."

Mrs Wyevale rose and paced the carpet. "My dear, where Richard and Anthony are concerned, there is always the threat of harm... "

"I am sorry..." she said in genuine contrition. "I should not have attended... but I thought that my painting for Caroline concerned neither of them and was simply a business arrangement between Caroline and myself..."

Hildegarde Wyevale looked at her almost pityingly. It was evident that she took the rivalry between the brothers as something to be dismissed. "Melissa, you must not accept invites from them without telling him... you must not go against him in this... no good can come of it."

"I see that now," lamented Melissa, though she did not entirely see, except that there was an enmity she underestimated in its gravity.

"He does not know... Anthony does not know of the visit," she added plaintively, "and I shall not tell him."

Her mother-in-law sat again, in a different chair, and stared at her with the kind of pained and weary sympathy one shows to recalcitrant children one has lost hope of curing. "But he does know, Melissa... Anthony does know... Richard made it his business to tell him."

Melissa gasped and was between several emotions: her *state of the heart, confusion* on whether or not to be pleased by the news was straining to express itself on her face... and not knowing quite which reaction to show: delight or trepidation! exhilaration or contrition!

"He is a viper!" she announced at length. "He had no business telling Anthony... he has done it on purpose. He is a snake in the grass..."

"Of course he is!" said Mrs Wyevale with more pitying and weary expressions. "But I thought you understood that much... amid the jests and witty jibes made by Tony... I thought you would have gleaned that much!"

"I am filled with contrition..." Melissa concluded. "I think I must have a sherry." She rose and went to the sideboard where she found the decanter empty.

"I am shocked and dismayed, Melissa..." Mrs Wyevale shook her splendid head of hair. "You must promise me not to go against him in this way with Richard or Caroline again."

It was like being twelve once more and receiving a scolding. She was beyond exasperation. She concealed her annoyance. "I promise you, Mama." She crossed to Hildegarde and kissed her cheeks and Hildegarde softened a little. She was aware that they played games, Melissa and Anthony. Not exactly dangerous games, but the kind which could get out of hand. "You must think of something to appease him by way of explanation..."

"I shall try!" said Melissa and checked the clock to gauge the time she had before he arrived home.

"And Melissa..." Hildegarde placed her hands in her lap and looked at Melissa with her translucent blue eyes until she had her full attention. "You must cease playing these kind of games... they are fraught with danger..."

"I do not fully understand what you mean!" said the artful wife of her youngest son.

"Oh yes you do!... you know you do! I am aware that you often purposely incur his wrath for your own... well, whatever you want to call it..."

Melissa gasped in mock horror and thought to protest but then sealed her lips and assumed a look of inscrutable secrecy, mixed with a sultry sort of longing. Hildegarde watched her carefully. Anthony was very closed about these games; they were possibly not of his choosing. Whereas Melissa was more careless about them.

Hildegarde stood, somewhat at a loss, and Melissa took her hands in their fingerless lace gloves, and held them. The last thing she wanted was animosity with her mother-in-law. "Do not worry, Mama... as I told you before our wedding, he will not harm me..."

Hildegarde was lost for words... and then she found some. "I know that, my dear!... but even so, you may go too far and cause a rift in your marriage..."

Melissa became a trifle smug and pursed her lips and deliberately made a face which showed she was refraining from comment.

"And..." continued Hildegarde, "the harm comes in this situation when he confronts Richard... which he might well do."

"That is Richard's own fault." she declared, recovering her self confidence. "If he will go about blabbing like a schoolboy and showing no discretion..."

Mrs Wyevale drew a sharp intake of breath and almost stamped her foot, her reticule held in readiness for departure. "He has no wish to show discretion, you foolish girl!... he is baiting Anthony... he has baited you too and used you."

Melissa saw the situation from all angles and it was overwhelming. She stared at her mother-in-law. It took a lot for a woman to be so honest on the subject of one of her children's grave character faults and Melissa admired her and felt for her in this example of betrayal and duplicity. "Perhaps I just needed to see for myself what he really is... what they both are..."

"Well now you have seen..." Mrs Wyevale strode to the door. "So you must be satisfied with that... and see also why Anthony wishes to keep them away from you. Do not go against him in this matter."

"I shall not do so," said Melissa softly and held Hildegarde's arm as they walked to the front door. "When did Richard tell him, do you know?"

"A few days ago, I think... I cannot be exactly sure... but Richard mentioned it to me this morning when he called to see me..."

So Anthony knew this afternoon, even as he stood in the drawing room and congratulated Susan and made small talk. He must have been incandescent with fury, his self containment as always without fault.

"In fact, I think that is the reason Richard called on me today..." said Hildegarde, descending the top step. "To make sure I knew of the event... in case Tony fails to tell me."

Melissa gazed at the leaden sky with its cold stormy weather. "It must be dreadful to have such an untrustworthy and conniving son." she told the other woman sincerely.

Hildegarde almost laughed as she waved to the coachman who stepped down from the carriage to see her aboard, then said. "Indeed... which is why I do not wish to have a conniving daughter-in-law on top of it." She raised her brows and softened her features so that Melissa would take the rebuke as well intentioned. Melissa began almost to giggle and Mrs Wyevale could well see why, but in order not to have her remarks taken lightly she refrained from amusement and boarded her carriage with the greatest sense of seriousness and dignity.

* * *

She forgot about the sketch and its disposal entirely. She had but a few minutes to think and she decided to go at once to 'High Lawns' and pretend to have work in her art room there. It was close enough to their own house and owned by her family's business estate. She could actually reach High Lawns in ten minutes if she sprinted at a fair pace – twenty or so if she took it at walking pace. She was accustomed to the walk, or the fast trot, and made the journey often. He had taken the trap or she might have used that. She did not ride, even though Melanie offered to teach her. Her husband never offered to teach her; *he thought women and horse riding were an activity best left out of the equation wherever possible.*

She set off immediately and arrived exactly twelve minutes later, breathless. The wind had risen and the air was assailed by intermittent sleet. Her hair was awry and her clothing damp.

She went firstly to the art room and then changed her mind and ran up the back staircase to the bedroom she had shared with him in their own rooms during the first weeks of their marriage, before Back Lane House was fit for purpose.

Summoning the maid to have a fire lit at once, she rested on the bed, as she had done in her erstwhile days of pre-marital status. It was blissful and she imagined stepping back into that time, longed to do so – perhaps just for a day or two – whilst she planned the correct approach to this latest catastrophic event of her own making.

Meanwhile Anthony Fairchild was quite seething with fury – well contained fury – but seething. He sat at his desk in the offices they inhabited in the town, above a bakery, on the second floor, overlooking the town square and the clock-tower and the place where the organ grinder lingered for half an hour or so each evening, taking refreshment before traversing the wider periphery of the town.

It was quite dark outside and getting on for six o'clock and he still had an hour's work to complete by the schedule he had set himself.

At length, an employee entered and asked him how much more of the lengthy document she was translating they needed copying before the day after next.  She was gratified on hearing that she may complete it by the end of the next day.

She was Dutch, and she acted as a translator on letters and other commercial export papers, and sometimes as a scrivener. She worked only two or three days a week. He judged her to be about five and twenty, although she had told both himself and Trimingham that she was thirty – obviously to sound more experienced and give herself the maturity she felt she lacked. She had told them that she was unattached, which he thought also to be a lie. But it worried him not at all... what she told him and the quality of her work, which was excellent, were not mutually inclusive. Single women of education were rare to come by.

"I will make of the moment one more coffee cup... and then I will make departure..." she said, her spoken English lagging woefully behind her ability to read and write the language. "Would you care also for that, Mr Fairchild?" she asked politely, "If I am to boil anyway."

He raised his head and looked at her, almost grinning at the grammar but refraining. He could have told her he would not care either way – if she made coffee cups or if she boiled!  But he would not give offence to a woman in that way, even in jest. "I do not mind, Miss Van der Creff, when you make coffee... and I would not care for any, thank you. I am leaving myself shortly."

Miss Van der Creff smiled, her face tilting slightly to one side as she made him a brief courtesy. Her mouth a small oval of satisfaction.

In his pre-marital days, he would have engaged her in conversation, he would have made more of her acquaintance. He would perhaps have bedded her, because on occasions it was obvious to him that she would be fine with that, perhaps more than fine. But he knew better than to mix business with pleasure. He was married now and could not countenance such behaviour in himself. Not at this precise stage, unless things went drastically awry with himself and his wife. Of course, the latest bulletin from his brother was enough to drive him into the arms of another woman, and who could blame him? But he would blame himself eventually.

He heard her chattering to Trimingham as she made the coffee on the small gas burner they kept in the tiny outer room, next to a large vat of fresh water and the coffee grinder and the jug of milk.

At length Trim entered his office, carrying a cup of the coffee made by Miss Van der Creff. He smiled ruefully and sat in the chair she had vacated.  "She is a lovely young woman... Miss Van der Creff... do you not find?"

"I do!" said Fairchild with brevity, not looking up from his papers. "You had better make your move if you are going to... if you are so keen... before you plight your troth formally."

Trim looked sheepish. "T'was never my way... troth plighted or not... when have you ever known me be unfaithful to Susan?"

"Well, I have not... but there is such a thing as the eleventh hour."

Trimingham laughed. "I was merely remarking how nice she is..."

"So you were, Timothy... so you were!  Perhaps you think it has escaped my notice?"

"I am certain it had not." Trim took out his pipe and lit it. "Betimes, she is spoken for, the town gossips tell me..."

Marrianne Van der Creff, it was believed, shared habitation with a young man, an artist who liked to paint in the Dutch style, and to whom she was a muse and a model... and whatever else the arrangement contained. But she liked also to keep her independence and earn money of her own.

"The fellow is a painter!" Fairchild commented. "Therefore, it may not amount to anything."

"Do I detect a slur on artists?" enquired Trimingham lightly, the pipe emitting essences of tobacco smoke, scenting the room and reducing the already sketchy light. "Your wife is among their fraternity, remember!"

"Yes, I am aware!"  said Fairchild darkly. "I have met a few of the male fraternity now, courtesy of Melissa's afternoon soirees with Monsieur Tisserand... and they are not the most conventional of people..."

"Good for them!" said Trimingham.

"My meaning is that the term 'spoken for' hardly applies here... they will sacrifice any principle for their art." Fairchild continued to scribble, then thought of what he had said. Melissa's own pursuit of her art to the detriment of their trust. "As will my wife!" He began to write faster to obliterate the thought.

"Are you thinking to work for much longer tonight?" Trim enquired.

"Why?"

"Because you seem fraught... not to say, driven... or even demonically possessed as you write..." said the laconic Trimingham.

Fairchild threw down his nib and then threw himself back in the curved wooden chair. "I am in truth besieged by wrath... I am quite beside myself with rage."

"I can tell." Trim's pipe became more efficient, and smoke billowed into the near space between them

"Timothy, put that out or take yourself off... you are ruining what little there is of the light!"

"I will fetch you a candle... what on earth ails you?"

"I need to finish this letter for my father-in-law's clerk... it needs to be done by midday tomorrow."

"Oh dear... and 'tis already five minutes after six on the day before!" rejoined Trimingham facetiously.

"Yes, but if I do not complete it now, I will be in no mood later...
"

"For the love of God!... what is the matter?... you will feel better for getting it off your chest."

Fairchild stood and left the letter and paced and then left the room and helped himself to coffee from the water recently brought to the boil by Miss Van der Creff. Irritated at the lack of milk on the day's end he sipped the coffee and looked from the window.

The organ grinder was still resting, his monkey on his shoulder and receiving adoration and affection from people passing who stopped to pet the animal. The organ grinder was encouraging this and listening to requests from small urchin children now gathered.

Fairchild prepared his words, diverted somewhat by the antics around the barrel organ. He had been told that the monkey was trained in the lifting of purses and wallets and other valuables from unsuspecting members of the public, but he was unsure how true that was, or how likely withal.

"Let us go for a gill or two?" Trim persisted.

"I cannot... I must sort this mess."

Trim raised his voice and himself from the chair. "Are you going to tell me what the blazes is the matter... or not?"

Fairchild swung around and allowed his rage to surface with some ferocity, but not too much. "She has visited the Wentworth woman... behind my back!" he said, and Trim paused to absorb the information.

"Melissa, you mean?"

"Yes... Melissa, my wife... "

"She has told you this?"

"Of course she has not... Richard told me... he waited for me yesterday morning and watched me come into the street here and then pretended to accidentally cross my path..."

Trimingham thought carefully how to react. Whether to speak of Richard Fairchild's interference first, or to broach the subject of Melissa and Caroline. Then, before he could assimilate words, his friend spoke. "Perhaps you would like to accompany me home..." Fairchild swung around again and looked at Trimingham. "I know how you love to save her from my wrath."

"Just once..." said Trimingham in a placatory tone. "It happened only once... and I was right to do so."

"Well you are not right now..." said Fairchild and slammed the cup down onto the desk so that the handle broke from the china vessel.

"I have not uttered!" replied Trim in his own defence. "I have said nothing as yet."

"Come to think of it, perhaps you had best go to find Richard... in case I manage to kill him..."

"I would wait and become calmer if I were you," said Trim. "You may play right into his hands... in one way or another... the odds are stacked against you... do you not find?"

Fairchild threw the broken china into the wastebasket and lifted the letter, and carefully placed it in the drawer between blotting paper. "If I wait until I am calm... and no doubt 'tis wise... but if I do, I simply afford her time to invent her excuses and fabrications to baffle the situation. She cannot have any reason for going against me in this way... she cannot."

"Well, perhaps not... but..." Trim faltered. He could see nothing worthy to say in her cause. No doubt, one of the infamous games was underway and had become unmanageable. "So you will not join me in a drink?" he asked hopefully.

"I shall decline, thank you," said Anthony Fairchild and patted Trim's shoulder as he departed for the day.

* * *

On reaching Back Lane House he found her to be absent, and he cursed himself for making the wrong decision. It was a direct choice between her coming here or going to her family's mansion. She had obviously gone to High lawns. He remounted the trap and made the five minute journey.

When he reached the mansion he found the large double doors unlocked and the butler in the hall awaiting visitors who were staying overnight with her parents. "Good Evening, Mr Fairchild." Jarvis greeted him.

"Where is my wife?" asked Fairchild by way of response. "Do you know?"

"She was in her art room, according to the maid, Sir... but that was an hour since, so she may not be there now."

He threw off his coat and gloves and handed them to Jarvis.

His mother-in-law appeared from the dining room vicinity and said "She is upstairs, I believe, Anthony... in the bedroom."

He bowed to Marguerite Shaw but could not bring himself to speak.

"She was very damp... having walked here," said Marguerite charmingly.

"She will be more than damp when I have finished with her..." muttered her son-in-law in low tones she did not hear.

He ran up the main staircase two at a time and the butler and Marguerite stared after him, marvelling at the speed at which he went. "What it is to be young and fit, Madam!" said the butler respectfully in jovial manner.

"Indeed, Jarvis... indeed." she concurred.

Giles Shaw appeared from his study at the sound of voices, thinking them to be those of his expected guests – business associates of importance.

"T'was Anthony..." said his wife. "What did I tell you over an hour ago!... they have rowed again... I think seriously."

"Leave them to it," said Giles. "They will get over it... they always do."

"I was not thinking of becoming involved." she said huffily, "I am sure I do not care what they do."

"As long as you find out all about it, I suppose." murmured Giles and winked at Jarvis briefly, a man of senior years like himself and of much service.

The bedroom door was unlocked – which surprised him. She was not expecting him. He went in and shut the door.

She was standing in front of the fireplace with a small sketchpad in hand but not doing much with it beyond looking at it.

"Gather your things!" he told her. "And let us go."

"I do not think I wish to go." she replied, having quelled her surprise at his entrance.

He raised his voice. "Whether you wish it or not, you will leave with me now."

"How dare you!... I have only just arrived."

"Do not begin *daring* me, Melissa... because you know I can *dare* a lot."

She retrieved her cloak, which was still damp, from the wooden rail before the fire only just beginning to thrive. If she refused, he would pull her out with him. And though she was not averse to being forcefully conveyed by him under certain circumstances, it was not favourable with an audience: the staff would see, members of the family would see, it would be ignoble to say the least. She dawdled in the putting on of her boots.

"Hurry up!" he said.

"Stop ordering me around! You know how I detest it!"

He ignored this, it was a veritable tired lament and he was used to hearing it. She took the cloak and draped it around her shoulders and it occurred to her for perhaps the first time how, when tempers had flared and they were at loggerheads, she ran always in the opposite direction whilst he charged right at her and into the fray. She smiled a little as she picked up her canvas bag and stuffed the sketch pad into it.

"I do not know what you find amusing..." he told her, taking her arm and propelling her through the door to the corridor. "You may not find it so amusing in a while..."

"Your threats are so tedious." she said, merely for something to parry with.

Downstairs in the hall her mother was greeting the anticipated visitors. He stopped in his stride and allowed Marguerite to make introductions. "This is our son-in-law... Anthony Fairchild..."

He bowed to them. "How do you do?"

"And my daughter, Melissa Fairchild."

She swept a brief curtsey. "Good evening!"

"We cannot tarry." he said in his even, charming manner, succinct and sincere. "Forgive us... we are late..."

Her father appeared from the study.

"I shall have the letter delivered to you by tomorrow evening, Sir!" Fairchild told him.

Melissa said. "Papa dearest..." but got no further with her diverting tactic as he took her elbow and led her to the wide double doors, held open by Jarvis.

"Out!" he said in a low tone and pushed her towards the steps. The visitors had disappeared into the drawing room and the welcoming fire.

"The letter will do by six of the evening!" Giles called to him and he lifted his free hand in acknowledgement, not moving his other from her arm. "I wanted to speak to my father... you boorish oaf!" she said.

"You have had the last hour to do that... and I would not begin with your insults at this point, if I were you!"

He pulled her to the trap where she stamped on his foot as he opened the door. He winced but did not let her go. He shook her a little and saw her into the trap and then went quickly round to the driver's side. The phaeton loomed forward in a dart of sudden movement and she clung to the door strap. "I know what is annoying you..." she said archly, thinking it best to *grasp the nettle.*

"Hush!" he told her. "Do not speak until we reach home... or we may have an accident..."

"May we?" she replied. "Your driving is not to be criticised normally."

"Be quiet... I am not speaking until home."

She was silent for three minutes and then ventured. "'Tis about Caroline Wentworth, I presume... Mama called to see me and she told me of Richard's tittle-tattling."

He groaned loudly. Women and their blasted news bulletins!

"Then if you know, you can save the rest until we are home."

She fumed and thought and nothing would occur in the way of ruses, defences or excuses. "I do not think I wish to be told when I may speak or when I may not..."

"I do not care what you wish..." He took a corner at high speed and she clamped her lips shut. It was perilous, and the trap may overturn.

They reached the turnpike, where he slowed the conveyance, and she thought she might spring out and run across the fields the remainder of the way. But he read her mind and grabbed her wrist to prevent her from moving. She was enraged and began to thump him with her other hand to make him free her. This never worked; seldom did he react. She twisted and pulled and carelessly slid off the seat onto the floor. She pulled her arm harder to free herself. If she ran over the fields, it may be wet and horrible, but it would give her time to think – she had already concocted half a tale – and she thought better when a deadline loomed.

"If you continue to struggle in that way, you will dislocate your shoulder, or your wrist..." he said, accustomed to these not infrequent skirmishes and quite unfazed. "Get up."

He held onto her until she was safely on the seat. "You think yourself so superior!" she threw at him. "You do not even bother to ask me my version of events."

"I will ask you at home!"

"I had a good reason for going to see Caroline..." she said over the heightened noise of the wheels as they cleared the home-straight on a wider road

"Then you have nothing to fear or avoid."

"I do not fear you... so do not puff yourself up in that way... you are far too—"

He cut her off mid sentence. "Melissa," he raised his voice and released her. "I have warned you not to begin with your insults..."

He drove straight to the small stable beside the house. "Stay there!" he instructed her as he alighted and began removing the horse from the shafts. When he had settled the horse for the night and laid the hay and saw the water trough was full, he saw her safely down. She shook him off immediately, but he seized her once more as they left the stable and propelled her to the porch.

He clanged the bell, having forgotten his keys, and the maid let them in, staring in her gormless and tactless way at the mistress and master of the dwelling, looking more like guard and prisoner. "Prepare a bath for Mrs Fairchild, please... with hot water, she is cold and wet."

"I do not need a bath!"

"You will take a bath!" he said. "Whether you need one or not. Your clothes were sodden when I collected you and you had been wet for a good while before that... you need to prevent a chill."

He watched her go upstairs, where she would take the bath in their bedroom. "I shall be up in a few minutes... and do not think to run from the house.... I shall be eating supper and I shall see you if you do. Have you eaten?"

"Hot broth at High Lawns... I am not hungry."

"Bring her some cold food for later..." he told the maid. "In case she is hungry then..."

"Peggy, do not trouble..." Melissa said. "I know when I need to eat, not my husband."

Peggy looked from one to the other, beset by bemusement. She rested her gaze finally on him and curtsied. She turned to Melissa and said in a voice of appeasement. "I'll bring you some light morsels, Madam... lest you be hungry after your bath... I be always ravished after sinking into water..."

She tried not to smirk at Peggy's vocabulary; always so amusingly awry.

"Thank you," he said, "... and the word you need is *ravenous*, Peggy... not ravished."

Peggy looked at him blankly, dismissing the amendment as soon as it occurred. She liked the word ravished better.

"Once the teacher..." remarked Melissa in her wake, "always the teacher... as if it matters what she says..."

"It does matter..." He went to the table in the hall and looked for messages brought in the day. "Do you think she does not have the right to correct speech because she is not privileged? Whilst you do!"

"I think she does not need to be troubled by it." She watched Mr Harrison carry up the water and the cook, to whom he was wed, pull another one to the foot of the stairs to follow.

Meanwhile, her husband threw non-urgent letters back onto the hall table. "Of course, left to you, everyone would run around uneducated, like savages!"

"If you are saying I run around like a savage... just because I do not tell you where I am going then -"

"Be quiet... I do not want to hear any more just yet."

He took up the second bucket of hot water himself and turned at the top of the flight. "Upstairs... now!" he said in his didactic way, which pulled her this way and that in an emotional reaction.

Once the water had been poured into the small hip bath in the bedroom, he retired again and came down to eat his supper. He checked his timepiece and thought he would give her ten minutes to bathe – the water was not hot enough for her to linger beyond that, but warm enough to erase the chill from her bones.

She lay in the water and reflected on his concern for her bodily welfare. It was the action of a thoughtful person. Or a husband who did not wish to lose a valuable asset in a wife. She was divided. Conflicted as to view and to feeling. Objectivity clashing with sentiment.

She climbed out of the bath and wrapped herself in the warm sheet provided, and then rang for Peggy who duly arrived with the male servant who carried out the bath to the sluice room along the landing.

She was wearing her camisole and drawers but she draped a heavy damask silk shawl around herself, until she had made up her mind whether she would stay upstairs or go down again. It would depend on what transpired next.

He entered as she was rubbing lotion into her calves and feet. He looked at her with the expression of a man who had only just made her acquaintance. "Well?" he demanded.

"Well, what?"

He took out his small cigars. "The excuse you have thought of for going to visit the Wentworth woman!"

"She asked me to make her a painting."

"Yes... and?"

"I thought I would accept the offer."

"Even knowing I had expressly told you to keep away from her... from either of them!"

"Even knowing that, yes... 'tis my entitlement as a free individual to make acquaintances as I wish."

"Is it?... and what of my entitlement as your husband?..."

The pause now was a lethal one; everything hung in it. She had baited the hook. "It was mere curiosity... I thought I could make an informed decision for myself... and I am glad I did."

He lit the cigar finally and threw the match into the fire grate where small flames danced, but did not heat the room much as yet.

"I have told you how I feel... and I have told you how I feel about you disobeying me on important matters..."

"I know..."

"I have a mind to give you the hiding of your life."

She made a scoffing sound but her insides quivered with tension. The hour of reckoning after almost nineteen months of prevarication, debate and deliberate misdirection on the subject – the subject of *her preferred method of chastisement.* A jest – and not a jest – a deliberate misunderstanding becoming etched in the marriage treatise

"I have heard no reason yet why I should not."

She picked at the cold ham sent up from the kitchen and the tomato on the side of the plate. "Do you expect me to beg for your clemency?" she said archly. "Because you will be disappointed."

"No... and it would do you no good besides."

"I am sure," she said.

He pulled on the cigar, and the end glowed and caught the flickering light from the oil lamp, turning it gold for a second or two. She watched it, thinking that he would not act now; his mood was growing calmer. She was wrong.

"I think I will retire to bed..." she said, looking at him with an invitation.

"Not yet, you will not..." He left the cigar in the dish on the dressing table and rose. She moved in a gliding way to the bed, still watching him. "Will you not join me?"

"No... you cannot seduce me into submission whenever you transgress... you cannot just easily detract from your behaviour with casual ploys of pleasure..."

"Casual ploys of pleasure!" She took off her slippers. "Is that how you see them?"

"The way they are couched now, yes... they are nothing short of manipulative and wanton."

She laughed; a huge error of judgement. He crossed to her and she moved sideways to avoid him and began to tread the carpet in the direction of the door, but he caught her arm and turned her round and slapped her hard on the behind. Then he slapped her again, harder, and she tried to free herself and moved them both in a circular motion – the door handle still some feet away. He brought her to a standstill and slapped her even harder. She squealed with shock and discomfort. The time of reckoning had come – just as Melanie had said it would. The time when he played his ace and took the game. She wriggled and writhed to gain freedom and her shawl fell to the floor. Now she was totally unprotected from the onslaught. "Let me go... let go of me..." she wailed, and even so kept her voice down so that the servants would not hear.

He ignored her and slapped her twice more, and she darted forward and lowered herself to avoid his hand. He pulled her to a stop and said. "If you disobey me, this is the consequence... I warned you before we married... and you decided to dismiss it as a mere threat... my warnings were tedious... so now you know what lies beyond the tedium..." He smacked her again and then again, and eventually she was exhausted from the wrangle and the shocks to her body. "I am sorry..." she cried, so that he paused. "Are you?"

"Yes... yes... I am truly sorry... you win."

"It is not about winning, Melissa... 'tis about quelling the battle..."

He slapped her three more times, and she thought she would weep from the sheer frustration of not knowing what was needed or what to do next. From the realisation of defeat in the face of merciless pursuit, when she had already given in.

"Please, stop!"

He did so. She became motionless and closed her eyes, and waited to see if this was yet another lull into false security. She was trembling from an assortment of reactions that would not be stilled or subdued, and threatened to leave her more vulnerable. "I am sorry," she said again. "Believe me."

He released her arm and moved away, and she heard the door close as he left the bedroom.

He had twice, when they were at school and quite rebellious, caned their behinds, merely flicking them with the instrument in truth, though they had made much of it and vowed never to forgive him. It had been as nothing compared to this; no one in her life had ever slapped her this hard, not even way back in her childhood. She was stunned with shock. It was little, perhaps in the greater scheme of things. But it was somehow everything in the landscape of where they had been and where they had yet to go.

She collapsed onto the bed and allowed herself to cry. Though It was the defeat in the game that upset her the most.

# Gossip and Garden Vegetables

They met in one of the less popular tea shops in the town – it was better than risking another meeting with Caroline Wentworth before they were prepared.

"I hope this doesn't mean we can never frequent the Pink Parrot again," said Melanie almost petulantly.

"Of course not... only for the time being," replied Melissa and pulled a face at the unappetising round bun she ate. "Certainly, we cannot be putting up with this substandard fayre."

Melanie discarded her own cake and called for the waitress. "So what exactly happened?"

"He has managed it at last..." said Melissa.

Melanie turned to her. "Managed it?... managed what?"

"What do you think?" replied her friend.

There was an elongated pause as Melanie wracked her brain and then made an expression of immense surprise and illumination. "You don't mean..." The waitress arrived.

"Sssh," hissed Melissa, and the waitress looked at them both.

"This is quite inedible," Melanie told her primly.

"Inedible?" repeated the waitress, as if speaking with someone from foreign parts. "Do you wish to explain further, Madam?"

"She means it is not fit to eat..." Melissa offered. "And this round bun is much the same..."

The waitress, an older woman with grizzled grey-black hair under a white broderie angle cap, assumed a disdainful expression, "None of our other customers have complained..."

"Then perhaps they are without discernment of palet..." said Melanie.

"Or too polite to make a fuss.!" added Melissa.

"I am sure they are not..." said the waitress provokingly, and Melanie looked at her mutinously. "Whatever... we shall pay only for the tea..."

"I don't think I have seen you ladies in here before..." ventured the waitress, as if this were somehow relevant.

"Nor shall you see us again." Melanie said, and she extracted coinage from her purse and threw it onto the table and rose. "Come, Lissy, let us leave."

The waitress became more amenable. "I can offer you something else to replace these items."

"No... Thank you. It will doubtless be as tasteless..."

They gathered their reticules and cloaks and left the premises.

"Now where?" said Melissa.

"The Pink Parrot, of course... nowhere else can be trusted to meet our standards."

"But..." Melissa hurried to catch her up, "but what if she is in there?... Caroline!"

"Then we face her and sort the matter out," Melanie explained rapidly.

"But he has destroyed the sketch of her aunt's residence!"

"That is not your fault... 'tis her own fault for not giving a true address where she might be reached... and besides, I doubt she will care..."

"But I am in the wrong of it..." wailed Melissa.

"No, he is... Atilla!" said Melanie, using her favourite nickname for Fairchild.

Caroline Wentworth was not in their favourite tea-shop, though Melissa was on edge in case she happened to arrive. They took a seat at one of their usual tables and were served with highly acceptable confectionery and tea.

* * *

Meanwhile, in Caroline's well concealed house, she shouted to Richard not to disturb her as she finished dressing herself and her hair in the bedroom – she could hear his footsteps, heavy and determined and measured, coming along the landing corridor. "Dickie, I shall be half an hour... I told you that a little while ago... except then it was an hour."

She disliked being seen before she was ready. Women needed to retain their mystique; they needed to be seen only when perfect – or as near as nature would permit.

"Don't be stupid, Caro... I need to talk to you." Richard Fairchild hovered outside the bedroom door, but hesitated to go against her in this way; she could be very aggressive when crossed.

"Then you must wait…"

"I have to leave for town in ten minutes!" he said in as firm a voice as he could muster.

"That will be sufficient… you may enter then, or I shall come down."

He sighed and made noises of exasperation – one of a multitude of men, he supposed, made to stand outside bedroom doors for vainglorious reasons which accomplished little.

The view from the landing window gave onto a wooded area which splayed backwards into a greater and denser forested area, into which he had never ventured. Perhaps no one had. It had perhaps not been traversed for hundreds of years. It disturbed him to imagine going in there after dark and he gazed into it, as the winter sunshine allowed access to certain parts of its interior – tangled with trees of all sizes and lethal looking green growth sprouting thorns and branches. Normally, when the sun was not high, one could not see so clearly its hazardous depth. A person could die if they ventured into such territory and never be found. It reminded him of dark fairy tales he had read as a child, procured from a library of them belonging to one of his cousins.

He became enthralled with the area in a way that had not occurred previously because he had not lingered on the landing with intent and in need of visual diversion.

An age passed, fifteen minutes perhaps, and Caroline opened the bedroom door. "You may enter now."

"So good of you…" he stepped inside.

"Well… if you will interrupt me when I am dressing."

"Dressing!" echoed Richard. "You might have dressed an entire village in the time you have taken…"

Caroline took up her ermine wrap and seated herself at the dressing table to finish with the powder brush. "How you do exaggerate!" She wafted the powder in a careless fashion, meant to be a light touch, over her features. The air was laden with it. He took out his kerchief in readiness to sneeze. "What is it you want?" she enquired.

"I want to know what you will do next…. about this painting and my brother's chit of a wife."

As the air settled and the powdering was finished, she laid down the brush, having given him time to adjust his irksome attitude to her generosity in admitting him to the room. "I have told you... I will do no more."

"But we need a signature... from her." He expostulated.

"Then you should have planned it better..."

"I thought she would readily accept your offer... we both did."

"No... *you* did!" emphasised his mistress. "I do not know the girl... and I never assume things about people with whom I am not well acquainted... unlike you!"

Richard huffed with impatience and examined a piece of her jewellery he did not think he had seen before. "Where is this from?"

"Never mind... put it down... stop prying into things which don't belong to you."

"But where is it from? I do not recall seeing it before... it looks expensive... the stone is a sapphire... amid small diamonds if I am not mistaken."

"'Tis fake..." declared Caroline. "And it is not your concern where it's from."

He dropped the brooch and looked at her dubiously. Her ability to acquire goods that were not her own was both worrying and impressive. "You will be the death of us!"

"Of us? I do not think I will ever need to embroil you if I am arrested." She surveyed herself in her dressing table mirror, turning her face this way and that to ensure there was not a demarcation line between her make-up and her neck.

"If only I could believe that..." he said and wandered to the bed and sat. "Betimes, I need you to reconsider..."

"Reconsider?"

"The matter of my sister-in-law and the painting."

"I have told you, I shall not!... she has made her decision, obviously."

"You cannot know that, as you have not seen her since... had you given her my office address, she may have replied in the affirmative by now."

"I feel sure she would have been out here again had she been willing... she would have wanted the advance on the work..."

"She may not, I doubt she is so experienced or business-minded." Richard remarked.

"Perhaps not, but that friend of hers would have advised her."

He saw the sense in these words, but still it begged a lot of questions.

"And what did he say, Anthony?... when you made sure to tell him the other day..." she enquired into his ruminations.

Richard looked omnisciently into the distance and could not help smiling. "Very little... he was quite understandably surprised by my arrival... he was quite tight lipped, as is his wont... he listened and said nothing beyond: *'I have told you to stay away'*..."

Caroline turned and frowned and shook her head, a pearl drop earring almost attached to one of her ears. "And you said?"

"I told him that I did not think an offer of a painting commission could be included in his structure at all."

She made a contemptuous noise and clipped on the other earring. "What a fool you are!... you should have stayed away from him... but you could not stop yourself gloating at her ability to defy him..."

"'Tis true... I could not," admitted Richard. "The look on his face, the one he failed to conceal, was satisfying in the extreme..."

"Then leave matters there!" advised Caroline, rising from the dressing table and taking a last look at herself in the mirror.

"I cannot... that was just a little token of glory... and I need her signature."

"You will not get it!"

Richard stood also and crossed to her and took her in his arms and caressed her back and nuzzled his chin against her face, the profuse powder irritating his nostrils, but he persevered. "If you went to call on her..."

"No!"

"If you just made a courtesy visit to see how she feels now about the commission..."

"Why me? You visit!"

"If Anthony is at home he will not attack you... he may very well attack me... he is liable to become quite beside himself during our spats... he has no self control... he never had."

"I think he has huge self control... I think he is noted for it... except where you are concerned..." she pulled away from his embrace. "And that, of course, is because you have bullied and tormented him unmercifully when you were boys, no doubt."

"No doubt," agreed Richard.

"But you are not boys now, Richard... and he may just decide to do you an injury... whichever of us goes to see her."

He heaved a sighing breath. "So long as I have a signature, I can live with that possibility."

* * *

In the tea shop, Melanie had now heard all the latest news from Back Lane House, delivered in the hurried whispering tone adopted for such updates, which regular customers were used to from the two young ladies when they frequented the shop, attracting more attention than if they had spoken normally.

"... I can scarce believe it... he has finally delivered on the threat...
"

"Yes..." snapped Melissa. "And I am at a loss what to think..."

"Perhaps that he has bested you?"

Melissa inclined her head in confirmation but then shook it vehemently. "Were it only that simple!"

"Well, he has! And it is!" said Melanie. "And I told you it would be unpleasant."

"I am not an idiot.... I knew that for myself."

"So how do you feel about it?"

Melissa picked up her fork and lifted a slice of vanilla and raspberry slice. "My behind still aches..." she said demurely.

Melanie laughed. "I meant about the occurrence in general..."

"I cannot tell... I am unsure how I feel."

"Perhaps you are satisfied now that he has finally given you what you thought you desired."

Melissa dropped the fork, which Melanie hated her to do; the vulgar clanging sound it made upon the table. "I have never desired it."

"Liar!" Melanie was occupied with her own confectionery and was beyond content with the taste. Melissa made her cat-like, inscrutable face and pursed her lips. "Although..." continued Melanie, "it has to be said that he could have delivered at any time during the past months of your marriage... had he wanted to... t'would not have been difficult for him..."

"You under-estimate me..." said Melissa sharply.

"I do not... but you overestimate your own power... he is bigger than you, stronger, and a male."

"Hmm." concurred Melissa through a delicious mouthful, her cat-like look seeming to centre on the food, though Melanie remained unconvinced. "'Tis somewhat true."

"'Tis entirely true..."

"What are you implying?" Melissa asked reluctantly.

"That this goes beyond the game.... this has angered him in the real and immeasurable sense... he could not prevent himself."

"He was undoubtedly very enraged," said Melissa, and Melanie watched her carefully. "I had to plead with him to cease."

Melanie laughed. "That should teach you!... but we shall see..."

"I am refusing to share a bed with him..." declared Melissa triumphantly. "So that will teach him as well."

"Maybe... maybe not... he could force you to that also if he chooses."

An astounded silence came from Melissa's side of the table; she was aghast and disgusted. "I do not think he shall..."

"Neither do I... but now you have cut off your nose to spite your face."

"Indeed... but what choice did I have?"

"You could just have admitted your folly... and apologised."

"I did... to make him stop slapping me."

"Not the same thing... he will be wise to that."

"Quite!"

"Has he complained of this bed separation?"

"No, but it has only been two nights... nor will he... we are both very proud..."

"Just so," said Melanie. "You are two sides of the same coin."

An age passed and far too much cake was consumed along with a gallon of tea. Melanie broke the silence first. "You were not hurling your uncivil remarks at him, by any chance?"

Melissa considered her response. "Perhaps a couple... but nothing serious... I called him a boorish oaf before we left High Lawns... then I told him not to puff himself up with importance..."

"You see... you provoke him at every turn. You obviously knew what may happen."

The fork dropped again to the table as she registered her silent objection and Melanie seized it. "Lissy, do remember where we are!"

Melissa took a fresh fork from the next table. "Do you expect me not to retaliate, for Heaven's Sake?"

"Not in a foolish unguarded way... I do not."

"He cannot just rule the roost in any way he decides..."

"But he can... and you always knew he would if it came to it!"

"Stop taking his side!" Melissa helped herself to a generous forkful of Melanie's half finished cream sponge in a fit of desperation and Melanie lifted her plate out of reach.

"I am not taking his side. I would sooner give up cake than take his side... but I am putting it to you that deliberately antagonising him is not aligning with some of your previous objections..."

"Ever since you married Geoffrey..." Melissa said, leaning forward to whisper even lower whilst pretending to smooth her skirt, "you talk more and more like a lawyer..."

Melanie's laughter was joyous and broke any tension. "Naturally, I listen to his addresses and summaries when he rehearses for court... he likes me to..."

"Well, stop it... 'tis very vexing... and more than a little affected."

Melanie emitted further merriment, this time more of a giggle – which felt quite wonderful. Melissa grinned and then made a polite face as she dabbed her lips and pushed away the plate to denote her repletion with the food. "Of course, I am already missing him in bed."

"Good God!... there is no gain saying you..." said her friend. "You had better begin seducing him back then... lest he look elsewhere for satisfaction. He will not have to wait long... we know that!"

Melissa was horrified at the thought and sat as if frozen to the spot. "I cannot!" she stated eventually. "I do have some self respect. I tried that before... before he..."

"What?... before he what?"

"Before he triumphed..." said Melissa carefully, "and he said I was wanton and manipulative."

"Yes, but that was then..." Melanie offered. "And doubtless he did not believe you were sincere..."

"But if I do not wish him to think he has won...?"

"He has won, Lissy!... this battle at any rate... and you had better accept it."

Melissa took out her purse and summoned the waitress. "I am paying today... so do not protest," she announced.

"Very well.  I suppose you must gain power from somewhere in the short term."

The waitress was nowhere to be seen, and the young girl assistant at the counter studiously refused to look their way as they waved to her. They gave up and waited patiently, and Melanie had fresh thoughts. "What is needed now, of course, is a diversionary tactic... in your house... to shift the emphasis."

"Such as?"

They stared out of the window and then at one another at the same moment. "Cousin Honoria..." Melissa said.

Melanie smiled. "Perhaps... let us seriously consider it as we walk through St. Mary's..."

"Must we?... 'tis very chilly!"

"We should... t'will be good for the digestion... we have over-indulged... I shall need to go and loosen my laces in a moment."

* * *

In the kitchens at High Lawns the gossip was underway. Peggy had called to select the produce from the gardens, of which Back Lane House were given a generous selection when it had been freshly picked. Mr Harrison had brought Peggy in the cart, as always, with his wife's list of the produce needed. And Peggy and the High Lawns' cook selected the vegetables and the fruit while he drank coffee with the footmen outside.

At once Matilda grabbed Peggy's shoulder and pushed her into the one chair at the work table. She placed tea in front of her - not coffee, which was cheaper - and Peggy looked suspiciously at Matilda.

"Now tell us the whole..." said Matilda as she brought the milk jug.

"What whole?" enquired Peggy.

The cook called from the stove. "Leave her be, Matilda... don't be poking your nose into things don't concern you"

Matilda, who was assistant cook, ignored her superior and took hold of the saucer as Peggy reached for it, as if to pull it away. "This kerfuffle John says they were in two nights back... their Lord and Ladyship... or I'll pour that tea down the sink."

"What Lord and Ladyship?..."

"The Fairchilds... you gormless wench..."

Peggy lifted the saucer near to her face, for safekeeping, and then the cup, and sipped.

"I don't know about it... I b'aint working here!"

"We know that... but he pushed her into their trap and took her home by force..." cried Matilda, watching Peggy steadily drink the tea. "You must have known about it over yonder..."

The cook stepped from the stove. "Don't speak if you don't want, Peggy..." she said, but paused to hear any opening words.

"He was angrier than I ever seen him... he let his supper go cold." replied Peggy in a forlorn manner.

"Yes, and?" demanded the garrulous Matilda. "We gathered he was angry... but what about?..."

Agnes, the maid entered, and said. "If you are talking of the argument between Mr and Mrs Fairchild, Tilly, then don't... 'Tis none of your business..."

Matilda turned from Peggy to Agnes, then turned back to the stove as saucepans boiled over, "How do you know of it then?"

"Their man has just told John... I heard them," said Agnes. "But neither should he be trading tales..."

Tilly looked again at Peggy and poured her more tea. Peggy had been warned before taking the position as maid – by Mr Fairchild's mother who was involved in the orphanage at which she had been raised, and by others in charge there – that she must never under any circumstances talk about her employers outside. But Tilly was as persistent as a wasp at a picnic and Peggy was no match for her.

"He told me to get her a hot bath set up... she was soaking wet... then he ordered her upstairs to the bedroom."

"And...?" said Matilda. "You must have been up there... or how did she get out of her laces?"

"She don't wear none ever in the day..." replied Peggy and blushed; she had revealed personal details of her mistress without thinking. "I took her clothes and she said she'd manage by herself from there... so I went to bed."

"Fancy wearing no stays," said Tilly. "A lady of her position..."

"She don't need 'em..." the cook said. "Her figure's lithe and slender." She spoke with pride, as if she were responsible in some way for the enviable figure of the daughter of the house.

Matilda scoffed, jealous of all good figures, and changed the subject. "He could order me upstairs any time he liked and have his way with me..." she opined.

The cook took umbrage. "If those saucepans boil dry, I'll be ordering you out of the kitchen... for good... and I told you a'fore, Tilly, don't be making those kind of remarks... the girl's not more than thirteen or fourteen."

"I be fifteen in three weeks," put in Peggy mildly.

"Even so... I won't have that smutty talk in here."

"Try and find out what he's angry about..." Tilly told Peggy and handed her a scone on a plate as a bribe. "Listen at their bedroom door if you must... then come over and tell us."

"Leave her be..." sanctioned the cook in a rising tone. "Prying into their private matters... if Mr Jarvis hears of it, there'll be hell to pay... you do no such thing, Peggy... take no notice of this one! If you get caught listening at doors, you'll be for it."

"What's he like to work for?" persevered Tilly. "The master over yonder?"

"He's right enough... so's she..." said the hapless Peggy through the first bite of scone. "He's kindly towards me... "

"O'course he is..." remarked the cook in a softening way, afraid of the repercussions of gossip. "He's a gentleman, that is why... not like some of 'em as just pretend to be and are really now't a pound when it comes down to it."

"He's always learning me words..." said Peggy absently, the scone almost demolished.

"The maid, Agnes, had been educated at a dame school and was literate. You mean he's *teaching* you words, Peggy..."

"What?" asked Tilly. "What sort of words? Swear words?"

"O'course not swear words..." said Peggy, offended. "Proper words... like when I says 'em wrong..."

Agnes and the cook shook with laughter. "He'll be at it a few years then!" offered the cook.

"He's a lingerist..." Peggy informed them. "He knows a lot of words."

"A linguist..." corrected Agnes, "not a lingerist."

Matilda gazed wistfully into various saucepans as she stirred. "He could teach me anything he liked... any woman 'ud be glad to have him close."

"Enough of that talk, Matilda!" bemoaned the cook in a louder voice still. "We don't want to hear any more ribald chatter..."

Then the butler came in, followed by John looking sheepish. "I hope there's no gossip afoot... nor any of your inappropriate remarks, Matilda," said Mr Jarvis.

"Those were just about starting, Mr Jarvis..." the cook told him – traitor to the cause of entertainment. "But I've put a stop to it..."

"Thank you, Mrs Blenkinsop... I will not sanction gossip about the family, as I have said to you before... and John, put those baskets in the cart and get about your business... you be off back now, Peggy..." instructed Jarvis.

Mrs Blenkinsop covered her concern with a maternal attitude and gave the girl an orange. "Now Peggy, give that note to Mrs Harrison... tell her that's the last of the peas and the broad beans... there's only sprouts, carrots and parsnips for the next few weeks."

"I shall, Ma'am," said Peggy and looked dully at the orange.

"And don't repeat anything you've heard in here back there... especially not from the likes of her..." She pointed a finger at Matilda. "It could cause bother."

"I shan't, Ma'am." Peggy bobbed a courtesy to Mrs Blenkinsop.

"Good girl," concluded the cook. Peggy was close to tears – she had said far too much about Back Lane House, and the thought of repercussions filled her with dread. Agnes looked at her sympathetically while piling cups and saucers on a tray for the drawing room. "Peggy, do not upset yourself... you have not yet said anything wrong... if we disregard the comments about Mrs Fairchild's under garments..."

"I have though..." Peggy lamented. "I've said what I shouldn't have... and I might be turned off." Copious tears rolled down her cheeks.

"No, no... we will always support you if it comes to it... t'was this trollop coercing you... she's shameless, as we all know," Agnes said.

Peggy was at a loss to know what 'coercing' meant and stared at Agnes through her tears.

"Agnes is right, Peggy..." counselled Mrs Blenkinsop. "No need to worry... you carry on working well and you have nought to fret over...."

Matilda turned on Agnes. "And who are you calling a trollop?... vicious old trout!"

"You awful Godless girl..." declared Agnes calmly while brewing the tea. Then Mrs Blenkinsop adopted a ruling stance and tried to organise her domain. "Matilda, Miss Cardew is senior to you in position and age... you will show some respect."

"Don't make her any better than me..." argued Tilly, a ladle held aloft like a weapon.

"That is a matter of opinion..." Mr Jarvis announced and urged Peggy to leave immediately and board the cart. She was followed by John, carrying the baskets. Mr Jarvis closed his eyes and drew a heavy breath. "I knew there'd been inappropriate remarks passed..."

Agnes Cardew and Mr Jarvis were quite friendly, being high in each other's estimation and both reasonably educated, able to communicate intelligently about world events and higher matters, of an evening when work was done. Though he was more than twenty years her senior, he was fond of sitting with her in his pantry, enjoying a glass of something and the sort of camaraderie shared by the like-minded in an otherwise barren wasteland. Agnes was the upstairs and personal maid to Marguerite Shaw. She and Mr Jarvis both knew their worth. There were three other housemaids, but Agnes Cardew was the eldest and most powerful, taking on some of the duties of a housekeeper and relieving Marguerite Shaw of the necessity of employing one. "She has reduced this poor girl to tears..." she informed Mr Jarvis in a dignified manner. "Making her say things she wouldn't otherwise divulge about Mr and Mrs Fairchild..."

Jarvis listened carefully to Agnes, as always, and then glanced at Mrs Blenkinsop. "'Tis true I'm afeared, Mr Jarvis!" the cook said. "I'm always telling her about her careless talk and lack of respect... until I'm blue in the face...

"I never made 'er divulge nothing..." persisted Tilly. "She was enjoying her tea and a scone..."

The two young scullery maids, each related to the cook, stood agog with fascination. "You two get on with your work..." Mr Jarvis told them.

"Oh yes, you did, Tilly..." contradicted Mrs Blenkinsop. "Threatening to take her tea unless she talked... telling her to listen outside doors..."

Mr Jarvis grew quietly scandalised and awaited more of the depressing narrative.

"Not to mention her comments regarding her shameless desires for Mr Fairchild..." Agnes put in.

John and Matilda, both lascivious by nature, exchanged eye contact; they made *shameless* comments about lots of folk and there was no law against it yet. Except in the kitchen, where Mr Jarvis issued dictats like some kind of self-appointed emperor.

Mr Jarvis was prone to firing Matilda on the spot, but she was assistant cook, and there was the lunch service to be gone through, and supper, and he was not so foolhardy or power-mad as to risk the efficiency of the dining room. He sat in the chair at the table and deliberated with all eyes upon him. Then Mrs Blenkinsop had a further thought and addressed Tilly. "I'll tell you something else, my girl... Peggy has come on a placing from one of his ma's orphanages..."

"What orphanage... I was from an orphanage..." interjected Tilly with the utmost scorn.

Mrs Blenkinsop continued with dignity. "Mr Fairchild's mother is involved in the local orphanage committee... she takes a particular interest in all her charges, so I hear... imagine if your remarks about her son were to get back... and herself wed to a bishop..."

"She's Swedish, I hear..." Agnes told Mrs Blenkinsop informatively.

"I believe she may be Danish..." Jarvis intervened, "... a very winsome and charming woman, to be sure"

"Good to gaze on, like 'im then..." said the irreverent Tilly. "Apples don't fall far from the tree..."

"Tilly!" reproved the cook. "Will you take heed of what you've been told..."

Tilly made a derisive sound. "I dunna care where she's from... or who she's wed to..."

John re-entered, having seen off the cart to Back Lane House and Mr Jarvis came to life again. "I will see you, Tilly, in my pantry after service... and as for you..." he turned to John. "You had better mind yourself..."

"I ain't done nothing wrong, Mr Jarvis," said John in a hard-done-to voice.

"Gossiping with their manservant!" snapped Jarvis. "So you may take this as a final warning."

"Yes, Mr Jarvis!" said John humbly, though he felt himself to be innocent. Tilly smirked, and Agnes glared at them. Mrs Bkenkinsop was always issuing warnings; they were like leaves falling in autumn, but the butler was another matter.

Matilda winked at John as Mr Jarvis turned to go, and John winked in return, and all might be revealed for consumption at the end of a long day.

# Sketches, Signatures & Oversights.

Three days later, Melanie watched her husband over the top of the newspaper he held, which stood between them like a shield. "'Tis so inconsiderate to read at the table," she told him, "at the very start of the day... before we have even had enough time to become bored with each other..." She paused and allowed the words to sink in. Geoffrey lowered the paper and smiled; his wife's satire was a source of delight to him. "Well, my love, 'tis the only chance I get to read the news... at the breakfast table."

She sighed. "By the way, I shall take my horse today, so I shall not need the trap."

The paper was lowered to the table. "What?... why?"

"I need to ride, of course..."

Geoffrey considered Melanie closely. "But I thought you said you might be with child again..."

"Yes... but 'tis early yet."

"Nevertheless... I do not think you should ride. In fact, I am telling you not to do so."

Melanie remained quiet and stared at him as he raised the paper.

He could not concentrate. "Where is it you think to go?"

"To a residence several miles away, and really it will be quicker."

He was suspicious, and being of an acute and wide-thinking mind, he landed on another concern. "Which residence? I hope you have dropped this business of the painting...you and Melissa! I hope that is not still the arch plan of the moment..."

"She has not mentioned the painting in a few days. I think she has rejected the idea..." This much was true, of course, and he was somewhat mollified. "I hope you are not encouraging her to quarrel with him."

"They need no encouragement from me, Geoffrey... 'Tis a veritable pastime with them... when they are not making love... I do not know why she agreed to marry him."

"Love is an imponderable," said Geoffrey from behind the paper. "People have been making bad judgments based on love since time immemorial... and undoubtedly, she loves him... anyone can see that."

"She certainly has some kind of affection for him... 'tis true" Melanie concurred. "God knows why"

"That is something only she knows," said her husband, the successful lawyer, with a kind of whimsical salute to professional experience. "And 'tis done now... so do not encourage her into poor wifedom."

"Poor what?" Melanie laughed loudly. "Is that a legal term?... *wifedom!*" Her laughter continued for several moments. Until Geoffrey Gillis was inclined to see the humorous side of his pompous statement, and grinned.

She needed the horse to ride over and survey the residence from which they thought to next extricate Honoria. A horse was the best way to traverse land, especially private land, and she waited to see if Geoffrey would return to the subject of her riding, but he did not, absorbed suddenly by an article concerning one of his clients. And then the maid came in to say that a clerk from his office was in the hall with urgent papers he had forgotten to sign the day before, which were needed imminently at court. He rose with some alacrity and left the table. She followed him to the hall, kissed him as he received the prepared nib from the clerk at the hall table, and went to check on baby Robert with his nurse, before she left the house.

The ride to the residence of Honoria's parents was a good few miles across country. She relished it. An accomplished rider since her seventh year – her father breeding and dealing in horses as a business – she took the journey at a steady trot and sang to herself as she went. She was certain she was with child again, but also certain that a steady canter on this mild and clement December day would not put her at any risk. Geoffrey was a worrier, and a careless rider (she could out-ride him any time), preferring, as he did, to take the trap or be driven when possible. He little understood the nuisances of horses and under-estimated her ability.

The ride to Honoria's home was longer than she thought. She was tired by the time she returned home and needed to retire to bed for two hours.

* * *

Peggy was in tears during the day, and Melissa was hard-pressed to learn the reason. Until Peggy could stand the tension and the secrecy no longer. Melissa was making her sit by her as she primed a brush with some kind of black ink at the dining table, and Peggy sorted the silver cutlery, sipping soda water with lime juice; a drink Melissa believed was good for the nervous system. She knew that eventually Peggy would be inclined to unburden herself. Then, suddenly, into the tranquility and the ocean of silence, Peggy blurted it all out, "I was talking and I shouldn't have been... at High Lawns."

"I see..." said her mistress, young enough to be her sister but old enough to employ her. "About what?" She continued to work, without looking at the maid. It was too chilly to work in her makeshift art room, so she was using the dining table.

"About some things Tilly made me tell her..." Peggy went on to explain the bare bones of the tittle-tattle and the row it had caused in the kitchen. Melissa told her not to worry. But Peggy did worry, and under this duress she confessed to telling Tilly, in the hearing of the others, that Melissa wore no corset or laces during the day.

Melissa was between astonishment and amusement. She laughed as she sketched. Servant gossip was something she had grown up with. It was a fact of life like interfering relatives. "Why on earth did she want to know about that?"

"She was saying I must know about the set-to you had with Mr Fairchild... 'cos I'd be assisting you with your laces when you got home and be bound to hear things... and I blurted out that you don't wear none."

Melissa paused to follow this logic and then deduced how Tilly's mind had possibly worked to gain information.

"Mrs Blenkinsop said you 'as a lovely figure and don't need to wear laces,'" Peggy said, brightening.

"That was nice of her," remarked Melissa absently. "What else was said?"

Peggy was reluctant to go on, but Melissa looked at her with raised brows. "I didn't want to say nothing, Madam, but Tilly was pressing me."

Melissa wrinkled her nose and then remembered Matilda from before she herself had wed. "Oh, yes... that dreadful girl... I can't think why they keep her on."

"Mr Jarvis doesn't like her, nor does Agnes. They say she's got a foul mouth..."

"Perhaps they will let her go now..." Melissa said lightly and carried her sketchbook to the light of the window to scrutinise more closely certain lines of the drawing. Peggy felt she could let it all out, even though Mrs Blenkinsop had told her not to. But Mrs Blenkinsop did not have to live with the worry of being 'let go' and homeless. "Tilly makes rude remarks about Mr Fairchild," she said, and Melissa stopped perusing the sketchbook and frowned and eventually enquired. "Rude? For example?"

"Like 'as how she'd love to go upstairs with him... and how he could have his way with her...'"

Melissa froze, extremely shocked for a few seconds – the brazenness of this woman was breathtaking – and then she saw it in the real sense, of ilk and society, and she giggled softly. "That is not a rude remark, but a lude one... and Peggy, you must not upset yourself over this... just do not repeat it elsewhere... to anyone else."

"But... but..." Peggy floundered. "Mrs Blenkinsop says there will be a lot of trouble..."

Melissa smiled at Peggy, a slow and dawdling creature, but good at heart. "Not unless you tell anyone."

"I would never do that!"

Melissa sat beside her again and sketched lightly. "Peggy, do you understand what Tilly meant by that remark?"

"A bit..." said Tilly. "But not altogether"

"You do not need to yet... but you must never agree to go upstairs with any man... until you are older and meet someone you wish to wed." She felt like a fraud. She had always wanted to bed her husband before marriage; she had scorned the question of needing marriage to be intimate with someone. But Peggy was of a different walk of life, with no protection if things turned bad.

Peggy looked at her with wide eyes. She couldn't imagine any man offering her marriage.

"You must not agree to letting any man... or boy touch you yet... do you understand?"

"Yes, Madam..." said Peggy. "I am truly sorry, Madam."

"You did nothing wrong... when you are a little older and feel you wish to know more about... about life and men... and men and women together... myself and Mrs Gillis, or Miss Darnley, will sit with you and explain things. Both of those ladies are excellent on female issues. They will put you straight so that you are prepared."

She knew that Susan, in particular, was zealous on the question of young women knowing about their bodies and the facts of life and not remaining ignorant, or solely in the hands of their prudish female relatives. Susan was a woman of forward-thinking reform and better welfare. Melanie, of course, was a woman who thought it right to enjoy life and sensuality.

"Yes, Madam... thank you..." Peggy was elated; it meant that she would not be 'let go' for gossiping, and that she might be with them in future times.

"And do not tell him either... Mr Fairchild... of what Tilly has said of him."

"The very thought of it..." Peggy shrieked. "I'd sooner die."

"Besides," added Melissa listlessly, "half the women of the shire wish to go upstairs with him... the only difference being they are careful where they say it."

* * *

The fundraising event was coming up, and she was busy preparing paintings to be sold or auctioned so that the money could go to the orphanage committee. Her cousin Gregory, with her long-time friend and his fiancée, Millicent, would play the piano, and other musicians or performers would give their skills. Money would be raised in plentiful amounts. They had already had one successful event of its kind last year, for the alms schools, of which Susan was the main organiser. But Susan might be very pregnant this time and not wish to be so involved. Melissa was looking forward to the event – she had enjoyed the last one and was ready to take on more responsibility for the running of the occasion.

She painted fervently, moving from one canvas to the next watercolour – two or three underway at one time – and worked in her chilly art room until the light faded in the afternoon. All this endeavour helped to keep her mind off the fact that she was in the midst of the first serious estrangement with her husband. It was four days now but felt like four years.

She was removing her paint smock when Peggy came to say Mrs Gillis had called. She went immediately to the hall to receive her and found Melanie in her riding habit. "I have called briefly..." Melanie launched at once into explanation. "To tell you, we may collect Honoria soon... I have visited the premises and crept about the gardens and took note of the entrances and so on."

"Did anyone see you?"

"Not that I am aware... I think we should do it before the weather turns... 'tis a good distance but the lanes are not too bad at present... perhaps tomorrow or the next day... Geoffrey is in London then and I may use the trap to come here. Though I think perhaps we should take your trap... seeing that she is your relative... but you should go in alone, and when you have been admitted, I will take the trap off and wait at the end of their driveway for you... then we can make a hasty departure."

"Yes. very well..." Melissa was emboldened as always by Melanie's enthusiasm and excellent planning. "Perhaps we should leave early afternoon... people are not disposed to receiving visitors in the morning usually... but I must think of a reason for our call, and for getting her alone..."

They hatched a more meticulous scheme with minor details and were pleased with themselves.

"I must go," Melanie said. "If I arrive after Geoffrey, he will question me about where I have been. I prefer that he does not know I have ridden. Betimes, 'tis better we keep this to ourselves."

"Yes, if we are successful and Honoria agrees to accompany me, I can tell people she is coming to visit for a few days... until we have a firmer plan."

"Does Atilla know of this?" asked Melanie.

"He is aware of her plight but thinks I am being overly dramatic... he was indifferent to the matter when we discussed it... though he has consented to my bringing her to visit."

"Good... after all, what harm can it do!"

"He thinks it interference into things which do not concern us..."

"Phooey!" declared Melanie. "If he were being held prisoner he would welcome someone's interference no doubt..."

"He does not believe she is being held prisoner... that is the overly dramatic part, in his view... but we are barely speaking, so he is not likely to be vocal on the matter, even if she arrives..."

Melanie made for the door and put on the rather strange-looking hat she wore for riding. Melissa stared at it as usual and wondered how it would look in a painting. "Perhaps you should take some tea before leaving... 'Tis quite cold now."

"I will survive... I cannot abide the taste of tea at present." She paused on the steps as Melissa opened her mouth in astonishment, then threw over her shoulder. "Did I mention I may be increasing again?"

Shocked into silence, Melissa gaped. "I thought I had misheard you..."

"You did not..." replied Melanie succinctly, and she watched her as she ran towards her horse grazing on the front lawn. "Melanie, you should not be riding now," she called, but knew she had been ignored.

* * *

At lunch next day she said to him, "I shall need the trap this afternoon."

"Oh shall you!" he replied, as usual perusing something in a scribbled language she did not recognise. His tone implied that she was high-handed in making this claim and assuming it would be met. "Perhaps it might be more polite to enquire if that is convenient," he remarked.

"I do not care what is more polite," she said coolly, rising and taking a piece of bread and cheese, and putting it on a plate to take with her. "I must use it to transport canvases for the fundraiser."

He looked at her, his distinctive green eyes narrowing as he thought.

"The reason is immaterial... your rudeness is not."

She might have known he would see it that way. She knew him well. She almost smiled; her rudeness was what had cemented their relationship. He exhaled wearily and began to scribble. "Are you going to persist in this attitude towards me?"

"Which attitude do you mean?"

"The one where you treat me as a near stranger."

"Isn't that a mixing of metaphors?"

His eyes again lifted, his lashes protecting his expression, and she was tempted to lean over and kiss him; it was like resisting blackberry jam when it was in season and on the table. "That very much depends on the way 'near' is meant," he said, playing her at her game.

"I shall take the trap... in a quarter of the hour..." she announced from the doorway. "If you object, you must realise you are jeopardising the profits of the fundraiser... you will be culpable."

"Oh yes... of course!" he said, faking serious concern and frowning and nodding judiciously.

It infuriated her. "Sarcastic pig..." she said under her breath.

He looked up. "I beg your pardon?"

"Nothing."

He continued to scribble. "I thought for a moment you called me a pig... I trust I am mistaken," he said smoothly.

"Very," she said and went swiftly from the room.

She was becoming worse with her insults and uncivil remarks, but he was not in the mood for chasing after her. He was tired and lacking in sleep; missing her in the bed as much as she missed him. He scribbled more ardently to try to induce concentration.

Not long afterwards, he was riding out of the gates when a phaeton paused to allow his horse clear passage before turning into their driveway. He glimpsed a woman driving the gig but did not recognise her. She had on an elaborate hat with a large brim covering her upper face. He thought she was perhaps something to do with the fundraising event, come to assist his wife, or perhaps another artist.

He took little notice and continued into the town at a faster gallop.

The woman was Caroline Wentworth, who ignored him in the same way he had ignored her.

Laden with canvases, Melissa staggered with them into the hall – the manservant busy preparing the trap. She would drop them off at High Lawns before carrying on to Melanie's home. When the doorbell clanged, she opened it herself and beheld Caroline with near horror.

"You!" she said unceremoniously.

"Indeed!" said Caroline. How uncivil this little wife of his was withal. *Perhaps that was the fascination. Opposites being known to attract!*

"May I come in?"

"No, you may not... you should not be here..."

Lady Wentworth feigned astonishment.

"What do you want? You have caused enough trouble already..."

"May I come in?" Caroline repeated, a little disdain mixed with surprise, and topped nicely with some chagrin.

"No, you may not!" asserted Melissa again. "If he comes back and finds you here, there will be more trouble..."

"*He?*" echoed Caroline. "Oh, you must mean Anthony?"

"Of course, I mean Anthony... who else would I mean? Now, please leave."

"Would it were quite so simple..." Caroline stepped adroitly past her and entered the hall. Melissa was bereft of words.

"Quite apart from your impoliteness over my visit, you are overlooking the intricacies of our arrangement..."

"What arrangement?" She was fraught with anxiety, not wanting to be late picking up Melanie when time was of the essence, and eager to deter this odious person for good. "I wrote to you saying I would not be taking the art commission, but it came back undelivered." She watched Lady Wentworth seat herself in the hall chair beside the Welsh dresser and remove her gloves. "You purposely gave us an address that is not registered with the dispatch office."

Caroline's eyebrows, as she removed her hat, shot up in two painted lines. "Why on earth would I do that?"

"I have no idea... perhaps so I could not refuse your offer... your motives being nefarious."

"But I am here in person now."

"Yes... and I am asking you to leave."

"Well, I have to say..." Caroline went on urbanely. "Your manner is rude in the extreme."

"I am often noted for it... I call it *plain speaking.*" Melissa grabbed a couple of the canvases for effect and summoned the manservant who waited next to the trap, now parked alongside Caroline's phaeton. He carried the canvases off and into the trap.

"Whatever you call it, Melissa... 'Tis not a fit way to greet visitors."

"You are not a welcome visitor, Lady Wentworth... according to reliable sources, you are not even reputable... and Richard Fairchild is a scoundrel."

Caroline was prone to smiling. She looked about her to disguise her feelings, and Melissa tapped her foot impatiently. "I am saying no to your offer."

"Yes, but... you still have in your possession the sketch..."

"The sketch?"

"Of my aunt's residence, the architectural drawing. Which is of some value."

Melissa began pacing and reflecting. He had told her that he'd been into the art room and then destroyed the sketch. She could not tell Caroline that and expect to be out of the house in a hurry. "'Tis mislaid," she announced.

"Mislaid? How very careless and unprofessional."

"Well, there it is..." She paced and put on her own gloves and assumed an arch expression which brooked no argument but a firm resolve.

"These things happen... now, can you please leave..."

"Not until we have resolved the matter."

She walked around the hall, checking the clock and cursing the timing of the visit. "You must know," she said, "that Richard and Anthony have antipathy."

"Ha! That is an understatement..." trilled Caroline. "There will be a fight to the death one of these days."

"Well then..." declared Melissa. "Why are you trying to precipitate the occurrence?  Please be more amenable to leaving matters."

Caroline rose but did not move. "That drawing is part of a legal document with which I am entrusted... if I do not return it, questions will be asked."

"By whom?"

"Lawyers, of course... have I not just said it is a legal document!"

"It cannot be helped..." said Melissa

Lady Caroline watched her and adjusted her approach. "There is a way it can be solved, I think."

"How?"

"If you give me your signature, asserting that you have seen it but misplaced it. That way, it will be known that it is entirely beyond any retrieval and be written off to happenstance."

Melissa wondered whether to ask Geoffrey first about this, but then realised that Caroline Wentworth may be loath to leave without it. It was her mess – her's and Melanie's. Besides, the less contact she had with this odious woman, the better. She sensed Caroline watching her and knew she would not succumb to defeat. What had been suggested was perhaps innocuous, innocent of any other implication, and without risk. "Very well... but that must be the absolute end of the matter."

Lady Wentworth brought forth a paper from her reticule, which advocated that she had surrendered said sketch to Melissa's temporary possession, and hurriedly, Melissa took a nib from the dresser and signed it. Caroline snatched the paper – rudely for someone who claimed to value politeness – took up her hat and gloves, and left.

It was only on her way to Melanie that she wondered how Caroline knew to prepare the document beforehand. How could she have known that the sketch had been mislaid!

* * *

It grew colder as they rode out to Honoria's parents' residence. The pace was increased as Melanie sized up the weather.

"Did you actually tell me you were expecting once more?" said Melissa as they flew around bends which Melanie claimed to know very well, "... as you were leaving yesterday?"

"I did."

Melissa laughed, for the first time in a while. "And you are pleased?"

"I am... we both are."

She wanted to reach to the side and squeeze her hand – if her friend was pleased, then so was she – but she refrained for fear of disturbing the motion of the vehicle. She was a nervous traveller compared to Melanie. "I am thrilled for you, my love!"

"I am perhaps about two and a half months..."

"Good Lord!... you will have a veritable brood in no time."

"Probably not... Geoffrey is not in favour of too many children."

"Nevertheless, it may happen!"

Melanie was one of those women to whom childbirth was little problem. "You may be like Granny," she said, referring to her paternal grandmother, whom she loved greatly. "She had six children and says that after the first, it was like shelling peas! "

Melanie laughed exultantly and flew round another bend, narrowly avoiding a plodding old-fashioned carriage coming in the

78

opposite direction. The coachmen on top cursing and shouting after them as they drove on.

"Mel, perhaps we are going a little too fast..." Melissa ventured. Her skimpy luncheon was threatening regurgitation. Melanie slowed marginally and said. "Well, you were late..."

"Yes... because I had a visit from Caroline Wentworth."

*"What?"* The trap slowed considerably, and Melissa breathed out. "She wanted the sketch... but he has destroyed it..."

Melanie reduced the trap to a mere trot and looked at her sidelong.

"So what did she say?"

"A great deal... the monstrous woman... that I was unprofessional and careless and so on... I signed some piece of paper to appease her."

"You did what?" For a few seconds, the trap veered to the right and left, and Melanie fought to get it on course once more. "What did it say... this paper?"

She went on to outline it roughly, but she was unsure now exactly what it said, and knew that perhaps she had not read it carefully at all.

"You should not have done that, Lissy!" Melanie sanctioned. "You should have considered who you were dealing with..."

"Perhaps not, but time was of the essence... and 'tis too late now."

Melanie did not increase the speed again, but sat silently and brooded. Eventually saying. "We could have asked Geoffrey..."

"I thought you said he was not happy with the situation."

"I did... but that was before things turned sour. He would have been willing to help at this stage."

"Too late..." she repeated, "'Tis done... and I am not going to think about it... I am concentrating only on cousin Honoria for now."

# While the Going is Good

Melissa waited on the porch for an age for a servant to answer the door. She watched Melanie turn the trap to take it to the drive entrance so that they may speedily depart when the time was right.

Eventually, the door was opened by an elderly female housekeeper, and Melissa remembered her lines. "Good Day... I am Mrs Ainscoe's niece, Melissa Fairchild... I am here to pay a call and deliver a gift."

"A gift?" questioned the housekeeper suspiciously. "Is it someone's birthday?"

Melissa stared her down – was it this person's business to pry into deliveries by relatives! "'Tis for my cousin, Honoria... please tell someone that I am here!"

The housekeeper swung the door open widely and stepped back. "You'd best come in then..."

The house was by far inferior to her own family home and even to her current residence. Her aunt and uncle lived on reduced means (according to her mother – her aunt's sister). The hallway had not been decorated since the Regency and had a distinctly musty odour and scuffed paintwork.

Her aunt appeared. Melissa did not give her time to speak. "Aunt Harriet... how are you?"

Aunt Harriet did little to conceal her shock and misgiving; unsociable by nature, she did not take kindly to surprise visits from richer relations. Her hair was in sporadic paper twists and pushed untidily under a day-cap, much greyed by washing. "Melissa... what on earth are you here for?"

"I was in this area, you see, Aunt... and I have a gift for Honoria. Is she here?"

"Indeed!" said Aunt Harriet. "Where else would she be?"

A good point, of course, regarding someone who was virtually a captive in their own home. Aunt Hariet summoned back the housekeeper – they did not keep a daily maid – and ordered tea before moving to the drawing room, which was cold and lacked a fire.

"What is it, this gift?"

"'Tis a dress. I do not care for the colour, but it would suit Honoria very well... especially with Christmas coming... I may not get a chance to call again before."

Aunt Harriet bridled. "She has enough dresses, thank you all the same... we are not in the business of accepting charity."

"Not charity, Aunt Harriet, I am her cousin. At least let her try it..." persevered Melissa. "May I see her, betimes?"

Then Honoria's father appeared. "Who is it, Hattie?" he enquired and peered at Melissa as if she were a stranger. "Who's this?"

"'Tis Melissa..." said Harriet impatiently. "Maggie and Giles' daughter..." She turned to Melissa. "Don't mind your uncle, his memory's not so good these days, nor his eyesight."

"Nothing wrong with either." Leonard Ainscoe bellowed, his voice resounding in the bleak room.

"She's here to see Honoria..." said Harriet and steered Melissa to a dilapidated sofa placed out of the draft of windows and doors.

"Honoria is not allowed uninvited visitors..." said Leonard unceremoniously. "Does she know you're calling?"

"I believe she does," lied Melissa. "I mentioned at Easter that I would call on her before the year was out."

"Then I shall be having words with her" said the patriarch. "She's no right disobeying me in this way."

"I believe she is four and twenty now..." replied Melissa and looked defiantly at Leonard who gazed defiantly back. "Surely it is her choice when she receives guests!"

The atmosphere now was colder than previously, notwithstanding the barren fire grate. "While she's in this house, she will do as she's told," bellowed the patriarch.

*Well, hopefully she'll not be in this house much longer,* thought Melissa, but inclined her head and gave him the advantage. This rescue was not a moment too soon.

The tea arrived, and obviously, in that short time could not have been brewed properly. "Where is she?" Leonard asked his wife.

"Upstairs polishing mirrors and windows..." Harriet replied unthinkingly.

"Fetch her down here," he told the housekeeper.

Aunt Harriet saw to the tea, pouring it from a very fine china teapot which perhaps only came out for people such as herself.

Then Honoria entered timidly, and Melissa rose to meet her, and Honoria ran to her and embraced her. Melissa held her away as if to survey her and winked broadly. "Honoria... how good to see you"

"And you, Lissy..." said Honoria in a flat voice. She was wearing an apron and a mob cap over her hair as she cleaned or whatever it was they had her doing.

"Honoria, have I not told you to let us know before you accept visitors?" said her father in his censorious tone. Though it was doubtful she had any at all in the usual way.

Honoria, easily chastened, did not speak, and Melissa said quickly. "As I have said to Aunt Harriet, she did not know I was coming today."

"She's brought you a dress, Honoria..." Harriet informed her, and Honoria's eyes brightened for a brief second.

"Perhaps we should see how it looks... and if it fits. Though we are quite the same size..." Melissa took out the blue muslin dress from the bag she carried, and Honora's face lit up. "'Tis beautiful."

"If you're the same size, it will fit." Harriet supplied suspiciously.

"Let us go up and see it on you," Melissa said eagerly.

Honoria looked at her father, whose permission she was used to seeking for all her movements, unless they were for the household's good. He considered matters, patting his copious belly while he perused. He had made his money in the family meat business, a wholesale concern with outposts across the region, and looked as if he had consumed half the profits. His waistcoat, which was garish and unfashionable, stretched across his broad mid-region and was afforded no room to move; only the top button was able to fasten these days. He sported side whiskers of a salt and pepper colour, unkempt and ragged-looking. He was as far removed from the rest of her mother's family in appearance and manners as it was possible to be. He had squandered money on poor investments: horses that did not win and property with dubious leases, and other miscellaneous ventures. Her father called him a *profligate waster* and could barely give him the time of day. Aunt Harriet suffered the stigma of having married beneath her. But the fact that she had married at all, at the ripe old age of thirty-eight, was a miracle she was grateful for.

They all waited for Leonard Ainscoe's approval of the suggestion, and at length he had come to a decision: his remaining money dwindling more and more and his estate in decline, and Christmas looming when some sociability was called for if only for appearance's sake – he was not averse to seeing his daughter acquire a new dress of quality for free.

"Very well... Honoria, take your cousin upstairs and try on the dress... but no more than fifteen minutes, mind."

"No, Papa..." said Honoria and led Melissa to the stairs.

On the second tread, Melissa grabbed Honoria and pulled her up to the bedroom swiftly. "The dress is a ruse," she said. "Do not bother trying it on. I am here to take you with me, but we must hurry."

Honoria was dazed – she entered the bedroom and Melissa followed. She stared at Melissa with abject terror. *"Take me with you?"*

"Remember... at Easter? I said we would get you out of here... well, the time has come."

"But... but... but I am afraid," said Honoria, unbuttoning her skirt.

Melissa stayed her fingers. "Do not bother with that. Put the dress back into the bag and fetch as much as you need in the bag with it. "

Honoria sank to her bed in the freezing bedroom and trembled with terror. Melissa watched her for twenty seconds while she absorbed the development. "Honoria, have you understood me? You must come with me now if you ever mean to live a happy... or even a normal life."

"But where shall I live?... And what will everyone say?"

"Never mind all that. You simply have to have faith... and trust."

"I cannot," said the desolate Honoria. "They will come and take me back."

"They cannot without your consent. "

"But... but..."

Melissa began opening drawers in the one cabinet, which seemed to house her cousins' entire wardrobe, and began throwing in her underwear and a nightgown. "Honoria... 'tis now or never perhaps. Melanie is outside with the trap, and you will be safe with us."

Seven minutes had elapsed already, and Melissa checked her timepiece. Still giving Honoria pause to make the decision.

"Do not let all our planning and effort go to waste," begged Melissa. "I know, and you know, that you can have a better life away from them." She threw a hairbrush into the bag and then some kind of threadbare soft toy, which may at one time have been a small bear.

Honoria bit her nails and made keening sounds of distress and coughed as if choking. Melissa had never seen someone in such confusion and terror.

"What... what about... what about your husband?" Honoria managed at last. "What will he say?"

"He will barely notice you. He is always so busy, and there is a room... he knows you may stay for a while."

"But what after that?" wailed the young woman in a hoarse voice.

"That will sort itself out as we go... there are all sorts of options..." explained Melissa in the calmest voice. Twelve minutes had gone by. She put away her timepiece, then Honoria jumped up and grabbed the bag, startling Melissa in the stillness of the gloomy, silent room. "Very well... I will do it."

"Excellent... now I will go downstairs and purposely spill the tea, and the housekeeper will be summoned, so you stand at the top of the stairs and when you hear her enter the drawing room and hear me say. *'How clumsy of me... I am so sorry...'* you must run through the kitchen door and along the drive as quickly as possible... you will see Melanie with the trap... I shall leave minutes later and join you."

Honoria was nodding in a mechanical way, looking about the room. "You are sure you understand all that?"

"Yes..." Honoria's voice was faint and her throat tight. "Yes... I do."

"I will go back down and say you are following and then spill the tea... listen for the cue: *'How clumsy of me'*... and don't forget your cloak... 'Tis growing colder."

Melissa went calmly down into the drawing room and sat. "The dress fits perfectly... but I do feel very faint of a sudden."

"Where's Honoria?" demanded Harriet.

"She will be down directly... she is hanging up the dress and putting on her own clothes."

"But we need to see her in it," declared Harriet pettishly. "It needs our approval... does it not, Leonard?"

Leonard Ainscoe smoothed his whiskers and huffed dismissively. "I'm sure it'll be right enough... you just heard her say it fits." He smiled at Melissa, his jowls beneath his whiskers bloating like sausages; glad to have acquired a good dress for his daughter for nothing. "How are your father and mother?" he asked in a contrived way. He detested her father and knew the feeling was mutual. And her mother, he knew, looked down on him.

"They are both in excellent health... they send their best wishes, of course."

"Of course!" concurred Harriet, imitating the new, improved manner of her husband. "Return ours to them."

Melissa sipped her tea and then moaned slightly. "Oh dear... I feel most unwell."

Aunt Harriet became animated. "I hope 'tis not the milk... it was fresh yesterday."

Melissa lifted her hand to protest and then dropped the fragile china cup to the floor. It remained intact and rolled, but the contents spilled onto the drab, once pale green carpet. Harriet was appalled, and Leonard sucked his teeth with impatience, and Melissa held her hand to her head and swayed a little.

"Martha!... Martha, come in now," bellowed Leonard and watched Melissa sway.

Martha entered and took in the scene. No one moved for quite a few seconds. "Clean up this mess," ordered Leonard, but Martha had her eyes on Melissa. "She may faint."

Leonard huffed and grunted, and then Melissa said in a renewed and louder voice. *"How clumsy of me... I am so sorry..."*

Normality resumed, and they all spoke at once, like a tableau come to life. "Fetch the smelling salts, Martha!" said Aunt Harriet.

"What about the mess on the carpet?" said Martha.

"Never mind that now... just bring the salts... we don't want to have to fetch a doctor... the expense of it!"

"Dear me, no..." said Leonard.

"In the top drawer of the sideboard, Martha."

Martha moved to where she was directed and saw Honoria dart past the doorway, but thought little of it. Harriet pressed the bottle of salts close to Melissa's nostrils, and she coughed as her head spun with the strength of the tincture. A horrid astringent shock to the system. How anyone relied upon them, she failed to understand. Leonard stepped nearer, and Harriet said. "Are you perhaps increasing?"

"I may be..." she replied.

"Good Lord above!" Leonard opined and stepped away again sharply, as if pregnancy in a woman was some rare contagious disease.

"Leonard, the brandy!" cried Harriet.

"No, no... that won't be necessary..." Melissa said. "I will just sip some tea... our groom is waiting in the trap to take me back."

More tea was poured, and she sipped it as they all watched Martha brandishing a cloth and intermittently dabbing at the carpet in front of them. Leonard and Harriet glancing at one another. Then Harriet said. "Where is Honoria?"

"She'll be down... she'll be down," said Leonard. "See to the girl first."

*The girl!* Who was she now? A waif and stray wandered in from the countryside! She sat upright and then stood, as if fragile. "I will be on my way... so as not to inconvenience you more... goodbye and keep well."

She hurried out into the hallway, her aunt scurrying after her in confusion while Leonard instructed Martha on how best to remove the tea stains.

"Goodbye, Honoria..." Melissa called up the stairs for effect, and then distracted her aunt from listening for the reply. "Goodbye, dear Aunt Harriet..." She pecked her on the cheek. "I feel sure we will see you at Christmas... my parents will look forward to it."

"You might," said Harriet. "Then again... we may just decide to have a quiet one here."

"What a shame," Melissa told her and threw open the front doors and ran out. Harriet was watching in bewilderment.

She caught up with Honoria a few yards from the gates of the house and grabbed the bag that was slowing her down, then pulled her along at a greater pace to where Melanie was waiting impatiently in the trap. "Quickly now!" she said, readying the reins.

Melissa threw the bag into the trap and pushed Honoria in so that she was between Melanie and herself as the conveyance took off at a speed beloved of Melanie's ambitious driving. Honoria fell against her and then against Melissa, hurtled about, unable to regain her balance. Melissa righted her and held her upright as she both wailed and laughed in a mixture of hysterical reaction to giddy events. The trap fell into a fast, steady pace, and they breathed more calmly.

"That was fun!" Melissa extorted, and Melanie shouted with protest into the noise of the wind and the wheels. "I am frozen stiff with waiting."

"I... I... I am sorry." Honoria stammered and began to shake with fear.

"Don't listen to Melanie... she does this kind of thing all the time," claimed Melissa.

Melanie glanced at the new passenger. "Think nothing of it now, Honoria..." She gripped the girl's cold hand with her own gloved hand. "I would not have missed it for the world."

* * *

In 'Golden Oaks' Caroline Wentworth glanced up briefly as Richard entered. She was sipping an expensive wine and helping herself to salted cashew nuts then licking her fingers and turning the pages of a book.

He rubbed his hands together and crossed to the fire which roared and crackled and showed red and orange flames twirling and twisting. The flames fascinated him and he was loath for a few moments to tear himself away.

The pages of the book rustled and Caroline spoke. "Move to one side, Dickie... you are blocking the heat."

He selected a handful of nuts and said. "Do you have it?"

"Of course I do," said Caroline.

"Where... give it to me please?"

"Just wait a moment... you are so impatient... I need to finish this chapter..."

"Caro, you are being deliberately difficult." He scanned the room and then caught sight of her reticule on the chair opposite. He went to it and picked it up. She tossed the book to one side. "Put that down... I will get it for you presently."

Ignoring her he opened the reticule and rummaged. His hand alighted on the slip of paper before he saw it and Caroline made a sound of abject disgust. "How very vulgar... going into a woman's reticule..."

He unfolded the paper and laid it on the small table near the window so that the lamp illuminated it. "Did you have much trouble?"

"Immensely so!" she lied. "It took an age of persuasion."

"Well, I never doubted you would do it."

"She is very suspicious... she called me disreputable... and you are apparently a scoundrel!"

"That does not sound like one of my brother's words... He is more likely to have called me a bastard and have done with it."

"Not to her, he would not!"

"How do you know?"

"He is far too mannerly and respectful of women."

Richard hissed his contempt. "So he would have you believe." His jealousy was about to consume him whole. He detested the fact that he could not dissuade Caroline's good opinion of his younger brother.

"She thinks we are of nefarious motive," Caroline said.

"Just imagine!" Richard tutted while examining the signature. "Being so distrusting of one's own family members."

"He must have warned her about us... she was terrified he would return and find me!"

"It matters not what she - or he - thinks." Richard had already taken up a nib and paper and was practising the perfecting of the signature, imitating the curves and flourishes of the letters. "This document serves us in two distinct ways, my love."

"She is quite spirited; you know..." said Caroline. "Not the meek manipulable little thing you perceive."

"I never said that," declared Richard. "I said she'd have values similar to his... that is all."

"Do you suppose she will tell him what she has signed?"

Richard straightened, satisfied with his ability so far to emulate the signature almost precisely. "That I do not know.... It remains to be seen."

* * *

Three days later Anthony Fairchild finished a light lunch and enquired of the maid. "Peggy, who is the young lady sitting in the drawing room?"

Peggy paused in the clearing of the dishes and took an age to reply. He was used to this and waited as he gathered documents together to take back into town. "I think she likely be one of Madam's relations..." said Peggy. "I b'aint that sure... but they's very friendly and they talks a lot about things from yore..."

"I see..." said Fairchild.

"She be always very pleasant..." Peggy went on, resuming the clearing in her snail's-pace. "she akses me if I needs help."

He cleared his throat and took his jacket from the back of the chair. "I see!... what an odd thing to do... so she has been before today?"

"Yes," said Peggy, unsure how to answer the question as to yesterday and the days before. *The intricacies of his language and her own did not quite gel, and things could get tricky during the act of conversing.* She smiled at him. "Mayhap you could aks the lady yourself, Sir."

"That would be crass..." he said. "And somewhat impolite."

Here was a case in point: *she failed to see what he meant... and 'crass' was not a word she had heard before.* She lifted the tray with the crockery and carried it to the door. He detained her. "And the word is ask, Peggy... not aks... *ask or asks or asked.*"

Another case in point! but she felt she might offer him a little information in return for his interest. "Mayhap her name be Caroline..." She saw him look up sharply. "No... no... I be mistaken... that's the woman Madam argued with t'other day... if there's nothing else, Sir, I'd best be about the chores..."

"Peggy... "He rose and called her back. "Which woman was she arguing with? Someone called Caroline? Caroline who?"

Peggy rolled her eyes upwards to summon memory. "I don't know her last name... I just heard Madam call her Caroline... then after that, Lady Some'atorother... I never seen her... she entered as Madam were leaving... then Madam had a job to get her out..." Peggy wondered why Melissa had not told him all this herself – it being an unusual occurrence – and she stopped immediately; she had perhaps spoken out of turn again.

"I see!" he said for the third time and waited to hear if the maid would add further detail. "Thank you, Peggy, that's all."

Melissa was in the small art room, where a fire had been lit – inadequate at best but better than nothing. He entered quietly, and she turned after a few seconds and saw him watching her. "To what do I owe this honour?"

They were still not on speaking terms. He decided to take it slowly.

"Who is that young woman sitting in the drawing room?"

"Cousin Honoria," she said lighty.

"What?"

"Cousin Honoria," she repeated.

"I heard her name... I meant, why is she here...so soon?"

"So soon!... 'Tis two weeks ago at least since I told you she would come..."

"I do not remember agreeing to it," he said. "I thought you meant sometime in the new year."

"I did not think you needed to agree... she is my relation. Had you wanted to bring a relation to stay, I would not expect to have to agree to it."

"When did she arrive?"

"Three days ago."

"Three days!" He stood next to her and gazed at the easel on which stood a small canvas containing a country bridge and an inn to the left of it, and three or four people looking over into the water.

"Why have I not seen her in the last three days?"

"Possibly because you are hardly in recently... and when you are, 'tis late evening and she is in bed. She rises early and retires early... she has her breakfast in the kitchen with Peggy and Mrs Harrison and goes directly out to walk, if 'tis dry."

He could not have looked more amazed had he been told she flew around the surrounding fields on a broomstick. He digested the information and frowned, and then asked. "Why does she do that?"

"Which?"

"Eat in the kitchen."

"I expect she likes the company of the two females... she has been much deprived of the company of any kind, remember!" He nodded his understanding but still frowned into the mid-distance. "And... she has not been allowed to roam free either... so she is eager to taste that too... which is why she walks as soon as she can."

"Yes, I see," he said at length.

She stopped painting. "Is she in your way or bothering you?"

"No..."

"Well then!"

He was lost for words. She turned and looked at him, her hair caught up in the scarf she wore to keep it tidy as she worked. He was struck by her beauty, as always, and almost distracted from his mission.

"Of course, you could have gone in and greeted her," she said, readying her brush. "Before now... when you evidently caught sight of her..."

"And you could have introduced us formally... I have never met her!"

"I do not see what difference that makes. Were a stranger in the house, I would approach them and make myself known."

She had wrong-footed him. His anger rumbled low inwardly, and he strove to contain it: *women and their ability to twist meanings to their own advantage!* "If I brought a stranger here, I would make sure you were introduced at the first opportunity... but of course you have been too busy entertaining Caroline Wentworth..."

The brush froze in her hand. Naturally, Mrs Harrison had informed him, or perhaps Peggy. "That is ridiculous... she was here for no more than five minutes!"

"Five minutes too long... she has no right being here at all."

The paintbrush began its journey over the canvas in small circular movements. He watched it, enthralled despite himself, and waited for an explanation. None was forthcoming. He moved away and put a distance between them, the fireplace offering comfort and warmth. "Well?" he said.

"Well, what?"

"What did she want?"

She slowed the brush and considered matters. It was not she who had destroyed the sketch, and she felt exonerated, almost glib. "The sketch... the one which you got rid of."

"And what did you tell her?"

"That it had been mislaid."

He paced, and she secretly watched as he looked down at the floor. He was angry but obviously not so much with her, or she would be hearing more of it by now.

"Peggy said she entered as you were leaving...and you had a job to get her out."

"'Tis so."

"So she forced her way in?"

"No, she did not force her way in. She assumed she was welcome and stepped past me!"

"The damned nerve of the woman."

Melissa said nothing; Caroline's nerve was a moot point in a sea of unfathomable reasons and mysteries.

"How did you leave things with her?"

"I told her I want nothing to do with her. I told her I thought she and Richard were disreputable... and that he is a scoundrel."

He lifted his booted foot from the fender and turned. "That is not a word I use to describe him!"

"No... 'tis quite comical withal... but 'tis how Geoffrey describes him."

"Geoffrey?  Geoffrey Gillis?"

"I do not know any other Geoffreys," she said tersely.

"What has he to do with the matter?... Do you mean you have discussed all this with him?"

"Only in as much as he knows of the offer of the painting commission."

Now he was quite furious, his rogue of a brother and his harlot discussed by all and sundry, and himself kept in the dark.

"He advised me, while I was sitting with Melanie, not to become involved."

"Oh, did he?"

"He does not think I should go against you and cause marital strife."

"How wise he is... and how kind of him to point this out," said Fairchild in his most biting sarcasm.

"Geoffrey is always kind to me... because of the closeness between Melanie and I."

"And I suppose, had he not given his noteworthy opinion, you might not have refused her commission? You needed him to clarify things... my word not being good enough!"

"You are being childish... and churlish. 'twas nothing of the kind."

She moved away from the easel to prime a second brush with a different colour of paint. He crossed swiftly to her and caught her elbow, and swung her round. "Leave that for now... I have had just about enough of this stupidity."

She shook him off but only partially succeeded. "Leave me..." Her grey eyes widened and blazed, and her face was fine enough for any canvas. "How dare you! I do not disturb you when you are absorbed in work."

"Do not begin *'how daring'* me, when 'tis you who brought the problem in the first instance."

She stared at him with her usual indignation.

"You bring that harlot to the door... install your female relatives without warning... and then expect me not to interrupt you and ask me how I dare!"

"I do!" she concurred. "You are never happier than when you have something to complain about."

"Is that correct?" he said quietly and watched her face as if it belonged not to the woman he was rowing with but to someone quite separate.

"Yes... 'tis correct"

Then he did something unexpected, just as she was preparing for a fight. He pulled her closer and kissed her. His mouth finding her's easily, as easily as he found the rims of cups and glasses to drink from. There was a moment of stiff resistance and then an easing of tension, and her lips softened, and she allowed his kisses to part her mouth. They kissed for several minutes, sating their individual hunger, as if not the same couple of moments ago.

She put her hands on his chest and pushed him a little, so that he stepped away. "I am still not speaking to you," she said. "You tricked me into doing so."

He dismissed this nonsense and thought for a second. "How did you leave it with her, Caroline?"

She sighed; it was not how she wanted him to respond. She thought of lying, but could not; too much to do now and to accomplish. Lying required energy and thought and constant attention to changing detail. "I signed a paper saying that I had received the sketch and lost it."

He was shocked back into reality. "You should not have done that, Melissa," he said, using the exact words Melanie had used. "You should have spoken to me."

"The woman was refusing to leave, and I needed to go for Melanie and then collect Honoria... time was of the essence."

He was quietly horrified. Her signature given to that wretched paramour of his brother! His brian reeled with possibilities. "God's Teeth!... 'Tis a blessing you are so well in with Gillis... we may need him in the future!"

Her innocence outshone her attempts at cleverness, and she displayed bemusement. Staring at him, the brush held in the air like a token of surrender. "How so?" she said softly.

"He has your signature... any number of things may happen." He turned to leave, then turned again. "How long is cousin Honoria staying?"

"Until we have decided where she will permanently bide... she will not disturb you."

"I shall go and introduce myself..." he said, his manners uppermost in priority as always. "And I shall tell her, if you have not done so, that she has no need to assist the servants for her keep..."

She laughed. "She thinks little of it because they have used her as free labour... my aunt and uncle."

"Even so, she does not need to play Cinderella here!"

She watched him straighten his jacket and then open the door. "And..." she added. "I am still not speaking to you."

"So I hear!" he said, and the door shut behind him.

She swore quietly; he now had the advantage. Standing back from the easel, she surveyed the canvas. It was coming on, but she was not about to become complacent with progress – in either project.

* * *

He had not destroyed the sketch, he had lied: though he preferred to think of it as omitting the truth. He detested lying and liars, in the normal way. He entered the drawing room, having just

94

silently glanced in an hour ago and withdrawn on seeing Honoria without her seeing him. She had been seated in an armchair and peering into a book and occasionally looking up and staring through the window, the chair turned to allow her to do this. She remained in the same position.

He coughed. She started and turned. Then she jumped to her feet, ill at ease.

"Please do not disturb yourself..." he began. "I have merely come to introduce myself... I am Anthony Fairchild... Melissa's husband."

Honoria smiled and her face was transformed. She was pleasant of feature, and more than a little modest. Her modesty may be mistaken for shyness he supposed. But he knew females too well to leap to any hasty conclusions. She wore a small silk cream cap, under which her hair showed minimally, pale red and perhaps in need of some more sophisticated attention.

"How do you do?" He made her a partial bow. She made him a slight curtsy and then gazed at him. Her smile a mere echo rapidly evaporating. She found him exceedingly good to look at. He was like to some of the princes and heroes she had seen illustrated in story books as a child. His light blonde hair, worn quite long and in wavy tendrils at the nape of his neck – she had never seen hair so wonderful on a man before and she stared at it, her vision moving in a way which took in its entirety, like a barber assessing the finished cut. He was aware of this singular inspection and flushed a little. Nor had she known that men could blush. She thought only females were allowed to blush. She moved her eyes to his face. His features were strong in outline: his hair an item of surprise in an otherwise masculine visage, a factor of fascination to the senses. His jawline was strong below a straight nose, his mouth generous, chiselled cheekbones and compelling green eyes. She had heard tell from Peggy and the cook that he was worth looking at and she was not disappointed. And suddenly he used the fingers of each hand and pushed his hair behind his ears, and the *fairy tale prince* illusion vanished.

"I... I... I shall not be..." Honoria floundered, she wished to say she would not be in his way but could not bring herself to express it.

Anthony Fairchild stepped nearer and took her hand and held it loosely. He did not kiss her fingers, he could see she was overly modest, barely at one with who she was, though she was four and twenty. He smiled and released her hand.

"I'm Honoria Ainscoe... but you may call me Honoria..." She sealed her lips again, as if she had been presumptuous, and looked away from him. He considered her from the side view and left a silence. She was wearing a dress that had once belonged to his wife, he recognised it, a little worse for wear now but it had been one of her favourites – when they had courted.

He spoke. "Please do not let me disturb you... I have merely looked in to make myself known, I apologise for not doing so earlier..." He looked down at her book and she looked at it with him.

"Birds!" she said with brevity. "I adore birds... I watch them whenever I can..." The book was obviously one of Melissa's from the bookcase, owned perhaps for artwork purposes; neither of them were bird watchers in the usual sense.

"A wonderful pastime!" He bowed again and then remembered. "And please do not think you need offer assistance to our servants... you are a guest here."

Honoria now flushed herself. It was a disgraceful thing perhaps, to come to somewhere like this, to a relation, and not know how to behave or what to do. "I... I... I did not..." She stalled utterly and he waited, until she had assembled her thoughts. "I like to be useful..."

There was no answer to that he could think of. "I may see you at supper later..." he said urbanely. "If you are still about... I hear you like to retire early..."

"I... I..." more faltering attempts before utterance. "Yes... I am accustomed to going early to bed... but if I nap for an hour this afternoon I shall be ready to dine when you dine," she said brightly.

"Then if you are at supper, we shall converse more," he concluded and smiled.

Honoria stood like a little girl, unsure and delighted and thoroughly without artifice. "Yes... I shall look forward to it."

No one had ever been eager to converse with her before... no one of his magnitude. It made her lightheaded, and she wondered how many other male people came here who were similar to her cousin's husband. The thought robbed her of strength, and she collapsed back into the armchair and closed her book.

* * *

He rode to his offices and collected from his desk the sketch he had taken from the easel. Then he went to see Edmund Shaw, Melissa's brother, an architect. Edmund's offices were in a street not far from his own offices, in a partnership with other architects.

Edmund was engaged with clients, as he had anticipated was a possibility, and he waited for half an hour or so in the outer office and sipped coffee brought to him by the clerk, while leafing through various journals on display and occasionally jotting notes in pencil for work of his own. Edmund and he saw each other frequently, both socially and in one of their respective places of work. Eddy Shaw was prosperous now, with many clients. But much of his work was involved with the family business, often in Spain – his and Melissa's grandfather having been Spanish and spawning commercial interests which would stretch down into new generations.

At length, Edmund was free, and they went into his office.

"Eddy, I come with a strange request... but you may be able to shed light..." said Fairchild and took the sketch from his inside pocket and unfolded it carefully from the middle of the paper. "Do you know this residence by any chance?"

Edmund perused it, turning it this way and that, and eventually gave an opinion. "I have seen the building depicted somewhere before... but I am unsure..." He raised his brows and waited for more information.

"Your sister has been asked to make a painting from it..." Fairchild said succinctly. "And I am a little suspicious as to its origin."

"Oh?" said Edmund in growing interest.

"My brother Richard is involved somewhere along the line."

"Ah!" said Edmund and grinned. "I see." He knew of Richard Fairchild's reputation, as did the rest of his wife's family.

"'Tis supposedly owned by his lady friend's aunt, whom she claims she is having the painting made for."

"If you leave it with me, Tony, I will make enquiries... one of my colleagues might know more about it."

He agreed to that readily, and they fell to discussing smaller matters for a while.

"Your cousin Honoria has arrived to stay with us..." he told Edmund.

"Has she?... did they allow that?... aunt and uncle Ainscoe?"

"No... she was liberated in some way... by Melissa and Melanie Gillis... I do not know the details, nor do I wish to particularly."

Edmund laughed. "Far better to remain in ignorance... but she is a quiet and sweet little thing, Honoria... she won't give you much trouble."

"Perhaps not... until she is tutored into bolder ways by the feminine front line..." He thought of Honoria and her modesty and bird watching.

"I doubt that will be accomplished in less than a year or two, knowing the timid Honoria," declared Edmund. "She has been too well suppressed by her father, Leonard the pig farmer... have you met him yet?"

"No," he admitted.

"My own father will not suffer him for more than five minutes... you may find out why..."

"Let us hope I will not," Fairchild said.

He did not have to wait long for more information on the sketch. The following afternoon, Edmund sent the clerk with news by letter.

It was thought that the building was owned by a Lord Neighsmith of Gloucester. Waiting to be auctioned once the gentleman's bankruptcy was settled. It was thought the sketch had been made before the place fell into dilapidation. And he doubted it was owned by Caroline Wentworth's aunt.

Fairchild wrote back to him by return. 'Just as I thought... a complete pack of lies... Eddy, I owe you a gill or two.'

# Honour and Awkward Moments

On the fourth day of Honoria's absence, it became obvious to Harriet and Leonard Ainscoe that she had not simply left on a whim or decided on a short holiday. But that she had left with the possible intention of staying away indefinitely – aided and abetted by cousin Melissa.

They set out after breakfast in their carriage to pay a visit to Marguerite Shaw, Harriet's sister, and her husband, Giles. Not knowing Melissa's new address since her marriage, it seemed the most likely move.

Marguerite was taken aback when Agnes came to the morning room to say that the couple were in the hall. "Are you sure?" asked Marguerite, annoyed by this occurrence and still in her dressing robe with her hair unarranged.

"Mr Jarvis received them, Madam, and he seldom gets names wrong."

"Where are they now?"

"In the drawing room, Madam..."

"Then I will go upstairs and make myself tidy... give them tea, please, Agnes, and say I will be down directly."

"Shall you require my assistance?" said Agnes.

"Certainly, but see to their tea first... let them wait. They have an absolute cheek calling at this hour... hardly yet ten thirty."

At length, Marguerite descended to the hall again, the Ainscoes having been waiting for almost twenty minutes. She hesitated outside Giles's study and wondered whether to inform him, but he was in a meeting with his estates manager and a tenant from one of the farms. He detested Leonard Ainscoe, could not abide him. Harriet, he tolerated for his wife's sake, and she usually came alone, once every *blue moon*.

She entered the drawing room in her visitor-receiving manner and smiled beatifically. "Sister dear... what a surprise!... and at this hour!"

Harriet looked sheepish; her elder sister's prestigious circumstances made her nervous and unconfident. "I apologise for the hour, Maggie, but 'tis rather an important –"

She got no further with her apology as Leonard cut in. "The hour is not the issue... what is the issue, Marguerite, is that your daughter has taken Honoria."

"What?" Marguerite thought she had heard this wrongly, but the couple stared at her with differing expressions, and Harriet was nodding. "Yes, taken her!"

"Taken her where?" she enquired, smiling as if this were a humorous little jest.

"If we knew that we'd not be here..." said Leonard, huffing and patting his belly as always. He had grown stouter than ever, and Marguerite had difficulty keeping her eyes from the size of his stomach.

"Had we Melissa's new address, we might have gone straight there..." said Harriet. "But she flew out of the door before we could ask her where she now resided."

"I do not understand what you are saying..." Marguerite's voice became shriller with simmering alarm. "Could you explain fully, Hattie... 'Tis a very early hour for these kinds of puzzles... where is Melissa supposed to have taken Honoria?"

"Ha!" said Leonard. "Are you saying you know nothing of it?"

"Of course she is saying that, Leonard." Harriet turned to her husband and cast him a withering glance. She had warned him to be polite and patient. The last thing they needed was for Giles to take exception to Leonard's way of handling matters. "Melissa came four days ago... with a dress for Honoria ../ very kind, I am sure..."

"Damned effrontery!" interjected Leonard. "We can buy her dresses when she needs them."

"... she went up to her bedroom with Honoria and then came down and said she felt unwell... and the next thing we know she is near to fainting..."

"A complete act!" barked Leonard. "A total sham... in order to take Honoria ."

Marguerite looked at them both and remained silent. It was not an impossibility now that she understood the circumstances. Melissa had huge sympathy for Honoria.

"Then we discovered Honoria missing..." Harriet wrung her hands and nibbled at her nails.

"But how do you know it was Melissa?" asked her sister.

"Because... because..." Leonard was struggling for words, but would not be shushed this time by Harriet. "Who the devil else would it be? Honoria sees no one and goes nowhere..."

"That is not right though, Leonard, she is four and twenty and should have friends and... and suitors... and so on," said Marguerite, as inflamed now as her brother-in-law.

"However, Madam," continued Leonard with raucous dignity in a louder tone, "as I was saying... we know 'twas Melissa because not five minutes after her departure we found our daughter gone... and some of her things gone with her."

"Did you see her leave with Melissa?" Marguerite queried.

"Do you think I would have allowed it if I'd seen!  No sooner had your daughter recovered from this so-called fainting do than she stands up and flies out the front door... to where the groom was waiting, no doubt."

"Well then... you cannot know it was Melissa ." Marguerite was standing her ground. Not because she believed Melissa innocent of any involvement, but because she did not want this drama to be in her drawing room.

"We are getting nowhere!" said the irascible Leonard. "Let us have Melissa's address and we will be on our way!"

Marguerite was wary. She needed to speak with Giles. "I do not have it to hand... give me a few moments and I will retrieve it from my bureau in the morning room."

"Rum how-do-you-do..." muttered Leonard under his breath as Marguerite closed the door behind herself. "Not knowing her own daughter's whereabouts... I suspect her to be in on it."

"Don't be ridiculous, Leonard!  Why on earth would she be?"

"They don't like us... we are not good enough for 'em... 'twas always the way... they look down on us... and doubtless they think Honoria ill done by..."

Harriet sighed – in a lot of people's opinion, Honoria was ill-done by – but she argued no further.

Marguerite tapped on the study door, and nothing happened, so she knocked louder until Giles appeared. "I'm busy, Maggie... can't it wait?"

"No... it cannot, Giles." She pulled him from the room, angered now by Leonard's infectious bad temper and the intrusion into her day's plans. "Leonard and Harriet have come."

"What?... well I don't want to see them... especially not that wind-bag, Ainscoe!"

"I know that, but they are saying that Melissa has taken Honoria away. "

They crept nearer the back staircase out of earshot as Marguerite explained in whispers what she had been told. Giles considered matters carefully. Then he summoned the butler and told him to take more tea into the study, and said to Marguerite. "Honoria may not want to go back."

"I know, Giles... but I do not know whether or not to disclose Melissa's address..."

He took Marguerite into the study and shut the door. "Excuse me, gentleman, we have a family emergency. Maggie, sit down and be calm."

Marguerite sat in the armchair near the fire and nodded to the two men in chairs at the large desk. Giles took paper and a nib and penned a letter to Fairchild... *'Better go home swiftly, Tony... your presence might be needed... possible unwanted visitors.'* He signed it and sealed it to make it official and give it priority.

"Who are you writing to?" Marguerite queried.

He went to the door and summoned the footman to have him ride to Fairchild's offices and deliver the letter. Then he penned the address of his daughter, but with the wrong lane name, to misdirect them. He gave it to Marguerite. "Let them go if they wish, but detain them for as long as possible to give Athony a head start. They'll be a while coming back from Nuttall Farm once they discover they have over-shot the turning..."

Marguerite smiled at him. It was at times like this when she knew why she had married him. "You are very clever, Giles," she said, and Giles shook his head, dismissing the flattery.

In the drawing room, she said to the relations. "I am sorry for the delay. I had a job finding it... I know the house by sight, but I forget the written address... an age thing I expect."

"Harrumph!" muttered Leonard.

"Betimes, I have ordered you more tea and some hot crumpets before you leave. You will have had a long ride here."

"That is kind, Maggie," said Harriet.

"Wasting time..." said Leonard.

"No, no, Leonard," opined Marguerite, "Melissa does not receive anyone until noon... she is painting quite prodigiously these days, you know."

"When she's not scheming..." said Leonard.

* * *

Anthony Fairchild was in his office, waiting for some Austrian clients to call and arrange terms on the translation of an agreement between themselves and another business. He stood and gazed from the window onto the town square, thronged now by late morning populace. He saw that the organ grinder had begun work somewhat earlier than usual and was accompanied by a young woman of foreign extraction who danced to his music. She was possibly of South American origin, dusky skin and waist length hair worn loose, swirling like a smooth black fan as she turned and gyrated. Intermittently she would kick out her skirts, revealing her bare legs, smooth and slender, while the monkey sat on the organ grinder's shoulder and clapped its paws as she moved with incredible lightness and speed. The coins falling steadily into the tin box. A crowd had gathered to see the spectacle, not unnaturally a great majority of it made up of men. Who did not enjoy the sight of an attractive pair of female legs, unexpectedly, at this hour of the day!

Then he spotted the footman from High Lawns ride into the midst of proceedings and dismount and leave his horse in the care of one of the rag-tag children to mind, before running over the road.

This could not bode well.

He received the missive and read it... *'unwanted visitors'* alarmed him. He thought immediately of his brother Richard and Caroline Wentworth and he went into the outer office. "Miss Van der Creff, I have urgent business at home... please ask Mr Trimingham when he arrives back to kindly receive the Austrians and do whatever is necessary."

Marianne Van der Creff looked up from her translating. "The letter just now come... I hope not bad news!" she said in her disjointed syntax.

He did not reply but ran down the stairs and around to the ostlers where his horse was stabled in the daytime.

Meanwhile, Honoria was in the kitchen at Back Lane House chopping vegetables with the cook when she heard her father's voice. She paused and dropped the knife, wiped her hands on her apron and said. "'Tis my parents arrived... I must run!"

"Run where?" said the startled cook. She was always very glad of the assistance from this young woman who seemed to be related to one of them, and not averse to getting her hands mucky.

"Anywhere!" replied Honoria and dashed around the work table, followed by the cook. "They will want to take me back... I am not going with them." She threw open the door to the courtyard and the cook grabbed her own cloak from the hook behind it. "Take this Miss Ainscoe... 'Tis freezing out there..."

Honoria took the cloak with an outstretched arm and continued her forward motion along the path. "Do not say I am here .

"Be careful... you scarcely know the district... you may get lost and..." the cook tailed off as Honoria picked up speed and disappeared.

She heard Leonard Ainscoe bellow at Peggy. "Where's your master or mistress?"

Peggy gawped at him as he strode into the greater part of the hall "They b'aint home, Sir." she said and shouted for Mr Harrison, who was not home either.

"Where is Honoria?" Harriet Ainscoe asked of the maid.

Peggy dithered. Then Mrs Harrison appeared, removing her apron to look more official in her housekeeper role, and frowned the couple down. "What's all this commotion about?"

"Mr Harrison needs to come..." said Peggy. "These two has let 'emselves in without being aksed."

"You stupid girl... Out of the way." Leonard looked around him like a bailiff with a warrant to seize goods.

"Excuse me, my good man, don't be calling her stupid in that manner!" cried Mrs Harrison. "Barging in here like you owned the place."

"Where's Honoria?" barked Leonard.

"She was in the kitchen... chopping!" said Peggy.

"Chopping?" echoed Harriet.

"You see..." Leonard told his wife, "they've taken her to use her as a scullery maid." He made his way into the recess from which the cook had emerged and located the kitchen, then emerged again. "She ain't in there..."

"She was two minutes ago... " Peggy offered.

"Peggy, hush! say nothing else to these beggars..." Mrs Harrison cautioned, "till we know who they are."

"We're Honoria's parents... who do you think we are?" Leonard looked around him as if the walls would render up his daughter.

"I don't care for your tone," said Mrs Harrison. "Peggy, tell Mr Harrison to send for the constabulary."

"He b'aint here, Mrs H!"

Mrs Harrison gave Peggy a glaring glance so that she would catch the need for the lie, but the girl was too slow on the uptake. "O'course he is... he's in the potting shed... go and fetch him." This would delay matters.

"There is no need for any high-handed moves," said Harriet in an ameliorative voice, stepping into the centre of things. "Leonard, calm down and stop bellowing at folk."

"Which bedroom is Honoria's?" demanded Leonard. "I will not be harangued and usurped by servants who don't know their place."

Mrs Harrison, a diminutive woman, drew herself up to her best height. "You'll be harangued by a saucepan if you take another step... you ignorant vile man!"

"Leonard, you are going about this all wrong," Harriet wrung her hands and clutched Leonard's sleeve to prevent him from assailing the staircase.

"Fetch my husband, Peggy," commanded the cook. "We'll see about this."

Fairchild entered the hall from the kitchen, having lingered unseen and listened to a few words of the exchange to assess the situation. "See about what exactly, Mrs Harrison?" he asked in his usual smooth tone.

They all stared. Mrs Harrison getting herself together first. "These two have barged in and –"

"We did not barge in... we were admitted by your maid," said Leonard, forestalling any more accusations.

"And who the devil are you?" He knew it was always best to diminish the significance of men like this by claiming ignorance of their identity.

"I am Leonard Ainscoe... and this is my wife... I am Honoria's father!"

Fairchild studiously ignored Leonard but turned to Harriet Ainscoe, as a woman, and made her a partial bow. "How do you do, Ma'am?"

"How do you do!" replied Harriet, fazed by Fairchild's impressive countenance.

"Where is Miss Aisncoe?" Fairchild asked Peggy nonchalantly.

"We've come to take her back with us," offered Harriet, her voice thin and not at all convincing.

"Have you indeed!" He removed his riding cape and gloves and handed them to Peggy, while Leonard made noises of unrest and half-formed sentences of outrage. "Perhaps you would kindly wait in the drawing room," he told them. "Is Miss Ainscoe not home?" he enquired again of Peggy.

"No, she b'aint," said Peggy

"Home!!" roared Leonard. "Her home is with us!"

"My good sir, please wait in the drawing room," said the master of the house. "In a civilised manner. Or I shall be obliged to ask you to leave."

"I've told Peggy to tell Mr H to fetch the constabulary!" the cook informed him.

"There will be no need for that, Mrs Harrison! The drawing room is the door to your immediate left." He addressed the Ainscoes.

Harriet took Leonard's sleeve to guide him to the correct door. He shook her off, but followed her even so.

"Shall I give 'em tea?" asked Peggy.

"No, thank you, Peggy." Fairchild stood to the side and allowed them to pass. "They were not invited... and will not in any event be staying long."

"Really, Mr Fairchild!" moaned Harriet. "I am Melissa's aunt and Marguerite Shaw's sister... I do not need an invite, surely."

"A moot point, Ma'am..." replied Fairchild and watched the couple move into the drawing room. He closed the door on them and ushered the two servants back into the kitchen. "Where is my wife?"

Mrs Harrison shrugged. "Out of the house, Sir."

"She be gone to collect Florna.." supplied Peggy.

He turned swiftly. "What?" His heart rate increased. "Who is she?"

The cook tied her apron . "No, no... she means fauna... flora and fauna for her artwork."

He let out his breath. For a moment, he thought he had heard the name of yet another female in need of rescue and refuge. "And where is Miss Aisncoe?"

"She ran out soon as she heard her pa's voice... like the devil was after her... she's a'feared of them taking her back." The cook resumed preparing vegetables. "No small wonder... listening to him out there."

He turned to the maid. "Peggy, come with me to find Miss Ainscoe... she won't be very far... take the town road and I will go in the direction of the Moss... tell her there is nothing to be afraid of... keep calling her, but not until you have left the grounds here... do you understand that?  Not until you are out of earshot!"

"I do, Sir." Peggy bobbed a curtsy.

"And put on a cloak..." called the cook after her. *They'll all be dead of the pneumonic if this keeps on...* 'she muttered to herself.

Harriet Ainscoe sat and rested, while her husband paced and fumed. She looked at the paintings on the walls, all Melissa's, probably. And then at the china in the cabinet – very expensive, *probably.* Then, at the rug on the floor which had been expensive, *probably,* and had seen better days. "Not as grand as High Lawns by any stretch!" she said. "But they are newly wed after all..."

Leonard ignored her and gazed from the window which gave a view onto the front of the house.

"That husband of her's is one of those campaigners... or reformers or whatever they call themselves."

"I know what he is," snapped Leonard. "Sticking their noses into everything and thinking the world bows to 'em..."

"Not into everything... only into education and poverty and poor schools and the like..." said Harriet in Fairchild's defence. "He used to be the deputy head at Barton Grange Academy!... you can well see why... that calm, authoritative way of his..."

"Damned upstart!"

"Giles apparently speaks highly of him..."

"Giles would," scoffed Leonard.

"His father's a bishop, so Marguerite says."

"I don't care if his father's Prince Albert... he won't come the high hand with me and get away with it."

"Don't be ridiculous, Leonard... Prince Albert is far too young to be his father," said Harriet with superlative irrelevance.

Leonard began to pace the room, looking without interest at the paintings and checking his repeater with monotonous regularity. He had decided to wait only so long before going himself to the upstairs rooms and searching. Though naturally he was wary of this legendary Mr Harrison, who might or might not have notified the constabulary, who might or might not look favourably on the do-gooding, politically misguided Fairchild, and act in his favour. The last thing Leonard Ainscoe needed was to be taken into charge and imprisoned – he would lose what little he had left.

"I think you should be more polite and gentlemanly, Leonard... you can see he's somebody of influence... with the local government and the like... according to sister Dorothea, he is learned and has attended Oxford University... and he might be asked to join the diplomatic services... or the foreign ministry... owing to his language skills and his –"

"Good God, woman!" interjected Leonard. "Anyone might think you wanted them to keep Honoria."

Harriet sighed and thought: 'No, but I can see why Honoria might want to be kept.'

* * *

Peggy found Honoria, lurking two lanes away between the wall of the flour mill and the low bridge, sheltering from the worst of the weather.

"Come back now, Miss..." Peggy did not give Honoria chance to argue before clutching a handful of her cloak and tugging her. "The master's home... and he says you are not to be afeared..."

"Have my parents gone?" wailed Honoria, her voice hollow and faint and carried off by the wind.

"No... but you must come back... the master says so... "

Honoria was unsure and took her cloak from Peggy's grasp.

"Come now, Miss..." said Peggy adamantly. "No telling where you'll end up if you keep on running... you could perish out here... or be taken by wrong'uns..."

This was true. Honoria knew it, and she turned in a desolate manner and followed Peggy.

Fairchild had ridden halfway up the Moss, which gave a one hundred and eighty degree view of the district, and he surveyed the landscape. He saw Peggy and Honoria trudging along the lower road, and he turned the horse and headed again for Back Lane House. Reaching home before them, he sat in the kitchen at the table used by the servants and ate cold chicken and leek pie and sipped coffee until they entered.

"I do not want to go with them, Anthony!" Honoria said desperately as she rushed in. "Please do not make me."

"No one is making you, Honoria... but you must make a declaration for yourself before them. You are an adult and a free citizen, and you have a mind of your own, and certain civil rights."

"But you don't know my father... he is... he is –"

"I can see for myself the ilk of man he is... I have met such men before!" He watched Honoria remove the cloak and hang it back on the hook. "Peggy, pour her some coffee... when you have drank something warm, Honoria, and are ready, we will face them together in the drawing room."

"Will we?" said Honoria, already in the habit of trusting her cousin-in-law and respecting his authority.

"Of course!... perhaps wash your hands first." He indicated her fingers, smeared with traits of earlier vegetable peelings, and red with cold. Peggy poured warm water into the large metallic bowl, and melted the soap and Honoria soaked her hands and dried them. "There's a good wench..." said the cook soothingly. "Do as the master says... he'll see you right!"

Her coffee half drunk, and eager to get it over with, Honoria accompanied him to the drawing room, and her mother sprang up and dashed forward and hugged her. "Honoria... why did you leave like that?"

Honoria was not about to reveal Melissa's part in things and remained mute.

"Because she was coerced into it by that witch of a cousin." Leonard declared. "We know all that..."

Fairchild stayed his anger and took a breath. "If you refer to my wife, I would ask you, Sir, to keep a civil tongue."

"But Melissa did urge her to go," said Harriet. "She had the groom aiding her. "

"She did not have a groom..." Honoria broke her silence. "Mrs Gillis was accompanying her and driving..."

"Mrs Gillis!... who the devil's she?" roared Leonard.

"The wife of Geoffrey Gillis Q.C.," Fairchild said.

Leonard was incensed. "See, what did I say, Hattie?... 'Tis a conspiracy... they have their lawyer involved."

"You are quite mistaken...  Melanie Gillis is Melissa's closest friend." Honoria informed him.

Fairchild stepped forward. "Honoria, tell your parents what you have told me. Make your declaration."

Honoria did not speak for a full two minutes, even though Leonard cajoled and harried her and her mother pleaded with her to see sense.

"What will you do for money? You foolish wench!" threatened her father. "You will be destitute."

"She will not be destitute." Fairchild said, seeing that Honoria would not yet speak. "She is capable of earning money in some capacity, and she can stay with us. Or with my brother, who is a vicar... to help with their children."

"Be a servant, you mean!" said Leonard.

And then Honoria found her tongue. "I am a servant at home, Papa."

Leonard and Harriet gasped as one.

"You ungrateful girl!" said Leonard.

"But 'tis true..." maintained Honoria.

"It is a vile untruth!" declared Harriet.

"But what do you think you were doing earlier? Skivvying in their kitchen!" Leonard pointed out in a wheedling tone. "Better to be working at your family home."

Honoria was gaining in confidence. "I was not skivvying... I was assisting the cook. I go there sometimes for company, and I chat with Mr and Mrs Harrison or Peggy... I have no one to talk to at home."

"Well... did you ever hear the like!" said Harriet Ainscoe to the room in general. "What are we then?"

"Whilst they use you to skivvy and fetch and carry..." persisted Leonard, his voice rising almost without his volition.

Fairchild cleared his throat. "I believe that on the day my wife called, Honoria was upstairs cleaning mirrors and windows... perhaps you consider that not skivvying?"

"This is none of your concern," barked Leonard.

"Honoria has made it my concern. As my wife's cousin, it becomes a family matter. I can find her more genteel employment if it comes to it... work more suited to her... she is literate and articulate, and I have many connections who will be happy to engage her." Fairchild stood and waited for the response while Harriet swivelled her gaze between them. Quite mesmerised. She had seldom encountered such a beguiling gentleman – his way of narrowing his shrewd green eyes and fixing his gaze steadily on whoever he was listening to, as if the intelligence of his understanding was given solely to that person. His undeniable sense of presence, his physique and his illustrious hair. How fortunate was her niece to have such a man as a husband! She took out her kerchief and began to weep.

"Stop it, Hattie," said Leonard. "Don't make a show of yourself."

"'Tis you who does that!" mumbled Harriet through her tears, trying one last attempt with her daughter. "Honoria, do come home with us!"

"No, Mama... I am sorry, but I do not wish to... I wish to stay here with cousin Melissa and Anthony... they are good to me."

"And we are not?" cried Harriet.

"You may think you are..." Honoria said generously. "But you do not know what I really want and how I wish to live."

"Good God above!" bellowed Leonard. "I never heard such piffle."

Fairchild touched Honoria's arm. "Perhaps retire now, Honoria... you may wish to rest after this upset."

She moved to the door. "Goodby, Mama... Papa!... I will come and visit you."

"You will not!" declared her father. "Our door will be closed to you if you do not return with us today... I will disown you."

"No, no! Leonard, do not make matters worse." beseeched Harriet, tearing at her kerchief in her anxiety.

"I think you may regret such a claim," said Anthony Fairchild. "You might wish to consider matters more calmly in the coming days... 'Tis a very hard thing to lose a child. For yourself as much as for the child."

"Arrogant upstart!" said Leonard and beckoned his wife to follow him to the door. "I don't need advice from you... whoever you may believe yourself to be with your reformist nonsense."

"I shall write to you, Honoria." cried Harriet up the staircase as she departed. "I pray you will not desert us."

Melissa had returned and was listening from inside the next room off the hallway. Fairchild stood on the front porch and watched them depart and board their trap and then re-entered, and caught sight of her peering out into the hall.

"If we were at High Lawns still, I think I might set your father's dogs on him." he said.

She laughed softly and moved to him, her eyes flashing wide in admiration of the result. He paused to gaze at her. She was dressed in her shabbiest clothes worn for trekking the countryside. She looked like a farmer's wife, but he was not sure he did not desire her more like this than when she was dressed to the nines. Then again, he desired her however she was clad. "I do believe 'tis my *witch of a wife*..." He was unsure if she had heard Leonard's remark but she had heard and she flicked his arm with her hand to show her disdain. He caught her hand as she lowered it and pulled her closer and kissed her, and remembered she was not speaking to him, whilst she made small noises of desire; vague sounds of unarticulated feeling.

He took her to the stairs, and she went without protest.

Not speaking to him was one thing, but making love with him was quite another. She was not betraying her pledge by satisfying her needs and his. A silent truce was called for – their wrangles for another time.

# False Calm Follows the Storm

Outside the bedroom they cast off their boots, leaning against the wall to do so, and allowing them to drop heavily to the floor, she losing her balance somewhat and toppling into the door and making it rattle. The noise attracted Honoria, who opened her bedroom door to make sure it was not her father returning. "I do beg your pardon," she said. "I... I... I thought –" Her stammering sentence was often relieved now, and he intercepted and said. "Do not worry, Honoria... 'tis only us..."

Honoria inclined her head briefly and disappeared. He pushed his wife into the bedroom and closed the door, locking it with the large key from inside. She began tearing off her clothes as he tore off his own.

"You are to cease these reckless schemes," he told her. "There are to be no more of them."

"What?... even though we have done such a good thing?"

"'Tis the means of how it was done..." he replied, not really wishing to talk of it and ruin his ardour.

"It was the only way possible. Melanie and I do not have all the time in the world, you know... we must make the most of opportunities."

"There are to be no more *adventures* of this kind, do you hear?"

"You loved having that contretempt with the detestable Leonard... you know you did."

"I did not!... it was vulgar and untimely... let it be the last."

"I don't have any more disadvantaged cousins," she said. "And Honoria already worships the ground you walk on, even without today's grandstand." She pulled impatiently at the tiny buttons of her chemise without complete success and loosened her hair.

He fell onto the bed, minus his trousers. "She shows gratitude that is all... she is much relieved of her old life... and I am not in need of her worshipping the ground I walk on."

"But you will begin to enjoy it." She pushed up her hair with two hands, as splendid as his in its health and vitality and differing only in colour, and then let it fall

"You are not to attempt any more of these kinds of things... or meetings with people I disapprove of, like Caroline Wentworth... 'Tis an inconvenience to all concerned."

"Anyway, I am not speaking to you..." she said, "but I will consider your words." She was almost breathless as she wrestled the final buttons.

"You will do more than just consider them," he told her, his voice lost in the shirt halfway over his head, "When I smack you so soundly, you will not sit at your easel with any comfort."

She flopped backwards onto the bed, removing her stockings from the horizontal position. "I never sit at my easel... I stand."

"Just as well." He pulled off his undergarments; time being of the essence.

"And besides," she added in a breathless sort of hiss. "You will not triumph in that way again... I shall defeat you. You simply caught me unawares..."

"Nonsense... you were in full awareness."

"I thought you were eating supper downstairs!... but whatever, next time, you will not win."

"We shall see!"

He pushed her chemise to one side and held her small, full breasts and sucked her nipples, and traced a direct line from there to her throat with his tongue. She arched her back and moaned, and he found her mouth and kissed her, his hand locating the moistness between her legs and the cherished spot which opened all the doors. She grasped his hair and removed her lips from his to suck his earlobe. He pushed her further down into the bed, and she wrapped her legs around his waist, and he entered her as she clung to him. Forgetting all about relatives and the potential problems they posed. The tension mounted with her surrender to the joy of her inner self until she shrieked with delight, a feeling accessible only in the act of union. He put his fingers over her lips to silence her. "Honoria is in the room opposite... she will hear."

"She will not mind," she mumbled into his fingers, nibbling them and then pulling his hand from her mouth and guiding it to her breast.

"She may not... but I do." He watched her until her vocal chorus had become discreet and then continued to ride her.

She bit his shoulder and clenched her eyelids tight to seal in all possible elements of pleasure. And then she climaxed in a slow, practised and sustained way until she was weak and her body tingled and hissed, alive with the unique and highly prized energy as old as time itself.

* * *

"Your father has sent a banker's draft with a note," he told her two days later. "For Honoria's domestic or personal needs..." He passed her the draft and the letter. It was a generous sum – more than some poorer people lived on in a whole year.

"Put it into your funds..." he said.

She looked at him. "I think he means it for the household expenses..."

"I do not want to accept money for that purpose..."

"You are too proud..." she claimed.

"I have self-respect."

It was a claim he often made, and she hid her satisfaction, for she liked the sentiment enormously, and then remembered she was not supposed to be speaking to him. He read her mind. "Even though Honoria does eat enough for three people..." He smiled to see if it would jolt her into a reply.

"'Tis because she is poorly nourished..." she said apologetically. "I doubt they spend enough on food... although looking at Leonard, no one would know it..."

He helped himself to coffee and checked his timepiece. "It must be hard for a pork butcher to be reduced to such lean rations!"

She began to giggle into her napkin – discarded but retrieved again to smother her humour. Her giggling was her achilles heel and quite ruined her vow of silence. He looked at her under his lowered lashes, pleased with the lighter mood. "She must require things... since she left in such a hurry."

"She is wearing my underwear and stockings... and a couple of dresses I may require... and some shoes which do not fit her properly."

"There you are then... that is what he meant the money for... and be sure to thank him"

116

She arched her brows and looked pained. "I do know common politeness, Anthony... even if I am rude by some of your exacting standards."

"Well, make sure you do it today... do not put it off in favour of the art... your father's generosity is not to be taken for granted."

She was now thoroughly shaken from her resolve to silence and leaned across the table. "Are you suggesting I take my father for granted?"

He levelled his gaze at her. She did take her father for granted; she took a lot for granted, things that he had been raised never to take for granted. "Well, are you?" she demanded, and still did not get a reply. "You see, that is just rude," she declared, and then giggled and could not help herself. He drew breath in an easy manner; he knew where he was with her when she giggled.

"I shall deposit the money into the household account, and then we know the coal and fuel for winter is seen too... plus the Christmas fayre."

It was quite enjoyable for her to think in this thrifty way; a novel change, because it would not be forever.

He snatched the draft from her and pocketed it. "I shall put it into your fund," he said. "We have a large contract in hand and can afford coal and food... so please buy Honoria what she requires."

Her father made her a generous allowance from the business, and she always had more than enough money. She was about to argue the point more – stuck between her need for the silence pledge and the need to prevail. Christmas was a mere five days away, and the fundraising event for the alms school planned for between Christmas and New Year. She needed to paint.

Then she was distracted from the disagreement by the entrance of Honoria, who had eaten before them. "Please excuse me," she said modestly. "I did not know you were still at table."

"That is quite alright, Honoria," he said.

"I wanted to ask you something..."

"Yes?"

"What is it, poppet?" said Melissa.

Honoria began to collect used dishes, and he put down his papers. "Honoria, leave those... Peggy will clear."

"Please allow me to help."

"If you wish..." said Melissa agreeably. "If you really want to..."

"I do... I like to be useful," said Honoria for the umpteenth time since her arrival.

He drew breath. "No, Honoria... please stop thinking you are a maid. I won't allow it."

Honoria looked abashed and stood back. "I... I... I apologise if I have given offense."

Melissa flashed him a look and pulled her lips into a thin line – a *now-look-what-you-have-done* expression. "Sit down with us, Honoria, and ask your question."

But Honoria was disinclined and perhaps near to tears. He mellowed his tone. "Honoria, you have given no offence... but I cannot have you clearing dishes. What you do in the kitchen with the cook to pass the time is up to you... but you are not to behave like the general maid... there is really no need."

"I need to repay your kindness."

"You do not... and not in that way." He smiled, and she was a little appeased.

"I do not mind..." she said quietly with the forbearance that was slowly more apparent in her nature as days went by

Melissa rang the bell for Peggy and indicated for her cousin to take a seat at the table. "You had better listen to what he says, Honoria..." she remarked skittishly. "I know 'tis hard to believe, but he is a terrible tyrant."

Honoria – used to her father, *the tyrant* – peered at him with curious surprise.

"Truly..." Melissa patted her arm. "You have not the first clue."

He tutted wearily and arranged his papers.

"Well, I... I... I do not..." They waited for Honoria to complete her sentence. Her stammer was lessening a little, but even so, it begged patience. "I do not mind."

Melissa made a sighing groan. "Lord above!... don't encourage him, he doesn't need it..." She smiled towards the window, and he waited until the sportive innuendo had passed and Honoria had assured herself of the wit.

Peggy came in and began clearing the table, and he said. "Peggy, make sure Miss Ainscoe does not clear dishes... or any other household chores beyond the kitchen... I have forbidden it."

Peggy curtsied and looked at him in awe, and then at Melissa.

"You see!" said Melissa to her cousin. "There is the perfect example."

He stood and picked up the papers. "It was an ironic jest, Melissa."

"Oh yes... his sarcasm is a language of its own... did I mention that?"

She gazed at Honoria to see if she appreciated this badinage. She seemed not to, and smiled perhaps simply to be obliging. "What was it you were about to ask?" she said, when the maid had gone. He sat again and they waited.

"I... I... I wondered if... I wondered if I might teach Peggy to read and write a little better..." Honoria blurted. "... in her spare time... seeing that she was kind to me the other day... and seeing that she has barely been schooled..." She lowered her head and feared she was being too presumptuous. "If 'tis very well with you," she added and looked at him for permission, rather than her cousin.

He pushed his hair behind his ears and stood, picking up the documents. "Now that is a completely acceptable undertaking... by all means teach Peggy."

Honoria beamed and nodded. Melissa clapped her hands together theatrically. "Yes, yes... education... he adores that... you know, he was deputy head at Barton Grange Academy?"

"I had heard," confirmed Honoria in grave seriousness.

"Indeed!... everyone has heard!... he will have you at the alms schools next, teaching there."

Honoria looked thrilled, and Melissa could see the witticism might backfire. "And there is another excellent suggestion..." he moved from the table. "But first you must let Melissa go with you to purchase everything you need."

Honoria once more looked stricken and swayed slightly from side to side in consternation. She had never in her life to date had everything she needed, and was not sure what it might consist of. And she had no funds. "But I... I... I do not have -"

"Worry not!... my father - your uncle - has made you an early Christmas gift for just such a purpose."

She flushed and he bowed briefly on reaching the door and left for his office, and Melissa let out peals of laughter and forgot she had broken her vow of silence. "Let us go forthwith to the town... without further ado... Melanie may call at four."

* * *

At the bank, to deposit the draft Giles had sent, he became aware of the attention of the manager. Obsequious in the way of all bank managers, the man approached him and bowed. "Mr Fairchild... quite a surprise to see you replenishing funds so speedily..."

"I beg your pardon?" He stepped away from the teller's desk and looked at the manager, an elderly man with bushy grey hair and side whiskers, and a ruddy complexion as if employed in an outdoor livelihood and not in a bank.

"After the removal of the sizable sum two days ago..." The manager continued.

"Forgive me... to what transaction do you refer?" He was somewhat annoyed at being delayed from business.

The bank manager was also now a little alarmed. "The servant who came on your behalf... on Tuesday!"

"Which servant?"

"The lady's maid to your wife..."

"My wife does not have a lady's maid." he paused with a sinking feeling growing in his stomach. "Only a general maid."

The manager looked around him, at the two other customers, one being served and one waiting. "Perhaps we should step into my office."

It seemed a woman, an elderly woman, had withdrawn several guineas from Melissa's own account, showing a letter written and signed by her. Melissa being apparently indisposed but needing the money quickly, for Christmas.

He sat with a blank stare and heard the man out. He showed him the signature – undoubtedly Melissa Fairchild's signature – and the letter in a good approximation of his wife's hand. "I do not think this is an authentic letter..." he said eventually and the manager blanched and called for the clerk who had attended on the withdrawal. And a second person to bring tea.

"I do not require tea." Fairchild said. "I need to go home and make some enquiries."

They bowed him out of the door, and he walked firstly around the town square to calm his misgivings and ground himself for further turbulence. He knew within a few minutes, his wits and his instinct heightened, he knew that this was his brother's doing. Caroline Wentworth either disguising herself as an elderly servant or engaging someone else to play the part. Having falsified the signature given regarding the sketch and copied the handwriting for the letter.

* * *

He wanted to ride home immediately, to make sure there had been no oversights or other omissions and that Melissa had not actually taken out money herself. Though it was unlikely, she had not left the art room much in the past three or four days, except to go over to High Lawns and to fetch Honoria. If he rode back now he may miss her; she and Honoria would have set off for the town to buy Honoria's clothing. He would lay odds on it – they would be unable to resist.

He climbed the stairs to his offices and decided to watch from the window to see if they came into the town square, the shopping streets all being located on or just off the square. He pulled up his chair and put his feet on the window ledge, and surveyed the two roads leading into the square from the surrounding area.

Then Trim entered and stopped in mock indignation at his idleness, when there was much work in hand. "Good God, have you fallen asleep?"

"I am watching for our phaeton... there is a crisis..." Fairchild said and felt morose at having to regale Trimingham with what he felt was his brother's treachery.

"What, another one!" said Trim. "What now?"

He outlined the set of events and watched Trim grow outraged along with him. "That is indeed soul-destroying, Tony... but are you sure 'tis Richard at fault?"

"I am almost certain!... who else would it be?" He went on to remind him of the sketch and the proposed painting commission, and the resultant signature. "'Tis as likely as not something to do with those two..."

"Perhaps you should go and see him!"

"What? And have him laugh in my face as he calls me a liar and threatens to sue me."

"Well, yes... you do perhaps require more evidence."

121

"Of which there will be none..." And then he saw the trap come into view, driven by Mr Harrison. It was distinctive now since it had a slightly inverted inner wheel owing to the madcap driving of Melanie Gillis while rescuing Honoria. He watched the two young women alight, and he rose. "I will attend to matters at the bank with her and then return, Trim."

Melissa and Honoria were heading to the next street and the bank as he caught up with them. "What is it?" asked Melissa, knowing by his face that something was very amiss.

"Money taken from your fund... by someone other than yourself, I assume..."

"What? Impossible!"

"Not unless you went in on Tuesday disguised as an old woman pretending to be your own maid."

She shaded her eyes against a shaft of winter sun and gazed along the road. "Why would I do that?" And then she had the realisation. "The signature I gave to Caroline Wentworth..."

"Indeed."

Honoria looked from one to the other in bemusement. "If there is a money problem, I do not need to buy new clothes at all..." she said. She was accustomed to hearing of money problems, had heard of little else for many a year now.

"There is no problem..." he said. "The draft from your uncle has been deposited... Melissa, you must take out enough for what you need for the festive season and for Honoria's items. Then we must put a stop to the account for now..."

"I suppose there is no telling what else they may do with the signature..." she said.

"None at all... but at least they will get no more from the bank."

She felt she might weep. "How much has gone?"

"Five guineas."

"But that is a fortune... and 'tis my fault." She sniffed back tears. "We should go to the constabulary and report it."

"Perhaps... but I may take measures of my own first."

"What sort?" She grabbed his arm and made him look at her. "Not with Richard?"

"Of course with Richard... first off... I cannot allow him to get away with this..."

"Caroline told me you would fight to the death one day."

"She is right, probably..."

"But supposing it was all Caroline's doing?"

"That is most unlikely!"

"I know but..." she was bouncing up and down on the balls off her feet in agitation.

"We will take Honoria to the tea shop and then go to the bank... and then you can go for her afterwards."

Honoria became fearful. "But I have never been to a tea shop. I do not know how to go on..."

He and Melissa exchanged glances, and for a moment, the sorrowful admission detracted from the crisis. That someone of her ilk should never have been to a tea shop by the age of twenty-four was a sorry state of affairs! He took Honoria's arm. "Come, this way..." He looked for Melissa to join them, and they crossed the street towards their favourite tea shop. "All you need do is drink tea, Honoria... and possibly enjoy some cake. You will be quite safe..."

"'Tis true, Honoria... only the best people frequent here... myself and Melanie for example and..." She stopped and looked at him. "... and Caroline Wentworth!... She was here the day she asked me to paint her aunt's house."

"Perhaps that is the only time she intended being in the place." he said. "And, by the way, 'tis not her aunt's house, it belongs to Lord Neighsmith of Gloucester..."

"How do you know?"

"I made it my business to find out... now come, we must hurry. I cannot spend all day discussing this. We must go to the bank."

They sat Honoria in the window seat, enjoyed much by Melanie and herself, and asked the waitress to keep an eye on her, being that she was new to the area and nervous. He tipped the waitress generously, and the waitress began at once to fuss over Honoria in a way Honoria had never before experienced, showing her a tempting array of confectionery. She was overwhelmed but looked longingly at the delicacies available.

"Do you know," he told Melissa on the way out, "I do believe she loves to eat almost as much as Trim does."

She tried to laugh, but the thought of the missing money was too devastating, and she managed only to smile.

# Silken Garments and Loose Threads

"Teaching the maid to read?..." said Aunt Dorothea – sister to her own mother and Honoria's. "Whatever next?... teaching her the intricacies of bridge or backgammon perhaps!"

This was Aunt Dorothea's idea of humour, and Melissa cleared her throat and looked studiously at the fire, not deigning to reply.

"Everyone should be able to read..." remarked her father who held the poker – his most beloved household artefact – with which to rake the coals, "... and that being the case, Anthony would encourage it... he's an educational reformer!" His tone narrowly skirted intolerance. "No point just the well-to-do learning if we are ever to progress... naturally he encourages the idea."

"Waste of valuable time," proclaimed Dorothea. "Those who need to read are taught when young..."

"Peggy is young..." Melissa pointed out. "She is fifteen, we believe."

"You believe!... does she not know?"

"No, aunt, because she came from one of the orphanages... she was placed there at two years of age... having been abandoned outside the old church near the turnpike..."

"Poor little soul," claimed Marguerite.

"But even so..." persevered Dorothea, "does she really need to read?... she will only pry into things which do not concern her."

"For Pity's Sake!" muttered Giles."

Dorothea glared at him with muted irritation. "And mayhap, Giles, they should refine themselves to more pressing problems, these reformers... not interfere with distressed relations and coerce them into teaching the serving classes..."

Melissa's patience wore thin; notwithstanding that she was just as scathing about his educational zeal in the usual way, she knew when her husband needed support. "It was Honoria's own suggestion... he has not coerced her."

"O'course he has not..." Giles flung down the poker in his favourite demonstration of annoyance. "He's better things to do than coerce folk... betimes, no one can argue against the basics of reading and writing... how is the world to advance if everyone has your view, Thea?"

Marguerite became fidgety: any moment now, there would be a tension which should have no place in any polite drawing room. Dorothea glanced at her sister and smirked a little. *Her brother-in-law's politics did not align with her own. He was in danger on occasions of sounding like a Liberal.* "And where is Honoria? I should like to have seen her?"

"She has stayed at home..." said Melissa. "For fear her father is lying in wait here..."

"That bellowing ne'er-do-well is not welcome at High Lawns," said Giles. "You can assure the wench he won't gain ·admission." Having legislated, he was unable to refrain from again picking up the poker.

"Poor Harriet..." bemoaned Dorothea. "How must she feel?"

"She could possibly try being glad that Honoria now has a better chance in life," claimed Melissa.

"Lissy!" chided her mother.

"'Tis the truth," said Melissa. "You might also agree, Aunt, had you witnessed Honoria cleaning in their upper rooms!"

Aunt Dorothea was clearly bested and drew her mouth into the disparaging shape which could not be mistaken for anything but extreme displeasure, both at her youngest sister's poverty and her niece's impertinence, but added. "Well, I expect she is now closeted with your maid, teaching her the alphabet..."

"Peggy knows that much already," she snapped, then said in a more ameliorative tone. "Honoria is actually mending some of my delicate silk under garments... and she volunteered for that as well."

"Lars!" said Dorothea. "Whilst shunning courtesy visits to her near relatives."

Remembering, she turned to appreciative themes. "Honoria thanks you, Papa, for the kind gift of money! She will do so in person when she sees you."

Giles frowned pointedly towards Dorothea to warn Melissa off saying more in her hearing. She would have plenty to say on that score, undoubtedly. But Dorothea had a contrary thought. "Perhaps the maid may benefit more from instruction in how to launder properly," she said, feeling she should recoup lost verbal ground.

"It has nothing to do with her laundering skills..." She was looking at the clock and deciding whether she could decently retire to the art room. "It happens elsewhere..." she said without thinking.

"Do not say you wear silk lingerie when traipsing round the countryside sketching!" proposed her aunt.

"Not that either..." she countered, and then realising her faux pas assumed her cat-like inscrutability of face.

"Where then?" persisted her aunt in pitiful ignorance of real life.

Her Mother, guessing where this might lead, said gently. "Silk undergarments are not a suitable topic of conversation, Thea, with Giles present! ... let us talk of other matters."

"But young brides need to know how to care for clothes and expensive items, Maggie... Money does not grow on trees..."

Melissa thought of lovemaking scenarios with her husband, and she grew mischievous. "'Tis one of the facts of life that even delicate items have a use which admits of their damage..." she declared, like a grandmaster at a chess match savouring victory for more than just the sake of winning, and her expression changed to the one which Marguerite knew to be a prelude to merriment. "I think we do not need to know more." she said loudly.

Her father cleared his throat and stood; in his experience, Dorothea would not gain understanding before more questioning and embarrassment was mooted. "I am going out, so feel free to carry on with the topic... I bid you good day, ladies."

"And I must repair to the art room..." she said.

Dorothea frowned. "Is it something I have said?"

"The question of underwear and the bedroom..." supplied Marguerite in a ludicrous whisper.

As she followed her father to the door, her laughter was nearing the unstoppable, and she heard her aunt whisper to her mother about the fall in moral standards in the young. Once in the hallway, she paused and gave in to a breath-taking bout of hilarity. "What a provoking little madam you are..." said her father mildly.

"Aunt Dorothea should not be so nosey..." she replied.

Her father harrumphed somewhat. "Better to ask the dogs not to bark!"

She linked her arm through his, and they moved at a steady pace along the hall. Then she recalled the fraud and the missing money and became grave. "But something worse has happened, Papa..."

He stopped in his tracks and prepared to listen before his estate's manager appeared immediately and sought his prompt attention.

"I will see you at the weekend, Papa... when perhaps Honoria can be persuaded to join us," she said, not wishing to delay him from business. "But she will most certainly be here over Christmas."

She had been in the art room for no more than five minutes, a cheerful fire ablaze in the hearth, when the maid interrupted to say the footman from the Gillis residence had traced her from Back Lane House and was bidding her to come at Mrs Gillis's behest. She was apparently having *'ladies problems'* regarding her expectancy.

She left her brushes uncleaned and fled the room and took up her cloak, and boarded the carriage with the footman, and they set off at speed.

* * *

"What on earth is it, Mel?" She launched herself onto Melanie's bed and took her hand; Melanie was never indisposed in this way. She was followed into the room by Geoffrey Gillis. "She is losing the child..." he said.

Melissa stared at her closest friend and she nodded confirmation. "I think so."

"Oh, darling..." Melissa squoze her hand and moved position to put her other arm around her. "I am so sorry... have you seen the doctor?"

"He came two hours since..." Geoffrey said. "And I have to leave imminently for the assizes in Birmingham in the morning. I must take the coach..."

"Go Geoffrey! I shall be fine." Melanie instructed.

"'Tis why I sent for you. Perhaps you would stay with her until her mother arrives... she will be here as soon as possible."

"Of course! I shall stay until she is come."

"There is no need to inconvenience anyone..." objected Melanie. "I shall be fine with just the maid... t'was a very early expectancy."

"Nonsense, Mel. You should not be alone for a minute... Geoffrey, go to the coach... I will be here."

He crossed to Melissa and kissed her hand, and then leaned in to kiss his wife. "I have left instructions for the groom to take you home as soon as my mother-in-law arrives." he told Melissa.

"Go... you will miss the coach and then things with your client will be awry." Melanie pushed herself up against the bedhead and blew him a kiss as he departed. Melissa arranged pillows behind her for greater comfort. "Are you bleeding?"

"A little... the doctor says it will be slow and steady... and may go on for a day or two... he is coming back in the morning but I am to send for him if it gets worse."

"What have you been doing?"

"Riding..." confessed Melanie. "But Geoffrey does not know..."

"Foolish girl!" chided Melissa lightly, as if it were a mere chill from running around in summer clothes during a storm. "You will perhaps take heed of advice in future expectancies..." And suddenly things did not look so bleak. "For there will be other babies... there are bound to be." Melissa continued.

"That is what Geoffrey says too."

"I imagine he does..." she retorted wryly.

And then they were giggling, the brighter side of the picture looming out of a dwindling darkness and commanding homage.

* * *

"I cannot think why Melissa is not back..." ventured Honoria to Anthony Fairchild in the drawing room of Back Lane House. "She said she would be only two hours, and that was almost four hours ago..."

He took out his timepiece and checked it with the ormolu clock on the mantle shelf. He glanced over at Honoria sitting at a distance across the room in her usual armchair near the window. It was almost dark outside but she liked anyway to look at the lilac tree and the rowan tree, their leaves withered but outlining their summer shape. He was seated at the mahogany bureau in the corner of the room, where he worked beneath the oil lamps – bright as daylight and better than the ones in the offices. "Where has she gone? Do you know?"

"High Lawns!" said Honoria. She was quite at home now, quite easy in his company.

He paused, the nib held at an angle which forbade the careless dripping of ink. He noticed suddenly that she was repairing lingerie,

128

expensive garments of silk and satin, his wife's lingerie, and he felt his face flush. Then Honoria looked at him, sensing his attention. "I am repairing some of Melissa's finer garments..." she told him brightly. "I cannot think how she has torn and ripped them so much..."

He froze as he heard this statement – her apparent inexperience, her oblivion to causes – and did not comment. Honoria was one of life's innocents; she may always stay that way. He allowed this realisation to overtake the first and then let his mind move to erotic and intimate thoughts of Melissa in her underwear. The fact that Honoria was making good on his damage and doing it with grace and willingness humbled him. Though he knew she needed words. "I cannot think either..." he lied. "Nor on her absence..."

Honoria cast him a look, as if she could see through the lie. But it may just have been that she wanted him to converse and did not know what to say. He wrote a few more lines in French from English and scanned the part of a page he had just translated, then gave up. "We will have supper without her if she is not back in half an hour."

"Is she alright do you think?" asked Honoira. "Perhaps we should wait... she will be hungry and glad of our company... she always looks forward to seeing you, Anthony."

*And not speaking to me*, he thought. And again, as if reading his mind, she said. "You two have not been speaking much, I perceive... but are now doing so a little more."

"A little more..." he agreed.

"Why have you not been speaking?" she asked, and then saw that this was an impertinent question. "I mean... I... I... I..."

"'Tis difficult to explain," he said, to save her awkwardness. "Ask her... she may tell you." He wanted to say: *because I smacked her behind...* but thought it prudent not to do so. Melissa might be furious and continue her ridiculous vow of silence. It was anyway not that simple; the real reason lay in her belief of his breaking the odds or the wager in some game she played – to which he had never actually willingly subscribed.

"I do not like it when you don't speak..." said Honoria

It struck him then that she saw Melissa and himself as surrogate parents, even though her cousin was three years her junior and himself a mere six or seven years older. Age had little to do with these matters. It was about the influence and assumed attitude, and the trust.

Honoria was humming to herself, and then she looked over at him. "We may eat whenever you are ready, you know..."

How obliging she was, this young woman. Perhaps it was a result of her parents' neglect. Or perhaps it was merely who she was naturally, and her parents' neglect a result of that! A tantalising hypothesis.

The doorbell clanged and presently Peggy entered to say that *Godfrey Gillis* had arrived and craved his attention. She handed him the calling card.

"This says *Geoffrey* Gillis, Peggy! The first name is Geoffrey... not Godfrey... but a good attempt..." He looked over at Honoria and nodded his approval of Peggy's early reading skills. Peggy and Honoria both began to giggle, in that annoying way of young women, as if life were one long farce, which in many ways it obviously was.

"Shall I be fetching him in?" asked Peggy, recovering and appearing self-satisfied with her ability to entertain.

"Indeed!"

Goeffrey Gillis entered in his buoyant manner and smiled. Fairchild rose. "Mr Gillis, how are you?" He extended his hand and Gillis shook it, right away explaining the situation with Melanie. "... just until my mother-in-law arrives... I have arranged for their carriage to fetch your wife straight home... but I thought you might not know."

"We did not know... thank you. We were only now discussing her lateness."

Gillis then caught sight of Honoria in the chair and the lingerie she was sewing – and hastily stuffing some of it beneath a cushion. He kept a straight face but was tempted to grin, not averse himself to the sight of delicate lingerie.

"This is my wife's cousin, Miss Ainscoe," Fairchild said.

Gillis approached, and Honoria extended her hand, the way Melissa had taught her to do – palm downwards, so that gentlemen may lightly receive her fingers. Gillis held them for a second or two and then bowed. "Your servant, Ma'am... delighted to make your acquaintance." His genial smile and winning way soothing matters. "The legendary Miss Ainscoe!... how are you now?"

Honoria had shrunk back into the armchair and watched him warily and did not speak. Fairchild spoke for her. "She is adjusting... but fearful of her father calling..."

Gillis became serious. "You do not have anything to be afraid of. He can make no claim on you... you are of age and have rights as a free person..."

"I have explained that to her," said Fairchild, "but 'tis difficult for her to accept all at once."

"Yes," confirmed Honoria, looking still at Geoffrey Gillis as if he might seize hold of her.

"If he tries to make any claims or hold you against your will, Miss Aisncoe, you have my word I shall intercede immediately on your behalf, if I am made aware..." He turned to make certain Fairchild had noted the assertion.

"Thank you... I... I... I am... I..." Honoria looked from one to the other.

"Not at all!" said Geoffrey, relieving her of the effort of speech, and aware of the constraints of time.

"I am mending personal items for Melissa..." Honoria said, suddenly finding her confidence and indicating the cushion which Gillis had been curious about. "I may need to become a seamstress in the future, for my existence."

He was not unaccustomed in his professional life to hearing strange claims and did not show a reaction to this.

"That is if I do not teach..." she said and looked at Fairchild, who also gave no clues as to what he thought.

"I think that may be unnecessary." Gillis smiled again and wondered whether to continue. "Should you care to accept invitations to dine with us on certain occasions, I shall introduce you to some very eligible gentlemen..." He saw that Honoria was as captivating as any young woman of society, and would probably become more so.

"Perhaps you will have a drink?" Fairchild suggested, diverting the conversation, which Honoria obviously found disturbing.

"I would very much like one, but I am in haste to board a coach... Birmingham Assizes first thing tomorrow..." said Gillis. "I merely wanted to let you know, so you would not worry about Melissa."

He followed Geoffrey Gillis into the hall. "'Tis bad news about your unborn child... I am sorry. I did not know your wife was expecting again."

The lawyer shrugged slightly and replaced his hat. "It was very early on... and I suspect she has been out riding..." he paused, to see if Fairchild might actually know of this via Melissa. "I have told her not to, but she pays me no heed."

Fairchild did not comment and Gillis went on. "They pretend to listen to what you tell them... they nod and agree... then they go behind your back and do it anyway..." He stepped into the porch.

"My dear fellow," Fairchild said, "I almost have a degree in the subject."

Gillis laughed heartily and bounded rapidly down the steps, pausing at the bottom. "I trust there have been no repercussions from that incident with the painting and the signature?"

"There have, unfortunately... but you are in haste so I shall not detain you with the details."

"If you have need of my services in any way please do not hesitate to contact me... there will be no charge." he said.

"That is kind of you," said Fairchild.

"Not at all. My wife was complicit in the start of this saga... so..." He tailed off, not wishing to prolong the subject. "And Melissa is godmother to my son... 'Tis the least I can do... she rushes to Melanie's side at the drop of a hat in times of trouble... 'Tis the least I can offer..."

"They are very firm friends." replied Fairchild, and Geoffrey Gillis adjusted his hat and pondered. "Perhaps over the next week of the festive season, you would care to come and dine with us... yourself and Melissa...?"

Hesitating, he thought of how to politely decline or reply. But Gillis was nothing if not astute and remembered the animosity his wife held for Melissa's husband, and possibly vice versa. "Then again... perhaps our wives are best left to enjoy their friendship in a space of their own..."

"I believe that may be the best... if somewhat fraught with danger," agreed Fairchild wittily.

Gillis was perusing the night sky and considering the comment. "They are clever women... perhaps it is less *dangerous* for them to enjoy these escapades... in the main... than grow bored with life... or ourselves!" He sprinted down the steps and Fairchild, in his turn, deliberated on the various meanings inherent in the remark; there was a dark and timeless wisdom in them. "Nevertheless, the offer of counsel still stands..." Gillis threw over his shoulder.

"I wish you a safe journey." Fairchild called after him, and watched the carriage drive away.

In the drawing room Honoria had resumed her mending. Her head bent over the materials, humming to herself. He sat at the bureau and resumed the work in hand. There was always work in hand. He realised that all his life to date he had made sure there was work in hand, to be completed at the expense of something else. What was that *something else?* It did not have one steady name. *The moment* perhaps! A distraction from pressing things in life commanding his fuller attention from the left or the right. A way to avoid himself? He thought of Lottie, his childhood sweetheart who had perished in the Irish Sea at the age of three and twenty. He thought of her less these days. But he still thought of her. Had he concentrated on the moment then, he may have prevented her death. Or perhaps it would have happened anyway - in another manner. The question was one of abiding torment. It could not be settled - the view of it held by the person left behind was obscured by a curtain of dense weave; it did not yield a reason on this side of life.

Then Honoria spoke. "Anthony...?"

He looked up from the uncompleted work. "Honoria?"

"Do you think Mr Gillis was suggesting I find a husband?"

He considered this and heard the clock chime. A reminder of time never waiting and setting its own agenda. An agenda only half perceived. "I think he was suggesting it as a possibility... he was reminding you to think of your entitlement as a woman."

"Do I have such a thing?" she said.

"Of course! everyone does!... it varies from situation to situation... it might be called *choice...* or it might be called *vigilance...* but it is an entitlement at the end of the day. To live one's life according to means and according to persuasion..."

She watched him and her eyes clouded. He had handed her, he realised, a philosophy and not a firm answer. People needed assurance, not philosophy. It was why he was not a clergyman like his father or his elder brother. Too euphemistic a pursuit for someone like himself. "But I think, Honoria, that finding a husband is not like beach combing." She laughed, not really understanding but seeing the analogy as amusing. "What I mean is that some things are inevitable! If you leave this matter open to possibility... and nature... a husband will come when the time is right."

"Do you believe that truly?" she asked, her face suspicious. He could see that she was not simply the child she had been forced into remaining, but a woman on the edge of a precipice of folly or wisdom. "Yes, I truly believe that."

He believed too that he did not want Honoria to leave the house as yet. She was a balm to the atmosphere. She was like the sister he had never had. A wholly different presence from his wife. The comforting presence of a caring relation, a constant gentleness needing only to be acknowledged. He was not prepared to see her go just yet. He needed to think he was protecting her in a way that did not demand a price. And in this sentiment, perhaps, intentionally and unintentionally, maiden aunts were formed! Spinsters and women who abided by the behest of others, fashioned from others' selfish lack of thought. Or from the deliberate calculation of those who would make use of the circumstance of the day ..

"Let us ring for supper now," he said, "I am famished... and it may be spoiled if we do not dine soon... Melissa may have eaten at the Gillis's house... and if not they can plate something here for her in the kitchen."

"Yes, let's!" She dropped the mending and jumped to her feet. "I am hungry also... I am always hungry though... as you will have noticed."

He proffered his arm, and she took it, and they proceeded slowly in mock formality from the drawing room to the dining room next door.

* * *

Melanie dozed and woke, and saw Melissa sitting a few feet away in the chair. She had found a small piece of paper and was sketching on the back of it. She never wasted an opportunity when implements were to hand. "You are still here, my sweet!"

"Of course..." said Melissa.

Melanie sat up and sipped some water and then she helped her change the padding and the cloth with which the doctor had bound her to staunch the bleeding, bundling up the soiled articles and dropping them onto the fire.

"I remember we should not have burnt those... the doctor wanted to see them in the morning..." Melanie said.

Melissa made a disgusted face and stood back. "Whatever for?"

"To see how things are proceeding..."

"What a ghoulish notion!" proclaimed Melissa.

"Yes, positively grizzly... I do not think I shall comply with him in that at all."

"Though he is a doctor..." Melissa countered.

"Yes, and a man... my body is my own affair.  He will have to be content with my summary of events."

Melissa watched her climb back into the bed. "Do you feel any better?"

"As strong as a horse... I shall be up and about tomorrow."

"I would not, Mel, if I were you... you need more rest... are you hungry?"

"I shall attempt a morsel or two... and have something hot brought up for you. I think we should also have some brandy..." She rang for the maid to bring a bottle of it and then settled back against the pillows. As soon as she closed her eyes to rest, she fell asleep and woke some fifteen minutes later with a start. Melissa had gone to see Robert, who was with his nurse, to play with him for a few minutes before returning to the bedroom.

"Good Lord, you should have woken me..." Melanie said, opening her eyes on hearing the door close.

"I was visiting my godson..." She poured brandy into a glass and gave it to Melanie, and then poured herself some. Then the maid brought in the small walnut table on casters from which they may eat, followed by two plates of food under cloches.

"Now tell me of what has been happening at Back Lane?" Melanie said.

She was about to recount the incident of the bank fraud when Melanie jumped in to enquire: "How is Honoria? I had completely forgotten about her."

"She is settled in, and quite the perfect addition... she likes to be useful all the time... mending my lingerie... and helping the cook. Though Anthony does not like her doing things like clearing dishes or polishing the furniture, even though she seems to love it... so instead she is teaching Peggy to read properly... and he has spoken to Susan about her teaching at the alms school after Christmas."

Melanie snorted and lifted a piece of fish with her fork. "Education! Learning and more learning!... they are fanatics, these people!... but Honoria may tire of it soon..."

"I do believe she sees him as a father,..." mused Melissa.

"Ridiculous!" said Melanie, "He is scarcely much older than her."

"Yes I know... but that hardly matters... her own father is dreadful so she may feel the need of a more suitable replacement."

"I hope she knows she is merely swapping one tyrant for another!"

"I told her that... phrased as a jest in his presence... she said she does not mind..."

Melanie feigned a horrified face. "She could be Millicent all over again."

"She is less confident than Millie... Millie was never as green as we thought... look how she captured cousin Gregory," said Melissa while cutting up tough runner beans.

"Do you think she knows the facts of life, Honoria?" asked Melanie at length.

"I am unsure... but I think not... she asked me the other morning if I knew how birds made their eggs."

Melanie coughed and swallowed several times to rid her throat of fish. "Birds!"

"Yes, birds... that is her other interest... beyond being useful."

"Then obviously she does not know the facts... we shall have to sit with her over tea and apprise her, I perceive."

"I agree," said Melissa and replenished her glass with Geoffrey's fine brandy. "We should perhaps include Peggy..."

"Peggy?"

"Our maid... she too is as innocent as the day is long. I have already told her that Susan may inform her... but you can tell her, along with Honoria."

"Why do we not just open a weekly class for virginal young ladies and have done with it!" said Melanie, supping more brandy.

Melissa pushed the beans to one side of the plate in defeat. "That is actually a very good idea, Melanie. But it could bring us too much notoriety of the wrong kind."

They ate and supped steadily and sat back finally, replete, and within minutes Melanie was dozing again and Melissa resumed sketching until Melanie woke up sharply with another start. "We are wasting chatting time, Lissy... my mother will be here shortly. I cannot stay awake unless you distract me... it must be the laudenum the doctor gave me for the pain..."

Melissa was aghast and dropped the pad. "You did not tell me you had taken laudanum... you must stop drinking brandy... the two together may be dangerous."

"Nonsense!... what else has occurred?"

"The fraud..." announced Lissy.

"Fraud?" Melanie sat up straighter in the bed. "Which fraud?"

"Don't interrupt me whilst I tell you... I cannot tell you the most important events for your interruptions about Honoria and sarcastic comments about Anthony..."

"It must be the laudenum..." chirped Melanie and swigged a good amount of brandy before Melissa snatched away her glass. "I cannot seem to stop talking..."

"Yes, the fraud!... it concerns Caroline. It seems he has discovered the house is not her aunt's after all, he — "

"How do you know? Are you speaking to him now?"

"Mel, you are doing it again!"

"Well, are you?

"Not properly... only when he tricks me into it... we merely make love now and then."

"*Merely!*... For heaven's sake!... not speaking to him but making love with him all the while... I never heard of such lascivious behaviour!"

"I cannot resist, I am afraid," said Melissa archly. "I have appetites to satisfy... he looks at me for long periods without speech, sitting across the room and emitting a silent mating call."

"For his own benefit! You must control your urges, Lissy, if he is to take you seriously in this strategy of silence..."

*"And cut off my nose!.... to use one of your favourite sayings... Mel, be quiet now while I tell you about the fraud!"*

Melanie made scoffing and scathing sounds of merriment and searched for the brandy bottle. Melissa found it first and took it out to the corridor and placed it on a high window ledge, and then returned to the chair and drank from her own glass. Melanie had now assumed an angelic expression, like a child waiting for a bedtime story.

* * *

Melissa entered the house and listened to the quiet amid the noises of the kitchen where crockery and pans were making a cacophony of clanking and clattering during the kitchen cleaning process.

In the drawing room Honoria was in her usual chair, her feet tucked under her skirt, reading. Her husband was in a chair farther along the room reading a book in a foreign language.

"I apologise for my lateness... I had to sit with Melanie, she is -"

"Yes we know...." he intervened. "Gillis called to tell us."

"Oh good... Geoffrey is a very thoughtful person." she said.

Honoria smiled at her brightly but then they both continued to read.

"Bookworms!" she said in a slightly disparaging manner, aimed more at getting their attention than criticising them. She looked at the book her cousin was absorbed in and saw it was an illustrated journal on garden birds. It was one he had obtained for her from the book shop he frequented where they ordered specific volumes of work for him from other countries, and textbooks of the most boring kind. Honoria was absorbed completely, looking happier than anyone else she knew. Occasionally sucking the end of her thumb. She had pale red hair which waved slightly and was most conducive to the forming of ringlets. Now and then she took hold of one of the side locks and stroked her chin with it, like a man with a shaving brush. She had a lot of these endearing habits, youthful and spontaneous and the very opposite of sophisticated.

He seemed very content always in Honoria's company – her undemanding presence in a cosy domestic setting. And she wondered for the umpteenth time whether she should give him a child sooner rather than later. Catering to his need for someone to sit unassumingly

138

near him and make innocuous conversation; someone to buy books for who truly appreciated reading.

She moved in a rather disjointed manner to the doorway to retire upstairs and Honoria said. "How is Mrs Gillis now?"

"She is recovering well." replied Melissa.

"Mr Gillis thinks I should find a husband..." said Honoria.

Fairchild came to life. "He merely suggested you might... as an alternative to earning your living."

"But I do not know..." added Honoria.

"Of course not." She paused on her exit. "Nor will you know until you meet the right man..."

"That is what Anthony has said." Honoria announced, as if that put the seal of approval on the wisdom.

"There you are then! If the all-knowing one has proclaimed it, you have to believe it..."

Honoria surged on. "Mr Gillis thinks I should attend dinners and so on at their house... as he knows eligible single gentlemen..."

"We have just heard what a thoughtful person he is..." Fairchild said and rose from the chair, discarding his book on the seat of it.

"Ignore him... he is jealous." Melissa told Honoria. "Geoffrey *is* a thoughtful person."

He grunted something inaudible and searched about for his cigars.

She said to Honoria: "It is perhaps a good idea... for when you are more rested and prepared... and when you have had a conversation with Melanie and Susan and myself..."

"Conversation about what?" he enquired.

She ignored him and watched her cousin.

"Yes... indeed," said Honoria with a bravado she did not feel. "Meantime, I shall content myself with birds... and books... Anthony kindly purchased this one for me... he is another thoughtful person."

He almost grinned and then tightened his jaw to conceal it. Melissa looked at him with arched brows. "How blessed we are to be surrounded by these thoughtful men..."

Honoria looked at her doubtfully, sensing an oncoming round of biting banter between husband and wife which she did not enjoy.

Fairchild moved nearer to her and sniffed. "Have you been drinking?"

"I have had a brandy or two... to keep Melanie company."

"I can see."

"Why? do you imagine you are the only one here permitted to drink brandy?" She took off her cloak.

"You never drink brandy and are not used to it."

"There was nothing else available." she replied and he thought this amusing and then saw that it was perhaps just the truth.

"I must go and lie down... I am fagged to death..." she said. "What with one thing and another today..."

"Not to mention the brandy!" he added.

"I hope you are not going to keep on about my having a brandy..."

"More than one... by the smell of it... and the way you are walking."

"Of course, you are careful never to be seen when you have had too much brandy... so we do not know how you might walk then."

Honoria frowned and fidgeted. She did not like any hint at all of them being at loggerheads. Peggy had confided to her that they played a game, and that it was often very intense and involved them arguing and Melissa running off somewhere. But Peggy did not know what the game really consisted of, or what the aim of it was. Nor did Honoria on hearing this. But it began, it seemed, with a tense kind of atmosphere in which barbed remarks were exchanged. And sometimes incidents or events happened – like the one where undesirable relatives called and were admitted to the house by the mistress, when he did not wish them to be admitted ever ..

Honoria was bemused amid it all. She stood now and handed Melissa her mended underwear. Melissa tore her eyes away from her husband who had locked his own eyes upon her's, and she smiled at Honoria and then kissed her cheek. "Thank you, my pet. How clever you are."

"Yes," said Honoria, again like a child with her parents. "I said to Anthony and Mr Gillis earlier that I might become a seamstress... and that was when Mr Gillis said I should find a husband instead."

Melissa nodded at Honoria in an encouraging way "You could do both, I suppose."

"Of course she could not." Fairchild snapped.

"Why not?" she flared, and stared at him.

This *flaring and staring* was definitely a bad sign. Honoria flinched as if someone had pinched her.

"No man of society wishes his wife to work as a seamstress..." he replied with laboured tolerance. "You are guiding her along a false path."

"And, of course, your path is obviously the right one?"

"I am talking of conflicting paths... not of right ones or wrong ones."

Honoria fell back into her stammer. "I... I... I did not mean to... I can not... I do not... I..."

"'Tis fine, Honoria." he said. "Just my wife as usual being perverse."

"I am being no such thing. I am expressing my opinion... and now I am going to bed."

Honoria went back to her chair and was relieved when Melissa left and he followed. The silence and tranquillity returning to the room, which was better than this tense atmosphere which Peggy had described.

He followed Melissa upstairs. "When are you coming back to the marital bed?" he demanded.

"When I am ready..."

"It had better be soon... or I will lock the door of your temporary bedroom and hide the key... and you will have no choice..."

"How dare you!"

"You cannot be serious!" He moved to block her path. "This game has gone on for long enough."

"'Tis not a game..."

"Then what is it?"

"Me not speaking to you..."

"When you are in bed I am not going to ask you for conversation..." he remarked smoothly. She thought of Melanie's words on the strategy of her silence becoming ineffectual. She moved around him and he caught her arm. She pulled it free and he caught her hand instead. "You are being ridiculous."

"I have something important to discuss at breakfast tomorrow." she told him. "Now let me retire."

"What is it?"

"I shall tell you tomorrow... I am drunk, remember."

"I have not said that, Melissa... please tell me now."

"Very well... but I must lie down whilst I talk... I am too tired to do otherwise."

"That is agreeable." He followed her into the bedroom where she removed her shoes and he helped her undo the buttons of her dress and the tight bodice beneath, without the assistance of Peggy. By which time his concern over where she might have called these past days to accrue the need for important discussion was less pressing, where other things were. Soon they were in bed, making love, as if they had not seen each other for a year.

* * *

Over breakfast next day she did not speak until he spoke.

"What is it we need to discuss?"

She gazed at him and he smiled slightly. She smiled in return, a tight smile, like the Mona Lisa, recalling their lovemaking overnight.

"This is Melanie's suggestion... regarding the fraud and the Wentworth woman..."

"I feel I already do not like it."

"Childish!" she said shortly.

He checked his timepiece and then the clock. "Get on with it... I must leave in ten minutes."

"Then it will wait until this evening... I am eating toast."

He gripped her free hand which rested next to her plate, not a firm grip – merely an encouraging grip, which even so could not be mistaken as his demand for compliance. "Tell me now."

"She has suggested that we... I... approach Caroline Wentworth and tell her that unless she puts back the money she stole with my signature we will inform this Lord thingy of Gloucester, and tell him what she was doing with the sketch of his residence..."

He sat back and released her hand whilst he digested the information. In principle it was a reasonable suggestion, and no one could doubt its potential as a weapon with which to try to recoup the loss. But it must have its flaws – he thought rapidly of what they may be. She continued to eat, buttering more toast with indifference.

"It has too many risks..." he pronounced at length.

"Such as?"

"She may outright deny it... she may say we are lying... and that leaves us open to slander suits, from my villainous brother... he could turn it against us."

"But why would we say such a thing were it false? Melanie has thought of all that... she is just as clever as you... just as deep thinking... though you will not admit it. You will go all out to refuse any help she—"

He intervened. "Melissa, this is not a competition about who is cleverer than whom... I am not interested in how clever she is, or thinks she is." It was unbelievable, this vendetta from way back. He placed the used cutlery onto his plate and left the table and went to the window and gazed at the bare branches of the winter trees. "If we say that Caroline Wentworth was in disguise we are in a worse position... they will claim that someone in disguise could be anyone and may never be identified... that we are only guessing."

"Who will say that?" she asked.

"Anyone whom Richard employs to protect them... lawyers and so on... the bank even. An elderly woman pretending to be your maid could be anyone..."

"Yes but there is the history of the commission and the tea room conversation... of which we have evidence, through my conversations with Melanie and Geoffrey. The art commission came some time before her obtaining my signature."

This was true. He paused to deliberate, twirling his first small cigar of the day between his thumb and finger but not lighting it. "The bad feeling between Richard and I is common knowledge in a lot of places... and he knows it as well as I."

Her turn to mull matters over. She poured more coffee while thinking. "But, Anthony, at the end of the day, the residence does not belong to her aunt as she claims."

"Yes... but it is not written anywhere that she has said it does not... even in the document you signed saying the sketch was in your possession."

She sat back, fairly stumped. Until she thought broadly about things.

"I think people like Caroline and Richard will not hazard that kind of exposure... if it went to law it might reach the broadsheets... or jeopardise their schemes elsewhere..."

He turned and looked at her, then inclined his head in agreement. "That is a valid point."

She smiled and drank more coffee. "I can see the odds here being on our side if we went to law... look at my father's position and assets... and your reputation with local authority and people of influence... why would we make up such a story and bring attention to ourselves?"

He paced the room a few times, checked the time once more, considered their position yet again. His wife... her family's prosperity and standing, her privileged entitlement within it!  The entitlement gave her automatic advantage in the eyes of some people – were she to go to court as a defendant. Society as a whole was snobbish about who was capable of what misdemeanour – it was undeniable. "Had you better run it past Gillis?" he said.

"Are you being facetious?"

"No...  he offered his assistance when he called last night... should we require it." He left the room and returned with his greatcoat and began shrugging it on. Followed by the woollen scarf he wore when riding in cold weather. "Perhaps ask his wife to tell him of the plan."

"Do you mean Melanie?"

"Does he have more than one wife?... of course I mean her."

"Then why do you not use her name!"

He sighed and turned. "What does she call me when referring to me, did you once tell me?"

She smiled. "Atilla!... or the Viking!"

"Then you will forgive me if I simply refer to her as *his wife!*"

"'Tis a nickname we had for you at school."

"You are no longer at school."

She shook her head and closed her eyes impatiently. "Then you do not like the plan!"

"I do like it..." He collected various items and pocketed them. "I am just not sure it will work without backfiring."

"Do you want to recoup this money or not?

"Ludicrous question... I am leaving."

"I may attempt it anyway."

He turned and came back across the room. "You will not... not without my approval. You most assuredly will not... do you hear me?"

"I cannot fail to hear you."

"Then heed me... I shall be beyond vexed if you go against me on this without further deliberation and discussion."

She finished her coffee. "I have to be fitted for the dress I shall wear for Trim's wedding," she said, changing the subject rapidly. "I must also be moving along."

"Yes... that is important," he agreed.

"So is the lost money... I do not like to be bested by Caroline Wentworth... she is a disgrace to womankind."

"I could not agree more." He pulled the muffler up to cover his ears and did not add anything further.

She stood and shook out her skirt. "And before we leave this... have you considered what else they might do with my signature?"

He stopped in his tracks, having forgotten that possibility, and he stood without turning for a few moments, and she allowed him to be riveted by the thought.

* * *

Some twelve miles away in 'Golden Oaks,' Caroline awaited Richard's arrival. He had travelled back overnight from business in Coventry and was probably taking a few hours of sleep. Although he might just be at the bank he owned with two other partners, detained by matters there. So she sorted through her jewels, precious and otherwise, and then locked the ivory box in which she kept them as the maid entered, hobbling badly today with arthritis. "A feller from the dispatch place is at the door again... they're upset about keep having to come up to see whether you're here and who is where... and the post keeps coming..."

Caroline looked over her tiny eyeglasses. "You are not making any sense, Miriam..."

"I ain't repeating meself..." grumbled the maid.

"Just tell them I am not in... and that you do not know of anyone with the name of whoever it is on the mail..."

"The young feller today says as how it can't keep on... all this coming out here up that steep hill and bad roads... you has to come into their office and name yourselves..."

"Tell him to go away," said Caroline firmly.

Miriam had had enough. She was wracked with pain and near to collapse. Winter was not kind to her. "Miss Wentworth, come and tell him yourself... I ain't lying to no officials no more on your behest."

"He is not an official, you silly woman... he is a dispatch clerk... and it's Lady Wentworth... how many more times!"

"*So many times don't make it true...*" moaned Miriam, hobbling back out, moving to the porch with unrelenting slowness, and looking up with her faded eyes at the young man in the uniform. "Get away..." she shook her dirty apron at him, as if shepherding hens. "Shoo... shoo..."

The young man stood, bewildered but determined, and attempted again to explain the situation. Miriam listened, as if actually taking it all in, and frowned and gave the impression of great patience under duress. The young man continued for some time, outlining the laws governing the delivery of mail. Then Richard arrived on horseback and dismounted.

"What is going on here, Miriam?" he asked in an authoritative tone.

Miriam gave a garbled account, and the young man filled in the blanks for his benefit.

"Be gone now, my good man..." Richard pronounced at length. "None of the people you name reside here..."

"Then who does?" asked the dispatch employee.

"That is none of your concern... now be off... harassing citizens of the borough in this way."

The young man was frozen to the bone, having ridden and stood in the draughty porch and waited. He blew on his fingers, his gloves covering only his lower hands. "We will not deliver at all, Sir... if this continues."

"Excellent..." said Richard portentously. "I do not recall asking you to deliver in the first place."

"Questions are being asked," said the disgruntled official, "about why mail is being directed here and not accepted."

"Then go away and answer them," retorted Richard Fairchild.

"In what way? There is no reasonable explanation."

"That is your problem... not ours."

"It is quite unacceptable... my superior is considering -"

Richard intercepted him, becoming more officious. "I am not interested in what your superior is considering... he can consider all he likes as long as you go away... now be off before I set the dogs on you." The banker indicated the higher ground beside the house where the dogs, which did not exist, were allegedly kept.

The young man turned and sprinted to his horse, having been assailed by dogs many times. And Richard ushered Miriam in and followed her. "Do not open the door if they call again," he told her.

"How's I supposed to see who's there without opening the door... I ain't got second sight..."

"You barely have first..." muttered Richard and Miriam hobbled away complaining.

"Oh, there you are!" said Caroline chippily as he entered the drawing room, dark as always with the curtains partly closed and only one oil lamp burning, the fire low in the grate.

"What is all this about the dispatch, Caro?" he enquired irritably.

She let out a long weary breath, as if constantly harried by dispatch men. "They are trying to deliver things I do not wish to receive... so I am telling them they have the wrong name."

"Dangerous," he said, taking off his gloves. "They are not fools, you know... they have ways and means."

"Why, have they begun employing sleuths now?" She picked up the red velvet pouch she had selected from the jewellery box and loosened the draw string. He watched curiously, not allowing himself to move away before all was revealed.

"Go and have coffee before we leave, as you always do..." she told him, turning her shoulder against his prying gaze. "Time is getting on, Dickie."

He moved to the door and then came stealthily back as she retrieved the bag's contents. She jumped when he came behind her, but it was too late to conceal the jewellery. He snatched the item from her – a gold chain with small diamonds and larger rubies dotted about its circumference. He held it close to his face. "These stones are genuine..." he declared.

"How surprising!" said Caroline urbanely.

"Where did you get it?"

"A jeweller of course... I did not steal it if that is what you think."

He did not believe her. "And what money did you use?"

She declined to reply and took the necklace back and replaced it in its snug holder. "Not with the money obtained from my sister-in-law's account, I hope." He glared at her as he sat down and refused to look away. She waved her hand dismissively. "You can be easy... I did not use that money..."

He was releasing his tension when she added. "I used her signature... to procure it on account."

He sprang from the chair. "Tell me you are jesting..."

"I am serious."

"Caroline..." he began in a dire tone, turning pale. "... that was a step completely too far..." He watched her laugh and then sip tea. "You have taken a step that is utterly without safety... you could see us in jail."

She laughed again and sipped more tea. "You are such a worrier, Dickie... I shall never, unfortunately, wear it outside... so do calm down."

# Rituals and Festive Cheer

"So, I thought we could go to late breakfast at about eleven to The Four Horsemen... my father and myself..." Susan was saying in the drawing room at Back Lane House, "and then drive to Lessingdale and arrive in time for the ceremony... in keeping with tradition"

"But it will be very cold weather, no doubt... why not breakfast at Lessingdale?" claimed her fiance.

"'Tis tradition that the bride should always arrive separately from the groom, Timothy..."

'Lessingdale' was the name of the Trimingham mansion where Trim resided still in his own rooms, and where he and Susan had shared their seven or eight years of courtship and intimacy, undisturbed. Although she mostly lived at the house from which her father, a local physican, held his surgery, and was in most ways the housekeeper. Her mother having died many years before.

"You have never before bothered yourself with tradition..." Trim said.

"But I am at heart very traditional... except perhaps in the length of engagement I have enjoyed." argued Susan.

It was the longest engagement anyone knew of and everyone smiled – or tried not to. Trim picked up his tea cup and looked at Fairchild who shook his head slightly to indicate the uselessness of arguing with women in these kind of details. The wedding was to be held at Lessingdale, a private ceremony rather than a church, but presided over by the Reverend Rupert Fairchild to respect Trim's parents' religious beliefs.

"'Tis a good idea..." said Melissa, and Susan's two aunts murmured approval.

"Is it?" asked the amenable Trimingham.

"Of course," said Susan's Aunt Virginia, visiting from Derbyshire for Christmas and the wedding. "She does not wish to be making breakfast and preparing for her own wedding all at the same time..."

"But why can the cook not prepare breakfast?" demanded Trim, aghast.

"Because she does not work on Wednesdays, Timothy... as you well know."

"I did not know that, Susan!... and can she not make an exception for that day?"

"No... she will already have worked hard preparing food for the visitors expected the day before... in addition to Christmas."

Trim sighed, and Fairchild subtly inclined his head to the door, indicating that they leave this tedious planning to the women. For now there was bound to be a unanimous vote against him on the matter of breakfast.

"I thought this was to be a quiet wedding..." Trim said to Susan.

"It is a quiet wedding... there will be only twenty five guests."

"Twenty five guests is not a quiet wedding, Susan." Trim persevered patiently.

"It is, considering how many more people might have been invited... all the people we know and have left out..." She placed her hands on her stomach, which was now quite pronounced with her expectancy; a time-honoured gesture she did not fully realise she copied.

"You could breakfast at Lessingdale..." Trim continued without much hope.

"The bride is not supposed to see the groom beforehand..." claimed Aunt Blanche, her father's twin sister, also visiting. "'Tis most unlucky..."

"Well, I could take breakfast here at a different time..." offered the groom.

"Give it up, Trim, you are outnumbered...." claimed Fairchild.

"I am thinking of her catching a chill driving about on the winter morning... and that inn never being too warm."

"How sweet and considerate..." said Honoria timidly, who until now had not commented. Fairchild sighed; Trim's sweetness to the opposite gender was legendary, so that they tended to walk all over him.

"Thank you, my love... but I shall be wrapped up well... my wedding dress under my winter cloak..." Susan told him more gently.

"And you may not be up in time for breakfast," Melissa said to Trim, to put the cat among the pigeons, "if you celebrate the night before..."

"There had better not be such festivity the night before his wedding." claimed Susan. "We do not want the place reeking of strong drink."

"There will be no festivity the night before... the bachelor do is to be the day after Boxing Day..." Trimingham looked at Fairchild. "Is it not?... have you invited everyone?... as best man!"

"Yes, all six are attending," said Fairchild.

"Besides, Lessingdale will be chaotic on the day of the wedding..." said Aunt Blanche. "There will be too much going on..."

"By far!" agreed Aunt Virginia. "You see, with the greatest respect, Timothy, 'Tis best to let the ladies organise these things... and Benjamin will not let her grow cold, I am sure."

"Thank you, Aunt Ginny!... my father is a doctor, you know, Timothy, he will not see me jeopardise my health!"

Trimingham gave in, and Fairchild murmured something which they all turned to hear, but he had closed his lips and assumed a vacant expression. Then Honoria ventured: "If I may enquire, Susan, what colour is your dress?"

Susan opened her mouth to reply, but Aunt Virginia broke in, laughing prettily and placing her hand on Honoria's arm. "No, no... she must not divulge that out loud... he is not to know any of what she wears beforehand... she may whisper it to you in a moment."

"I... I... I am so sorry... I... I did not think," said Honoria and suffered her arm to be patted more by Aunt Virginia, who was seated beside her on the sofa. "You must remember that for when 'tis your turn, my dear... which will be soon, I am sure... bridegrooms do not need to know the dress details until the ceremony... so they may better appreciate the stunning beauty of the bride."

"Shall we retire to smoke, Tony?" Trim said, before he lost his patience.

It was the day before Christmas Eve, and all was festive; the tree and the garlands and the sprigs of holly and the atmosphere of muted anticipation. Christmas and a wedding! Everyone loved a Christmas wedding.

But then Susan had a diverting thought and turned to Honoria. "Honoria, you are still of a mind to try taking a class of the youngest ones in January... at the alms school?"

"Indeed," said Honoria with eagerness.

"Thank you... we are so grateful... if you could do Tuesday and Thursday mornings?... shall you come with her?" she asked of Fairchild.

He paused and looked with a pained expression at Trimingham, who sat back resignedly. "For what reason, Susan?"

"For one thing, I shall not be there..." Susan said. "You cannot just throw her into it..."

"Where shall you be?" asked Honoria in alarm.

"On my honeymoon... and I do not intend to re-appear until after the happy occasion."

"But I thought your wedding was the happy occasion," Honoria said in her innocence.

There was some shuffling and throat clearing, and no one knew what to say. Susan's pregnancy was never referred to directly, except by Trimingham and her father, the esteemed doctor, and that was quite different. Fairchild intervened to save Susan having to talk about the birth of her child. "I can bring her..." he said. "But I cannot linger above fifteen minutes... we are under pressure at present and there will be deadlines to be met, with Trim absent."

"Yes," confirmed Trim. "Quite so."

Susan sighed. "You can spare an hour surely?"

"What is this?" queried Aunt Virginia, so that the question of Honoria teaching at the alms school for a trial period with the youngest children was explained by Susan.

Trimingham was slightly put out that her attention could go so easily from their wedding to her passion for the school, but he strove not to show it. Farchild rolled his eyes at him and then shifted his gaze deliberately to the door again, but Trim was not quick enough picking up the hint

"I think you should be there." Aunt Virginia said suddenly to Fairchild.

"Forgive me... be where?" he asked, his attention shredded by never-ending witterings on one thing and another.

"'Tis a large responsibility to ask of someone without previous experience," elucidated Aunt Virginia.

"Certainly..." put in Aunt Blanche. "Supposing these children are too much for her! Supposing they refuse to do as she tells them?"

He realised they were again talking of Honoria and the school. He was trying not to grow exasperated at this interference from Trim's in-laws on a subject not connected with weddings. "They will not refuse. It is explained to them on their first day what is expected of them and Donald Aldrige will be in the other classroom."

"And who is he?" enquired Aunt Virginia nosily.

"He teaches the older children... but leads the school..." said Susan, "the only male member of staff... the head... if there is such a thing at the school."

"Well, I hope there is such a thing." Aunt Blanche said. "Imagine a school without a headmaster!... even a ragged school."

"We try not to call it by that name, Aunt Blanche..." chided Susan.

"Which name?" asked Blanche.

"Ragged school!... 'Tis very hurtful to the children."

"Well, that is what they are... and however you call them, Miss Ainscoe cannot be expected to go in there and face them alone."

"Yes, but she is not alone... Mr Aldridge will be next door if there are any problems..." said Susan, also now exasperated by her aunts.

"Fear not, Honoria." Melissa offered in a droll tone. "There will be at least one tyrant in residence..."

Trimingham grinned, and Fairchild cast her a withering look. The aunts looked at her curiously, unsure how serious she was being.

"My wife thinks all people in education are tyrants..." Fairchild told them evenly.

"Yes, I actually married one," she added brightly, "for revenge..."

Trimingham snuffed quiet laughter while the aunts exchanged bemused glances, and Susan dismissed Melissa's sarcasm as an unnecessary incursion into a profound subject. Melissa felt her giggling growing inside her – like indigestion – and took out her kerchief.

"Oh dear!" said Honoria in a quailing voice. "Perhaps they will not listen to me. Perhaps I will fail..."

"They are not quite barbarians, Miss Aisncoe, and Donald Aldrige is not a tyrant... merely a believer in good behaviour," Trim said.

"As are we all..." confirmed Susan.

"But these sorts of children are often without manners or much idea of conduct," said Aunt Virginia argumentatively.

"Not when Mr Aldridge is about..." claimed Melissa, and Fairchild moved behind the sofa from his standing position at the large fireplace and squoze the back of her neck. "Stop it," he said softly so that her amusement grew worse.

Seeds of interest were now sewn, and the aunts had new thoughts regarding Honoria's entry into this meritorious pursuit. "How old is he?" asked Aunt Blanche, "Mr Aldridge... this tyrant?"

"He is not a tyrant," declared Susan defensively in a louder voice. "Melissa is teasing... she often makes these remarks, knowing that we are teachers... Mr Aldridge does a sterling job... we are fortunate to have him at his time of life."

"But how old?" persevered Aunt Virginia. "Is he married?"

"He is a widower, I believe... and his age is his business," Fairchild commented and was ignored.

"He is probably seventy... or thereabouts... no one is entirely sure!" said Susan to be obliging.

"God bless him!" announced Aunt Blanche, dropping the idea of him as a possible suitor for Honoria.

"Quite!" said Fairchild, hoping to conclude the subject.

"We are hoping that after next week's fundraising we may be able to afford another paid member of staff... another male for when Mr Aldridge is taking time off," Susan added.

"I am sure you shall..." Melissa told her confidently. "If I have anything to do with it... after all, you cannot have too many tyrants on hand."

"Melissa, do stop saying that!" Susan implored.

"Your wife seems taken with this idea of tyrants..." Aunt Blanche said to Fairchild, and he kept his neutral face but inclined his head to her politely. "Indeed, Ma'am... 'tis her favourite subject."

"Really?" queried Aunt Virginiam, peering at Melissa. "How curious!"

Trimingham laughed loudly, knowing the history of the jibes and the humour... which might or might not be humour at all. "She is in jest, Ma'am."

"So you may like to believe..." said Melissa, beaming impishly at Trimingham, then turning to Honoria to detract from this private area of curiosity. "The worst thing, in truth, is the odour... though these children cannot help it, they perhaps only bathe once a month, some of them."

"Dear me!" opined Aunt Virginia, her fingers rising instinctively to her nose. But Honoria was hopeful. "I shall not mind that so much..."

"No... 'tis easily cured... I use my kerchief soaked with cologne and hold it to my nostrils now and then." Melissa said. "So should you, Honoria."

"Do you teach at this ragged school too?" asked Blanche with astonishment.

"Alms school!... " amended Susan vehemently. The school was her pet project and occupation, beyond her herbs and tinctures.

"Not teach exactly... I draw with them perhaps once a month... sometimes with pastels..." Melissa said.

"She is another godsend..." claimed Susan. "They love her to come... most of them will never draw in their lives... unless with someone like Melissa."

"She allows them to do as they wish..." said Fairchild lightly. "In her eternal commitment to freedom for all... so naturally they love her to come..."

"Yes... I am the entertainment value... Melissa countered, "amid the oppression... and the tyrants!" She giggled a little, for the benefit of everyone's peace of mind, and he squoze her neck again and wound his fingers tightly in her hair. She put back her head and looked at him with a seductive face which made him remove his hand... before he could become aroused.

The aunts now were a little more satisfied by the facts, and Trim was daydreaming, but Susan was already counting in her head the probable donations to the funds and the acquisition to the meagre staff.

"Oh well there we are..."

"How wonderful..."

"How good of you, my dear... and you Miss Ainscoe!"

"'Tis heartening to hear of such devotion to public life..."

The mood had changed to one of goodwill and glad thankfulness.

"Trim!" said Fairchild in a stronger voice. "The smoke we agreed on..."

"Yes." Trimingham rose and bowed to the women. "Ladies, excuse us, would you!"

But the outer bell clanged and everyone waited until Peggy came in to say that the parson had arrived.

"Which parson?" asked Trim with evident annoyance.

"She will mean my brother..." Fairchild said.

Then the Reverend Rupert Fairchild entered, smiling widely in his convivial way, accustomed to such gatherings – both pre-nuptial and parochial – and Anthony Fairchild and Timothy Trimingham grinned at him thankfully. "Rupert, how good of you to come," said his younger brother.

Rupert continued to smile and bowed to the room. "Not at all... 'Tis part of my job... or I'd be at home now hanging decorations with my wife and keeping the children from the fireplace and the garlands and burning down the vicarage..."

"How many children do you have?" enquired Aunt Virginia at once. Part of the fun of visiting was the insight gleaned into the lives of perfect strangers.

"We have six, Ma'am." replied Rupert and another chorus of approval and interest went the rounds.

Rupert Fairchild bore only a passing resemblance to his brother, in certain lights and with certain expressions; his features favouring his father, unlike Anthony who was almost the male facsimile of his Scandinavian mother. Rupert was taller by a couple of inches with dark blonde hair, not light blonde like his younger brother's, but of the sandier variety, straight and thick and combed behind his ears, except for a frontal piece which swept his forehead and fell over his eyes. Without his collar and clerical robes, as today, it was hard to imagine him as a vicar. But once in his company for any length of time and hearing his approach to people and his amenable manner, it was easy to recognise his calling. He was seven or eight years older than Anthony Fairchild and mellowed by life and his strong faith. He seated himself in the spare armchair nearest the fire and became attuned without qualm into the conversational flow and atmosphere.

"Rupert," said his brother. "We are absenting ourselves for ten minutes... make yourself at home and enjoy the fire... Peggy will bring you whatever you want by way of refreshment and Melissa will make the introductions... and perhaps we shall have sherry and mince tarts..."

Aunt Virginia clapped her hands gleefully, like a young girl at the thought of a ball. "Mince tarts and sherry... how splendid!"

"Timothy, do not disappear completely..." Rupert said. "I shall need you in a moment whilst I explain the formalities for next week... you are the bridegroom, after all..."

"I shall not let him disappear," said Fairchild. "He has had enough reprieves over the years as it is."

Laughter followed them, and Melissa kissed Rupert's cheek. "Rupert, let me introduce you... ladies, the Reverend Rupert Fairchild, my brother-in-law, who will officiate at the wedding... Rupert, this is Susan's aunt on Doctor Darnley's side and her other aunt on..." and the niceties flourished as they made their way to the small conservatory to smoke.

"Good God! I feel as though I have been married three times over." Trim said.

"I have been trying to extricate you for at least fifteen minutes but you have not been taking the signals..." said his friend.

"I did not see any signals."

A hoarfrost had lingered on the bushes and shrubs beyond the conservatory windows and Trim rubbed a square in one of the panes, where the condensation was itself like a faded white curtain, and peered into the garden. "Susan's aunts are quite infuriating. They always want to know the ins and outs of the cat's arse and cannot let anything go inside of a half hour."

"'Tis quite useless to argue with women on these occasions." Fairchild said, lighting his small cigar. "They are not seeking your opinions... they are merely informing you of theirs... so you just waste your breath."

The conservatory was freezing cold but quiet and remote. They accepted the temperature change gladly and rubbed their hands briskly for warmth. They had slept in dormitories this cold in boarding school as boys.

"Thankfully Rupert is here now. He's an old hand at these meetings..." Fairchild remarked.

"The only one not taking things too seriously is Melissa..." continued Trim doggedly.

Fairchild scoffed and pulled on the cigar. "Melissa scarcely takes anything seriously... you surely know that by now... and that is why I have a momentously stressful situation..."

Trimingham was startled into stillness. "What? More stressful than being best man at my wedding?"

"I am severely compromised by Richard..."

"In what way compromised?" said Trimingham, tamping tobacco into a pipe.

"He has used the signature they obtained from Melissa to take money from her trust account..."

Trimingham stared at him. "Are you sure?"

"Quite certain... 'twas the Wentworth woman doing the deed... obviously in disguise of some kind... in the bank."

Trimingham assumed the expression of feeling for another man's anguish in the midst of betrayal, and lit the pipe. "I did not think he would ever sink this low," he said softly.

Fairchild hit the door frame with the flat of his hand. "I swear to God, Trim, I shall kill him one of these days with my bare hands..."

Trim pulled open the old stiff and resistant door to the outside, as if they may run into the overgrown garden and escape life. Then he brightened, as was his way, and grinned, having heard these threats on and off for years. "Yes... but please do not let it be before Wednesday and my wedding..."

* * *

"I never thought he would sink so low..." said Rupert an hour later, echoing Trimingham almost word for word..

"God knows why not!" Farichild claimed bitterly. "He is hardly a paragon of Christian virtue, Rupert..." Then he mellowed his tone. Rupert abounded with those virtues in a genuine way. As if one person in a family carried an excess of some values and others felt obliged to forfeit them completely.

"What will you do?" asked Rupert.

"The bank wants to go to the constabulary... they feel they are culpable... but they need my sanction upon it."

"I see..." Rupert sat on a rickety chair – the conservatory was hardly used, except in summer and for Melissa's art when the light outside was right.

"'Tis why I am telling you now..." Fairchild watched his brother. "The repercussions if the bank proceeds... not that I think they have much chance... and your position as a vicar of the parish..."

"My position as vicar is one which admits of human frailty..." said Rupert stoically and his younger brother tried to curb his impatience.

"Yes, but Rupert, in the real world people are not so forgiving.,."

Rupert smiled – this inference that the church was not part of the material world was something he heard all the time. Whereas the first place some people ran to in times of trouble – in their *real world* – was the church.

"Then there is Mama... it will cut her to the core... if this turns bad."

"She is made of stronger stuff, Tony!" Rupert said. "She has not spent her life kneeling before an altar, but out in the wider community ministering to the needs of the *real world...*"

"Yes but she is getting old now..." he said with mounting anguish, "and the ministering within the community has a different value than her own family."

"Does it?" said Rupert.

"Of course... however much you dress it up..." He stopped; any moment now they would be disagreeing over theology and doctrine and veering from the point. "She is wed to a bishop, Rupert..."

"And even he, as a bishop, is bound to see the fallibility of mankind... how do you think he became a bishop?... Richard's villainy is something they are aware of."

"Oh, so you admit he's a villain?"

"He has fallen by the wayside without a doubt... many years ago," said the Reverend Fairchild.

He laughed then, despite his attempt not to, and gave up the attempt to save Rupert's reputation. "*Fallen by the wayside!...* I fall by the wayside when I drink to excess and need to be helped home by friends who may or may not also have fallen by the wayside... or when I lose too much money I cannot afford to lose on a horse!... But I do not indulge in some of the schemes and exploits in which our brother indulges."

"What do you want to do?" said Rupert shortly.

"Kill him, of course..." He waited a beat and then continued, not expecting Rupert to sympathise or endorse the statement. "I have wanted that for some time."

"He is Uncle Charles all over again... without the brutality or thuggery perhaps, but there are similarities." Rupert claimed.

"I said that to mother just before I was wed... Melissa heard me... and mother denied it... and we know how that story ends!"

"We should perhaps try among ourselves to talk to him..." Rupert said, "about this latest business... and see where it leads."

"I can tell you where... with him playing us for fools."

"'Tis Christmas... let us wait until after..." Rupert stood, as though the matter of approaching Richard Fairchild was decided upon. "I must get on with matters to hand... I have much to do at the church and at home... let me pray on it..."

"If I do not do something Melissa will take it upon herself to try her own methods of reclamation... though I have forbidden her from doing so, she will doubtless defy me... and then things may become worse."

"Perhaps... but there is less likelihood of bloodshed in that..." said Rupert.

He reacted sharply. "Are you suggesting I should use my wife to deal with this matter... in the same way as he uses that jade of his! Are you actually proposing that Rupert?"

"No, I am making an observation, Tony, and I implore you to remain calm... and not to let your temper rule you in this."

"Why do you not just add that *God will find a way...* and that *faith will bring me through...* just to sustain me over Christmas!"

Rupert watched him calmly. His brother's lack of faith was a source of sadness to Rupert, as great as was Anthony Fairchild's perception of Rupert's perceived naivete. At a time when the church was losing ground to the fad for modern science, Rupert saw the divide constantly and knew how to span it. It was an ongoing speculative problem for many, but for him, it was all part of a greater whole.

"Shall I appeal to him?" Rupert said. "Shall I visit him and appeal to his better nature?"

The laughter of his youngest brother, even though muted, was the hardest thing to hear. It brooked no optimism. "Yes, yes... do..." he said equivocally. "Better to have tried... before he ends up in Newgate or worse."

"You have to remember," said Rupert. "We are not our brother's keeper..."

"Is that a witty pun, Rupert?" He was shivering with the cold from the conservatory interior, with the added emotions of the subject matter. "Is it meant to be ironic in the biblical sense?"

Rupert smiled thinly but did not reply.

"I badly need a drink now," he said, "and the blasted sherry in there will not suffice... unless I drink a full bottle or so..."

"You see, we are fallible in different ways!" claimed Rupert, and heard the door slam behind his brother.

*  *  *

At roughly the same time the next day, early Christmas Eve, as Melissa was riding with Melanie back to Golden Oaks, Anthony Fairchild was on his way to see his mother. Whom he hoped would be at home in the bishop's palace.

She was, and he divested himself of his riding cape to the butler and waited for her to leave late breakfast (or perhaps early luncheon) with her husband. He could hear them – her distinctive laughter and the deeper tones of his step-father. They were happy in their second marriages and he was glad for them, though it had taken him a few years to reach that point; his resentment of her love for this man was something he was not proud of and strove to overcome. He was beckoned by the butler into the smaller dining room.

"Good Heavens, Anthony... is it Christmas Day already!" she said.

"No, Mama... and you must forgive my intrusion..." he kissed her warmly and took the chair next to her.

"Good morning, my boy..." said his step-father. "What brings you?"

"'Tis not pleasant tidings, I am afraid." He said straight off and then cursed himself for precipitous speech. These were elderly people – he should have more tact and allow them time to adjust to his arrival.

"Should you care for something to eat? We have only just finished... there is more left," said the bishop.

"No, nothing, thank you. I have eaten."

"Whatever is it?" claimed Hildegarde.

"I must speak to you, Mama... regarding Richard." He may as well come straight to the point, seeing that she requested it. Her features, still etched with her earlier beauty, clouded over. "Tony, what is it now?" She intoned, stirring her tea with intent. He hesitated, and the bishop said. "Take him into the drawing room, Hildy, there is a fire in there... you won't be disturbed."

"I apologise for taking her away..." Fairchild told him. "And at Christmas."

"Not at all... I will see her all over the festive season, and no doubt you too at some point... how is that little wife of yours?"

"She is tolerably well, thank you, Sir." He thought of how amused Melissa would be at being referred to as the *little wife,* though it was meant to convey her comparative youth rather than her size, which was if anything tall.

"Excellent!" said his step-father and waved his fingers to Hildegarde to urge her to go quickly.

The drawing room was decorated to perfection, expecting all and sundry to be gracing it. The tree was huge and magnificent, and the baubles expensive, as befitted an elder of the Church of England. The holly and mistletoe were profuse, and the large floral... arrangements opulent. This did not resemble the vicarage he had grown up in; this was the higher echelon of the religion itself. He looked about him and appreciated the luxury but reserved his judgement as he seated himself.

"I expect you would like coffee?" she said. "Rather than tea!"

"I would, thank you."

"Are you all prepared for Timothy and Susan's wedding on Wednesday?"

"Yes... I think we are."

"Good." His mother seated herself in the small curved armchair next to the fire. "I think Eleanor and Matthew are delighted... those two taking their vows at last."

"I am sure they are!"

"And Eleanor has the fundraising only two days later... after the wedding celebrations... she will be glad to rest at New Year."

Trim's parents were old friends of his own parents, and now of his mother and her second husband.

"She has told Melissa she finds the period between Christmas and New Year very flat... so she is glad of the fundraiser to quicken the pace... and Melissa is taking all the responsibility for the visitors, assisted by Honoria and the maids..." he told her. "And I shall be around the whole while... as Trim is absent."

"Oh, splendid..." Hildegarde then had a second thought." Who is Honoria?"

"Her cousin... she has brought her to stay with us... indefinitely."

"What? When did that happen and why?"

He sighed. "'Tis a lengthy story, Mama, and we should broach the matter I came about..."

"Good Heavens'... there is hardly a dull moment... Melissa is a whirlwind of activity in one way or another..."

"You have no idea..." he said.

"But she makes you happy?" queried his mother, crossing her ankles beneath her expansive skirts and becoming more comfortable.

"She... she is..."

"What?" she asked impatiently. "She is what?"

"She both infuriates me... and gives me great pleasure... she is an enigma "

"She always was... even before you married, if I remember well."

"Yes... yes, but we cannot get into that now."

There was a pause of some seconds, and then he wasted no time in outlining for her the dilemma and the conversation with Rupert. She sat very still and stared at the far wall, where the painting he had gifted her and her husband, one of Melissa's own, hung over the cabinet in the alcove.

He noted firstly the tears in her eyes, and sensing this, she swiped at them with her fingers. "I am sorry, Mama."

"It is not for you to be sorry, Anthony... 'Tis Richard who needs to feel contrition..."

"I doubt he will... he never does."

He loved his mother. He could never bear to upset her or see her distressed. The tears welled more profusely in her translucent blue eyes, and he rose and crouched in front of her and took her hands in his. "We have to act on this... and I need to know that you are -"

"Of course you must..." interposed Hildegarde Wyevale in her strongest tone. "He cannot be allowed to get away with it."

"There is the possibility it may be all Caroline Wentworth's doing..."

"That dreadful creature..." she stood abruptly and turned her back. Her anger was an unwelcome guest at Christmas. "I rue the day he ever took up with her."

Returning to the sofa, he cleared his throat. "Mama, you must allow of the consideration that had he not taken up with her, it might have been another female like her..."

She turned and stared, for that had not occurred to her, and it did so now with a resounding clarity. It made her feel faint, this revelation. It verified the wrong thinking and criminality of her middle son. She straightened her posture, almost proudly. It was the truth, and she knew that the truth set one free. "It was most likely his idea..." she uttered at length. "She would simply be the instrument of it."

"This is what I think..." he said, as the coffee arrived, and he watched the man servant pour it. This was the bishop's palace (so called), and the servants seen in the house were mostly male, of the most efficient and respectful of staff available. Their mother, likewise, was of the most sensible and fitting of wives for a bishop, having previously been married to his father.

"We thought we may at first try dealing with this from within the family..." he ventured when the man had left the room.

"Tell me the finer details of the matter," she said and sat in the chair again to compose herself.

* * *

"We are lost once more..." cried Melissa, holding onto the reins of the trap, which this time was the Gillis' conveyance. "I knew we would be..."

"You should let me drive..." Melanie protested. "While you look around and try to remember the lie of the land..."

"You are still recovering."

"Phooey... it simply needs me to sit and hold the reins..."

"I cannot allow it," said Melissa airily.

"You see... you have already caught the tyranny disease... from him..." Melanie laughed loudly and it was stolen by the wind and dissipated in the nearby forest. *"I cannot allow it!... I cannot allow it!"* she imitated and laughed in a yet more raucous fashion, enjoying the freedom and the venture as usual. Then she stopped suddenly and sat bolt upright. "Look, over there... that is the turning... quite concealed but I remember it."

Melissa turned the horses to a sharp left angle so that the trap lost the grip of its right wheels for a second or two.

"Jesus Christ!" wailed Melanie, clutching the door strap.

"Stop blaspheming... 'Tis Christmas..." said Melissa gaily, and the trap righted itself and carried on up to the short driveway, fringed with poplars, the large oak trees apparent in the woods beyond. The weak sunshine glinting between high barren branches.

"That is why they christen it 'Golden Oaks'..." Melanie said, "the sun turns the trees to that kind of bronze colour at certain times..."

"They call it that when the fancy takes them..." scoffed Melissa, "The rest of the time they call it whatever they will."

They stopped at the top of the driveway and deliberated, deciding to leave the conveyance with the horses tethered a little way into the forested area where the flat ground permitted, and then go on foot the rest of the way. It was a similar manoeuvre to the one they used on rescuing Honoria. "We do not need to turn the trap, we can head out onto that lane when we leave... see!... this leads back onto it from the other end..." Melanie pointed with satisfaction and Melissa shaded her eyes to survey the land and nodded.

"We are so good at this kind of thing now..." Melanie boasted as they sprinted to the house.

"We are not making a habit of it!" said her friend in a censorious manner.

"Why not? Think of what we could accomplish," rejoined Melanie.

Melissa slowed down to consider the meaning of the comment, but was pulled along by Melanie, and they moved into the trees surrounding the driveway to approach the house unseen.

"Slow down, Mel... you should not be running too fast, being still weakened.

"Phooey!" said Melanie, "I am right as rain..." But she heeded the advice, and they proceeded at a slower pace.

The small manor seemed to be deserted. No sign of horses or other conveyances and no sign of human activity. They crept around the outside of the building and tried peering into windows, which were all shuttered by blinds or curtains. The one window they could actually see into was at the rear of the house, and gave a view into a small scullery, dilapidated and in need of a clean. Within a few seconds, they made out the figure of the ancient maid, slumped in a rocking chair, sleeping next to a small fire grate.

"Look... 'tis that poor old Miriam," Melissa whispered.

Melanie gazed at the slumbering figure and then tapped at the window. Melissa pulled her hand away. "No... she will tell Caroline and they will not admit us... we must think what to say to gain entry."

Miriam had not moved or shown signs of hearing. "She is fast asleep," Melissa said. "But I will lay odds she has not locked the kitchen door."

The kitchen door lay to the west of the structure, a few feet from the window and around the corner of the building. Here, there were two doors side by side, and Melanie held onto Melissa's arm to stop her trying the first, then kicking at the overgrowth of thorns and grass round the oldest looking door and finding a low glass pane. "The cellar," she declared, and then quietly lifted the latch to the other door. It opened immediately. She turned and beamed at Melissa for guessing rightly about the unlocked door.

They let themselves in and peered at Miriam, who snored lightly, creeping past her and opening the door to the main hallway. "Can you remember where the drawing room is?" Melanie queried.

"Yes... 'tis second on the left."

The hall was eerie this time, far more eerie than on the first visit. It had a hollow ring of desperation and doom about it. Nothing stirred besides the ticking of an unseen clock. "If we are discovered..." whispered Melanie, "we must say that we could not make anyone hear us... we must say we tried the door by chance and found it open, so that we cannot be prosecuted for unlawful entry and trespass."

Melissa stared at her. "In truth?"

"Yes... remember Geoffrey is an attorney."

"How could I forget..."

The boards of the floor creaked, and they paused on every two footsteps, but no one appeared. Then they saw the crack of light from the door of the drawing room.

The room was dark, one oil lamp burning, the fire dying in the grate, the heavy curtains closed. It took an age to adjust their vision.

The chaise longue was placed next to the small table, which held the lamp, and upon it lay Caroline Wentworth, also slumbering it seemed, her legs sprawled haphazardly, one foot on the floor and the other on the pink upholstered seat. Her dyed black hair covered in an elaborate scarf of some kind, with stray locks of it escaping onto her face and neck. Her face, without powder or paint, was grey and harrowed and without any trace of beauty. There was a strange heavy musky odour in the air. "Lady Vulture is almost falling from the nest..." whispered Melissa.

"She may actually be older than Miriam." Melanie hissed.

Their laughter came over them unbidden, and they stifled it as Melissa tip-toed to the small table on which there was a small brass receptacle, oriental in design, lidded but with a protuberance coming from it, like a single tentacle of a small octopus, a lip-shaped nozzle at one end. They gazed at Caroline together, like visitors to an invalid, and she gave a small shudder and murmured something, but did not rouse. They stood very still and took stock of the room and its contents. "Caroline..." whispered Melanie, "Caroline... wake up... you have visitors."

But Caroline did not stir, although her eyes flickered open for a second, displaying a blank unseeing look.

"I think she is an opium eater..." Melanie stated.

*"What?"* Melissa came nearer to look at her. "What is that?"

"She is addicted to the drug opium... look at the pot and the thing coming from it."

Melissa was tempted to lift the nozzle and sniff, but refrained. She had seen such equipment in drawings and paintings from the East and from Arabia. And then Melanie accidentally kicked the foot of the chaise longue and Caroline stirred and woke a little. She attempted to stand but fell back, her body refusing to obey her alarmed mind. "What are... you... doing here?" she managed to say, her mouth as slack as her limbs. "Get out."

"Not until I have my money..." said Melissa, the room seeming to echoe with her normal speaking voice. "You took money from my account."

"Don't... know... what you are talking... about..." slurred Caroline Wentworth, unable to keep her eyes open.

"I think you do, Caroline," said Melissa, "and if you do not make good what you stole, we shall go to Lord Neighsmith and tell him how you are using his house for fraudulent gain."

Caroline shifted position uncomfortably. Her exotic scarf unwinding from her head and trailing over her shoulders. "Never heard... such... outrageous nonsense..." she drawled. But her own voice had given her life, and she attempted again to stand and then fell back into a sitting-lolling position on the chaise longue.

"Hold her shoulders..." said Melanie. So Melissa pinned her from behind and kept her from moving. It was not hard. Caroline could not fight, her body and mind wandering in clouds of drug-induced realms between reality and dream.

"Where is Richard?" said Melissa.

"Who?" echoed Caroline, her head already lolling onto her chest.

"Richard Fairchild... where is he?"

Caroline mumbled something and fell back into a deeper drowsing state. Melissa shook her without success.

"The house is empty, obviously," said Melanie. "Keep her still while I go and search."

"Be careful for God's Sake."

"Where is the safe?" said Melanie to Caroline in a loud voice.

Caroline's eyes flickered again. "Safe?"

"Yes... the money safe?"

Several seconds passed, and they waited, without much hope, and then she said. "The bank!" and tittered, the sound quite lost in the folds of her scarf.

On the sideboard, Melanie found a candle with matches and lit it. "I shall go and search."

"Supposing she rouses?" Melissa cried.

"She will not... she is drugged and it apparently takes an age to wear off."

Melissa turned in consternation to look at Lady Wentworth and when she looked back to the door, Melanie had disappeared. Caroline had lapsed into slumber, and Melissa walked the room and tried to find a drawer or a cupboard that might hold money. If she found a sizable amount, she would seize it and count it later. She was determined now not to come away without the amount she had been a party to carelessly losing. She thought of Anthony and how furious he would be if he knew what she was doing. How long would it take him to get over it? But then again, he might be pleased that the money was returned. She need not tell him how it was obtained. He would question her relentlessly, of course. He would slap her behind until he had the whole story. She thought of him at Barton Grange, all those years ago – seven years, but feeling like longer. The way he would try to get to the root of things, misdemeanours, and the things they did to deliberately annoy him. He was intrepid and unswerving in his quest for reason and truth. She smiled to herself; the game they played, which she knew was really her game, one she had invented to which he seemed to subscribe but denied complicity within.

She gave up her quest for the money and sat next to Caroline on the chaise longue. Caroline, like Miriam in the kitchen, snoring slightly and intermittently murmuring. The room grew very cold, and Melissa rose and threw a log onto the fire from the basket in the hearth.

Then Melanie returned, carrying a large hessian bag with leather handles. "Come... let us go."

"What is that?"

"I have not looked thoroughly, but it has Caroline's effects in it... and a wig." She pulled from the top of the bag a grey wig, a theatrical prop designed to convey old age. Beneath it were other dresses and costumes, also theatrical props by the looks of them.

"This wig is what she wore to the bank," Melissa stated.

"Undoubtedly!" said Melanie.

Melissa then saw around Caroline's throat a necklace of some kind. "Look at this she is wearing... it looks expensive."

Melanie stepped closer and held the candle near. "They are real gems, by the looks of them... diamonds and rubies... probably worth a fortune."

"Should I snatch it?" Melissa reached out for the necklace.

"No..." Melanie pulled her hand back. "False entry and theft is a serious charge... it could see us imprisoned if we are caught."

"Oh God!" uttered Melissa. "You are right... money is one thing, but this is..."

"Something else entirely... she may herself have stolen it... if we took it to a jeweller, they may inform the constabulary... if we are found with it, we would be co-conspirators."

"Yes... you are right," concurred Melissa.

"Now let us leave quickly... we do not want to linger here... we do not know who may come... and besides, I have to finish my Christmas shopping before I return."

The last claim seemed incongruous and absurd in the circumstances, and Melissa was inclined to giggling. She held onto the chaise longue to suppress the merriment, and Melanie shook her arm fiercely, unamused. "Did you search this room?"

"Yes, and there is nothing of note."

They went back along the hall to the outer door through which they had entered. Miriam, like her mistress, was still dead to the world.

* * *

It being Christmas Eve, all was in progress at Back Lane House. People had called with gifts and flowers. Honoria was hanging more garlands and enthusing about the fig and apple tarts with butter cream, which she and Mrs Harrison had made that day. "Have you bought dates and nuts?" she asked of Melissa while descending a short ladder perilously, in one of the full skirts purchased with the money gifted from her uncle.

"No, I forgot... is Anthony home?" she asked carefully.

"I think he might be... he—"

"Yes, I am!" he said, leaving the drawing room. "Where have you been?"

"Out and about shopping."

"Obviously not buying dates and nuts... so what have you bought?" He looked about for bags or packages, deliberately accentuating the lack of them.

"That is a very personal question," she said and took off her cloak with haste and removed her bonnet.

170

"But a natural one..." He followed her to the stairs. "Where have you been? Not shopping evidently!"

"I have been with Melanie at the dressmaker."

"Late on Christmas Eve afternoon?... I do not think so."

"I shall not be interrogated..." she said archly and ran up the stairs.

"Oh, but I think you shall..." He bounded up the stairs and passed her on the landing and blocked her way. "Now tell me what you have been doing?... no, let me guess... you have been to see Caroline Wentworth or Richard... or both of them!"

She halted but did not turn to look at him. How had he found out so quickly? Or was he guessing? Thankfully, Melanie had taken the bag of Caroline's effects home with her to hide. She would ignore him. She turned and headed across the top of the stairs to where the landing joined the back staircase, avoiding the bedroom. "Do not walk away from me, Melissa..." he said in his even tone, which meant little in the way of his encroaching anger.

She wanted to stop; it was the best thing, but she could not. He may see the mud on her skirt hem and her boots from the trek over wet ground. "Melissa, you will tell me what you have been doing... I know you rode out on the Lichfield road... you were seen driving a trap... but not ours."

"By whom?" she demanded.

"Damien. I met him in the town earlier and he told me he'd seen you..."

She became furious. Her detested brother, Damien. "That tittle-tattling bellwether!... that blabbermouth... his word cannot be trusted at all... he is mistaken."

He sighed and shut his eyes. "Have the graciousness to admit when you are caught in the act..."

"I shall not... and how dare you take his word against mine!"

"And do not try to detract from the issue with that... now just tell me where you have been!"

"No... I shall not..." She tried to move quickly to the back stairs, and he came after her. "I think you shall..."

Their voices had grown louder and could be heard downstairs.

"Think what you will..." she said and picked up her skirts in readiness to run. Then she paused. "No... on second thoughts, I will lay you odds that if you find me within three minutes, then you have won and I will tell you."

He slammed the bannister with his hand. "Do not try to turn this into one of your blasted games... 'Tis not a game... I will not stand for that." He moved across the top of the stairs to catch her, and at the same time, Honoria ran up to the top step and the level part of the corridor. "No, please..." she called, and then she and he collided. She losing her balance and staggering backwards on the stairs. He reached for her swiftly and pulled her upright to safety. The scene was frozen for a moment or two.

"Honoria..." His voice was hoarse with shock... "Have more care... you might have fallen and broken your neck."

"I do not want you to fight," cried Honoria with spirit. "Please stop it... 'Tis Christmas Eve." She looked from him to Melissa and made gasping sounds of fear... "Please be friends... I cannot bear it if you fall out."

"Now look what you have done!" Melissa told him censoriously.

He released Honoria's arm, unable to comprehend what had happened. *"What I have done!"*

"Yes, you!... you are never happier than when giving orders and upsetting everyone!"

"Stop it." Tears ran down Honoria's cheeks; the shock of the near fall and the probable collapse of Christmas cheer was overwhelming her. She sank to the top stair and sat with her hands covering her face. Melissa was speechless. He was speechless. But he found words first. "Honoria, do not distress yourself like this..."

"I... I... I cannot help it..." gasped Honoria, "I... I hate it when you row."

"'Tis just a game..." said Melissa cheerfully. "Do not be upset."

"It is not a game!" he said in a low warning voice.

He gave Honoria his handkerchief, and she blew her nose noisily. Melissa nodded at her with approval. "We shall eat some of your tarts in a moment... that will cheer you."

"You will not eat anything until you tell me what you have been doing," he claimed carefully, keeping his tone even so as not to upset Honoria more.

"Do not tell me when I may eat in my own home!" she said.

Honoria began crying more profusely, and Melissa looked at him with a disdainful and satisfied face. "You see, just look at the way you have distressed her."

"Not nearly as much as you will be distressed if you do not tell me where you were."

"You despicable tyrant..." she stood in a majestic manner at the top of the staircase and gazed at Honoria, who then lifted the kerchief. "He is not a tyrant, Lissy... my father is a tyrant, but Anthony is a good man."

Disconcerted amid this diverse feminine emotion, he shifted his position and tightened his jaw – in the way she so loved – flushing a little, self-consciously.

"You see..." she claimed. "Honoria is in love with you now... in common with half the women of the county."

He flushed more, to the roots of his hair. "Don't be ridiculous."

Honoria rose with purpose. "Of course I am not in love with him, Lissy!... I... I... he is good to me... I care for him like a brother... but I am not in love with him."

"Oh, what a shame!" she said airily. And Honoria began weeping again, but more quietly.

"You are the one distressing her..." he continued calmly, "with your flagrant disregard for the feelings of others... and your utter inability to do as I ask."

"I do not like it when you fight..." Honoria whispered.

"Of course you do not," he countered. He was flummoxed and beset by remorse for her cousin, and she felt relief flood through her. Honoria had deflated the situation.

"I am sorry..." said Honoria. "I should not have interfered... but I... I... I do not want you to fall out on Christmas Eve... when we have made everything in the house so nice... and so I... I...I..."

They waited and watched her, but nothing more coherent emerged. Then the door bell clanged and Peggy hurried into the hall from the kitchen. The carol singers from the nearby church had arrived

*'God rest ye merry, gentlemen... let nothing you dismay*
*Remember Christ, our saviour was born on Christmas Day.*
*To save us all from satan's power*
*When we were gone astray...*

"They wants coins I 'spect..." Peggy called to the tense threesome on the landing.

"There are some on the dresser..." he replied equably. "Melissa, take Honoria down... she may enjoy the carol singers."

Honoria clasped her hands together below her chin, her face brightening. "Oh yes... I adore carol singers."

"There you are then..." he claimed and relapsed into an inescapable defeat..

They tripped down the stairs, Melissa leading the way. "And we must give them something nice to take with them..." she said, "... they have a detour to come here and a long walk down the drive... some of your tarts perhaps, Honoria?"

"Will there be enough?... I wanted some for Aunt Maggie and Uncle Giles tomorrow."

"How many are there?"

"Three dozen!"

"Good Heavens, Honoria... that is more than enough to feed the neighbourhood..."

He paced in a tight circle on the landing and listened to the chatter. Women with their ability to change the mood to their whim and liking. Now the conversation had turned remarkably to tarts and Christmas hospitality. He had lost control of the moment.

Melissa took a handful of loose change from the brass plate on the dresser and gave it to Peggy to put in the collection box, and then turned to her cousin and began to whisper excitedly... "Wonderful, Honoria!... that was a marvellous intervention... just in the nick of time..."

"But I think..." began Honoria, and then the carol singers stepped into the hall, six of them, men and women, and the singing grew loud and hearty. Peggy joined Melissa and Honoria, and then Mrs Harrison came along. They all stood appreciatively and smiled at each other.

*'Oh tidings of comfort and joy... comfort and joy...*
*'Oh tidings of comfort and joy....'*

# New Year – 1853

# Relative Values

Melissa finished telling Melanie the finer details of Susan and Trim's wedding as they sat in the Pink Parrot and drank tea. The fundraiser for the alms school was taking place the next day, the day before New Year's Eve. "Did you go through Caroline's bag of effects?" she enquired next.

"I did... there are no useful pieces of evidence, beyond the wig... and I doubt that will be useful... except perhaps to coerce her with..."

"She is too hard-faced to be coerced," Melissa said.

"Perhaps... and it could be said that the wig was taken from anywhere and could belong to anyone..."

"That is what Anthony says. He is against going to law on it."

"Does he know we went to Golden Oaks on Christmas Eve?" Melanie asked sharply.

"Not for definite... he was demanding to know where I had been... but thankfully there was an intervention by Honoria."

"Honoria!... she has become very spirited since her arrival, has she not!"

"Not that kind of intervention... she is still timid and humble... but she hates us rowing and she came running up the staircase and then bumped into him and almost fell down the stairs." Melissa went on to outline the events of that hour, and Melanie listened in fascination. "I still cannot tell if she planned it to end like that or whether it was happenstance."

"If 'twas not..." Melanie said, "She may prove to be very useful in future times when we take on other daring pursuits in the name of rightness."

Melissa coughed on the crumbs of her sponge cake and did not want to think of what kind of *'pursuits'* Melanie had in mind. So she began summarising Honoria's more gentle side to deter her friend from gaining the wrong impression. "Honoria is so useful to have in the house... she completely takes the wind out of his sails when he is becoming full of his own importance..."

"How?" asked Melanie.

"I do not exactly know... with her innocent charm and guileless attitude to life, I suppose... her winning ways... she is besotted with him... but not in a romantic sense... and when she says things in that child-like manner of hers, he becomes docile and biddable."

"Docile!" echoed Melanie in a loud tone which she was quickly obliged to reduce. "Surely not!

"Perhaps that is the wrong word... but sort of more reasonable and loath to continue with any animosity afoot..."

"Good Lord!" said Melanie. "Are you sure they are not bound for an affair?"

"I think not... she says she cares for him like a brother..."

"That means little..." Melanie buttered a scone and assumed a contemptuous face. "Besides, there are many brother and sister relationships which are incestuousness, or so Geoffrey tells me... he hears about it often during family matters turned to legal wrangles."

Melissa paused to consider. "I doubt they will enter into anything like that. It would ruin the peaceful note of their liaison..."

"We shall see..."

"I know him well now... he does not see her in that way... he sees her as... I know not precisely, but perhaps she is like a sister to him... neither of them have a brother or sister. 'Tis a novelty for them."

Melanie surveyed her across the table. "Lissy, you are truly a woman of bohemian values these days..."

"I just see a new side to him in her company... and it suits me. I can do or say as I please and then rely on Honoria to deflate the situation... 'Tis quite satisfying... and everyone benefits." She smiled widely and sat back in the chair with aplomb.

"I see!" said Melanie, trying to imagine it all in Back Lane House. "Pity then she was not at Barton Grange Academy with us years ago... she might have exerted this magical influence and saved us from suffering."

"She would not have been able to then... she is older now... and betimes, I love observing this other side to him... 'Tis fascinating... watching them being homely and agreeable to each other is very comforting."

"You could be all that with him... if you tried."

"I doubt it... we are too volatile and passionate and altogether given to different attitudes..."

Melanie took out her purse. "What a wise woman you are becoming... I will pay today... so do not argue."

* * *

At Back Lane House meanwhile, his cousin Isaac had called. They had not seen each other for a number of years and were catching up on news and family affairs. Isaac was the son of his uncle, one of his father's brothers who was also his godfather. Isaac was three or four years older, a graduate of Oxford and also an academic. Different kinds of men with different characters and personas, they had in common the one love of serious study. Isaac Fairchild had never shown the interest in the opposite sex the way Anthony Fairchild did and was a bachelor still, not hopeful of ever settling down with a wife and family. He had firstly studied medicine and then changed direction and turned to natural history, travelling to far flung parts of the world in pursuit of his vocation. He was now a professor in the subject, but as a sideline he had also become an investor, a shrewd one, and had amassed quite a tidy sum from a small beginning, though few people knew of it; he was modest in all his ways.

He had wavy light brown hair which was thinning somewhat. Mild features and a disposition which matched; he was genial and easy going and fitted in wherever he went and so was shaded somewhat by mediocrity, until one engaged him in personal conversation.

"What of Rupert?" enquired Isaac as they sat in the drawing room. "How is he?"

"The same. You know he has six children now."

"Good God!" exclaimed his cousin. "It is quite an accomplishment!"

"Is it? I imagine 'Tis easy if you throw caution to the wind."

They enjoyed some covetous laughter and began talking of things from years ago. Of Anthony's mother's second marriage, of their uncle Felix and all his daughters – their cousins – who they never saw and did not miss. "Do you remember Philida?" Isaac said. "And Cassandra?... how very disruptive they were!"

"Brats the pair of them!" declared Anthony Fairchild.

"Though Cressida and Penelope were quite behaved and amenable... same parents, same upbringing, but so different..." Isaac mused.

"Nature over nurture!" said Anthony shortly. "No telling... look at Richard and myself... and for that matter Rupert, myself and Richard."

"Or myself and Jacob!... yes, yes, 'Tis a mystery..." Isaac crossed his ankles and steepled his fingers in the professor-like way which gave him the relevant aura. "How is Richard?"

"Do not ask... I prefer not to talk of him..." said Anthony Farchild. Isaac looked pained, and so naturally he continued. "He has taken money from Melissa's account by fraudulent means."

His cousin reacted in a drastic manner and looked even more pained. "You jest!"

"I wish I did... but he will rue the day... I do not know how yet, but be assured, he will regret this latest piece of villainy..."

Richard and Isaac were the same age and had played together much as young boys, though very different characters. "He was always inclined to the dangerous side of rebellion when we were but young lads..." Isaac said. "Does your mother know of this?"

"Oh yes... she knows and she—" He paused as the door slowly opened, giving no immediate clue to the identity of the newcomer as it swung to a slow ninety degree arc on its hinges and then stopped.

"Hello!... a ghostly visit," said Isaac with whimsy.

"Who is it?" Anthony Fairchild called in an impatient voice.

Then Honoria's face appeared round the edge of the door. She stared, and sensing this was rude, came fully into the room but did not advance. "I... I... I am sorry... I did not mean to interrupt... I... I was looking to see if Melissa had returned..."

"Honoria, come in." He rose from his seat, as did Isaac. "Let me introduce you..."

Honoria tip-toed to the centre of the floor, as if in a sacred place of some kind where no sound should be made.

"This is my cousin, Isaac Fairchild... Isaac, this is Melissa's cousin, Miss Honoria Ainscoe."

Isaac bowed, and Honoria curtsied and then flushed and twisted her fingers together in semi anguish.

"Quite a meeting of cousins," remarked Isaac wittily and stepped towards her cautiously. She offered him her hand in the prerequisite manner. "Delighted to meet you, Miss Ainscoe."

Honoria thought him to more resemble Rupert Fairchild than Anthony. They regarded one another, feeling it easy to do so. Then Anthony Fairchild had a stunning thought. "What a fortunate thing you came in, Honoria... Isaac is a natural history man... and an ornithologist..." He turned to him and raised his brows.

Isaac dipped his head self-effacingly. "Only in passing, Tony!... ornithology is not my specialist subject..."

"A mere detail... you have written papers on the subject... he is being modest, Honoria."

"I see." Honoria opened her eyes wide and was looking at Isaac with a fastidious gaze, as if he were one of the garden birds she had yet to know more about.

"Honoria watches birds..." he told Isaac. "She is passionate about them..."

Isaac lifted his head and looked at Miss Ainscoe, and Honoria lifted the illustrated book she always left on the arm of her favoured chair, as if needing to prove what was said as a fact.

Two shy people meeting for the first time.

Isaac stepped yet nearer to her and peered at the book. "May I?"

"Indeed," said Honoria and passed the book to him. "I have two such books now... Anthony bought me this one when I first arrived, and then he and Melissa gave me another for Christmas."

Isaac Fairchild was at once taken out of himself. Out of his self definition as a dull citizen, much appreciated by relations and friends but not readily by those who did not have his acquaintance. He cared little for that dull history when there was someone who shared his passion for the winged creatures gifted to mankind by nature.

"How... how... I... I mean..." Honoria faltered, and both men waited. Isaac tore his eyes away from the colourful pages to behold the voice trying to express itself. "How wonderful to write about them." Honoria managed at last.

Isaac did not reply, but smiled and blinked and again waited politely for more of her thoughts.

"I think I saw a nuthatch the other day in the garden..." Honoria ventured. "But I cannot find it listed in here."

"They are commonly mistaken for finch..." Isaac offered, "and they are not often so close to human habitation..."

"Really! What then is the major difference between the two species?"

"May I?" enquired Isaac once more, indicating the sofa and for Honoria to seat herself beside him, while rifling through the pages of the book. "If we compare the two, in the main they are not..."

Fairchild excused himself softly and was not heard. He went from the room and grinned and made an approving shape to his mouth as if to an invisible onlooker.

Peggy came around the corner of the hall and saw him. She was forever catching him unawares. He straightened his face and looked at her, and she switched her gaze to the wall to save him embarrassment. *She talked to herself a lot, and it was awful when others noticed.* "Miss Ainscoe has come in from the garden... I thought as how you might like more tea... for her and your cousin?" she said, her eyes still on the wallpaper.

"No, Peggy, thank you... leave them be for now. They do not require tea at present," he said and smiled.

* * *

In the aftermath of Christmas, Caroline was coming down to earth once more; it was not pleasant. She entered the main drawing room of Richard's town house and said. "I have still not found my effects... the ones in the hessian bag..."

He sighed. "Well, I have not had them."

"I think they were stolen by your sister-in-law."

"What?... when?"

Caroline took on a superior expression, knowing she had been in a deplorable state at the time and determined not to feel ashamed. "The afternoon of Christmas Eve..."

"But you were in the dream then..." he said, referring to her habit. "So how could she have gained entry?"

"I know not... but I feel sure that her and that friend of hers were standing over me making accusations... and they would not go away."

Richard groaned wearily and summoned his manservant to make ready his carriage. "Caro, that is preposterous... the notion will be the result of the state you were in..."

"She held me down by my shoulders..." Caroline said impatiently. "I felt it and could do nothing about it."

"You take too much of that stuff," he countered. "I keep telling you... one day you will not return at all."

"Stop being so sanctimonious." Caroline helped herself to his whisky and sat. "Where have the effects gone then?"

"I have no idea... but it is impossible to see how they gained entry. Miriam would not let them in."

"Perhaps they climbed through a window..." said Caroline pettishly.

"Which window?"

"Does it matter?"

"If you are going to make these wild claims, you have to be able to substantiate them..."

"I do not have to do anything of the kind, Dickie... you either believe me or you do not... all I know is that the costumes are missing and I shall have to go to the bother of replacing them."

Richard Farichild did not for a moment believe her; that the wife of his brother and daughter of a prosperous land owning business would break into her house and steal! "You have not searched hard enough."

Caroline threw her fan at him, and it caught him on the shoulder at speed and broke the slender wooden frame.

Neither of them seemed to care. "She wanted the money back..." Caroline continued smoothly, as if not having lost her temper.

"Of course she did..." Richard re-tied his neck cloth at the mirror and then re-tied it again, trying for a more elegant look. "I believe I saw her yesterday on the road to Leek, dressed as a highway man."

Caroline looked about for something else to throw, but he pulled her to her feet and ushered her to the door. "Fetch your cloak... or whatever you are wearing. We shall be late for dinner at the Dalgleish's."

"Bores, all of them," she said.

"Yes, but wealthy bores... now Caro, improve your mood or I shall be vexed."

Caroline made a stupid and ghastly face, a grimacing mask, and jiggled herself about in a contemptuous carefree fashion like a feckless teenager. Richard took the whisky from her and said. "Do you remember what you have to tell them... once we have dined?"

"Yes, yes, yes..." She trailed after him into the hall and stamped her foot to slow him down. "Betimes, you do not know what those girls will do with my theatrical effects, Dickie..."

"It matters not... they cannot be traced to you, can they!... unless you have sewn your name into them..." He laughed heartily and then stopped, and she waited with alarm to see if he had thought of something. And he had. He made an exaggerated hand gesture. "Yes, that's it... they are going to go to the bedroom and play dressing up... pretending to be little again..."

"Too glib... you are too glib about important details... it will be your undoing one day."

They had descended the flight of wide, shallow steps to the street when a Hansom cab pulled up across the way and a man alighted and shouted Richard's name. Caroline and he turned and stared into the darkness, illuminated only by the dim gas lighting.

It was Isaac Fairchild.

Richard Fairchild groaned but said loudly. "Isaac, my dear fellow... what brings you?... we are just out to dine with friends."

"I need only five minutes of your time, Richard... I shall be brief, but I must speak with you." Isaac was slightly breathless; obviously not from running this mere distance but from some kind of stress.

"About what?" He released his cousin's arm, where he had grasped it in a fake warm greeting. One relation to another, obliged to seem glad of an unexpected encounter. "I did not know you were back in the country."

"I leave again in three weeks..." Isaac looked at Caroline and bowed.

"Lady Caroline Wentworth..." pronounced Richard, "Caro, this is my cousin, Isaac Fairchild..."

Caroline inclined her head and extended her hand.

"Your servant, Ma'am." Isaac partially bowed and took his attention immediately back to Richard. "I crave just five minutes of your time... let us go inside, Richard, this is not the place."

"Oh, very well... but only five minutes... 'Tis such bad manners to arrive late for a dinner engagement... Caroline, do you mind?"

"Not at all..." Caroline was already remounting the steps, "'Tis not as if I were looking eagerly forward to it, now is it?"

Isaac and Richard followed her, and Richard shook his head to denote his disquiet at the temperament of women in such circumstances. "I shall have the whisky you deprived me of..." Caroline said to him over her shoulder once they were in the hall."

"Do not have more than one..." commanded Richard.

He took Isaac into the study and closed the door. "Well?" he said sharply. He was already suspecting the worst; his cousin Isaac and he had not remained friends since their boyhood – they led different lives and had nothing in common.  "Well, spit it out, Isaac!" he said after a few seconds of silence.

"I have come to ask... no... I have come to beseech you..." Isaac paused and took out a handkerchief and mopped his brow. It was cold weather, but he was sweating profusely.

"What?" snapped Richard.

"... to return the money you have taken from Anthony... or more precisely from his wife's account."

Richard pretended severe shock and drew himself up and squared his shoulders, lifting his chin in a defiant manner. "I beg your pardon... I cannot have heard you correctly, Isaac."

"I think you did, Richard... you cannot in all faith keep that money and live with yourself..."

Richard maintained his stance and took in some deep breaths, preparing his words.

"Whatever possessed you, I do not know, but you cannot keep their money..." Isaac went on quickly, pre-empting any excuses or lies.

"How dare you!" said Richard at length. "How dare you accuse me of such a thing... you are quite mistaken."

Isaac regarded Richard over the central space of his study, a look of tormented sadness in his eyes, and was truly distressed. "There is one thing Tony is not, and that is a liar."

Richard smiled, a bitter smile which became a subdued laugh. "Of course... you would believe him over me..."

Isaac had no words; he formulated a few but did not express them. He followed his cousin with his gaze as he moved, saw him turning so as not to give away his thoughts. "I would not be here if I thought there was any chance he was mistaken... they are newly wedded, Richard, and he is trying to make good for the future... how must this look if it becomes widely known... for the good name of our family?"

"Get out," Richard said urbanely. "We have not met for a number of years, and the first time we do, you have the gall to accuse me of—"

"I am here not for myself but for Anthony—"

"He has put you up to it, no doubt."

"He has not... he is not that kind of man... and you well know it."

"I have asked you to leave!" said Richard majestically.

Isaac moved towards the door and then paused. It had taken courage for this mission, and he felt his resolve deserting him. "Your actions now speak volumes regarding your guilt," he said quietly. "You would not be so calm if you knew nothing of it... you display no surprise in your manner... nor any curiosity."

"Have you proof?" demanded Richard coolly, and Isaac registered amazement; the question was tantamount to a confession.

"You are a banker with a reputation to uphold... if this is brought to court and proved you will be ruined... whatever is driving you..."

"And you are a naive fool, Isaac... now leave!" Richard's voice was rising and his manner growing alarmist.

"Richard, your complicity or guilt in this is all too apparent... and I am ashamed of you."

"Please go!" Richard said, mastering his alarm and opening the study door, and then the front door, and waving away his butler.

Isaac ran down the steps and looked this way and that along the street, unsure after some years of where he might gain a cab back to his family home.

* * *

The fundraising response this time was almost overwhelming, Melissa as she strove to cope without Susan and with more people than ever attending; the popularity of the last two events had become known, and the well-to-do and those who valued their position within society prepared to contribute handsomely. The door at Lessingdale was manned by several volunteers over the day... Melissa, two of Trim's sisters, Mr Aldridge, who ran the alms school, the Trimingham's butler, and finally Anthony Fairchild, who arrived in the mid afternoon. "I am so glad you have come..." she told him, "Honoria cannot be spared from the kitchen and the demand for refreshments. Perhaps you would mind the door until the butler returns?... I am needed to talk about my paintings... people are bidding for some of them and I am frazzled."

He had brought with him two of his elder nephews. He looked around for them and saw them at the refreshment table, naturally taking an interest in what they may eat. Then he saw Melanie arranging chairs for the seating in front of the small stage where the recital would be held. Melissa's cousin Gregory and his fiancée Millicent were to play professionally, and they had brought along a three piece string ensemble who had volunteered their services for free. Later on, two ballet dancers – friends of the musical ensemble and travelling with them – had offered to give extracts from certain ballets.

"Give me five minutes, Melissa, and I will oblige... Mrs Gillis should not be doing that!" he said, and he whistled to his nephews, who looked across, along with several other people.

"Anthony..." she admonished. "Please! They are not dogs... how vulgar..."

"I cannot make myself heard over the throng otherwise... unless I yell, and that is more vulgar," he said casually.

The two boys came over, their mouths full of delicious pastries made by Honoria and Mrs Harrison. They were Rupert Fairchild's sons, ten and twelve in ages. "Come with me..." he told them. "And clean your hands first... you are not here to eat." They grabbed dampened napkins from the maid officiating at the table and followed him.

"Mrs Gillis!..." he said to Melanie, who turned from placing one of the small chairs, perfect for performances in the ballroom. "Good afternoon, Anthony..." she replied without breaking her stride.

"I cannot allow you to continue moving furniture... my nephews will do that..."

She paused and looked at him with merry disdain. "I shall not keel over and die... they are light enough chairs."

"Even so, 'Tis not work for a lady when there are young boys about... take over from her!" said Fairchild to his nephews, and the two boys began lifting chairs stacked one on the other. "Note how Mrs Gillis has placed them and follow suit. And there is to be no larking about or skulking off..."

"No, Sir," said Thomas, the eldest, and they began at once to do as he had instructed.

"Show them how you need the rows to go," he said to Melanie, "and they will finish this..."

"'Tis very courteous of you, Anthony." She made a pert shape with her mouth – a parody of feminine acquiescence. "I shall go and see if Honoria needs help in the kitchen... she has already run out of cakes..."

"And that is the other thing..." Fairchild said to his nephews. "Do not help yourselves to any more confectionery, or there will not be enough for the guests."

Thomas stood with a chair held aloft. "The lady in the kitchen is putting some by for us... she says there will be more coming from Back Lane soon."

Samuel joined in enthusiastically. "Those will be the apple, fig, and butter cream tarts... everyone's favourite..."

"That will be Miss Ainscoe in the kitchen... when you are finished helping, you may eat, and have my apple whatnots. I cannot abide the thought of more of them!" He checked his timepiece to see how the schedule was proceeding and had a second thought. "But do not tell Miss Ainscoe I said that about her tarts!"

The nephews smirked, and Melanie laughed and made her way to the kitchen and waved to Melissa, who was temporarily stuck at the entrance until the footman could be found.

Gregory and Millicent had now mounted the stage and had begun testing the piano, playing opening bars from well known symphonies, moving seamlessly from piece to piece. Even their preliminary tuning and rehearsing was a gift to the ears of music lovers, and people stopped talking to listen.

In the kitchen, Honoria was covered in flour and her face bright pink from the boiling of kettles and the preparation of scones... and she was never happier. Melanie entered and took the used plates stacked by the maid to the large sink. "Do you not wish to go into the main room and look around, poppet?" she said to Honoria. "Surely you can give yourself a treat now?"

"No, no..." Honoria shook her head adamantly. "I do not like to be on view..."

"Good Lord, Honoria!... do not be not so shy... there are some nice young gentlemen attending who would love to see you."

Honoria shook her head more vehemently – the world was suddenly full of *nice young gentlemen* whom she was not ready to meet. "I think not... I am not looking my best... thank you all the same, Mrs Gillis."

Melanie poured water into the sink. "Call me Melanie..."

"Thank you... Melanie, where is Anthony?"

"He is instructing his nephews about the chairs and generally taking charge where there is a need... we do not call him Atilla for nothing!" she added wryly, and Honoria was puzzled – not knowing anything about anyone called Atilla. "Why? did you want him for something?"

"Only to see if he would prefer pastries or scones... before they all go..."

"I see..." Melanie was remembering how much Honoria revered him. "You had best go and ask him..."

"Could you do that... please?" Honoria said.

Melanie began drying her hands. "I doubt he will trust me with the question... he will believe I am poisoning him."

Honoria stared, more puzzled. "Surely not?"

"A little jest, Honoria... I will ask him in a moment or so... when I go back to door duty."

At the front entrance to Lessingdale, more visitors were arriving. "This cash tin is overflowing..." Fairchild said to his wife. "All this money..."

Melissa clapped her hands excitedly. "I know... 'Tis marvellous... Susan will be overjoyed."

"Could you ask Honora for a piece of cheesecloth..." He began stuffing bank notes into his inside pockets. "I shall take all the money so far and put it into the Trimingham's safe... it is still coming in, but we need paper or cheesecloth to wrap the coinage..."

She went for the cheesecloth, and Melanie took over on the door. "I doubt we have enough chairs..." she said.

"It matters not, people without tickets will have to stand if they wish to listen to the recital," he replied.

The footman had arrived on the scene. "I believe, Sir, that there are some spare chairs in the small barn... across to the right of the grounds... but I am unsure how clean they are. I can go with these lads and we will bring some and dust them down?"

Fairchild surveyed the small space still available in front of the stage. "Excellent... we have room for perhaps another twelve or so."

Then Mr and Mrs Harrison arrived, carrying more trays of pastries and cakes, and Mr Harrison accompanied the footman and the nephews to the barn to fetch the chairs whilst Melanie held the door. "I can stay only another twenty minutes..." she said. "Then I must return for Robbie..."

"I am so glad of your help, Mel," Melissa said, watching him stack the coins in the cheesecloth and tie them into bundles.

Melanie turned to him. "Honoria needs to know your culinary requirements, Anthony. She asked me to ask you, scones or pastries?... or perhaps a roasted ox?" she added skittishly.

He closed his eyes and partially grinned but stifled it rapidly. "I shall not require anything, please tell her."

He had removed his jacket and loosened his neckcloth for the lifting of chairs and the shifting of heavy objects. Working in his shirt sleeves like a fashionably attired tradesman, the sight of him was alluring, attracting much attention. Matronly women cast him admiring glances on their way to other places. A group of very young women were surveying him from yards away, giggling and whispering in hushed tones. Melanie indicated them with her eyes, and Melissa turned to look. It was true, he was desired by at least a quarter of the region's female population, but it was her name on the marriage certificate with his. And for the first time, perhaps she gleaned some satisfaction and pride from her marriage. She had not wanted marriage at all in the beginning; it had not been her first choice.

Donald Aldridge had returned, having taken a rest with Matthew Trimingham (Timothy's father) in the drawing room. He was running a *'find the lady'* table, and performing other swift conjuring tricks, for contributions – much to the surprise of all who knew him, finding they knew him little at all. "Shall I take over from you, Ma'am?" he asked Melanie, and she told him she had another quarter hour to spare, so he proceeded to the table allotted to him and began at once to attract an interested audience.

The musical ensemble were bringing in their instruments, the butler appearing from nowhere and hastening after them. "Perhaps

you could take those in through the back of the house, gentlemen!...
to avoid too much of a crush in the hall..." He clicked his fingers to
the footman, who looked flummoxed. "I was going for the rest of the
chairs, Mr Salter."

"Those can wait... assist these people first."

The musicians disappeared with the footman around the side of
the mansion. One of them paused ahead of him. "It is not
necessary..." he struggled for the next words, being Hungarian – all
Gregory's connections in the musical world were from foreign parts.
"We are... how do you like to say?... wanting to carry our
instruments... each one of us..."

The footman halted to make sense of what had been said and
screwed up his face and held fast to a violin case, before realising the
man had meant they preferred that no one touch their instruments
cases. But the footman remained adamant; Mr Salter was the
authority around here, not these entertainers. The young musician
grabbed the violin case and put up the palm of his hand to prevent
further intrusion by the footman, who looked mutinous. Fortunately,
Gregory then appeared and lifted two of the instrument cases, and
was trusted to do so, while explaining the taboo to the harassed
footman.

Mr Harrison was being badgered by both his wife and Mr Salter
at the same time – *the extra chairs versus the additional cakes!* The
cakes won out, and he brought two more trays from the trap and took
them into the kitchen.

Patrons were still arriving. The grounds were clogged with
conveyance of every kind. A five or ten minute period where it
seemed that chaos had descended.

Fairchild jumped into the door-keeping with Melanie, and the
two of them received payments, and at the same time, he directed
people to various places. And as suddenly as it had begun, the chaos
was over and all was manageable again.

"Now for the last of the chairs, Sir." Mr Harrison announced.

"The lads are making room for them at the back..." Fairchild
said, leaving the door and scooping up excess bank notes and shoving
them into his pockets. "Keep an eye on the money box..." he told
Melissa and turned to the butler. "Please, stay here with my wife until

I return... one cannot be too careful on days like this... word gets around to the wrong sort of people."

"By all means, Sir," said Mr Salter. "I shall stay here at the door... have no fear."

The musicians and the pianists had begun tuning up in earnest, and divine sounds arose around the place. Eleanor Trimingham (Timothy's mother) appeared on her first floor balcony, smiling magnanimously like benign royalty, and looking down over the hallway. Melissa waved to her, then nudged him to acknowledge her. He bowed, and she lifted her hand and called out. "I shall come down presently for the recital..."

"Make sure Mrs Trimigham has a seat," he told the footman, preparing to place the additional chairs.

"But not at the front..." added Mr Salter. "She dislikes being at the front of anything... reserve her a side seat... nearer the front... but neither will she object to being at the back."

Melissa felt her giggling coming on, and Melanie was already making low gurgling sounds. It was all too amusing – the way people went on when out to frolic and play, especially old people.

Mr Harrison returned with the boys, carrying the extra chairs. "There's a gentleman loitering around asking for you, Sir... says his name's Fairchild too..."

He looked at their man-servant curiously. "Who... not Reverend Fairchild?" Then turning to his nephews. "Has your father come?"

They shook their heads, and Thomas said. "He's in a parish council meeting, so 'tis doubtful."

Melissa and he exchanged glances. "'Tis Richard," she said. "I just know it."

He replaced his jacket and loosely tied his neckcloth. "What the devil does he want?"

"To return the money, perhaps!" she ventured, and he gave her a pitying look. "Well, you never know," she said.

"I do!" he retorted.

Melanie called after him. "Tell him I have her wig... Caroline's..."

Melissa was startled by this admission and opened her mouth to protest, but he had gone out of the large front door.

"I shall creep along and listen to what they have to say!" Melanie told her.

"Indeed," said Melissa and pushed her towards the doors, angling her around three elderly ladies just arriving who were all stout and clumsy in making their entrance.

* * *

He made his way carefully over the grounds immediate to the entrance and pondered Melanie's comment about the wig. He did not think he would pursue it – they had probably obtained the item by nefarious means, possibly on Christmas Eve, in the absence his wife was loath to explain – and it would merely lead to further wrangling. The matter could wait.

He saw Richard pacing near to his own phaeton and watching the people still arriving.

Fairchild spotted him first. "What the hell do you want?" He waited, his shielded gaze levelled at his detested brother.

"I shall be brief... as cousin Isaac said when he came on his mission last night on your behalf."

"I did not send him on any mission... I fight my own battles... as you well know!"

Richard made a long inhalation of breath, faking enforced patience under duress. "I am here, dear brother, to deter you from making any more of your slanderous accusations regarding money you say is missing from your bank account."

"Do not bother with your lies, Richard... and if that is all you have to say, I suggest you leave!"

"You do know there are laws against slander?" returned Richard, fiddling with his shirt cuff and avoiding eye contact.

"I know there are laws against thievery... and embezzlement!"

"How dare you accuse me..."

"I accuse you because this whole thing has history... you have Melissa's signature, obtained under false pretences."

"Can you prove that?"

"I can if I go to the trouble... but I am in no doubt."

"You may be highly educated, Tony, but you are not that clever."

The day was dulling overhead, clouding with the rising of the temperature, which threatened rain later. He looked towards the sky.

"What a piece of work you are, Richard!... who would have dreamed you would sink so low."

"I am warning you not to say any of these things about me again to others."

Anthony Fairchild assumed a dismissive tone and watched the clouds. "I have the takings so far from today in my jacket pocket... perhaps you would like to relieve me of those too... before you slither off around the ground to make your exit."

Richard stepped from his leaning position against the phaeton and grabbed his arm, then swung his fist. It glanced off his younger brother's cheekbone, and still he did not release his sleeve. "Let go of me."

Richard released him then and made to turn away, but his younger brother pulled back his arm and jerked his elbow up towards his face. It jarred his jaw, and Richard groaned and staggered and put his fingers to his chin. "You might have broken my jaw... or even my neck."

"Perhaps next time," he said and stepped back to show his withdrawal from the conflict.

"You smug bastard!" Richard muttered, mounting the phaeton. "You will regret this."

In the Lessingdale mansion, he paused in the hallway and heard the musical recital rendering Chopin, with which Gregory always liked to begin such performances, moving to more rousing pieces as time went on.

Matthew Trimingham had descended into the downstairs. "Ah, Anthony, how are you?..." He looked at his face where a bruised redness was already showing. "You have been in the wars, dear boy?"

He smiled. "A slight contretemps with a carriage door, Sir."

"Perhaps you should get something put on that wound... Salter will oblige you," said Matthew Trimingham pleasantly. "I shall join my wife for the excellent music." He made his way into the ballroom – having witnessed the altercation from an upstairs window – and on seeing the butler, he said confidentially, "If Richard Fairchild attempts to gain entry, he is not to be admitted... have someone make certain he has driven away... I do not want that villainous wretch on the premises."

# Out with the Old

His cheek had swollen the next day and there was a deep cut above the cheekbone. Melissa tended it carefully. "Perhaps you should see Darnley... or another medic!"

"'Tis a scratch... his ring grazed me when he hit me."

"I could shoot him myself."

He laughed. "That may be a step too far."

"Would it though?" *She thought of Caroline saying they would fight to the death; but whose death might it be!* "I shall put some of Susan's ointment on it... 'Tis quite miraculous and it will prevent it from turning septic." He allowed her to dab on the foul smelling stuff which hurt like blazes but lived up to its glowing reputation.

"She will be home in two or three days... and she can look at it."

"She will not need to trouble."

"She will insist!" said his wife.

"Only if she is told..."

"She is bound to hear of it," said Melissa, who knew quite well that Matthew Trimingham had seen the fight. She leaned down and put her lips on his and kissed him so that he forgot the discomfort. They were kissing ardently when Honoria came into the drawing room and doubled back on seeing them and closed the door. A few minutes of tranquillity reigned while she sat on his lap and he enjoyed the fact that she had forgotten her 'silence vow' and they deliberated on whether to go upstairs. Then the outer bell clanged and Rupert Fairchild eventually entered, without his collar, announced by Peggy who called him the *Relevant* Fairchild. Melissa doubled with laughter and he tried laughing without the use of his facial muscles, to save the pain, and failed.

Rupert halted a little way into the room and winced on seeing him. "The fight yesterday, I presume?"

"Indeed." he said.

"But fear not, he all but broke Richard's jaw." she added, knowing he would do so himself. He laughed at her and then winced. The wound burned and throbbed and felt as if it were splitting open again. "Keep your cheek still... Susan always tells people to keep wounds calm when they have applied the tincture."

Rupert Fairchild stood with closed eyes, and they wondered if he was silently praying. They watched him, partly from fascination and partly from respect. When he opened them again they were staring at him. "Have you seen a doctor?" he asked, as if there had been no lull in proceedings.

"He will not," said Melissa. "He fears they may stitch the wound and make a bad job of it... so that he is then scarred for life."

He did not argue – there was some truth in it. "I think I shall trust Susan's remedies... Darnley may keep me doped for two weeks."

"He saved your life before we were wed that time!" she pointed out.

"Surely that was God's doing... was it not, Rupert?"

"You will not draw me into that theological argument at this time of day..." Rupert demurred.

"How did you know of it?" Anthony Fairchild asked, "the altercation!"

"The boys, of course... they were watching you through the hall windows, apparently... they were re-enacting the scene last night and elaborating on it, naturally... 'Tis now one act of an opera..." Rupert smiled ruefully; the foibles of young boys and reckless siblings.

"Regrettable... but they are to be men and should know how to defend themselves," said Melissa sensibly.

"That is what Bella says too," said Rupert. "You have risen in their estimation to almost heroic proportions... they do not care for Richard..."

"Why is that?" Melissa enquired suspiciously. *Richard Fairchild had now become a focal point of life requiring much scrutiny and consideration.*

Rupert deliberated, loathe to fuel family enmity. "He is very critical of them... the lads..."

His young brother gave a hoot of unamused laughter. "That is sooner than look at his own conduct."

"... and he is too fond of clouting them, with little cause." added Rupert.

Anthony Fairchild lit a small cigar. "Uncle Charles all over again... I have said as much before."

"I will not let that happen..." Rupert conceded. "I have sworn it to Mother."

There was a pause of moments. She thought of what Susan had told her over a year ago, and of Hildegarde's words a few days before. "Perhaps Charles Fairchild's spirit enters Richard." she said tentatively and they looked at her with differing expressions. "Granny would offer it as a possibility..."

If they were alone now they may debate this as an interesting hypothesis; their shared beliefs in an afterlife, but they were not alone and he told his brother. "She is talking of Jemima Shaw... and her Cornish pagan beliefs."

"We do not know what happens after death, do we?" she said. "None of us really does." Rupert did not comment, he seldom criticised the beliefs of others: his was not an indoctrinated faith. "But what of the missing money?" he asked. "What have you decided to do?"

"I am still contemplating matters... and I will have no time until next week, owing to Trim being on his honeymoon." His tone was closed and Rupert knew it was futile to press him. He decided to change the subject and turned to Melissa. "So you had a triumph yesterday... according to the boys ?"

"Indeed..." She became enthused. "Rupert, it was an utter success... the amount of money we raised was three times the sum we raised last time... and more!... and your sons were of enormous help!... as was your brother here."

"I may have contributed somewhat..." He was trying not to grin and strain the injury.

"He oversaw the event from half way through..." she told Rupert. "For 'Tis now grown to beyond a good cause... gathering to almost a festival occasion."

Rupert declined tea or coffee but stretched out his legs for better rest. The Christmas period was arduous for clergymen. "You do know, Melissa, that they will want you as patron and committee member to the alms school?" he said. "They were talking of it at the parish council meeting... they will press you for it..."

Anthony Fairchild raised his forefinger. "And remember that your father's business standing and wealth will have a little to do with it..."

"In case I become too cock'a'hoop with myself!" she laughed.

"It is a pertinent fact, Melissa..." Rupert conceded. "But it will be your attention to matters and your presence they require... not your father's."

"What will it mean for me?"

"You will have to give serious consideration to weighty subjects..." declared her husband.

"I shall decline." she said quietly.

Rupert was quite astonished and looked at his younger brother who became flippant. "She cannot be seen to be pandering to the modern fad for education, Rupert... at the expense of fun and freedom... come along now!... do you not know of her views on this!" He was taking a comical facetious tone and the mood had broken into one of informal chat and was more manageable.

"I will stay as I am, thank you..." she concluded. "There is enough pomp and parade about the place without me fuelling it... Anthony is right, I cannot be seen to lean into petty bureaucracy... I am an artist, not a social campaigner."

"Surely you can be both!" said the Reverend Fairchild with sincerity.

"No, no... 'Tis impossible... I would be compromised."

"Perish the thought!" said her husband and was secretly relieved that she was eschewing local politics.

"I shall just do what I can from the truth of my soul," she told them and Rupert could not find words to praise the sentiment enough. Instead he inclined his head in her direction and remained silent.

"Why do you not stay and dine with us?" she asked Rupert, who considered for a mere second and then declined. "I have promised to be at home this afternoon with Bella and our older children... we are playing one of those games you gave them for Christmas..." He made an apologetic face, and it was not certain whether it was the game he regretted or the lunch invite. "These sort of days are as rare as hen's teeth, of course, in my line of work... so I dare not be absent... but... I think I might have a small glass of port, if you would be so kind, to celebrate the success of the fundraising... and the fact that 'Tis New Year's Eve..."

The astonishment was palpable as Melissa rang for Peggy to bring the port – her abstemious brother-in-law calling for liquor at just after mid-day. It was not a drink her husband usually partook of unless at dinner somewhere else, but they kept it in for male visitors:

* * *

After Rupert's departure he began trawling his memory of the day before and the hectic events at Lessingdale. He watched her as she sketched on a pad with pencil, her feet curled up beneath her on the sofa.

"Where did Mrs Gillis obtain Caroline's wig?" he said suddenly into the silence as the flames crackled in the hearth and consumed the logs.

She looked up, startled, previously believing he had not heard the comment or forgotten it, and she heaved a weary sigh, as if to say: *not this now!*

"Melissa..." he said. "The wig... where did she obtain it?"

"I am obliged not to tell you."

"Oh really!"

"Really!... and you will not make me." She raised her eyes from the pad once more and stared him down.

*Perhaps this was the inception of one of her game challenges... it was hard to know!*

"Well, what if we make one of your famous wagers!" he proposed experimentally. "I will give you a twenty second start... but if I catch you, you will tell me."

"I am not in the mood for the game." she sighed.

"That's a pity... because I am!"

He rose and she stuck out one foot from beneath her skirt to push him away without dropping the pad.

"It will give you an appetite for lunch." he said and grabbed her ankle and pulled her slowly from the sofa. She squealed, but softly, so that the servants would not hear. Then subsiding to the carpet she flung the pad to one side and dropped the pencil. She rolled onto her knees and he held her hips and would not let her move away. "Too late..." he declared in some triumph.

"You told me I had a twenty second start!"

"But you were too long in agreeing the odds... so it is no longer your advantage... now tell me."

"NO!"

198

"Yes!" He tugged her shoulders and she fell backwards into a semi sitting position so that he could lift her and carry her.

"No! I have not even agreed to the game."

"Neither do I most times... but that does not stop you."

She was unsure of how to gauge his mood. Unsure if this were sport or some serious attempt to score and gain information. "You will tell me... or you—"

"You will win..." she interjected loudly. "I feel sure... so I do not accept the wager."

He stood back and considered her, his fingers running through his hair and his gaze shielded to allow no discernible expression.

"You have been to see her, have you not!... I think 'twas Christmas Eve... and why you were so late in."

"Then you must think that!"

"Did you steal the wig?"

She remained mute and rose from the carpet. He took her elbows and pulled her backwards into him, putting his face into her hair and speaking into her ear, his breath warm. "Come on!... why are you suddenly running scared of the wager?"

She pulled away by inches, beginning to giggle but determined to be silent on the question of the effects in the bag. "You will win... so I reserve the right to refuse the odds!"

He let out a long breath and released her. "You know that only because you are sure how much I need the information... you do realise that I often allow you to win?"

She turned and arranged her skirts to sit. "I am not sure I want you to do that..."

"What??" There was an intense silence. "Are you implying what I think you are implying?"

"It depends what it is you think I imply..."

"If you are then it changes the fundamental approach I take to these wagers in the future... if you are really saying you are using a strategy towards an end that you cannot otherwise bring yourself to admit to desiring then we—"

"You are over complicating it..." she cut in haughtily.

"You seem to be saying you wish for the enjoyment you may gain from my triumph in the wager." he continued.

"I am not saying that... not at all."

She had tied him in knots. He had no time for it. He picked her up swiftly to carry her upstairs.

"Put me down... you are cheating... claiming unfair advantage!

"Unless you explain your deeper meaning here, I shall not put you down... because you leave matters wide open for my deliberate understanding of only one consequence you really can want."

She threw back her head and scoffed. "Were it that simple, do you imagine we would have not come to this before? Do you think I would not have made it easy for you to win!"

He looked into her eyes, grey like dove's wings, widely staring back into his. "I am unsure... women are complicated creatures."

"Quite... there you have it!"

"I am done with these riddles. I will now have an answer to the wig question... one way or the other..."

She struggled and partially fell and he picked her up again, her skirts and legs akimbo and her position untenable. "Put me down, Anthony..."

"No... we shall go upstairs and continue this... I will have an answer!"

"You are bullying me!" she screamed.

"No... I am managing you... there is a difference..."

"Only in your view... put me down." She struggled more, partly falling again and clinging to him as she did.

"You leave me no other choice..." he said. "So tell me now and I will put you down... otherwise you risk the consequences in the bedroom..."

She grabbed for his hair with outstretched fingers and took a handful and he winced and tried to free himself.

It was then they saw that the door had opened, and Isaac Fairchild had entered, stopping just inches inside the room. He dropped her immediately – inelegantly – and she landed once more on the carpet. He quickly helped her up, his eyes on his cousin, hoping he had not heard his last threat, which was open to huge misinterpretation.

"I do most humbly beg your pardon..." Isaac became immediately flustered. She gathered herself together and laughed encouragingly. "We were larking."

"Yes... please come in Isaac, do!" he said. "As Melissa says, we were playing the fool."

"Well 'tis the season for it..." Isaac stepped forward, not meeting their eyes. "You must forgive my bursting in on you in this indelicate manner... I did knock but you... you were..."

"Otherwise engaged!" she supplied merrily.

Isaac ploughed on regardless. "Your maid was out on the front, sweeping the porch steps and told me you were in the drawing room... I did not for a moment think you.... you would be... I do most sincerely apologise..."

Anthony Fairchild looked from his cousin to her. "How fate does protect you from these direct exchanges of fact within fiction..."

"And you also, it has to be remarked. You are not exempt from motive..." She turned to Isaac. "We are pleased to receive you, cousin Isaac." she said prettily. He had been introduced to her over Christmas at his parents' house, and was comforted by her lovely gaze. *He had heard that theirs was a passionate and volatile relationship, and that they played games which were often verbally introduced at random wherever they found themselves, subtle and unfathomable to onlookers. It was odd behaviour within a conventional marriage.* She seemed less disconcerted by the intrusion than Anthony. Though Anthony, he knew, was perhaps of a more conservative disposition.

Isaac made these summary observations whilst smiling at them both in turn and enjoying the pleasure of their company and waiting to see what would transpire next.

"Please be seated..." said his cousin "and excuse this highly irregular welcome..."

Isaac sat. "I must begin, Tony, by saying how sorry I am for my untimely interference with Richard... I felt I had to do something... and I tried, perhaps unwisely, to seek redress on the matter..." he turned to Melissa. "Richard and I played together a lot as young boys and I hoped he would—"

"Think nothing of it." Anthony Fairchild interjected.

"But I heard last night that you had fought with him... and I possibly see for myself the injuries resulting, do I not!"

He touched his wounded cheek, and before he could respond, Melissa said. "Yes, but you should know that Richard almost had his jaw broken." She looked at her husband cheerfully, and Isaac took this in his stride. "I fear I have made matters worse."

"They could hardly have been much worse..." rejoined his cousin.

A moment's silence and then they all three laughed. Life was comical after the event. Otherwise, tragedy was a constant companion.

"Will you take something to eat? We were just about to sit down to the table," said Melissa.

Isaac held up his hands in a surrendering gesture and it was then that they saw his outer pockets bulging. "Thank you, but no... in point of fact, I was wondering if I may have a few minutes with Miss Ainscoe... I have some journals she may like to see..." He patted the conspicuous pockets confidently.

"Of course... she is somewhere around." Melissa went into the hall and sought Honoria.

Honoria came from the kitchen at once, and on seeing Isaac blushed profusely, ripped off her apron and smoothed her hair.

"Miss Ainscoe," said Issac, bowing formally. "Forgive my unannounced arrival... but I have some literature for you... birds of a rare breed which you might be able to see signs of in the nearby woods..."

Honoria was at once enthralled. "'Tis good to see you again... and you will be glad to know we have just made blackberry and rhubarb pies... so you are in good time to try some..."

"Excellent..." said Isaac, forgetting his previous refusal to eat, and rubbed his hands in anticipation as they retired to the bay recess at the window where the chair was placed for Honoria's bird watching.

"You will excuse us, I hope..." said Melissa to their backs. "I will have tea sent in to you directly... with some pie, of course..."

"Those will be too fresh as yet, surely... you will give them indigestion..." Fairchild remarked airily and she pushed him towards the door which they closed behind them.

"Well, well, well..." he said, when they had entered the dining room, his brows raised and his memory for the time being having dropped the matter of the wig.

"Just so!" she laughed and picked up the ladle to serve the hot broth from the covered bowl placed on the table. Peggy entered with a platter of warm soda bread and deposited it and went to leave.

"Peggy, a moment please..." He waited for her to pause and turn.

"Could you make sure in future that you leave whatever you are doing when visitors call..." he asked her pleasantly, "... and announce them to us first before allowing them access to the drawing room."

The maid looked bemused. "Oh yes, Sir... if you mean your cousin, I was sure he would be fine to enter... he'd not steal nor nothing..." she added, thinking of the recent gossip about fraud within the family.

"Well no..." Fairchild said. "Of course he would not... but what I mean is that we may not be quite... we may be not..."

"We may not be ready to receive guests!" Melissa interposed politely. "So we need notice of them."

"Oh... I see!" said Peggy and closed one eye and pulled down her mouth in a wise expression of *'say no more!'*... having now been apprised, along with Honoria, on the facts of life by Mrs Gillis. Though she thought privately that had she been fortunate enough to have cousins, or relatives of any kind in this lifetime, she would be only too ready to receive them, whether announced or not.

They looked at each other in surprise, speechlessly, and he sliced a piece of bread. "Why is it that I am constantly made to feel wrong-footed by the females in this establishment?"

She made an arch face and buttered her own bread. "Because, now you are a respectable householder... and a married man... you cannot just do what you wish when the fancy takes you... you cannot just grab hold of people... not even your wife... and begin behaving in a boorish manner..."

"Is that so?" He tasted the broth.

"Yes, 'tis so!"

"We will see about that when I have finished this meal."

She stuffed an enormous piece of bread into her mouth and chewed, and then smiled at him with the bread between her lips, showing in the place of teeth. Her eyes in the most seductive expression.

"Good Lord... I have scarcely seen anything so vulgar in a dining room."

Her mouth full of the soda bread, she mumbled, "It has to be said, you have scarcely seen anything yet... hurry and finish your meal."

* * *

Their lovemaking was quite long and frenzied, both of them with their driving needs. They were now exhausted and drowsy and reluctant to leave the bed.

"Do you think Isaac thought you meant to rape me?" she enquired languidly, "having overheard your last threat!"

He sighed ostentatiously. "God's Teeth, I hope not..."

"You had better reassure him."

He turned onto his elbow to look at her with horror. "I cannot raise a subject like that with Isaac.... he is too... too..."

"Too what? He is a man and knows the facts of life."

"Yes, but he is very... very particular in his ways and morals..."

"All the more reason."

"It will embarrass him painfully... he is not Trim."

"I will reassure him then..."

She expected him to react fiercely but he did not. He looked at her long and then said with some irony. "You cannot do that, my love, without explaining the nature of your game... and your ultimate desire and motive."

Her laughter was subdued; it made him easy and relaxed as if this were another life. "*Your* motive and desire... not mine."

"Nonsense!" he proclaimed, as usual.

"Anyway, I shall find a way around it without going into all that!... for shame, Anthony, do you not believe me capable of such tact?... he shall not learn anything from me that you do not know... and you know very little on the matter."

"Is that correct?"

"It is!" She put her hand on his thigh and began to trace a circle with her finger until she found his penis, and then she took it and held it and he was gently aroused but not pushed beyond limits.

They lay for ten minutes, dozing and pursuing their own thoughts and then he said. "Now... I want to know about the wig."

She sprang from the bed and put on her robe and came back and sat on top of the eiderdown gazing at him. His male beauty; his hair awry and longer again nowadays, curling damply on his forehead.

Lying in his rumpled shirt which he had not bothered to remove and was now only fit for the laundry. He stroked her arm and watched goosebumps rise on her skin and waited.

"Very well... but you are to remain calm and not say anything accusatory about Melanie..."

He assumed a composed expression and shifted his attention to her face.

"It was in a bag of effects we found in Caroline's house..."

"Found?" he intercepted. "You mean you roamed around her house?"

"Shush... do not interrupt... we let ourselves in by the back door... it was open and the aged maid was sleeping in the kitchen... Caroline was in a haze on the chaise longue... she uses opium..."

He listened in apparent fascination to this tale of daring and do. It did not surprise him, but he had trepidation about anyone finding out. "We cannot use the wig... it was obtained unlawfully... you stole it." he said eventually. "It would not be viable evidence in a court of law... it could be argued that you had presented any old wig."

"Yes... but 'tis at least some slight evidence that she was in the bank that day!"

"Only to us... not in law. Ask Geoffrey Gillis, he will tell you."

"I think he has already said that to Melanie!" she admitted.

They talked of it for another ten minutes and then washed and dressed and went downstairs.

Isaac and Honoria greeted them as they entered the drawing room. "We have waited for you..." said Honoria in her child-like breathless voice and Melissa and he exchanged glances.

Isaac cleared his throat, "Yes, Tony... I wanted to ask if 'tis well with you that I take Honoira to the Caldon Valley tomorrow... it promises to be a dry day and there are some winter birds of a particular variety I think she would enjoy seeing..."

He looked at Isaac in bafflement, "Certainly... yes... 'Tis not for me to say where she goes and with whom..."

"Perhaps not, but she is living under your protection and I thought it only right to ask you..." said Isaac.

"By all means..." he glanced at Honoria who was nodding approval to Isaac's statement. And then he glanced at Melissa and his expression gave the confirmation of what he had told her earlier about his cousin's very modest and correct ways.

Even so, she ventured. "Isaac... on a separate subject, you must not put any score by what we were saying when you entered today... Anthony and I, we were simply being silly and we don't—"

"My dear..." Isaac interjected hurriedly. "It has nothing to do with me what you do... I mean, what a man and his wife do in their... I did not for a minute think... anyway I am unsure what was said... and even so I..." they allowed this floundering to go on for a few moments as Isaac became more flustered. Then Honoria stepped in to save the day. She put her hand comfortingly on Isaac's arm "They were doubtless playing their game..." she announced with assurance. "...so disregard it..." She looked almost proudly at the couple and Melissa looked at her husband, prompting him into speech.

"In reality they are more Melissa's games... I simply become embroiled... she leaves me little choice."

"Such lies!" she uttered quietly, gazing to the ceiling, where the paper streamers were coming a little unravelled with the passing days to twelfth night.

"You do not need to explain... it is really none of my..." Isaac began floundering again, and once more Honoria jumped in. "Yes, but it can be disconcerting if you do not know of it... they are a lot like children..." This statement seemed to make her happy, and she beamed at them and then at Isaac, as her cousin and her husband stood, caught in the glare of unwanted attention. Neither knew what more to say, or whether to deny what Honoria had said, or admit to it.

Isaac rubbed his hands together to show ease within something he did not for a moment comprehend but took as one more obscure facet of a strange world. "I shall take my leave now... and I shall return tomorrow at about twelve thirty to collect Honoria."

# Paved with Good Intention

Hildegarde Wyevale sat in her eldest son's drawing room and watched her smaller grandchildren playing on the floor. Whatever the problems, children were always an answer to cares; representing the fact that life went on and was little if not the flow of eternal change.

"There is nothing to be done..." said the Reverend Fairchild. "I can see no way of recouping that money... the signature is fake, but that cannot be proven."

"There has to be a way," his mother claimed. "He has to be made to give it back voluntarily."

"He has firstly to be made to admit he has it..." said Rupert.

"The thought of this blight on the family name is untenable..." bemoaned Hildegarde. "What will the Shaws think?"

"That every family has a bad apple!" Rupert rose and closed the curtains on the gloaming. "No one is immune... besides, Tony has told them about Richard's more nefarious traits."

"They were thinking to purchase a new house of their own, you know, next year. Did Anthony tell you that?"

"Yes, but that will not be affected... that will be with his own money..." Rupert lifted his very youngest son away from the fireguard, while his mother remained impatient with the logic. "Yes, but Melissa will wish to furnish it in a certain style and add touches that will require expense... she would have done that with her own funding. She told me so herself."

"Well, she will have to wait... 'Tis not the end of the world."

"To you as a man, perhaps... but to her as a female, it is a devastating blow."

"She does not show it... she seemed happy at Christmas."

"Of course, she has that sort of disposition..."

"According to Tony, she sulks..."

Hildegarde closed her eyes and shook her head. "No, no... that is with him only... 'Tis part of the game they have going on."

Rupert screwed up his face and wracked his memory. "I really do not understand the ins and outs of this game you talk of..."

"No one does... except perhaps Melanie Gillis... but the point is, Rupert, if you go along that route of her not caring, you will begin to say Richard's behaviour matters not..."

"Will I?  I do not think so..."

Hildrarde rose. "Never mind... you either sympathise or you do not... it remains that he cannot be allowed to get away with this... for his own good he must be held to account... or where will it all end, this propensity to fraudulence and criminality?"

"In the dock of the Old Bailey, perhaps?..." remarked Rupert unthinkingly, and she rose and crossed the room to the door, waving her hand behind her as she moved – a gesture to denote sheer exasperation, and one to which he had become accustomed over the years.

He caught up with her in the hall, a couple of children trailing after him. Then Rupert's wife, Bella, came down the stairs.

"You are not going already?" she enquired of her mother-in-law.

"Yes, Rupert is about to worsen my mood."

Rupert looked helplessly at his wife and held up his hands in wounded desperation.

"He fails to understand what a blow this is to Melissa's wishes on any new home... and what a terrible smear on our family name."

"That is not the case, Mother," said Rupert in futile protest. "I merely pointed out salient facts." He looked from right to left in a beleaguered way.

"I shall employ a sleuth!" said Hildegarde, opening the front door for herself. And Rupert and Bella exchanged agonised glances. "What does His Grace say?" he asked anxiously.

"Do you mean William?" she snapped.

Rupert liked calling his step-father by his official title; it was something he was naturally proud of, a bishop in the near family, though he wondered if other family members felt the same.

"Nothing much... he fears upsetting me... like you, he hopes the problem will go away..."

Rupert sighed again. "I have not said that... merely that there is little to be done."

"I think there must be something..." Bella soothed Hildegarde by stroking her arm, and Hildegarde, considerably taller than Bella, smiled at her with appreciation. "We must put our heads together and think carefully..." added Bella.

"Oh Lord!" Rupert glared at his wife. "I do not think or like—"

"Yes, yes... quite, Bella!" cut in Hildegarde. "I am thinking certainly to employ a sleuth..."

"Too costly!" Bella said.

"And what exactly would he do, this sleuth?" asked Rupert.

"Look into Richard's private affairs... find out what he has hidden."

"I think it unlikely they will succeed in that!" said Bella sadly, and Rupert turned on a weary breath and went to the side door of the vicarage, calling. "Goodbye Mama... I shall see you in a few days."

Hildegarde addressed Bella while inspecting her appearance in the hallway mirror. "I shall not give up so easily... there will be something to be done."

Bella laughed and led her back into the drawing room. "I know... I merely said that to appease Ru on the question... come and have more tea and tell me of your news."

* * *

Agnes, the maid from High Lawns, had arrived at Back Lane house, spared for the afternoon by Marguerite Shaw – to whom she was personal maid – in order to show Peggy how to dress Melissa's hair. And the hair of other ladies who may need her services in the future. Peggy was excited for this tuition – reading and writing and now hairdressing! there was no telling what skill she might acquire next!

Agnes placed her in front of a mirror in the small room next to the kitchen, which was seldom used, and arranged her hair. One or two styles were shown but Peggy had relatively short hair, which was not really suited to many styles. They called for Honoria to see if she would volunteer. Honoria was eager and agreed willingly. Deprived of sociability and company for so long in her life, any diversion of this kind was acceptable to her. Especially one which enabled her to improve herself. And her longer curling hair was excellent for the lesson. Agnes worked on Honoria and then had Peggy copy her. The first attempt did not turn out well.

"You must hold the brush like this..." said Agnes irritably. "You are not grooming a horse..."

209

Peggy found this hilarious and Honoria was inclined to agree. Both of them giggling, and Agnes, being a lot older and of a serious nature, waited for them to become attentive and sober again.

The second attempt by Peggy was coming on well, but then the doorbell chimed and Peggy was obliged to answer it. "I hope there are not many such interruptions..." moaned Agnes. "We have not got all day..."

Peggy hurried out and attended the door and then went to where Anthony Fairchild was seated in the drawing room ingle-nook, scribbling at the bureau he tended to use as a desk. "There's a gentleman here to see you, Sir." she said. "I ain't never seen him a'fore, but he says as how he's related to the Mistress."

"What's his name?" he asked suspiciously.

Peggy fished a card from her pocket, engraved with the information scrolled in flourishing script which was almost unreadable. "I am sorry, Sir, 'tis beyond me to read his last name... but his first is *Gerjary*... or something..." Peggy scrutinised the card again rapidly and handed it to him. He began to laugh quietly even before he had read the card. "Peggy, no one is called *Gerjary*,... this perhaps says *Gregory...*"

"That's it..." said Peggy. "He did announce it, come to think."

*What would they do for intermittent comedy once Peggy could read proficiently!*

Gregory bounced in on the balls of his feet in his usual loping carefree manner.

"Gregory... to what do we owe this honour?"

"I hope I do not come at a bad time... I shall be brief," said Gregory and searched the deep pocket of his stylish velvet jacket – reminiscent of composers and musical virtuosos in general. As always he was dressed for the part. His hair was long but immaculately groomed. While the moss green velvet of his jacket suited the festivities and enhanced the decorations.

"I need a translation or a missive – 'Tis in Hungarian and I cannot read it."

"Regrettably, I do not speak Hungarian..." Fairchild told him, "but if you leave it with me I will endeavour to have it transcribed for you by the day after tomorrow."

Gregory bowed low, another of his affectations as a performer. "I would esteem it a favour, thank you."

"Would you care for coffee... or a drink?" It occurred to Fairchild that he was expected now to make sociable small talk for a while. He detested this kind of interruption, life was too short, but he had discovered that family life was prone to it constantly, and he succumbed to the occasion for his wife's first cousin whom she rated highly.

"Coffee, if you please..." Gregory seated himself at one end of the long sofa. "Is my cousin about?"

"No, she is not, unfortunately... did you wish to see her particularly?"

"Not specifically... only if convenient..." Gregory looked around him, as if seeking out the nearest piano, and Peggy came in again to the summons.

"Coffee for Mr Montalbein, please Peggy."

"I shall get Mrs Harrison to bring it, Sir... I am having a hair lesson from Agnes..." she announced importantly.

Fairchild hesitated. "I beg your pardon?

"Miss Cardew is learning me how to dress the mistress's hair... and other folk who might need it... Madam at High Lawns sent her... but she only be here for an hour... and she's impatient at interruptions "

Both Gregory and Fairchild stared at Peggy and then Fairchild said. "Is she, by God!"

"Yes... she has not got all day!" Peggy said, repeating Agnes' phrase word for word.

He thought about his mother-in-law and deemed it best not to offend her maid. "Well then, you had best hurry back..." He turned to Gregory the moment the door had closed. "This is what it has come to, Gregory... ordered about by the female staff."

Gregory laughed, his glossy brown hair falling over his right cheek.

"You have it all before you, dear fellow... when you marry!... living in the midst of the womenfolk and their doings."

Gregory laughed again cheerfully, looking more innocently youthful than ever, and said. "I am eagerly anticipating it."

"How is Miss Bromley?" Fairchild enquired, politely.

The younger man began to speak in a hushed reverent tone. "We are betrothed... she has my ring now... but my father does not know... we do not speak to each other much, as you are perhaps aware. Hopefully, we shall wed as soon as I have my inheritance... three years from now. Though the lawyer says he may be able to bring it forward..."

"Excellent! My heartiest congratulations," said his host, and listened to minutes more of Gregory's financial circumstances and nuptial hopes while mentally ruminating on the translation he had been working on before the interruption.

Mrs Harrison entered with the coffee tray. "Now then, gents!... here we are..." She busied herself setting out the crockery and the plate of macaroons.

"Mrs Harrison, we are much obliged... do you know where my wife is at present?"

Mrs Harrison pondered. "Last I saw; she was up at the top land sketching one of them cows that comes near..."

"Of course she is!" said Fairchild sagely. "Where else!"

"If you ask me, 'tis a bull... but she insists 'tis a cow." Mrs Harrison reported.

Both men looked patiently at the cook, who continued. "I soon as not she didn't encourage it... whatever it is... they break the fencing and come close as I'm hanging the washing... making that lowering bellowing noise...it fair curdles the blood."

"It will be a bull then, probably..." said Gregory with authority.

"Could you send for her and tell her that her cousin Gregory is here?..."

Mrs Harrison straightened her back with a grimace and pondered. "Well, Sir, not meaning to be disobliging... but I got so many pans on the stove and daresn't leave 'em too long, and Harrison's out at the gates sorting the milk churns..."

Fairchild rubbed his eyes with the tip of two fingers rather than show his irritation to either person present.

"And as you know..." continued the cook, "the light's fading, so he must get done for tomorrow's delivery..."

He heaved a long breath. Oh for the smoothness of life in Mrs Anstey's lodgings in his old pre-marital days!

"Please do not trouble," Gregory announced amiably. "I will go myself to see her directly I have finished my coffee..."

Mrs Harrison curtsied. "Much obliged, young Sir." And then the doorbell clanged once more. "Now see..." she said, as irritable as he felt. "There's no one to answer but me... and the dishes will spoil."

Fairchild rose and cursed silently and crossed to the door, and called Honoria.

"She's in on the hair doing lark as well," said Mrs Harrison.

He had had enough of this domestic disruption. "Well, one of them will need to break off for a moment. For I am not receiving anyone else this afternoon," he said testily, and called a second time in a calm but carrying voice for Honoria.

Honoria came, her hair in tight little curls held fast by tiny combs, looking like something from a children's story book. "You wanted me, Anthony?" She looked quickly at Gregory, who stood and enthused immediately. "Miss Ainscoe... how the devil are you?" He took her hand and she stared at him in bewilderment. "You remember me, surely... Gregory Montalbein!  We met at many parties when we were younger... mostly at Uncle Giles' house!"

The doorbell rang out ferociously a second time.

"I do remember you now..." Honoria dropped a swift curtsy. "I recall us playing hide and seek... and your brother cheating by looking through his fingers at where everyone went..."

"That's right..." Gregory stepped back delightedly, releasing her hand, and they both laughed. "That would be Justin... he cheats at cards now instead... for a lot of money."

"No!" said Honoria, quite horrified.

"Yes, I am afraid so, 'tis true..."

The doorbell clanged like a firebell and was ignored. Mrs Harrison had disappeared, and Fairchild was hard-pressed to get a word in.

".... I remember you playing piano for musical chairs and later for sing-songs..." Honoria was saying. "We would have been about nine or ten... but perhaps I am a little older than you... I hear that you play professionally now and are very successful!"

Gregory bowed again – his most accomplished genuflection – still more delighted, both with the flattery and the renewed acquaintance. "Have you met Miss Bromley? Millie?... my fiancée?"

"I believe not... have I, Anthony, and possibly forgotten?"

"Possibly at the fundraiser..." said her cousin-in-law succinctly. Or this reminiscing and connecting people might go on for a long time.

"Yes... of course. I heard you playing but I was so caught up and frazzled in the kitchen, I did not..."

"No, of course not," enthused Gregory. "You were far too busy to see us... and your refreshments were delicious."

"Well... well... I... I merely... they were..." Honoria began to falter under the praise. "They were done by myself and Mrs Harrison... I only officiated on the day at the kitchen work table."

"But that is everything... is it not, Tony?"

"Everything!" agreed Fairchild in a dull, obliging voice which lacked conviction, though they did not notice.

The doorbell was now an accompaniment, reminiscent of intrepid church bells on a Sunday morning. Gregory and Honoria appeared to be deaf to anything other than their own conversation. He leapt to his feet and took her arm. "Honoria, I regret spoiling this reunion but I require you to answer the door... just tell whoever it is to go away... unless 'tis close family, of course. I cannot be bothered with more interruptions today. Begging your pardon, Gregory, I do not refer to you..."

"Of course," said Honoria, and skipped from the room. "I shall be back in a trice, Gregory, to reminisce more..."

But the trice brought bad news, and Gregory broke off from relating his father's recent woeful behaviour in gaming rooms and places of ill-repute as she re-entered, her hands clasped at her throat to illustrate an alarming occurrence. "There is a jeweller at the door... he says he has urgent business."

"What??... With whom?" said Fairchild.

"With Mrs Fairchild... something about an expensive necklace..."

But then the whispering became unnecessary as the jeweller's man entered the drawing room unbidden. He was rapidly losing control of his own domain. Gregory and Honoria both gaped at the audacity as the man stepped forward. "How may I assist you?" Fairchild demanded of him.

"Perhaps by paying for the necklace your wife bought before Christmas... or returning it to us... today!..." said the intruder.

Fairchild indicated the sofa for him to sit, his mind already conjecturing possibilities.

"Gregory, perhaps you would be so good as to fetch Melissa... ask her to return immediately, please."

"Certainly!" said Gregory.

Honoria offered. "I will come too, in case we need to search... just let me change my slippers for shoes..."

"Don't delay him... let him go ahead," instructed Fairchild, for the length of time that would take a woman was legendary.

"I will catch you up..." Honoria told Gregory as he left.

The man now had taken out a toothpick and was prodding his teeth nonchalantly. It was evident he was not a jeweller himself, but some kind of debt collector or henchman. An uncouth type of fellow who performed his personal ablutions in the homes of others.

* * *

At length, during which time Fairchild did not speak to the man who was content to sit in silence and pick his teeth, Melissa hurried in still wearing her cloak but cast it onto the nearest chair "I can guess what all this is about..." she said to her husband. "I can tell him exactly where to find the—"

"Not right now..." he interjected, taking her arm and squeezing it to silence her. "Let us hear what he has to say..."

The jeweller's man looked her over: not the usual kind of toff's wife he was accustomed to seeing but fetching and pleasing to the eye. He drew breath and put away his toothpick. "Your wife, this lady no doubt... a Mrs Fairchild, at any rate, took a diamond and ruby necklace on account just prior to Christmas. The payment has now become due... overdue in fact."

Fairchild looked at her, eyebrows raised, but spoke for her. "I doubt she did, in actual fact."

"I have her signature here..." The man took the paper from his pocketbook and showed them.

"Indeed... but 'tis a forgery..." Melissa said.

An expression passed over the visitor's face, depicting the weariness with which he was obliged to listen to these sort of pathetic denials and fabrications, and how patient he was while being heartily sick of them. He appeared like a judge in a courtroom on his eve of retirement, surveying defendants. "I dare say..." he intoned. "But someone has to pay for it..."

"Are you calling us liars?..." Fairchild asked in some astonishment.

There was no immediate reply, and the man screwed up his mouth and stared at the Christmas tree for something to look at rather than make a response. He was accustomed to dealing with toffs and gentry and found them to be tighter than clamshells when it came to producing the blunt.

"... because I can assure you, we are not those sort of people."

"I dare say..." repeated the man, this time with heavy tolerance shielding a jaundiced opinion.

"He scarcely believes us!" declared Melissa with alarm in her voice. She pulled her husband to one side and whispered to him. "Caroline was wearing it the day we went into her house... I saw it clearly."

He nodded and put his finger to his lips to silence her again.

"Allow me two or three days, and we will have your jewels for you," he announced and straightened his shoulders to square up to the man.

"I hope so, my dear sir..." drawled the henchman. "Or matters may take a turn for the worse... one way or the other."

"Yes, yes... you have no need to make veiled threats of intimidation... we are aware of the gravity of the matter." He walked to the door and spoke over his shoulder so the man would follow. Which he did, bowing slightly to her as he left.

She had sunk into a chair, defeated, and was watched by Honoria and Gregory, who had entered with the man's departure. "I should have snatched it from her neck..." she told him, almost in tears. "I wanted to, but Melanie said it would be theft with false entry if they found out..."

He laughed despite himself. "Oh, the irony..."

"I should have just taken it..."

"You know what they say about *hindsight*..." he helped himself to whisky and held the bottle up to Gregory, who declined. "We must think carefully now on the situation," he said casually and controlled his incandescent rage while thinking of Richard.

* * *

"So, how was it, the honeymoon?" He asked of Trim in the office on the day of Trim's return.

Trim grinned and took on a soulful look. "It was very similar to other holidays we have taken in Wales... there is not much difference, you know, from how we have been the past few years..."

"Yes, no need to gloat!" Fairchild said jestingly.

"Apart from the fact that Susan couldn't walk as far as we normally walk... her back aches and she has indigestion... and all the other symptoms of her condition..." he smiled, again soulfully. "The honeymoon was expected of us... 'twas necessary for appearances sake."

"Indeed!" said his friend. "One's duty no less."

Trim gulped coffee and paused. "If all goes well we shall perhaps have two more... and then stop."

"Two more what?" He turned in confusion. "Two more honeymoons?"

"No, two more children... three is the number we have agreed upon."

"God's Teeth!" claimed Fairchild. "The first one is not even in the world as yet!... your organisation is astonishing!"

Trim's grin changed to laughter, and he carried his empty cup into the outer room. Returning in good humour. "Anyway, is it not time you and Melissa got busy in the bedroom and did your duty?"

"We are always *busy in the bedroom,* as you put it... but we manage somehow to avoid begetting issue..."

"Yes, but you cannot be—" Trim was interrupted by Miss Van der Creff's entrance to announce a visitor.

"What sort of visitor?" said Fairchild suspiciously - no one was expected.

"A lawyer, to see you... he has a card... but I do not want to touch with inky fingers..." she twinkled her fingers prettily to show proof of the ink. Fairchild felt relieved that it was not another deputation from the jeweller. Then he learned that the lawyer represented his brother, Richard, and the relief was short-lived.

"There has been a theft of a necklace..." he told Trim hurriedly. "Richard or his harlot... one of them... on Melissa's signature."

"Christ!" Trim was horrified. "Whatever next?"

"Perhaps you can tell me!"

Trim left the room and the lawyer's clerk was ushered in and took a seat. "I will be brief, Mr Fairchild... your brother, Mr Richard Fairchild, is issuing you with a written warning... you are to cease making slanderous allegations upon his good name and character. Or he will sue."

He almost laughed and was beyond surprise, beyond anger, beyond reasoning on the subject. It was a farce of dizzying and spiralling proportions. A bad dream. He turned his back to face the window. "Get out!" he said to the man, not bothering to look at him. "Get out now... before I throw you out!"

The man left hurriedly and he turned around to see the letter left on his desk.

# Cousins and Conflict

"We must go back again..." Melanie said as they strolled through the town park gardens, freezing ground and frosted tree branches, and people shivering and hurrying to and fro.

"Go back?..." echoed Melissa.

"To Golden Oaks... or whatever they are calling it now.."

Melissa gasped and looked mortified.

"Tis the only way... we must gain entry... as we did the last time... without drawing attention and then somehow locate the necklace..."

Melissa was speechless, opening her lips and closing them without forming words, her face ashen with dismay and cold.

"But... 'tis such a risk..."

"I know... but what is life without a risk now and then!... we will find a way in... we will think of something."

"Will we?"

"Yes, look how competent and inspirational we have been so far," Melanie claimed airily.

"But supposing Richard is there... supposing they tie us up and call the constabulary... supposing—"

Melanie grabbed Melissa's gloved hand. "Supposing hell freezes over tonight... what if... what if... life is full of *'what ifs'*... is there a better idea?"

"No..." admitted Melissa.

"So let us repair to the Pink Parrot and plan."

* * *

His concentration was shredded – he could think of nothing but the predicament with Richard. He left the office matters to Trimingham and dealt only with translations within his command, which required a different part of his mind.

Two days after the large twelfth night celebration given at High Lawns – a tradition they valued as much as Christmas Day itself – he sat in the small recess of the drawing room, working, when Peggy entered.

"There's a gent to see you..." she announced.

"Yes?..." he raised his eyes expectantly and waited. "And does he have a name?"

She looked doubtfully at the space where the Christmas tree had stood, leaving a sad empty gap in the room. "Yes, but I didn't rightly hear it..."

"Does he have a card?... otherwise he has no business calling at my private residence..." he said impatiently.

"He's related to you someways..." explained Peggy. "He's yarnin' with the mistress in the front garden..."

"What are they doing in the front garden?... no, let me guess, she is sketching something?"

"Yes... and he's yarnin' to her."

"Do you mean speaking to her?" said Fairchild. He could not abide these colloquial terms sprinkled like confetti into important exchanges.

"Yes, that an'all" said the maid in desultory fashion.

He sighed. "His name, Peggy, please?"

Peggy looked constrained and twisted her apron hem to aid her thinking. "Sounds like *Mr Mottlebin,*" she said at length.

He gazed at her, his lips twitching and ready to grin; some people did have peculiar names, but no relatives he knew of with that name. "If he is talking with Mrs Fairchild then show him in please..."

Seeing that Melissa had not hurried in with bad news he did not feel too concerned. And after a while her cousin, Jasper Montalbein, strolled in. Closely followed by Peggy to ascertain any of his refreshment needs.

"Jasper..." said Fairchild and rose to greet him. "Have a seat..."

Peggy waited to one side and her employer said. "Peggy, this gentleman's name is Mr Montalbein... 'Tis French... Fetch us tea, please? Or would you prefer something stronger?" he asked of Jasper.

"Stronger, of course," said Jasper.

Peggy left and hurried to the kitchen to share the humour at her own expense with Mrs Harrison. *Mottlebin was a much more comical and interesting name, even if it was not posh and French.*

"I called at your offices, but Trim said you were at home today. I need a translation of a letter to the Spaniards in a hurry, and of course, he is not the Spanish expert... you are!"

"Indeed... will brandy do?"

"Nicely!" said Jasper Montalbein.

He was tall and dark and favoured in looks his French ancestors. He had a broad, high-bridged nose and strong features with thick eyebrows that defined his face. A full generous mouth and a deep and melodious voice – refined and polished at the best places of education. He was altogether a gentleman and one of society. But still single, a good catch for any woman; those harbouring marriage prospects... and possibly those who did not. He was Gregory's oldest brother, and they were in no way similar.

"I need it to be ambiguous..." Jasper was explaining, and Fairchild was immediately on his metal. "But obviously so 'tis acceptable in language and sense."

"Obviously!" said Faichild. "But ambiguous?..."

"So it might be read one or two ways, for now..."

"Good God, Jasper. I am not in the business of mealy-mouthed jiggery-pokery..."

"No, no... nothing to compromise you. I have written an explanatory brief herein..." He pulled out a sheaf of two or three papers and stepped to the bureau and left them. "Read them at your leisure... but not too much leisure... I need it by Friday mid-day, if possible."

"I cannot promise... on the ambiguity, I mean... not the deadline."

"Do your best!" said Jasper and smiled.

The brandy was poured and savoured, and Fairchild rang for Peggy to bring him coffee. He was partaking of the brandy only for politeness, having vowed to lessen his drinking since the festivities.

"Where is the delightful Honoria?" Jasper asked at length in a light manner, and his host looked at him sharply as Jasper examined his ruby signet ring and rotated it around his little finger.

"She is hereabouts somewhere?" Fairchild told him.

"Splendid... I am desirous of seeing her again.... what a curious and wondrous little thing she is..."

Fairchild remembered that Honoria had attended the twelfth night celebration, though not to his knowledge fraternised with Jasper Montalbein. They talked of other matters, and eventually Honoria entered and then immediately turned to leave. But Jasper rose to his feet. "Miss Ainscoe! What a wonderful surprise to see you again."

"Is it?" Honoria looked wary. "Did you not know I now live here?..."

Jasper was unsure how the remark was meant. Clearly, it was a rebuke of some kind. He was an impressive and charismatic character, given to charming women, whoever they were. He was clever and quick-witted beyond the average. Twenty nine, and very much the financial light of the Shaw empire. All the men in the family thought well of him and respected his economic genius.

However, in this situation, he was taken aback. Unaccustomed to such a plaintiff response from ladies on innocuous openings of light conversation. "Yes... we did not have time to discourse much at twelfth night... and we do have much history in common."

Honoria remained unhelpfully silent. It was disconcerting, and Jasper turned to Fairchild to save embarrassment. "Honoria and I are unrelated by blood but connected by family... as I am sure Melissa has told you..."

"I am aware."

"Our aunt and uncle being the common tie. I am related to Giles and Honoria to Marguerite..."

"Indeed..." said Fairchild, wondering where all this pedigree was leading.

"We saw each other often as children... did we not, Honoria?... though I am older by a few years..." Jasper continued intrepidly with more references to his brothers and her cousins, countering, he hoped, the awkwardness of her not wanting – or not knowing – how to reply. He was unsure as yet which it was. Unsure whether her eccentricity was a deliberate rebuff or a characteristic of her nature.

Honoria, wearing one of her newly arranged hairstyles courtesy of Peggy, was baffled by his attentions and impatient to leave and make haste to the garden to look through the small retractable telescope – given to her by Isaac Fairchild as a Christmas present – for some small birds which emerged now and then from the hedgerow.

Jasper addressed several polite questions to her, of the kind he thought women enjoyed, and she replied in a monosyllabic way whilst remaining uncomfortable.

"I am on my way to a tea dance..." he announced next, and Honoria noted his pale lavender shirt with excessive frills, and necktie of a deeper but similar hue, and his dark blue velvet jacket. "Perhaps you would care to accompany me?" he ventured. "Seeing that I am unpartnered."

Melissa had entered and was listening to proceedings and saw Honoria's extreme trepidation written in her expression.

"I do not have anything to wear..." Honoria lied.

"I could lend you a dress if you would like to go..." Melissa offered.

"I do not think I... I do not dance!" Honoria finally told Jasper to put them both out of their misery.

"You do not need to..." he rejoined. "The dancing is quite arbitrary... even irrelevant."

"I think not..." Honoria moved as if to rush from the room, but hovered in a *ready-to-run* sort of way. Jasper remained steadfast but somewhat pained.

"'Tis not the dancing... or the frock primarily..." Melissa told him. "But the fact that she will dislike being questioned about herself and her background..."

Honoria did not deny this, and Jasper seemed more hopeful. "Oh yes, your dreadful father and his financial distress..." he said. "Fear not, my dear Honoria... my father is also quite the *elephant in the room*... but I do not allow it to deter me from enjoying life. I simply change the subject when they begin questioning me. When all is said and done, we can none of us be held accountable for our parents!"

"I do not know of your father," Honoria said in a near whisper.

"He is Gideon Montalbein..." announced Jasper in slight hesitation, and a bravado which usually stood him in a more confident position with the critics.

Melissa spoke in low tones to Honoria, outlining briefly the character of Montalbein senior and his torrid history.

"I see... then you have my sympathy..." said Honoria to Jasper, and Jasper was much amused and looked at her with appreciation. "'Tis not your sympathy I desire, Miss Ainscoe, but your company."

"Oh!... why?"

Again, he was unprepared and paused for a few seconds. "So I may get to know you better... and because I think I will like your company."

Honoria turned her attention from him. "Anthony, should I go with him?"

Fairchild was stunned to silence, as always when his guidance was sought by her. Jasper jumped into the pause. "Yes... I forgot for the moment that he had appointed himself as your guardian..."

With one of her intermittent bursts of confidence, Honoria informed him, "He has not appointed himself... I appointed him."

Jasper smoothed the frills of his shirt cuffs and turned to Fairchild. "Anthony, give her your consent to accompany me and have done with it."

"She does not need my consent... she pleases herself."

An intervention was now overdue. Melissa rose and paced a little. "Jasper... I think you are not quite grasping the problem..."

"The problem?" repeated Montalbein with feigned innocence.

"The differences between yourself and Honoria," she said.

He laughed softly, his dark eyes surveying both women. "The only difference is that she is a woman and I am a man... no other difference matters."

"You are in difficult waters, Jasper!" said Fairchild. "Give it up."

But Jasper Montalbein was not about to accept defeat. "Perhaps I could call on you another day and take you to tea?" he asked of Honoria.

"For what reason?" she responded, her sincerity an alarming flag of unwanted truth.

He smiled widely. "My dear girl, you cannot be so sheltered or so gauche!... you are tormenting me on purpose!"

"No, you are making fun of me..." Honoria turned away and spoke to the wall, which was easier. "I do not understand what you are alluding to or the reason for your interest in me..." she said in mounting dismay. "And betimes, I have promised to observe some birds for Isaac and make notes this afternoon, so I cannot be -"

Jasper cut her off. "Isaac!... who the devil is Isaac?"

"Anthony's cousin... he and I share a passion for birds."

Jasper had never encountered such bizarre retorts from a female. He looked firstly to Melissa and then to Anthony Fairchild, who said, "I would throw in your cards now, Jasper, were I you."

But Jasper stood and held out his hand tentatively to Honoria. She ignored it and stood very still and he re-thought his position and watched her as if much entertained. "There is a rival for my affections," he said in a contrived reverential tone.

"You are being ridiculous..." Honoria told him quietly and without rancour, blushing to the roots of her hair.

"He is!" said Melissa. "Disregard him, Honoria... let us go into the garden while the sun is still out a little."

"He is making fun of me." Honoria was close to tears.

Then Jasper became earnest, taking them all by surprise and changing the mood. "I assure you I am doing no such thing, Miss Ainscoe... you entirely mistake me... and if I have offended you I humbly beg your pardon."

Honoria stared at Melissa, and Melissa slowly closed one eye to her in a careful wink. She had tried to warn her of the kind of rhetoric some men used when pursuing women. It was often the only way forward in a false and highly engineered society.

"Well, I... I... I do not... do not ha... have... I do not have..." Honoria's stammer had returned, and Jasper now was quite full of self-recrimination. He bowed to her. "I shall perhaps call again in a while... and we will renew acquaintance on more conventional and safer terms. We can perhaps take some tea and talk of birds... or whatever you wish!"

Honoria made him a brief curtsy and allowed him to take her fingers. He held them and stroked them subtly with his thumb in a way that disconcerted her and made it impossible for her to pull her hand away. He met her eyes and gazed into them quizzically, and then lifted her fingers and kissed them. She was both soothed and confused, and she snatched back her hand and left the room.

Jasper re-seated himself and breathed out. "God in heaven!... That was awkward. I never felt so wrong-footed... I need another brandy, Tony, to fortify me for further encounters with the ladies today."

Melissa wished to do more sketching while the light held. "It serves you right, Jasper," she said. "Do you imagine all women... even shy and rusticated women... are going to fall at your feet?"

"I do not..." said Jasper in exasperation. "Or else where is the challenge!"

She picked up her small easel to exit, but then thought twice. She deposited it next to the door and turned to her cousin. "Jasper, hear me out!... you are not to trifle with Honoria. She will be terrified of you."

Jasper looked at Fairchild in mock horror. "Am I so repulsive?"

"'Tis nothing to do with that!" said Fairchild smoothly. "She is overwhelmed, that is all!" He was not about to explain further. Jasper was assuming a role, and he would not waste his breath. *Having discarded his intense business head, Jasper had taken on his engaging and diverting drawing room persona. Next may come his talent for comedy genius... but Honoria was not mature enough to appreciate that as yet.*

Melissa continued. "She is not some artful debutante in society, no more than I was... nor is she looking to be courted or entertained... you will send her back into her shell when we have only just managed to coax her out... she will not engage with a man until she wishes to take him seriously."

"How do you know I do not wish her to take me seriously?" said Jasper with slight umbrage. He took the brandy offered and swigged half of it. "When I marry, I require someone sincere and modest of countenance..."

"You are not seriously telling us you have Honoria in mind for marriage?" Melissa paused on the verge of her own exit.

"No, not as yet... but she is the kind of female I may like as a wife... I thought that when I saw her on twelfth night... I remembered her from childhood, you know, at your parents' house... and being quite interested in her then... but she was, of course, too young... and I not old enough."

Melissa was sceptical. "Really?... or did you just think she was a change... and a novelty?"

Jasper held back his frustration and blinked slowly.

Melissa exchanged glances with her husband as he drank coffee and kept his counsel. She manoeuvred her easel for easier transportation. He would not allow Jasper to toy with her cousin, as much as he disclaimed any influence over her. She knew it too well and was not overly worried.

"And what does this Isaac have that I do not?" demanded Mr Montalbein next.

"'Tis more what he does not have!" returned Melissa skittishly. She stood with her equipment balanced and waited a moment or two.

"He does not have an exaggerated opinion of himself... for one thing... nor a flamboyant wardrobe... and perhaps not a barouche which takes up half the lane!"

Jasper was inclined to laugh but assumed what he thought of as a rightfully offended air. He gazed at Melissa wide eyed as she gazed back, and then he looked at her husband. "Tony, I had hoped you might have cured her of her scathing tongue by now... but instead she seems to have grown worse..."

Fairchild shrugged and tightened his jaw against his grin. "Jasper, you must know what they say about Rome not being built in a day?..."

They looked at Melissa together with fond and contained amusement.

"How dare you both!" she said, re-arranging her equipment as she left.

In the garden, Honoria and she strolled a little while, Honoria now and then raised her telescope to the trees. "You must not mind my cousin..." Melissa said. "It is after all a compliment to be sought after by gentlemen of his calibre."

"Is it?" asked Honoria. "Why?"

Honoria asked these sorts of questions frequently – questions to which there were no real answers. "Because he is thought to be eligible in the extreme... handsome and accomplished... growing wealthier by the year."

"I see!" said Honoria as if that made no sense but ought to do so.

"His paternal grandfather was a French nobleman..." Melissa supplied. "But his father has frittered away the family coffers... as I told you briefly. His grandparents were guillotined in the revolution..."

Honoria froze before clutching Melissa's arm and making her almost drop the easel. "But that is truly dreadful!"

"Yes..." Melissa sighed as she collected various pages of dropped sketches and righted things, and Honoria remained oblivious to the mishap. "Of course, it happened to a lot of French aristocrats, you know!"

"So Jasper is an aristocrat?"

"Only vaguely. and only by lineage. He officiates in our family business... though he is successful in affairs of his own."

"It makes it even more imponderable," Honoria remarked, her telescope to one eye.

"Makes what imponderable?" Melissa asked and thought now to move on alone, but Honoira was still gripping her arm with her free hand to detain her.

"Why he would want my company?"

"Well, obviously because he is a man... and you are a desirable woman..."

"I am not," said Honoria scornfully, "not next to the ladies he meets in society."

"Honoria, beauty is in the eye of the beholder... all artists know that... and I am an artist"

"Indeed you are, Lissy... and a fine one," said Honoria proudly. She gripped Melissa's arm more possessively and marched them both forward, feeling happier now and even somewhat heartened.

* * *

In the drawing room, Jasper had recovered tolerably well, swapped back to his *business head,* and moved to the question of his required letter. All was understood but with a little more time bought by an intervening and preliminary letter to slow down proceedings.

"I hear you have a problem within your immediate family!" he remarked eventually. "One of your brothers!... or so Eddy tells me."

"I do!" Fairchild confirmed and was reluctant to enter the painful subject.

"Outline it briefly," said Jasper.

He did so, finding it difficult; how disconcerting it was to admit to one's own brother being a common criminal.

Jasper listened and perused and watched out of the window, arrested by Honoria's distant form clad in a cloak and a becoming bonnet – even more alluring to him than before.

"Would you like me to do something...?" he asked.

"Do something?"

"To reclaim your money?"

Fairchild ceased studying the end of his small cigar and looked over. "What sort of thing?" he asked dubiously.

Jasper emitted his well-known laughter, which was never in short supply. "Nothing deleterious, dear fellow, don't look like that."

"Then what?"

"You know your brother is acquainted with my father?"

"Yes... I did know."

"They are both of them cut from the same cloth... though your brother is younger and has a way to go before becoming so sunk in infamy as my father... he is not, as far as I know, given so much to the excesses of drink at the wrong times... or of gaming to the extent of bankruptcy..."

"Perhaps not!" said Fairchild reluctantly.

"Even so... they are both of them to be avoided... and I believe are quite easily managed by men of superior character and strength..."

"What are you suggesting?"

"Why do you not leave it with me... how much does he owe you?"

He named the sum and explained the necklace while Jasper ran his hand through his hair and knitted his dark brows in thought. "The necklace may be a thing of the past, regrettably, and harder to obtain... but the debt of money, leave to me."

"Is this in return for Honoria's hand, by any chance?... because I do not have that sort of influence!... nor do I wish it." Fairchild opined.

Jasper stood in a dignified manner. "I am appalled that you should ask that, Tony!... I am well versed in the ways of women and romance... and the disappointment they can bring."

"I apologise!" said the other with sincerity. "I sincerely apologise."

"Leave that to the fates..." Jasper relented visibly and inclined his head to him, with just as much dignity. "And once again, if I have given her strife, I apologise... But anything I do for you is because you are family... and family is everything."

Fairchild held out his hand. "No, forgive me, Jasper, I have wronged you in suggesting it. I take it back unreservedly..."

Jasper accepted his hand. "You are a good man, Anthony... like Uncle Giles, and cousin Eddy, and your friend Trimingham, and your brother the reverand... You are all the best of men. You do not deserve to be used so ill... by family of all people."

Fairchild turned away to hide his feelings, moved now by all the developments, to an emotional level he did not enjoy. "I am accustomed to Richard and his venomous ways... we all are."

Jasper eyed the weather from the window. "Nonetheless, there are lines that most definitely should not be crossed... or civilization crumbles... and men who cross those lines lose the right to sympathy and respect... and that apart, he has defrauded Melissa of money which came from the business to her fund... so as accountant for the business it makes it very much my concern, would you not agree!"

They broached the increasingly cold day from the porch steps, and on the driveway, Jasper halted and gripped his shoulder. "And one last thing, Tony... whatever you or Melissa think, I am not my father... I am not Gideon Montalbein... I will not ill-treat any woman the way my father did my mother."

"The idea had not crossed my mind..." said Fairchild. "Nor Melissa's, I am sure."

Jasper struggled to continue and sought words. "However... I do seem to be struck by some... some deep and abiding feeling for her... Honoria!... 'tis quite disconcerting, I admit... and it must be explored... I am that sort of man... but I shall not distress her or cause her worry... have no fear on that count! I can see she is a fragile and sensitive little thing."

Fairchild made a dismissive gesture to signal an end to the discussion, which neither of them knew best how to conclude. "Is she much taken with this cousin of yours?" Montalbein enquired nonchalantly.

"I believe she might be... and he with her..." Fairchild admitted.

The accountant considered things. "Then... what can I say!... *all is fair in love and war*, is it not!"

They continued to the stables, where Jasper bowed briefly and saw the bow returned, before disappearing to collect his barouche... *which took up far too much room on country lanes.*

* * *

Later in bed, she said sleepily. "Jasper, harbouring marriage wishes towards Honoria!... did you ever hear such nonsense?"

"I know of stranger matches..." he remarked.

She turned to him. "Do not encourage him, please... he will make her miserable."

"He has promised me he will not... he may even make her happy."

She was dog tired, her eyes closed. "Have you taken leave of your senses?..."

"Besides, he may tire of her before too long... if she resists his charms."

"Or he may become more ardent in his pursuit... he is not known for easy defeat," she said.

"Perhaps not in business... but his feelings are another matter."

"Does he have feelings for her? Has he said that?" she asked more urgently.

"He has known her since their childhood," he replied, rather than betray Jasper's confidence.

"Yes, but only very occasionally and not that well..."

"Does that make a difference?" he said. "To a man it does not, I think." He decided to lighten the mood and told her of Peggy mistaking Jasper's surname for *Mottlebin.* It was a few seconds before her giggling began, and soon the giggling had overtaken her and went on for five minutes or more. "That is so comical!"

"Hilarious!" he agreed in a sombre tone.

She yawned. "And now I am truly exhausted..."

"You mean I have a reprieve from duties?"

"Yes... for now."

"Unfortunately, I cannot allow you the same concession." He pulled her to him and began kissing her and enjoying her limp reclining body. But she was almost asleep, and he arranged her for better comfort and pulled the sheet over her shoulder, and turned to sleep himself. He did not enjoy unresponsive love making.

Some hours later, she awoke and put her arm around his waist, and gradually he stirred. She wondered whether to tell him of the plan she and Melanie had hatched for the re-visit to Golden Oaks. But she knew it was risky. He may take great exception and absolutely forbid her to carry it out, and then, when she did carry it out, there would be endless trouble. She remained silent on the subject, even though she lay for hours thinking of it. When she felt him stir again, she whispered. "What are we to do about the necklace? They will take us to court?"

"I do not know..." he replied quietly. "But the money will be almost certainly returned!"

She sat bolt upright and looked down on him in the almost darkened room, save for one small oil lamp burning in the corner. "How do you know this?"

"I know it..." he assured her, "now let us go back to sleep. I have a language tutorial at the Grange first thing tomorrow with the upper form boys. Though he had resigned a while ago from his role of deputy head at the academy, he was still engaged by them to tutor languages at senior level on a fairly regular basis."

She subsided back under the bedclothes and pondered – he had his secrets and she had hers.

* * *

A week later she was waiting until he went out before setting off to meet Melanie. He was sitting in the dining room at the far end of the large table where his latest translation work – of some volume and impressive in size – was spread, whilst he scribbled rapidly. He had said he was due at the office by noon. It was now ten past the hour. She walked about and pretended to casually inspect the flowers in the vase on the sideboard. "Are you not going to be late?" she enquired casually, finding it hard to keep the impatience from her voice.

He looked up and did not seem to hear. "Who is with Honoria in the drawing room?"

"Your cousin Isaac," she replied impatiently.

"What, again?... that is the third time this week."

"Well he is returning to the Scilly Isles next week... so he will not see her for another month!"

He sighed, and then she sighed. Both for differing reasons. If he did not leave soon she would have to postpone the expedition. Perhaps it was no bad thing. But then Melanie would be annoyed with her. Wasting time, which was precious, when they had it all planned.

In the drawing room, Honoria and Isaac were sitting comfortably, Honoria in the chair and he on the arm of it, gazing from the window together to where two larger birds of yet unspecified origin were prancing from branch to branch. "I cannot think what they are..." said Isaac.

"That is unlike you..." she replied, lifting the telescope. "But then you cannot be expected to know every species..."

"I should know the English birds..." said Isaac in his calm and quiet manner, not unlike Anthony's, but different in timbre and inflection.

"You will go away soon?" she said, phrasing it like a query, even though she knew the answer, to the very day.

"Yes... but I shall return soon... perhaps one day, Honoria, you will agree to travel with me... to see different places... and different birds?"

She became ecstatic at the thought, and then afraid, and then curious. "But, it will not be quite seemly... me travelling with you... will it? People will gossip about us."

He stared at her overlong. Not knowing now how to proceed with his perceptions and thoughts on the matter.

"For how long will you be away?" she asked.

"For a few weeks, I expect..." They knew each other well now in a companionable and easy sense, like people who had been long acquainted. "You are quite alright, are you not? You are happy here?" Isaac queried anxiously.

"I am very happy... except..."

"Except what?"

She hesitated, and he took her hand and squeezed it to encourage her. "Honoria? What?"

"I am now obliged to sit and take tea with Jasper... or walk with him in the garden..."

Isaac reacted as if stung. He turned to look at her sharply. "Jasper Montalbein?"

"Yes..."

"I did not know this... obliged by whom?"

"I really do not know...by myself I expect... he is Melissa's cousin and in my Uncle Giles' business... I cannot easily refuse. So I have agreed to receive him for afternoon tea and so forth.  He has called twice."

Isaac was appalled and aghast. Then he became quite animated, which normally was not in his temperament. "There is no reason for you to feel obliged to him, Honoria."

"I think it is not such an imposition, Isaac... I do not mind. He says he wishes to be my friend..."

"Does he?" retorted Isaac in arch scepticism and laughed in a way she had not heard him laugh before. "I think he wants more than that. He is a young man of means and strong character."

This announcement had fired him to rousing heights. Assuming his greatest confidence and positivity and *grasping the nettle,* he stood and paced the room. "He is desirous of you... obviously!"

"I do not think so," she lied, and her face told a different story as she looked down at her hands and flushed.

"I now have to speak out," Isaac said, and cleared his throat ominously and straightened his shoulders. Honoria quivered a little; it was exactly what her father did when he was about to say something objectionable. She felt tears come to her eyes and closed them tight to prevent them. He was about to say he could not meet her any more. Because of Jasper Montalbein. Her heart beat into a painfully accelerated motion.

"When I return..." Isaac went on. "I shall move into a modest home of my own. As you know, I live with my parents when I am here... but the time has come for me to put down roots... so I... so I have been thinking, Honoria... your name suits you so well, you know!... you define the word *honour* itself..."

"Do I?" she asked, opening her eyes to look at him.

"In every way..."

"I do not care for my name much."

"That apart, it epitomises you... a name you should be proud of."

"My mother would be pleased, t'was her choice... my father wanted me to be called Victoria... and my mother scarcely gets her own way, but she prevailed and he -"

"Honoria," interjected Isaac. "Do not interrupt any more, please... this is important." He waited with a serious face, which made it impossible for her to keep her eyes on him. "I was wondering whether you... it may be too soon to ask... you might be disconcerted by this... but I wanted to ask you to—" He was interrupted by the door opening quickly and then closing again before he managed to see who the visitor was. Honoria turned and peered at the door. "Perhaps someone wanted to use the room."

"Never mind... they can wait."

"But... I... I..."

"Honoria," he began.

"Yes?"

He had lost his nerve and his concentration and paced about in an agitated manner. And now Honoria felt an overwhelming illumination of instinct. She shook herself mentally but could not get past the knowledge. It was written there in the air; it was given to her by some divine guiding power from above. It was undeniable.

Isaac felt ridiculous. He was thirty four years of age, not a callow youth. His experience with women was limited, but he knew how not to behave, how not to be seen as facile and inept. He took his courage into his throat and began again." I will not get down on one knee... 'Tis a ridiculous posture in my opinion... so I shall just..." He paused and took her hands and pulled her up. "I wanted to ask you if you would... if you would consider... just perhaps consider..." He broke off; that was the wrong phrase, the wrong approach entirely. He was overcome once more with fear and confusion and a sense of hopelessness.

Honoria smiled, and in one of her new, brave displays of fortitude, she ventured. "Yes, Isaac. I do."

He lifted his head and looked into her face. "You do?"

"Yes, I do... though that is not the correct answer for now. That must wait until the church..."

He embraced her and twirled her around, and began to dance with her, slowly around the room. They smiled at each other and hummed music to accompany their movement.

* * *

Melissa crept out to the garden to gaze through the window to see what was happening in the drawing room, having almost disturbed them at a vital moment. She crouched under the window and then peered above the ledge, while the two occupants were oblivious. She flew back into the house and to the dining room where her husband was again pondering his translation.  "Are you still working at that?" she said. "It would appear so." he replied laconically. "It is what I do to keep us in house and home."

A more *provocative* approach was called for. "You know, my sweet, if I accepted the commission to paint the race horses of that associate of my father, it would pay us enough money to live on for a month... then you would not need to do all this."

235

"All this is what I do for my profession." He told her. "I choose to do it... and no man wishes to hear that his wife can earn more than himself." He declared. "But, if you wish, accept the commission... 'Tis your private fund which will benefit. Just do not take it on my account."

She did not actually *wish* to take it. It would mean sitting in a cold and draughty stable for hours. She wished only for him to leave the house immediately. She changed the topic. "They are dancing..." she told him. "Honoria and Isaac... they are dancing. I think he may have moved to a firmer or more binding arrangement..."

This gave him pause and he stared across at the fireplace. "Then obviously she has greeted the proposal with far more joy than you did..." he muttered.

She stood at the mirror and looked at her disarrayed hair – and Peggy nowhere to be seen. She would need to cover it in a bonnet. But then it mattered little since Melanie had suggested they disguise themselves. "Perhaps because cousin Isaac is not a despicable tyrant... perhaps that is why." she said.

He sighed. "Melissa, stop saying that kind of thing... 'Tis ridiculous... and some people may take you seriously."

"So they should!"

He flung down the nib in irritation. Now they were getting somewhere! She moved to him and put her hands on his cheeks and then in his hair. "Leave my hair alone!" he commanded. "I know what you intend."

"Your precious hair?" she purred, and twirled locks of it in her fingers in a loving manner. "But you are a tyrant..."

"I am not."

"Well, you were."

"In your mind perhaps."

She clenched her fingers and pulled his hair tight so that he winced. "I am warning you, stop that now."

"You are not warning me surely?" she purred. "Surely not!"

"Melissa!... I have to finish this work."

"You always have to finish work..." She tugged harder and he grabbed her wrists as he stood and then pulled her arms around, so that the rest of her followed. He lifted her bodily and moved with her into the centre of the room, her legs kicking out and she trying not to laugh but to sound threatening. "Stop it... you are becoming a tyrant again... you despicable fiend."

"You are a menace at times... and a vixen.. and a shrew..." he told her, "and I won't have you disrupt—" The door flew open and Honoria burst in, Isaac following more sedately at the rear. "Oh... never mind!... they are at their game..." Honoria said quietly.

"We are not at any game..." Fairchild informed them evenly and he dropped his wife onto her feet.

"We can come back later..." proclaimed his cousin politely, "if you are... if you have other matters to attend to."

"Isaac, we are not at any game... 'Tis Melissa, she is causing mayhem, as usual."

"Liar!" Melissa said gaily and shook herself into a semblance of respectability. "'Tis he who is suddenly the tyrant again..."

"Stop using that word!" he complained.

She smirked and gazed at the couple. "How nice to see you, Isaac..."

Honoria had revived her eagerness. "Isaac has something to ask you, Anthony!"

"I see," said Anthony and smiled pleasantly at his cousin while indicating the sofa.

"I have offered marriage to Honoria... and she has agreed to it."

"Very good..." Fairchild said, as if listening to the weather forecast. "My heartiest felicitations."

"Indeed!" echoed Melissa with a satisfied look at her husband; the joy of being right and second guessing the future moment.

"But we need your blessing!" pronounced Isaac. "We need your approval."

His face went through a series of expressions before he spoke. "Isaac, as I have said before, I am not her father... nor her brother... she does what she pleases."

"Yes, yes..." Isaac was undeterred, and took this as mere generosity of spirit. "But as *I have said before,* she is under your protection. She looks on you as her guardian. I need to have your blessing on the proposal."

Honoria was nodding and raising her brows and looking expectantly at Anthony Fairchild.

"Yes, of course... 'Tis understandable..." Melissa coaxed. "Him being the tyrant he is... one does not wish to cross him."

He turned swiftly and stared her down. "Cease with this nonsense immediately..." he said in a low hoarse voice. She laughed delightedly and he closed his eyes and turned back to Isaac. "Naturally, you have my blessing... both of you... I am very glad for you." He crossed to Isaac and shook his hand and then kissed Honoria's cheek.

"I shall go to the Scillies and be there a few weeks... but when I return we shall announce the engagement. I intend to purchase a house nearby... so I shall be able to look after her as she deserves to be looked after."

Honoria was blushing and looking as brides-to-be should look, Melissa supposed. How marvellous for her. And how speedily it had happened. He was right when he said Honoria had more eagerness and pleasure in the proposal than she had ever had in the prospect of marriage.

"We will not marry at once... we shall enjoy a decent engagement..." Isaac told them and beamed at Honoria, "In case you are thinking this very precipitous in our association."

"I trust it isn't to be as long an engagement as Trimingham's..." he remarked drolly, and Honoria needed to explain to her fiancé about Susan and Trim's betrothal over many years. Isaac duly smiled and shook his head. "Indeed not... I am not so patient in these matters." He took Honoria's hand and squoze it. They gazed at each other with pride and complicity, as if they had pulled off some miraculous coup.

"Betimes..." said Isaac to her. "We should get about watching the trees over yonder..."

"Yes," said Honoria with enthusiasm. She turned to Anthony and said softly. "Thank you, Anthony."

He waved his hand dismissively. He felt as ridiculous as Isaac had felt minutes before. This idea of patriarchy descended upon him from nowhere and gained in strength. Melissa was nodding and making an approving face, encouraging the notion for perverse reasons he could not fathom. It was obviously a facet of the game she orchestrated in her imagination. Not that she liked the idea of patriarchy in the usual sense; it was merely one of the enigmas of the game itself, which she found useful, and he was not allowed to understand.

Isaac went swiftly to the door, taking Honoria's hand as if afraid of losing her. "So you can get back to... to the game!"

"There is no game!" His cousin repeated with heavy tolerance, before realising how this may be misconstrued. "'Tis Melissa being... being..."

"Playful!" said Honoria, and Melissa grinned impishly and waited for him to agree the suggestion. He did not agree with it, and murmured. "I think she means antagonistic."

When they left, she stared at him challengingly.

"Saved again, in the nick of time!" he remarked. "You have the knack of that down to a fine art."

"How popular is Honoria these days... since Melanie and Susan and I have been coaching her on womanly virtues..." she said, dismissing his last remark. "And with her new fashionable hair arrangements..."

He sat again in front of his cursed translation, and she sighed without sound. "I expect he had to beat Jasper to the finishing line," he said. "And she is more suited to Isaac... nobody can deny that... although, it has to be said, she is a wifely little creature... all the virtues a man may want..."

"Unlike me!" She watched him from her side vision.

"Oh, you... you are a..."

"Say it once more... I dare you!"

He shut his eyes against the challenge. "You will be more like Honoria when I have done with you... have no fears."

"How you do puff yourself up..." she declared. "I will lay down odds right here that it will not happen... in fact, if you will take the wager I may..." He felt her come closer through his closed lids, then suddenly he sprang up. "No Melissa I am not listening to any wagers right now... I do not have time for this... so do not bother laying any odds." He moved away from her, not to be seduced into staying.

*Eureeka!* Now he would leave and de-camp to the town, and she could leave for Melanie's home, giving him a five minute start from the stable and along the driveway.

# Ladies Day

"It has happened again..." Melanie shouted into the rising wind as they drove to 'Golden Oaks.' "This magic of bringing people together under your roof..."

Melissa held onto her unbecoming bonnet, large enough to not show her face from the side view, the floppy loose brim copious enough to shadow most of her face. "I suppose it has..."

"The magic followed you from High Lawns... you and him... Polly and McCarthy... Millicent and Gregory... and now Honoria and Isaac!... who next, I wonder."

"I wonder," said Melissa obligingly, and briefly thought of her erstwhile maid, Polly, and her husband's work colleague from the school, Dominic McCarthy, gone now to live in Ireland. Though as she always pointed out, they met in the large town park, strictly speaking.

An age passed and her main preoccupation was the proposed visit, where they planned to gain access the way they did before – through the kitchen door – and then search for the copy of Melissa's signature, in any drawer in any room. It was a lottery, though Melanie thought it would be the drawing room, Caroline being a woman and not needing a study and doing all her business in the drawing room, unless there was a smaller morning room... she was lost in reverie and they were almost there and then Melanie spoke, loudly above the wind and the wheels.

"Do you imagine he still thinks of Lottie?" she asked suddenly, "the childhood sweetheart."

Melissa started at the sound of her voice and the mention of Lottie and arranged her mind to the moment. "I think he does... In fact I know he does... I can tell when he is refining upon her!"

"How?"

"I do not know precisely... but something about the set of his face... I know his every expression and facial movement... I love to study him in that way."

"And you do not mind?"

"No... I think it heartens me in many ways. The fact that he can love Lottie after all this time, if love it is!... If he can do that, then he must be able to love me too... in the here and now... he is capable of much love it seems.”

Melanie made a contemptuous face – not about to give him quarter though it was food for thought. It was a fascinating subject.

“It is not as though she bothers us at all...” concluded Melissa.

“Not that you know of!” said Melanie darkly and Melissa made a horrified face, but then the carriage lurched to turn into the lane leading to Golden Oaks.

* * *

Purely by a twist of fate, and at the same time as they made their way on this third visit, Mrs Wyevale was also in transit to visit Golden Oaks, from the opposite direction. Her face a mask of disdain as she viewed the countryside from the carriage window. Driven by her husband’s coachmen and nicely wrapped in fur rugs for greater comfort, her open book lying on her knees as the conveyance gathered speed on the open road. She thought of what she would say, how she would deal with Caroline if her son was absent. She would not leave without a conclusion, that was for sure. She would secure some payment at least against the money stolen. If not the full amount. Richard might be well into his thirties but he was still her off-spring and she would make him listen to reason.

She had the advantage in the journey over the two younger women in that her coachmen (the bishop’s men) were experienced drivers who knew how to negotiate the roads and the layout of the countryside. But even they were not prepared for the rugged, stony and isolated approach along which a conveyance had to travel to reach the house in question.

The two men, one young and one a lot older, stopped in perplexity and stood for several minutes staring up the unwelcoming siding and talking between themselves. Eventually Hildegarde grew inpatient and climbed down – the elder of the men rushing to assist her. “What appears to be the problem, Stephen?” she enquired, but then saw for herself that the lane was too narrow for the carriage – if lane it could be called. “Too narrow, Ma’am!” said Stephen and looked for his colleague who had disappeared into the surrounding trees. “Not just that this sign don’t say ‘Golden Oaks’ neither... ” he added.

Hildegarde looked at the sign on the verge which announced in faded lettering on a small piece of wood: 'Four Cedars.' She fumed and made one of her disparaging faces, her lips turned to an angle expressing extreme annoyance. "For Heavens' Sake... do I mistake the house name my son gave me!"

"Which son?" asked Stephen to be helpful, as if that was relevant.

"The youngest!" replied Hildegrade, not to seem churlish. "He is always very precise with his words... being a linguist."

They stared together along the rocky incline, as if it may magically widen for them. Then the second coachman came back, holding a larger sign post on a heavy wooden stave, obviously pulled from the ground. He turned it the right way round so they may see it. 'Golden Oaks' it boasted, in newly painted copper plate sign-writing.

"Aha..." said Mrs Wyevale with great glee. "So that is what they do!"

"There must be a way up there, Ma'am..." claimed the older man, "for they must needs take up heavier stuff... furniture and the like."

"And the coal wagon has to deliver..." Simon offered.

"Mayhap they only burn logs though." the older one pointed out.

"Nonsense... they will burn coal at some point... Richard is not the kind of man who will welcome chopping logs... he is far too idle... and I know they do not have above one servant for the most part, and that a female." advised Hildegarde in tightly controlled anger. The thought of Richard's shady ways was quite intolerable.

"There has to be another way round..." claimed Simon, the younger man, and ran to the right of the lane and surmounted a smallish incline and then sprung onto a low hanging sturdier tree branch for better surveillance, while they waited and stamped their feet against the cold.

At length he returned. "There seems to be open flat ground at the back and a couple of cottages to the left... if we find a way onto that land we can approach from there..."

"There will be a way round." Hildegarde affirmed. "There has to be..."

They returned to the coach and assisted her in and the older man said. "If the cottages is to the left of the open area, the entrance to the flat ground must be round there... we'll head that way." Simon made sure she was comfortable in the carriage and enquired politely, "Why would your son not have the correct sign at his gate, Ma'am?" Realising it was impolite but being too curious not to ask.

"Because he's a devious individual," replied Hildegarde drily, "and certainly the most untrustworthy of my sons..."

The men exchanged glances. "Never mind, Ma'am..." said the elder man in a gentling tone. "You just sit tight and hold on to the door straps... it looks to be bumpy up there!"

Hildegarde straightened her posture against the upholstered seat and shook her head. "I do not care, Stephen, how bumpy it is... just deliver me there."

"Right you be, Ma'am," said Stephen, a long time in the bishop's employment. His employer, the bishop, had told them not to allow Mrs Wyevale out of their sight for a moment. Not that he did not trust her to Richard Fairchild, but that the people Richard kept company with, from all accounts, were not to be trusted.

* * *

Miss Van der Creff looked up as Anthony Fairchild entered the offices and smiled at him welcomingly.

"Are you well, Miss Van der Creff?" he enquired, not pausing but continuing through to his own room, necessitating her to follow, which she did without too much reluctance. He took off his outer coat, and she watched him hang it and noted the clothes he wore today. The line of his thigh and the shape of his calf muscle in the trousers he wore, which were closely fitting as usual. She breathed out slowly, as much unaware of her own body language as he was with his back turned. She imagined running her hands through his hair, freshly washed and with the loose curl that would not be so curled in a few hours.

Sensing her eyes on him, he turned and raised his brows. He knew something of her thoughts and strove to keep his own in check. Otherwise, he might succumb, as in days of old, and all kinds of problems would ensue.

"Where's Trim?" he asked quickly.

"He is gone somewhere with Mrs Trim..." said Miss van der Creff, imitating the shortened name. "I think to an attorney... a family matter of some kind."

"Oh yes!" The changing of her father's will and estate, "he did say."

Miss Van der Creff hesitated, still feasting her eyes on him. "Was there something else?" he enquired.

"A jewellery man has been..." she told him.

He was immediately on his metal. "What do you mean by a *jewellery man?* What did he want?"

"He says he will not wait longer for payment... a necklace missing... if not paid within the week the bailiffs will come."

He stared at her, uncomprehendingly. Until she was minded to say more. "He says two months the necklace has been with your wife and no payment... now they don't wait any more after the end of week."

He opened and closed his mouth and could not get out the relevant words. His embarrassment at the predicament was overtaking him. "He is coming back later to find your answer..." added Miss Van der Creff indifferently.

Slowly he was becoming incandescent with fury. Miss Van der Creff watched his face show the highly controlled signs of anger, which she found captivating. "Perhaps your wife may give it up... to save us from the bailiffs... if you ask her."

He came to life. "My wife does not have the necklace... my brother stole it using her signature." He felt foolish and tawdry and not believed.

Marianne Van der Creff stared, a look of incredulity on her features. "I see..." she said at length, in a manner which clearly told of her disbelief. *Obviously this wife of his had him duped, wrapped around her little finger, and could bamboozle him with any tale; such was the nature of men when beguiled by love... or lust.*

"'Tis a long story..." he said at length. "If he comes back, this man, tell him you are instructed to get money from the bank forthwith... ask him to call back within the hour and then lock the door and go home."

"And what if he does not like to leave?"

"Then lock the drawers and leave him here and go to the constabulary..."

She became tense with fear. She did not like authorities of any kind. "Constabulary!... to say what?"

"That you are in danger... they will let you wait in their offices while they will come and get rid of him... or take him into charge if the papers are not in order."

"Where are you going?" she asked, watching him put on his coat again and not following the story or its details or making sense of any of it.

"To the 'Feathers'..." he said. "I am in need of a drink... while I think of the next move."

"So, you do have this necklace?" said Miss Van der Creff.

"No... I do not."

He scribbled a note for Trimingham to let him know where he had gone and left it on his desk, then moved to the main door, fastening the buttons of his coat.

"I will not stay... I will come with you!... This man, he might be dangerous... he might attack me... I am coming!" insisted Miss Van der Creff.

"It is better that you do not!" he protested.

"Why? Do you mean it is better that you are safe and I to be in danger?" she cried with incredulity.

"No, no... but 'tis better you go to the tea shop or home... not with me!"

"Why not with you?"

It was no easy matter to explain the expected English niceties of women and hostelries and married men to girls like Miss Van der Creff in times of crisis. He abstained from doing so and went along the passage, hoping she would not follow.

She grabbed her cloak and locked the door and ran to catch up with him on the stairs. "I will come with you." she said adamantly and ran in front of him to await him on the pavement while he locked the outer side door giving entry to their offices.

* * *

At 'Golden Oaks' Caroline was again in her dream. She heard a banging on the front door and the bell clanging for all it was worth. But she was almost beyond caring – almost but not quite. Having begun the substance some short time before. She was between worlds, not oblivious but not entirely coherent. Not concerned but not without the awareness of some intimidating outer presence pressing for her attention in the vicinity of the room.

She squeezed shut her eyes. She heard the aged maid lamenting in a croaking voice about having to come down the stairs and the stairs creaking as she descended.

Outside in the porch, Mrs Wyevale continued to clang the bell. Convinced that those inside were hiding from her, Richard and his paramour. And Simon watched from the rear in the garden, a few yards away from where Stephen stayed with the bishop's prestigious carriage.

Miriam shuffled at last to the door and opened it fractionally to behold a stately looking lady of mature years staring at her, pleasantly.

"I am Mrs Wyevale... allow me entry please?"

"No..." said Miriam cantankerously. "Who the blazes be you?"

"The mother of Richard Fairchild!" announced Hildegarde, still disposed to pleasantry.

Miriam screwed up her face into a thousand wrinkles and put her hand to her lower back.

"You are in pain, my good woman?" enquired Hildegarde with civility.

"I's always in pain, lady!" said the beleaguered maid.

"You are too old to be working..." Hildegarde informed her, sliding past the slight  and distressed form of the very old woman. "Allow me in... then show me to your employer."

"Who?" She peered up at her from her bent position.

"Mr Fairchild."

"He b'aint around..."

"Then who is?"

"You'd best be off..." said Miriam for lack of anything more informative.

Hildegarde swept past her and smiled as she did so. Disgraceful – it got more deplorable by the minute. She would see to this dreadful exploitation of the aged and infirm at a later point.

On entering the drawing room, dim as a deep cave, she saw that Caroline was slumped on the chaise longue with her eyes half open, watching as Hildegarde made her entrance. She did not immediately recognise her – would not easily recognise anyone while in the dream.

"Where is Richard?" asked Mrs Wyevale, seemingly not surprised by the other's wretched state. "Where is he, Caroline?"

Caroline heard her name and fathomed that the interloper knew her and was not an assailant or other malevolent stranger.

Hildegarde looked about her at the darkened room, the lamps so low it was hard to see a hand in front of her face. The place reeking of a strange odour she could not place, until she saw the container with opium and the snaking pipe with the silver nozzle from which Caroline was imbibing. She shuddered and called for greater strength from on high.

Richard might be hiding from her somewhere else in the house – he always had as a child. Cunning little wretch that he was. She sat in a chair and calmed herself, staring at Caroline and thinking.

Melanie and Melissa arrived a few moments later, having left the trap where they had tethered it on the last visit, and ran up the unwieldy incline by foot. They crept around to the kitchen entrance, just like the last time, knowing they would not be allowed entry formally. The door again was not locked and Miriam was nowhere to be seen, having gone into the small room off the kitchen, which served as her bedroom, to lie down. Tired out after the unexpected confrontation with the woman calling herself Richard Fairchild's mother. They crept into the hallway and stood outside the drawing room, listening to the voices from within.

"Where is my son?" Hildegarde was asking, then in a louder voice. "Have him fetched now, Caroline." Lady Wentworth had become a little alert and vaguely knew the woman in her drawing room, but she remained unresponsive, and Hildearde began to pace the room, peering at things and looking at the obje'd'art and the paintings – almost impossible to view clearly – trying to assess monetary value in general. She was totally unsure of Caroline Wentworth's current financial status or position, and it was something she needed to know before taking further action.

"It sounds like my mother-in-law's voice," hissed Melissa.

"What?" Melanie looked askance at her. They had not anticipated anyone other than the couple themselves being present.

"We must think what to do now..." said Melissa.

Then a step was heard behind them, heavy and purposeful, and they turned to see Richard. His riding cape about his shoulders and a little damp from the recent shower, and his gallop to the house. "What the devil are you doing here?" he said angrily. He did not immediately recognise them; they were wearing large shapeless bonnets of an inferior cloth, and tatty cloaks, like skivvies or maids of all service from the lower classes. He grabbed Melissa's shoulder and swung her round, and peered at her. Then he did know her and smiled slowly. "So, 'tis Mrs Fairchild the younger – *again!*... and in bad disguise..." He peered at Melane. "And Mrs Gillis, no doubt!"

Melanie thumped his arm above the elbow. "Take your hands off her..." she said. "How dare you!"

Richard smirked and noted the irony of the situation.... *'How dare he!'*

"You have once again broken into the house, as before Christmas when you did the same... according to Lady Wentworth."

"We came through the back door..." Melanie announced proudly. "We have not broken in anywhere."

"But you were not invited, so it amounts to the same thing," Richard said laconically.

"Not in law, you will find..."

He took a long breath and surveyed them. Of course, the Gillis girl was wed now to a Q.C of some renown. He had to be a little careful. "I think you need a lesson in manners!... barging into the homes of others in this way..." He took hold of Melissa and began to lead her along the hallway. "Take your hands off me..." She struggled against him to no avail.

"Where do you think to take her?" asked Melanie with a calmness she did not feel.

"I am locking her up whilst I fetch my brother... he of the impeccable values and censorious attitudes... so he may see how his wife disregards the rights of other people. I shall secure her, and then fetch him to collect you." He shouted for Miriam, who was nowhere about. "We will see what he has to say... he may then climb down off his high horse."

Melissa kicked him on the shin with the pointy toe of her boot (the only piece of wardrobe not resembling poverty), and he disregarded the pain. "Take your hands off her!" yelled Melanie and went behind him and kicked him more stoutly on the back of his leg. He turned around to push her away and only partially managed to derail the attack. "Leave her be... you vile man!"

Melissa was pulling and tugging and trying to free her arm from his grip, cursing him all the while and making idle threats. "Go to the front of him and poke him in the eye!" she cried to Melanie.

But Melanie hesitated, and wondered if that was not too violent a repost. She wanted only what her friend was entitled to and not the risk of blinding someone  "I will give you one last chance, Richard…" she said majestically. "Let her go, or I will do as she suggests."

"I do not think that will be necessary," said Mrs Wyevale, coming from the drawing room. "Richard, let her go immediately…"

Richard stood very still, but did not release her, taken aback by his mother's sudden appearance. "Mother? Is that you?"

"Yes, Richard, it is me."

"So, you have come as a deposition!" he remarked, and Melissa tugged her arm free of him. "What on earth can all this mean?" His tone had changed to one of quiet outrage and dull effrontery. He feared his mother considerably, feared her ultimate rejection of him constantly, while still craving her attention and affection.

"You know very well what it means!" she replied. "We are here to collect the money you have stolen… though I did not know the two girls were coming."

"Let us go into the drawing room…" he said. "And be civil."

"We do not have time for all that…" Melanie objected. "Just fetch the necklace and the money, and we will leave…"

Richard laughed throatily, as if this were a prank or a charade of some kind carried on from the Christmas festivities. He stepped into the dimly lit space of the drawing room and looked over at Caroline, almost collapsed now on the chaise longue, the drug having taken deeper effect. "Your mama is about somewhere…" she drawled. "Your dearest, sainted mother…"

"Caro, try to pull yourself together," he admonished, and then shook her by the arms.

Mrs Wyevale gazed with disgust at Caroline. "I do not think she will be pulling herself together any time soon," she said. "And I hope you are not about to offer everyone tea…"

Richard chuckled falsely and blinked at his mother, flattering her wit in the absence of any other strategy. Melissa and Melanie stepped through the doorway, and Mrs Wyevale stared at their clothes. "Why on earth are you dressed like that?"

"Disguise!" said Melissa shortly, and Richard laughed louder.

Caroline hiccuped audibly, and Hildegarde said, "Just give me the money, Richard... a banker's draft will suffice."

Richard pretended great astonishment and threw his arms wide to an imaginary audience. "To which money do you refer?"

"The money you obtained fraudulently with my signature..." Melissa cried and swung her comedy bonnet around in frustration as if fanning a small fire. He stared at her and then looked balefully at his mother. "I do not know of this money."

When Mrs Wyevale approached him, it was carefully and deliberately with a menacing air, causing him to step back. They waited in anticipation, sure she was about to slap him; it was in her expression and her salient intention. But she did not; she lowered her eyelids and raised her brows and stared him in the eye. Caroline hiccuped again, and a crackling slurping noise was emitted as she inhaled more of the drug.

"What am I supposed to have done with this alleged money?" he asked no one in particular, staring at the bust of a Roman emperor on the sideboard. The emperor lent him insuperable inspiration in the face of the onslaught.

"Richard, if you do not make good this theft, you will not be welcome in my home again. My husband... your step-father... is a bishop of the Anglican church. We simply cannot have this kind of slur upon the family... "

"I do not have their money!" said Richard, and Hildegarde turned her face away in temper and loathing

"Because you have spent it, no doubt," supplied Melissa quietly.

"Perhaps if you ask the Dalgleishs..." Caroline drawled from the depth of her haze, "they may return it... if the investment is not yet made."

"Caro, be quiet..." He turned and hissed at her. "You do not know what you are talking about... she doesn't know what she is talking about!" he repeated in a laughing manner for the benefit of the three women. "'Tis the drug..."

"Yes, I do..." breathed Caroline, her voice barely audible. "I was present at dinner with them when you -"

"Caroline!" he yelled, his voice in the dim and quiet enclosure shredding any hope of calm. *"Shut your mouth now."*

Lady Wentworth sank down into the recess of the chaise longue and seemed to be shrinking into its upholstered back, unperturbed by his words.

"And there is the necklace..." said Melissa after an awful silence. "That is far the worst thing... the jeweller has sent bailiffs..." She watched Caroline lift her hand and touch the skin above her neckline. The necklace around her throat was one of rubies and small diamonds.

"That is it," she told Melanie. "She is wearing it again. I told you we should take it before Christmas!"

Eagerly, Richard clutched at this lifeline. "Caro, give them the necklace..." he said and Caroline again lifted her fingers, like someone in a trance, and clutched at the lower part of the jewellery protectively. "Mine!" she muttered. "'Tis mine..."

"No, it is not!" said Melissa angrily, "It belongs to a jeweller in Stafford..."

"Are you sure it is the one?" asked Mrs Wyevale, seated uneasily on a small velvet chair.

"It has to be... it fits the description... and who else would take it on my signature?"

"Indeed... there is that!" said her mother-in-law.

"Supposing she has two such necklaces though?" Melanie pointed out, and Melissa rasped breath through her teeth in annoyance. "Mel, I do not care if she has twenty two such necklaces. This one will do for now... it looks valuable."

Richard stepped towards his mistress and prised her fingers from the necklace. She batted his hand away weakly, but he moved to the side of her neck and chose a place where only the gold chain hung and quickly yanked it so that the chain snapped and fell away.

"Here!" he said to Melissa. "Have it, if it pleases you so much... 'Tis worth nothing anyway... 'Tis fake."

"Liar!" said Caroline, stroking her throat as if to sooth it after a great loss.

He threw the necklace towards Melissa, and it landed on the floor. She retrieved it hastily and put it down into her bodice for safety. "That will suffice for now." She put back the shabby bonnet and nudged Melanie, whom she knew would be enjoying proceedings

– diverting as they were. "Let us go... he is not about to admit to the theft of the money."

"Not presently at least!" said Hildegarde.

"Not ever..." said Richard, and Caroline tittered from somewhere in her torpor.

"He does not need to for now... "Melanie said. "I shall speak with my husband and see what he suggests..."

"Shall you be alright, Mama?" asked Melissa, approaching Hildegarde and touching her hand. "If we leave you?"

"Of course I shall!" said Hildegarde. "My coachmen are waiting outside." She turned to her son, "You may offer me tea now, Richard, if you wish."

Caroline's eyes were closing against the soporific effects of the opium. "Tea's no good, Mother-in-law!" she mumbled. "We need something stronger!"

Hildegarde cleared her throat. "I am not your mother-in-law, Caroline.... nor do I wish to be..."

"Not good enough for you, I suppose?... I am not good enough, Richard. I always told you that." Caroline slurred.

"A genius observation!" said Melanie, and Melissa grabbed her hand and pulled her from the room before more argument could be seeded.

"If you see my coachmen, tell them I shall be out shortly," Hildegarde called to them as they left. "After I have taken some tea."

"Miriam is not about, Mama..." said Richard urbanely. "So tea is not an option, I fear."

"Miriam?" repeated Hildagrde. "Oh yes... the maid!... and that is another matter... that poor old woman you are exploiting."

"Oh God!" opined Richard in a harrowed voice. "Is there no end to the list of charges!"

* * *

Meanwhile in The Feathers, Miss Van der Creff was downing her third large glass of gin in less than an hour – to his two tankards of ale. He watched from his side vision, appalled. There was little he could do. He could not force her to leave in the face of her refusal. She was enjoying herself. Nor did he wish to run into the jeweller's man who might be lurking around the high street. He sat a distance away from her along the wooden bench, and to all intents and purposes had nothing to do with her. Except when occasionally she slid along to cosy up to him, whispering in his ear. He shrugged her off each time and groaned extravagantly.

Now and then, Mrs Walters, the landlord's wife, looked over at them disapprovingly. She knew of Anthony Fairchild from the tavern and the town: a respectable young gentleman of letters and business, and married of late to the daughter of a wealthy and prestigious family. Normally behaving in a proper manner and not consorting with women of loose reputation – even if occasionally becoming foxed, which was quite understandable and acceptable. Eventually, she could not contain her curiosity and crossed to where they were sitting on the pretence of wiping the table. "Who is this person with you today, Mr Fairchild?" She asked lightly – it was after all her hostelry. "I have not seen her in here with you before."

"She is a translator... she works for us." he said, mastering his embarrassment

"And why do you need to know?" Miss Van der Creff enquired of the landlord's wife. "What business is it of yours who he drinks with?"

He shifted uncomfortably and glared at his employee to silence her.

"All things taking place in here are my concern, young woman, my husband is the landlord." replied Mrs Walters proudly and smiled for his benefit. "I was worried she might be a doxie... playing her hand and prevailing on your good nature." she told him, ignoring the employee – so called.

"Mind your tongue, old woman..." said Miss Van der Creff in a venomous kind of growl. "Or I will drown you in a keg of your own ale."

He glared at his translator and kept his voice low. "Miss Van der Creff, please! Remember you are in a public place..." He addressed the landlady. "My apologies, Ma'am. She is not a doxie. She is simply not accustomed to English propriety."

Mrs Walters sniffed and looked down her nose. "Yes... I thought she was foreign."

"She is not a doxie!" he said adamantly. "She is just passing time."

"And swelling your takings... so do not presume yourself, you overweight beer peddler!" said Marianne Van der Creff, her English becoming less proper but more colourful. "Go and wipe your arse... instead of the table."

He blushed and groaned and looked at his translator with abhorrence. "Miss Van der Creff... I implore you to be quiet."

"I may have to ask you to leave..." Mrs Walters told him, "if she keeps on this way!"

"Yes... again my apologies. She is inebriated... but we are leaving any minute."

Mrs Walters moved off, her smugness diminished momentarily, though she was not unused to vulgarity, in this place of revelry.

Then thankfully Melissa rushed in, looking about her fervently, the tavern being almost as dim as Caroline's drawing room but quite full of customers. She spotted them and hurried over. "Who is she?" she asked, echoing the landlady's sentiments.

"This is Miss Van der Creff..." He turned to Marianne. "This is my wife!" he said in desultory tone, defeated by circumstances and expecting the worse.

Miss Van der Creff looked Melissa over with cheerful contempt. "Oh yes, the jewel thief!"

Melissa bridled and stared at her. "How dare you!"

"She is not a jewel thief, Miss Van der Creff. Please stop saying that..." He stood and took Melissa's arm. "Come... let us go. I need to -"

"How often has she said it of me?" Melissa interjected, pulling back to prevent movement.

"Unfortunately, we had a visit from the jeweller's debt man... to the office..." he explained.

"Well I now have the necklace!" she announced excitedly and opened her shabby cloak and delved into her bodice to retrieve the jewellery to show him.

"What are you doing?" he admonished in a hushed tone. "This is a public tavern... cover yourself!" At this rate he would not be able to show his face in the place again.

"Why is she dressed like a pauper?" Miss Van der Creff asked him in a loud voice, disregarding the production of the necklace. He blinked slowly. "I have not the faintest idea... but no doubt I am about to find out." He took the necklace and inspected it.

"The chain is broken..." Melissa said. "Your brother yanked it off Caroline and threw it to me..."

He was speechless and had the unsettling feeling of a bad dream. The necklace was glistening and heartening, flashing some kind of redemption to events with all its gem facets.

"That can be easily mended." He murmured. "But where have you seen Richard? You have not been to that house again, when I expressly told you not to?" He looked about him furtively; customers were watching, no doubt under the impression he was a receiver of stolen goods or other criminal type.

Melissa gathered her cloak around her and pulled her bonnet on more securely. Doing so haughtily and exuding defiance to onlookers, as if dressed in her finest. "Do not have the effrontery to lecture me about my conduct... when you are in an ale house supping with this drunken slattern..."

"Be careful who you are insulting... you jewel thief!" announced Miss Van der Creff.

Melissa turned pale and Mrs Walters passed with her damp cloth. "Who is this one now?" she enquired skittishly. "Another translator, I suppose!"

"My wife!" he said shortly, losing the battle with appearances.

Mrs Walters opened her mouth in astonishment and then smirked, imagining it to be a joke. Just as Trimingham entered, out of breath from running through the high street to catch up with Melissa.

"Thank God you have arrived..." said his business partner. "Miss Van der Creff needs escorting home, Trim?... she is about to destroy our good name entirely."

"What has happened?" Trim enquired, unable to look away from Miss Van der Creff and her degenerated state of lolling and grinning inanely at all and sundry.

"We have the necklace..." His voice was so low that Trim had to lean in to hear him above the murmur of general conversation in the tavern. "I must get it back to the jeweller... before the henchman turns ugly."

Marianne allowed herself to be pulled by the elbow as Trim lifted her from the bench, weaving slightly from the effects of the gin.

"And would you be so kind as to pay the bill?" Fairchild said, handing him silver. "If we drive quickly, we can make it to the jewellers before they close." Then he had a thought and halted. "Are you certain it is the right necklace?"

Melissa tutted and stamped her foot. "I do not care... 'Tis a necklace, is it not? And it looks expensive and fits the description... so it will have to do."

"Where is this jeweller?" queried Trim, Miss Van der Creff leaning heavily on him, her head on his shoulder.

"Stafford..." he replied, "but if we drive smartly, we will be there before they close."

Trim guided Miss Van der Creff to the counter, where she once again leaned inelegantly and glared around in a challenging manner at the male customers – all gawking and grinning.

Mrs Walters handed him his change and refused to look at Marianne. "And who exactly was that woman he claims is his wife?" she asked in a highly dignified way, as if requesting the salt cellar at a dinner table.

"She *is* his wife!" said Trimingham. "She is well acquainted with my own wife, who dines with me here some days and can vouch for her... I shall bring her in to do so, if you wish."

Mrs Walters assumed a wry face and looked to the barmaid, who pulled a face of her own. "Dressed as a nun, no doubt!" she said sagely, and she and the barmaid succumbed to silent amusement.

Trimingham smiled and nodded, as if amused. He tried in vain to straighten Marianne Van der Creff from her dependent position, but she flopped against him, putting her arm through his and singing in Dutch. He was as good as his business partner as a consort. "We will find a cab," he told her, "to take you home... before there is any more gossip..."

"Goodbye, goodbye..." called Miss Van der Creff to the whole tavern as she left. "Mind how you go..." She leered at Mrs Walters. "And if you can't be good, take more water with it... as you English say!"

Trim tugged her onwards. "That is not what the English say... now come along and stop drawing attention..."

Miss Van der Creff laughed raucously and waved at anyone who might be watching, rotating her hand in circular motion like royalty.

Cabs were in short supply at this time of day. He peered up and down the street, all the while trying to keep her upright so as not to advertise her drunken state.

"We can walk..." she said. "'Tis only a short stroll... and the weather is mild."

"No, we cannot walk..." objected Trimingham. "People will wonder why you are linking arms with me and swaying about... they will think the worst."

"The worst!" echoed the lady, "what is that to be?"

He ignored her and spotted a cab, which slowed, and he bundled her in and sat beside her to make sure she did not disembark before reaching her destination.

She squinted from the window, leaning over him, to ascertain whereabouts they were. And eventually she found her address. A solid and spacious detached dwelling on a corner, in need of some repair, standing in overgrown garden and sporting many windows, through which easels and drying canvasses could be seen

Before he could get her along the path, the front door opened and the artist with whom she resided appeared, dressed in a shirt unbuttoned to his midriff with billowing sleeves and ostentatious ruffs and altogether not of the usual mode of dress of local townsmen. Every inch the fashionable painter, he shook back dishevelled hair from his unshaven face and assumed a condescending expression of amusement, "Ah, there you are, Marianne... where the devil have you been?..."

Miss Van der Creff made no reply but leaned more heavily on Trimingham's arm.

"She is the worse for wear, I am afraid..." Trim said.

The artist looked at Trimingham with disdain. "I thought you were running a translation service..." he said laconically, "not a bawdy house!"

"We *are* running a translation service!" Trimingham felt his temper rising. "She has taken it upon herself to become intoxicated."

"Really!" said the fellow. "I don't see how... being that she is short of the blunt just now..."

"She obtained alcohol on our bill... we could not prevent her."

"Did you even try?" offered the self-opinionated Jermain.

"Be quiet, Jermain!" said Marianne. "He is one of my employers... do not offend him."

The artist took her by the elbow, away from Trimingham. "I assume she has had gin?"

"I believe so... but I did not arrive until the last minute..."

"You should not have allowed her any gin! It always has this effect on her..."

"We did not *allow* her... we could not stop her." Trimingham was about to see red and express his greater annoyance – a rare occurrence for him – when Jermain spoke first, to Marianne. "Mr St.John has been waiting for half an hour... he expects you to sit for him."

Miss Van der Creff made a disparaging hissing noise and shook Jermain's hand away. "He will be disappointed... I must lie now... before I fall down."

Jermain grabbed her by the back of her cloak and held her upright. "Now we will lose revenue today... you should not let her anywhere near gin..." he said to Trimingham, with the self righteous air of someone who was receiving his daughter or sister home in a torrid state.

Re-adjusting his hat, Trimingham drew breath. "I have already explained to you, my good sir, that it was impossible for us to prevent her drinking..."

"Then you will know for next time," said Jermain loftily and pushed Miss Van der Creff further into the hallway.

"I do not know who you think you are speaking to... but there will not be a next time," said Trimingham with an overweening patience underlying his displeasure.

"So you are dispensing with her services?"

Trim hesitated. He wanted to affirm this but knew it was the wrong move; they needed a Dutch speaker and one who had another language besides, and Marianne was the only candidate in this provincial town. "Well, no... but we are not in the habit of going to the tavern in the middle of the day... there were extenuating circumstances..."

Jermain paused and turned, waiting for more details, but Trimingham faltered and wondered how to proceed.

"Mr Fairchild's wife... a renown jewel thief... has landed them in the shit!" explained Miss Van der Creff gaily.

"Mrs Fairchild is not a jewel thief," Trim said angrily, and Jermain lifted his brows. "Not Melissa Fairchild?"

"Yes... her!" said Marianne. "She dresses as a beggar and goes about snatching expensive jewels..."

Jermain took a step backwards in astonishment. "I have met her, whilst with Jacques Tisserand... she is an accomplished artist, and a woman of means. She has no need of such an activity..." he argued.

"'Tis merely an unfortunate misunderstanding and has now been cleared up..." Trim countered.

"Naturally it has!" said Jermain with superlative contempt. "Of course, the translating business offers the perfect cover for such practices..."

"Now listen here..." Trimingham stepped closer to Jermain to remonstrate, but Jermain was quicker and closed the door on him before anything further might be added.

* * *

Back at 'Golden Oaks' and some hour before, Mrs Wyevale had seen success from her vigilance – sitting on the chair and telling them she would wait all day if need be, in order to obtain more information about the money.

Richard had tried lying, wheedling and pleading with her to leave it in his hands. But his mother was implacable. Then he had fled upstairs, unable to take the stress any longer. Unable to withstand the mounting tension.

And Mrs Wyvale had then triumphed.

At length, Caroline had also caved in under the discomforting surveillance, felt even from her distant haze, and pointed to a small cabinet in the corner of the room, containing one tiny drawer. Hildegarde snatched it open and almost immediately discovered several samples of Melissa's signature in differing sizes and inks, on several pieces of paper. She took them and put them securely in her reticule. As soon as she reached home she would write a declaration on where she had found them and what they were, and lodge them with the attorney for safekeeping.

"Now, I am asking you, Caroline, woman to woman." She sat in front of Carolione's recumbent and drug-addled form, "to stop all this fraudulent activity... and to leave Melissa and Anthony in peace... I have the ear of several influential men... through my husband's position... and you will soon regret your nefarious doings. You will end up in jail. Do not be led more by Richard – if indeed 'tis him who does the leading... think carefully about your future..."

"Whatever you say, Mama," said Caroline lightly, seizing the nozzle of her pipe and sucking on it with desperation. "Just go away..."

"And do not call me Mama..." Hildegarde paused en route to the door. "And one more thing... where is your maid?"

Caroline frowned. "She will not do any of your bidding... she scarcely does any of mine."

"Where will I find her?" snapped Hildegarde.

"In the kitchen... dozing most likely..." Caroline's eyes were closing again, thankfully into oblivion.

Hildegarde went along the hallway and eventually located the kitchen, knocking on the door and calling Miriam's name. Miriam looked up from her rocking chair, sleep blurring her eyes. Hildegarde watched her with a mixture of sympathy and disdain, and perched herself on a wooden stool from the table, "Miriam..." she began. "I hope I may call you Miriam?..."

"Call me what you will, lady!" said the maid. "But if you wants tea or coffee you'll be unlucky. I'm tired out..."

"Indeed... I can see that. You are near to collapsing, if I am not much mistaken... so I have come to offer to take you from this foul place to one of rest."

"What do you mean?" Miriam demanded sharply, fearing abduction.

"You cannot work any longer... you are beyond it and will die."

"I's been working since I was a young wench." Miriam pulled a ragged soiled blanket up about her face and neck for protection.

"I am sure..." said Mrs Wyevale more gently. "But you are no longer a young wench. Why do you not let me take you in my carriage to safety?"

Miriam made a grumbling sound and surveyed the other woman. "What? To work for you?"

"No, no... not to work... I am wed to a bishop of this diocese... and we have a stipend for the upkeep of aged and infirm people... such as yourself... who need assistance... they can look after you."

"I don't want no charity, thank 'ee all the same, Mrs!"

"But Miriam, you cannot keep on in this way. You're not fit or well enough..."

It took a lot to get Miriam to see reason. It took patience and a lot of explaining and re-phrasing of words until the old woman could begin to see sense.

"Listen to me, my dear..." said Hildegarde, removing the verbal kid gloves, and aware of the time constraints and the bishop requiring his carriage for five p.m. "Your employer, Lady Wentworth... and my son they -"

"She b'aint no lady!" Miriam declared angrily. "She pretends to be, is all."

"Yes, indeed... she is a charlatan... so is my son, in truth! They are villainous... and they may be in serious trouble soon..." Hildegarde paused to allow Miriam to absorb this.

"With the dispatch office, I s'pose," said Miriam. "For giving false names on the house."

"No, far worse than the dispatch office... authorities higher than that," said Hildegarde. "They could be taken into charge... or forced to flee from here... and then you will be left alone... you may starve to death and no one will know. And I cannot keep coming back to check on you... 'Tis too far. You must come with me today... or you will perish here."

Miriam's small gimlet eyes grew large in her face which then crumpled into lines of muted distress. She closed her eyes and appeared to sleep. Another period of valuable time passed and Hildegarde was about to rouse her when she came to life and sat bolt upright, as if stunned. "Where's this place you talk of?"

"'Tis next to the cathedral... well, not far from it... 'tis an alms building... supported by wealthy people... churchgoers and others with philanthropic inclination... now and then given a grant by the ecumenical council... but mostly it is run by volunteers."

Miriam struggled to follow it all and did not understand half the words used. "What'ud I need to do there?" she interrupted sharply, her brain whirling from the intake of strange vocabulary.

"Nothing... if you did not wish... or you could perhaps polish and sweep in the cathedral... or various other churches, if you felt so inclined... you could also cook a little in the communal kitchen... if you felt strong enough, but no one will force you to do anything..."

And then suddenly the old lady relented and struggled up from her chair and went into the small room beyond to collect her meagre belongings. Hildegarde followed and was dismayed by the state of the unwashed bedding in which the woman slept, and the filthy bit of carpet that had been down for perhaps half a century, and the damp stains on the plaster walls. The cold, the drafts, the sheer degradation! She shut her eyes tightly, feeling the tears oozing behind her lids. It was beyond anything she might have feared in this house of villainy and degeneracy, encouraged by her middle son.

Eventually she was able to help Miriam down the steps from the kitchen door and around the side of the house, and saw the younger coachman pacing about impatiently near the carriage on the flat ground some fifty or so yards away.  She waved and he came running. "Where is Stephen?" she asked.

"The front porch, watching the door, Ma'am."

"Then kindly go and fetch him... we must help this lady into the carriage and leave instantly for St. Peter's Grove..."

"As you wish, Ma'am..." Simon sprinted through the neglected flowerbeds to find his colleague as Miriam hobbled in her badly fitting boots beside Hildegarde and they proceeded slowly along the lawn, which may at one time have been immaculate.

Richard, spotting them from upstairs, ran down and out of the house to them. "Where are you taking the maid?" he asked in a civil manner, as though it were an everyday occurrence to see his parent assisting his servant.

"To somewhere you cannot work her to death... now stand aside, Richard," said Hildegarde. "I cannot bear to look at you."

"Will you not let me offer some explanations?" cajoled Richard, "things are not as bad as they appear."

"No, they are far worse, and I do not want to hear any explanations... until you are able to decipher truth from lies... get out of my way!"

Simon was coming onto the grass with Stephen close behind. "Out of the way, if you please." he told Richard. "We will deal with this from here."

"How dare you!" said Richard grandly, "you may be the bishop's coachmen but you have no authority here..."

Stephen took Miriam's boney elbow and indicated for Simon to take the other, and between them they lifted her a little way off the ground, carrying her across the land, her feet dangling in her cumbersome boots and Miriam chuckling as if in her second childhood. already tasting the exultation of freedom. Mrs Wyevale following at a sedate pace behind.

"Did you not hear me, my good man?" called Richard, sprinting alongside. "Put our maid down at once." He stepped into their path.

The elder coachman halted the march. "I'll be putting you down if you don't clear off... nor will you be getting up for a while. Your mother's wishes are to be heard." He pushed Richard to one side and they carried on with the transportation of Miriam to the carriage and lifted her in. Assisting Hildegarde in after her. She gave Miriam a rug to put around her legs.

"Who do you be, again, Lady?" asked Miriam of Hildegarde once they had set off. "You b'aint from these parts. I can tell from your speech betimes."

"I am married to the bishop of the diocese." explained Hildegarde again.

"Is that like a duke?" enquired Miriam politely.

"No... but perhaps similar in terms of rank and influence... I came originally from Denmark."

"Aaah..." sighed Miriam triumphantly. "I think I been there once... just past Hastings, b'ain't it?"

Hildegarde laughed merrily and handed Miriam a barley sugar sweet, hoping to deflect more questions. "Yes, Miriam... 'Tis somewhere out that way."

Miriam was satisfied and watched with eagerness the scenic countryside flying by. Not having ventured from Golden Oaks for many a year.

A ten minute period passed in tranquillity and Hildegarde dozed and dreamt vividly. The motion of the carriage at high speed always induced sleep and dreams. She dreamt that she was standing on the shoreline at Hastings and watching Richard on a small sailing vessel moving out to sea, waving and beckoning to her to sail out to him. She had sailed a lot as a girl in her seafaring village, and she looked about her and saw a rowing boat which she knew from experience she could manage alone. But William, her husband, was standing with her, she thought... or was it Rupert?... or Anthony?... or even perhaps Joseph, the father of her sons? She was about to run to the boat and began removing her boots when whichever man it was grabbed her to prevent her leaving.

She awoke with a start and found Miriam clutching her arm and looking at her beseechingly

"What is the matter?" she muttered, coming from the confusion of sleep.

"You sure you b'ain't taking me to no workhouse?" said the old woman. "I don't want to end my days in one of them places. You swear it won't be a workhouse?"

"No, Miriam... it is not a workhouse. It is an alms house... belonging to the diocese."

"You promise?" said Miriam.

Hildegarde shook her head to rid herself of the dream and sat upright and cleared her throat. The old woman still clutching her arm with a claw-like grip. "Miriam, I am wed to a man of God and am a practising christian... I do not tell lies or take people to places they do not wish to go... I promise we are going to St Peter's Grove, an alms house... if you wish I will let you out of the carriage before me and you can go inside and look for yourself before I join you."

Miriam hummed and aaghed and swivelled her eyes around the coach interior. "I believe you... I think you's a good woman. So's I trust you."

"Indeed!" said Hildegarde. "You can trust me!... my son, of course, has given you reason to trust no one ever again... along with his paramour... but you can trust me, Miriam... be assured."

Miriam released her grip and settled back into the seat, before turning her head again to the bishop's wife and smiling, revealing gums with no discernible teeth. "One more thing?... a'fore you doze."

"Yes?" said Hildegarde politely.

"Please can I have another of them sweets?"

* * *

In 'Golden Oaks' Richard had removed Caroline's drug from her and was attempting to make her drink coffee. She spat it out as he poured it into her mouth and it dribbled in a sickening manner down the front of her dress. He gave up in disgust and paced the room. "Caro, we have to leave." he told her ominously. "Now try to stand and walk about."

"Do not... be... so fatuous!" drawled Carolione. "I can... no more stand... than I can fly to the moon."

"You must! Or I shall leave you here..." He began collecting things from drawers and cupboards and pushing them into a large case. Then he came upon the small cabinet. "Where the devil are the signatures?" he demanded.

Caroline seemed without comprehension of the question, her head lolling about on the back of the chaise longue.

"Melissa's original signature... and the forgeries!" he repeated in a louder voice. Then he crossed to her and shook her vigorously so that her head rolled on her shoulders. "Think Caro... where have you put them?"

"She has them?"

"Who?"

"Your mama... she took them with her."

"What?... how did she find them?"

Caroline was coming round a little, the room and her life coming into immediate and bleak focus. "How should I know?... Perhaps she has supernatural powers."

"Did you tell her where they were?"

"No." she lied.

"I do not believe you... you gave in to her pressure, did you not? You let her know where they were!"

"I did not... but perhaps I glanced in that direction."

Richard seethed and rubbed his chin with quivering fingers. He looked from the windows helplessly, where the encroaching night had eclipsed the daylight to form the country darkness. "You feckless bitch." He slapped her and then pulled her upright and walked her about in the drawing room.

"Don't you dare touch me..." she screeched, her steps faltering so that her body sagged and hung from his arm. "'Tis my house, not yours."

He walked with her until she could move in a straight line. "Miriam..." she yelled. "Miriam, come here at once."

"That is no good... she has gone! We have to do what we need for ourselves now."

"Gone!... gone where?"

"With my mother, of course... to some place of charity, I expect. Rescued by my parent, who cares more for her plight than mine."

Caroline chortled and sank to her knees in exhaustion. "Your plight?... you have no plight... you idiotic selfish man."

"Caro, we have to leave... quickly, this night."

"Why?"

"Because she will show the signature to someone in authority... and those two girls will swear witness to what you carelessly said. One of them wed to a Q.C..."

"So dramatic!" bemoaned Caroline. "She may say nothing to anyone. You simply have to stop meddling with Anthony and his wife now, that's all."

"She is done with me... we will be taken into charge on a number of accounts."

"I do not think she will do that... much as she may wish to... she is your mother, after all."

He pulled her upright and led her up the stairs. Half carrying and half dragging her. "They will prevail on her... Anthony will prevail on her, and so may Rupert... not to mention her husband, the bishop. I am a blight on our family."

"You would be a blight on anyone's family," sneered Caroline.

"You must pack some things." He pushed her into the bedroom.

"Pack some things?"

"Yes... we have to leave... in case they come in the early morning before it is quite light."

"Where do you think we will go?"

"I do not know yet... France perhaps."

Caroline's knees were buckling beneath her, and she collapsed onto the bed. "I do not wish to go there..." she said petulantly. "I do not care for it there... they are too snooty and aloof... they gabble away in French and they do not -"

"Caroline!" interjected Richard. "It matters not... we cannot stay here. Or you can stay alone if you wish. But I do not intend to spend years in jail... or worse!"

She looked up at him from her recumbent position. "Well, you go alone then... leave me to face the music. If you must. I am not going to France."

"Holland then?" said Richard. "But get up and pack... or I will leave you here."

She made an unflattering curl of her mouth and fluttered her eyelids, and was altogether not in the right frame of mind to think. "Holland?... I do not know... possibly... but certainly not France."

# Every Cloud

Melanie frowned and tutted about the lack of variety in cakes and confectionery at the Pink Parrot. "Hurry up and choose..." Melissa said. "We don't have all day!"

"Oh, very well... the sponge cake... but not if it has strawberry jam. I prefer raspberry or blackcurrant..."

"You will eat what you are given..." Melissa chided in a parody of her grandmother in former days, and as the place was two assistants down, she went to the counter to give the fresh order.

"Your mother-in-law is a force to be reckoned with..." Melanie told her as she poured tea. "She is truly a Viking woman!"

"No wonder she produced Atilla!"

The cake arrived, with the wrong jam, and Melanie scowled again. Melissa swapped their plates so that Melanie had the marble cake and looked a little happier. "'Tis like being with a five year old." Melissa sighed.

Melanie smiled, aware that her food fads could be tedious. *Geoffrey had stopped indulging them and recently told her she was lucky to eat at all, given the state of the country, and that she was not to encourage Robert or any other of their children into such demanding culinary habits.*

"Anthony once told me that his mother's strength was why his father was so successful in his vocation." Melissa said, "her work within the community as the parson's wife... and people's trust and respect for her... and you know, I believe that is real strength when a person can do that."

Melanie was now not entirely happy with the marble cake, and she stared at it on her plate with a bite taken from it, as if it could answer for its own shortcomings." Of course, Hildegarde was serving her own ends as well, with all this selfless service..." she commented.

Melissa paused in her eating and deliberated; there were definitely two ways to look at it. "But if it helped everyone involved, it was the right thing, surely?"

Melanie disregarded the philosophy and drew breath. "I think we should ask her to think of the next move..." she said, flapping the menu in front of her friend's eyes to gain her attention. "Lissy, are you listening? *Is Lissy listening!*"

"Move with regard to what?"

"The question of the missing money..."

"She will say she does not know... and to seek advice elsewhere."

"But then she will really know what the next move is... and be putting on an appearance of innocence, I imagine," supplied Melanie. "In her guileful... or *competent* manner!"

Melissa sat very still and did not offer a reaction. It pained her to think of the matter. She still had not informed her father. Though her cousin Jasper knew and it was surely only a matter of time before he told him. It was Easter next week in late March. "It has been more than two months now... since they took that money!" Melanie said.

"I am aware!" rejoined Melissa. "But they will not obtain any more... Hildegarde has lodged the evidence with her solicitor... the church's solicitors, no less."

"Does the church have such a thing?" queried Melanie.

"Of course... they are not idiots."

"But she has done nothing with the evidence?" Melanie gave up on the marble cake and picked up the menu.

Melissa gazed from the window. "Richard and Caroline have disappeared from 'Golden Oaks,' it seems... so it is supposed pointless to take any further action."

Melanie dropped the menu in shock. "Disappeared where?"

"Idiotic question!" Melissa remarked, not turning from her observation of the street.

"And why are you only just telling me this?" Melanie put the menu to one side and frowned heavily, then hurried over to the counter and called to them to bring other confectionery.

"How do you know they have disappeared?" she said as she sat again.

"Jasper told us... his father is embroiled to some extent in Richard's bank. He learned it from his father... Also, Rupert and Hildegarde tried paying a visit to 'Golden Oaks' and found it deserted with boarded up windows."

Melanie was agog with disbelief. "But what... what about that old lady, the maid?"

Brightening perceptibly, Melisa giggled and said. "Hildegard rescued her that very day... took her to St. Peter's Grove..."

The cake arrived, delivered by a harassed looking girl of thirteen who normally stayed in the kitchen. "Thank you, poppet." Melanie handed her some pennies.

The girl looked surprised and then guilty, and then around at the counter to see who was watching. She was not supposed to keep any gratuities. "Thank you, Ma'am," she said and bobbed a curtsy.

"That was good of you." Melissa lifted her tea cup and Melanie hers, and they clinked them gently together.

"Nonsense..." said the ever generous Melanie and changed the subject. "I would not have been surprised to hear Miriam was taken to your house... and has since found a suitor from your enchanted woods!"

Melissa carrolled laughter. "Even I would struggle to match Miriam now... she must be eighty at the very least."

"There is always St. Peter's Grove... think of the destitute and distressed elderly gentleman she might encounter there."

It was not a highly amusing suggestion, but would do as a source of today's amusement, so they giggled unrepentantly. When Melanie had recovered, she became grave in the opposite way. The new cake had nearly all vanished, and she made a playful fork grab for the last piece and won. "I still think we should take up sleuthing..." she paused, and Melissa shut her eyes tight to denote patient disapproval. "Not this again... there is my art to consider."

"Yes, but what better cover... a young lady artist with an easel... you could use it as camouflage..." said Melanie skittishly.

They had discussed the topic some weeks ago, from a humorous and a speculative perspective. It was appealing whichever way they looked at it – if somewhat outlandish. But then again, stranger things took place in this bizarre world.

"If we plan it carefully... no one will know we are behind it... we simply examine the findings and use our brains... and of course see to the finances," Melanie repeated for perhaps the sixth time.

"And what if Geoffrey and Anthony find out?... they will not like it."

"We make certain they do not."

"Preposterous, Mel!... things like that are bound to become known!"

"Think of the good we could do..." said Melanie, not ready to give up as yet. "We would work only for other ladies... think of how many women there must be in need of that kind of service... who have no recourse to help or rights but need to obtain knowledge..."

Melissa had finished eating and was chewing the skin beside her thumbnail, as an aid to contemplation. "But you want more children... and I have commissions and will have more... where is the time?" She opened her reticule and took out her purse, and summoned the main assistant in order to pay.

"Lissy, we would perhaps only have one or two cases a year... to start with... until we are known. We could be discerning about what we choose to take on!"

Melissa stared at her with a hard look, frowning. "Hmmm."

"It would occupy hardly any time at all... but would be diverting. It would stop us from growing bored or complacent."

"We could do something else to prevent that."

"Like what?"

"I do not know as yet... but this will never be accepted... or acceptable."

"Only if our identities became known... 'Tis not as if we are considering a millinery shop on the high street..."

"Should you like to do that?" asked Melissa, watching the waitress disappear with the money for the bill.

"Certainly not... I can think of nothing worse..."

"Obviously not, with your history! Fourteen hats in twenty minutes and counting... 'Tis enough to discourage anyone!"

Melanie ignored the wit, though it was true, in favour of serious discourse. "Besides, that would be trade... whereas the sleuthing would make us professionals."

"Meddling busy-bodies, you mean!..."

More giggling and then a straightening of blouses and skirts prior to leaving.

"I can see you are quite tempted..." Melanie offered, holding the door for Melissa to exit first.

"Perhaps... but that doesn't mean I am confident or willing..."

Melanie stopped abruptly, causing the other girl to collide with her on the pavement. "You see, we need not charge... not at first... we could work for nothing unless we had success."

"You mean... like a hobby?"

"Yes... a philanthropic pursuit for the good of those who require it..."

"Hmm," murmured Melissa again and pushed Melanie slightly so that she would begin moving and not clog up the entrance to the shop. "You make us sound like angels of mercy... indispensable to the larger community."

"Just so..." Melanie began her brisk walking pace and spoke over her shoulder. "You see, Lissy, women who are clever and talented like ourselves should not waste it on silly drawing room pursuits... or embroidering altar cloths and tray cloths... and the like. We should be furthering the cause of our own gender in ways that are necessary..."

Melissa stared at her before relapsing into merriment. "I suppose you see yourself giving chase to some miscreant or other devious character on one of your father's faster steeds before it is sold."

Melanie tossed her head. "Do not be ridiculous... I would be trotting behind a seasoned rider at a sedate pace and keeping a low profile while they did the dirtier business!"

They were using Melanie's coach and watched it slow up as it reached the near kerbside to allow them to board. "Well... let us refine on it a little," Melissa concluded. "In fact... I think we should discuss it next week... but not in the Parrot."

"No... nor in either of our houses." Melanie agreed with a brighter expression. "Perhaps in the large cemetery ... since the weather is growing milder by the day... we could stroll around there before the tea shop and not be overheard."

The large cemetery was a favourite place to walk. Many large trees and arboretums, and lawned areas with monuments and benches.

"But not on Tuesday... or Thursday..." Melissa put in as the carriage began moving. "My mother and Aunt Dorothea are fond of walking there on those days..."

"What on earth for?" Melanie lost her bright face and grimaced.

"To inspect the new graves and the recently deceased names and so forth..."

"How very morbid!"

"They are both inclined to morbidity in the extreme... especially Aunt Dorothea... surely you know that by now?"

The coach swerved to avoid a young boy pushing a barrow full of vegetables, and they held fast to the seat edge as the groom leaned out and cursed the boy roundly, then begged their pardon for the language. "Besides, they have so little else to occupy their time... there must be a limit to the shops they may visit." Melissa continued.

"You see... we do not want to end up like them!" declared Melanie in some triumph.

"No, but we will not... whether we sleuth or not!" retorted Melissa, trumping her ace. "Your mother is not morbid in the least is she!... and she leads a very quiet life."

"Only because she lacks imagination!" said Melanie glibly. "What about Wednesday next?"

"Yes... Wednesday... but let us change the subject now. Your groom may be listening."

*  *  *

At Back Lane House, meantime, Honoria was pursuing the peaceful and highly acceptable passtime of mending torn pillow cases and other delicate items. While occasionally breaking her needle rhythm to gaze from the window at the birds. The birds were profuse now in the small garden encompassing the house. And she eagerly awaited the return of Isaac Fairchild from his travels. Now and then fearful that he may have changed his mind about becoming wed to her. Anthony and Melissa had both assured her that would not happen. His cousin, said Anthony, was not a man of fickle whim or precarious promise. He was steadfast and reliable. And Melissa told her that no gentleman did such a thing. '*But why not?*' she wanted to know. If women did it, why could men not do it? It was different for men, Melissa told her. It was just one of those accepted things, mooted in the aeon of time in polite society.

Honoria was vaguely aware of hearing carriage hooves a little before the doorbell clanged but did not rise to answer – chaffinches were abounding, and she had just spotted a Eurasian bullfinch, she thought! – and anyway Peggy loved answering the door and announcing peoples names; usually quite wrongly.

At length Peggy entered to say that Mrs Shaw had arrived, with her sister and another lady, who was heavily veiled. Honoria discarded the sewing and rose and greeted aunts Marguerite and Dorothea, both smiling – suspicious in itself that Dorothea was smiling. But Honoria smiled back and curtsied briefly.

"Anthony and Melissa are not at home presently, Aunts..." she said, "That is very well. 'Tis you we are here to see..." said Dorothea. "And we have brought a visitor."

The heavily veiled lady was her mother.

Honoria gasped as she revealed herself. "Are you in mourning, Mama?"

"No, no... " Her mother smiled, rushing forward to embrace her. "Simply not wishing to be recognised lest it get back to your father that I have been here."

Honoria suffered herself to be hugged and kissed by her mother and smiled thinly in some trepidation. She was not displeased to see her parent, but unsure of her welcome in the house overall.

"How splendid you look..." said Harriet, holding Honoria at arm's length. "How you have blossomed."

"Have I?" enquired Honoria modestly.

"Indeed... you are quite transformed."

"That is what happens when a girl is allowed to be a young lady... rather than a servant!" murmured Dorothea through tight lips.

Harriet flushed and said, "That was none of my doing, Thea!"

"Even so..." persevered her eldest sister, not one to shy from the truth. "You did nought to oppose it, as far as I can see."

"Let us not quarrel..." Marguerite interposed and looked Honoria over.

"I hear you are engaged to be wed!" said Harriet, holding onto her hand as if she may flee. "To Anthony's cousin."

"Indeed, Mama... I am."

"How wonderful."

"Yes, I am very happy."

"And you have another admirer... so your aunt Maggie tells me..."

"Do I?" Honoria looked puzzled. "Oh, you do not mean Jasper?... do you?"

"Yes, Jasper Montalbein..."

"No, he was never serious about me."

"I think he was, my dear," argued Dorothea.

Honoria blushed. "He is not someone a lady may easily take seriously."

"Perhaps not..." said Marguerite, looking around somewhat disapprovingly at the less than immaculate chairs and faded decor, "but many ladies would love the chance to do so... he is already quite well off, and as my husband's nephew will grow wealthier."

"Is your fiancé wealthy?" asked Harriet with assumed innocence.

"I am not sure... he is not penniless, certainly..." said Honoria. "He is a professor of natural history... and an ornithologist."

"Not wealthy then," concluded Harriet on a down tone.

"No. no, Harriet!... do not presume! Melissa tells me he has acquired money from sound investment... and he has his parents' legacy to inherit, of course!" supplied Marguerite

Harriet brightened and smiled and nodded and was lost for words as she gazed more upon her daughter, saying at length. "I will tell your father of the news, now I know more..."

"Please do not, Mama," opined Honoria. "He may try to come here... and will not be welcome."

"But he is entitled to know of your engagement," complained Harriet.

"If only to see if he may borrow money..." added Dorothea in an aside and was nudged by Marguerite. *The poor girl was disadvantaged enough by having Leonard Ainscoe as her father without having further insult added upon his name.* They all turned to surveying the room and what Melissa had made of it. And then Melissa herself arrived and was amazed at the unannounced visit.

"I hope it is alright for Mama to call..." Honoria said to her cousin anxiously. Melissa shrugged off her cloak and kissed them all in turn on their cheek. "Of course it is," she assured. "As long as she has not brought your father along..."

Harriet cast her eyes downward, and Honoria blushed. "That is what I have just been saying... that he must not be encouraged to call."

Marguerite, as always, took the peace-making role. "There is no need to be so churlish about the man!" she said. "This is to be a joyous reunion."

"There is every reason, Mama!" countered Melissa. "He offended Anthony quite badly and I do not know how the next visit may play out if he returns... Anthony cannot abide vulgarity and impoliteness."

"Indeed!" chorussed Honoria. "Anthony must not be offended a second time by him."

Marguerite shared a brief exchange of glances with Dorothea, whom she had already informed of Honoria's adoration of her son-in-law. Dorothea twitched her lips to denote minor amusement, then raised her brows. "I am sure he will cope. A gentleman of his accomplishment."

"Oh, he will! He is able to deal with all kinds of people, given his campaigning experience and lobbying skills," affirmed Honoria. "But that is quite beside the point."

Marguerite now enjoyed another glance with her elder sister after this ringing endorsement, and Melissa said. "But fear not, ladies, this shall be a joyous occasion... I shall go forthwith and organise refreshment... if you have not already had such."

"They have not..." Honoria hastened to the door herself. "And 'tis fortunate that we have made date plum and ginger muffins, only this morning..."

"So you still bake whilst here?" queried Harriet.

"Oh, she does!" affirmed Melissa. "She undertakes a lot of domestic tasks... I do not know how we will go on without her... and everyone looks forward to her confectionery delights..." She thought of her husband as the main exception to the rule, who invented excuses to avoid the rich and overly sweet produce Honoria tried tempting him with. "In fact, I do believe 'tis her apple, fig and butter cream tarts which won over Isaac's heart... not to mention his stomach."

"I do hope that is not true," Honoria said.

Some polite laughter at the jest, and Honoria and Melissa left for the kitchen. As soon as the door had closed, Harriet turned to her sisters. "Is this Isaac as good looking as his cousin Anthony?" she whispered.

Marguerite was about to retort when Dorothea said. "By no means... he does not have the physique, or hair, and is a little round shouldered... though he is pleasant of feature... do you not agree, Maggie?"

"I have not had time to properly assess him, except briefly on twelfth night," said Marguerite, "but he seems a pleasant man in all ways."

"And one cannot have everything..." added the pragmatic Dorothea

"I do believe..." whispered Marguerite, "from what I am told, that Isaac is wealthier than Anthony presently... overall."

"My, my!" gasped Harriet in some awe. "Nonetheless, instinct tells me that Honoria would prefer to be wed to Anthony... were he not already spoken for."

"Possibly true," said Marguerite vaguely. "She looks up to him as a paragon, in all things, it seems."

"Let us not be coy..." muttered Dorothea, twitching her lips again in even greater amusement. "Any young woman might prefer to be married to Anthony... given the chance."

Soft and subtle merriment ensued from the sisters, alone in the drawing room, as if they were young girls again.

* * *

In his office in town, *the paragon* himself was sitting with his feet on his desk and watching Jasper Montalbein swig claret, seated opposite in the visitor's chair, listening to the rumour of a sighting of his detested brother in a lakeside village. "Are you sure," he asked, for the third time, "that this is reliable information?"

"As sure as damn it... and the source from which—" Jasper paused in mid sentence as the door opened and Miss Van der Creff entered. She smiled at Jasper in the most sanguine of ways and he smiled in return.

"Yes, Miss Van der Creff?" said Fairchild briskly. "I thought I said we were not to be disturbed."

"I did not hear that!" replied the translator in her haughtiest tone, her eyes still on the visitor and warmer than her voice. "But the clerk of the bank has called... they require a second signature on something. You must attend tomorrow at your first convenience."

"Must I?" Fairchild said facetiously.

"That is clerk person speaking,... not me!" added Miss Van der Creff in her quirky vernacular.

"Please lock the office door... I do not require any further interruption today." summarised Fairchild.

"In fifteen minutes I shall be not here..." supplied Miss Van der Creff. She backed out of the room, winking at Jasper Monalbein as she did so. Jasper took a moment – he was unused to females in commercial positions enticing him in such blatant ways. It was barely four of the clock. "Who was that?" he asked.

"A translator..." said Fairchild.

"But more specifically, if you please? She winked at me."

"She is not English..."

"Does that matter?"

"She makes those kind of gestures to many men who call."

Jasper considered the issue. Having been gently spurned by the gracious Honoria, his roving eye had opened once more.

Fairchild laughed and said. "Do not tell me you are perceiving Miss Van der Creff now as the wifely sort?"

"No, obviously not!... but perhaps..."

"Perhaps what?... sport?"

"Yes!" said Jasper and gave into a wider grin.

Fairchild reneged on his previous resolve and brought another glass in which to pour his own claret. "She might be too much, Jasper!... even for you."

"You surmise so?"

"Depends how you feel about women in states of inebriation. She loves to quaff."

"Oddly enough, Tony, so do I!"

"Yes, but she does it at the most ill-conceived times and inappropriately... she all but rendered it impossible for us to go into the Feathers after a display she made a few weeks back."

Jasper swirled the wine about the glass and deliberated. Perhaps he would call in again on some pretext. But then perhaps he had enough on his personal agenda. Perhaps he merely sought a balm to his heart – somewhat bruised, he was astonished to find, by Honoria's recent betrothal to a man she had barely known for more than a few weeks, as opposed to himself whom she had watched mature, albeit from a distance, since childhood. He needed balm perhaps from the kind of woman who would not take him seriously and he would not need to cherish. Honoria's rebuttal of his well-intentioned charms had put him off the wife trail temporarily. *Supposing she had accepted his suit simply to prosper herself, and then spurned him after marriage! Such things happened all the time, with ruthless females and foolish men.* He was more sensitive on the matter of women, it seemed, than he cared to admit. He stared into the few remaining dregs of wine and looked morose.

Fairchild said. "Jasper, you do not need to begin hunting them so zealously... you will not find the right wife that way. Allow things to happen naturally."

He looked over at Fairchild, who had yet again displayed the knack of reading another's mind. It had been noted in the family; in business meetings and other more informal occasions: he seemed to possess the ability to penetrate what was not being said. Giles Shaw spoke of it, praising it as shrewd. It was more than shrewd. But Jasper hesitated to put a name to it. Anthony Fairchild was a boon to the art of second guessing what associates and others were thinking, even though languages were his main remit. Or perhaps because they were his remit. Jasper stared at him without speaking. "And," Fairchild continued more softly. "On the question of Honoria... you are better off not marrying her... she might not have made you happy. You are too unalike."

"Perhaps not." He considered the possibility. *Honoria was family to his Uncle Giles who gave her consideration now, in the way he gave Melissa consideration, and his sister Amaelia (Jasper's own mother) and his other sisters. Giles had grown up with many sisters and loved his feminine relations to be about him. Honoria was fond of bringing Giles food she had made herself and leaving them with the butler... grapefruit or rhubarb marmalade... syllabubs... exotic pickle... the delights were endless! Giles adored receiving these gifts made specifically for him; Jasper had noted his delighted expression on occasions when the butler had shown them to him before taking them to the kitchen. No other of the females around did such things for him and he was moved by it. If he married Honoria and she was unhappy, Giles would take it badly. His own lauded position in the family business may then suffer. He could see that clearly from the current point in time...*

"She is eminently better suited to Isaac..." his cousin-in-law was telling him. "He is far more..."

"More what?" snapped Jasper, his jealous rivalry springing from nowhere. "What?"

"Well, homely perhaps," said Fairchild. "They sit together discussing the birds and other trivia and are quite content."

"Homely!" Jasper sat up straighter. "From what I have heard he is never in the blasted country!"

"Yes... but only because of his work... and that will change when he marries her, he will -"

"I can be homely if I choose!" cut in Jasper.

Fairchild laughed. "For an hour perhaps... but then you would be bored. Isaac is never bored with her."

Jasper grunted tetchily; here was that grain of truth he was loath to swallow and was unequal to denying right now.

"Or you might have made *her* unhappy... which is worse... no man wants an unhappy wife... no good comes of it." Fairchild was uncannily reading his mind again.

"Indeed! But Honoria is the kind of woman who introduces a man to his own soul... and makes him gentler... do you not find?"

Fairchild's turn to stare. "I do... I could not have phrased it better myself."

"So I am heartsore, I am ashamed to admit..." conceded Jasper.

"Do not be ashamed on my part..." Fairchild offered. "I have been so heartsore in years past, I almost put an end to myself." Jasper raised his brows and waited. "There is no shame in it... unless a man has known sorrow he may remain only half a man."

"Yes, so I now need some sport." Jasper said.

"That will be easy enough to ascertain." replied the other off-handedly.

"Oh it is!" agreed Montalbein. "And you must concede, Tony, that few men can resist being winked at by fulsome flaxen haired females of mature years but not yet old?..."

Fairchild frowned and did not reply. He was conjecturing seriously but then knew it to be wasted effort. He cleared his throat. "So... returning to this rumour." He said. "When exactly was this sighting?..."

"Last week, I think."

"He may be gone now."

"Yes... or in hiding."

"Was she with him?"

"Caroline?... no, not in evidence anyway."

"I may go over there."

Jasper rose. He should not have said anything. "Tony, leave it... the money will be returned. I am certain of it."

"How can you be so certain?"

He tapped his nose with his forefinger. "Just leave it with me."

"What is it you are not telling me?" said Fairchild.

Buttoning his coat, the other man paused. "'Tis something like my recent dilemma with Honoria... the consequences of remaining ignorant and doing nothing are less threatening than risking triumph but losing."

# In Praise of Marmalade

They were strolling in the large cemetery. An archaic and somberly majestic place, where costly monuments and mausoleums stood in various sizes. Glimmering in splendour in the sunshine. Gravestones sporting winged angels... white marble saints with outstretched arms... headstones bearing glass photo frames depicting the inhabitants of the graves. A cemetery favoured by the well off. It was hard to know, when walking around, what to look at next.

It was almost Easter. Melissa was inspired to share her feelings in this hallowed place and the conversation turned to emotions and husbands. "I used to think 'twas his physical beauty I loved so much... now I see 'tis not actually that at all... that is merely a trick of the light." she told Melanie as they seated themselves in a shadowy glade where a dilapidated bench gave a reclusive view onto everyone passing without them readily being seen.

"Surely not?" retorted her friend, who did not quite understand the abstract thinking. "How can a person's look be a trick of the light?"

"Easily... ask any artist... or actor, perhaps."

"What, in all manner of light?"

"Yes... my experience has taught me it was just that... 'Tis his character and mind I am drawn to... it reflects on his face, of course, which helps..."

Melanie screwed up her own face for contemplation; she was always at a loss to really understand how her closest friend had become permanently attached to her oldest enemy. But she never let it come between them.

"Let us talk of the sleuthing?" Melissa said.

"It will be an inquiry agency." corrected Melanie. "That is what it is to be called."

"Inquiring into what?"

"Whatever needs inquiring into which cannot be done under normal circumstances."

"And what makes us equal to the *abnormal* circumstances?"

"Our wits and cunning and our ability to think cleverly, of course..."

"Does it not somehow conflict with Geoffrey's work? He may be adversely affected by it if it becomes known." Melissa said.

"If we run into anything illegal or criminal we will refuse to have any more to do with it."

Melissa stared straight ahead at a newly arrived funeral procession proceeding deep into the grounds of the cemetery, all dressed in black, like a flock of giant crows. "What if we do not succeed?" Melissa asked.

"In what?"

"In any given case..."

"Then there is no charge..."

"I thought you said there was no charge anyway?"

Melanie smiled and stared up at the dense foliage of leaves above them, entanglement from many decades of growth. "That was only to soften your concerns... of course there will be a charge... but we can give it to charity if you wish... to the alms school, for example."

It was coming on to rain and dampness pervaded the air. Melissa frowned. "And where do we hold the office?"

"Nowhere... we place adverts in journals and papers and are contacted by letter at a post restante... and then we perhaps meet in places of designated convenience to clients and ourselves..."

There was an elongated silence, and then Melissa opened her mouth and her eyes wide, as if stunned by revelation. Suddenly she saw how it might all work.

* * *

"So, I thought we could use this as a trial run... for our first inquiry." she said, some days later, concluding the report of Jasper's possible sighting of Richard Fairchild.

Melanie looked at her and held little Robert's hands as he made his tentative walking steps. "Well... if you are sure!... but is it wise, a circumstance so close to home?"

"I will just take that chance... as I always do..." Melissa reached for Robert's hands and took over the walking exercise which was excruciating to the lower back after a while.

"'Tis certainly tempting!" Melanie sank onto the sofa. "Do you know where this place is?"

"Not really, beyond the general direction... but there are signposts along the roads no doubt... and we have a large map in the bureau drawer... and tongues in our heads. It is not more than twelve or fifteen miles away, according to Anthony."

The maid was summoned and tea was brought. They said nothing more until the tea arrived and Melanie was pouring. "It might be a half day of travelling, all told... but it strikes me that it's a perfect opportunity on two counts..."

"It struck me that way too," said Melissa.

They drank the tea casually and watched Robert crawl and attempt to stand and fall back and start all over again – as in so many of life's challenges.

At length Melanie replaced her cup and gave a relenting sigh. "Very well... if the weather is fine on Saturday, let us leave about eleven o'clock? If 'tis a small place it should only take an hour or so to ask questions and look about."

"Very well... I can say I am at High Lawns and then at High Lawns I can tell them I have gone for art materials."

"We must think of plausible reasons why we are gone so long though... in case we are delayed." Melanie pronounced.

"Indeed..." Melissa sprang up swiftly and kissed little Robert and said. "Ones that cannot be proved or disproved... I will depart, before the trap is needed urgently at home."

* * *

Saturday morning dawned bright with clear skies, a slight breeze and that constant feeling of sun somewhere near the horizon but never quite manifesting. It was actually perfect weather for driving the trap. Melissa was about to rise, having received a first cup of coffee in bed as usual from Peggy. She put her feet out of bed and stretched and frisked her hair with her fingers and yawned and then was surprised as he approached silently, not yet himself dressed. "Where are you going?" he asked quietly.

"I am rising, is that not obvious?"

"I have other ideas for you..." He climbed in beside her, and she sighed with impatience which he took to be desire in some form. Normally she loved to be detained in this manner in the morning, but not this one. He pinned her down as she wriggled to escape and looked at her with undisguised longing. "I must go to High Lawns..." she told him.

He began kissing her and nibbling her neck and she was resisting the urges this brought. "Not until I have finished with you..." he said into her neck, his mouth finding her exposed ear.

She would just have to miss breakfast and that was not the worst obstacle in the world. She made love with him, furiously matching his ardour with a rhythm of hunger and a longing to reach orgasm.

"Slow down!" he told her. "We are not in a race."

"I cannot..." She thrust her hips upwards and squoze his penis with her perineal muscle to spur on his climax.

"Why?" He caressed her nipples with just the right kind of pressure. She was quickly succumbing to the kind of bodily languor which would not disturb itself for anything. It was beyond her control. "Oh, stop..."

"Why?" His voice was a soft growl, his tone not serious, his question politely indifferent.

She remained silent, giving in to her need for satisfaction. Her eyes closing and her senses withdrawing from the outer world and the tyranny of time. He rode her for several minutes and she lost herself, along with previous intentions to meet schedules.

Then came unexpected interruptions. The doorbell clanged. Timothy Trimingham and Jasper Montalbein arrived simultaneously, their voices audible on the porch below the window and then in the hall. It gave him pause and he slowed his ardour but did not withdraw from her.

"We must get up... I think that is Trim and possibly Jasper." she whispered.

"Let them wait..."

She was on top of him now, partly lying on the bed and partly twined around him, his mouth on her throat and his hands on her breasts. "They can sit in the drawing room..."

"Is it not rude?" she whispered, her voice husky with satisfaction.

"'Tis Saturday!... so, no... and it is but ten of the clock, at the latest."

But the mood was diluted. Their ardour fighting the demands of polite society. Their hunger diminished by lingering echoes of the presence of kith and kin below.

At length, he rolled onto his back and closed his eyes and groaned, and she fell onto her side and tried to ignore the downstairs intrusions. Then Peggy knocked on the door.

"What is it, Peggy?" he called. "We are busy." He did not scruple these days to disguise their bedroom activity under any pretext and Peggy understood. "Mr Mottlebin and Mr Trimingham are here... Mr Mottlebin says he can wait but fifteen minutes..."

"Good of him." muttered Fairchild, then in a louder voice. "Tell them I shall be about five minutes... and Peggy..." he paused until Peggy replied. "Do not call him Mr Mottlebin to his face... the correct name is *Montalbein...*"

They heard her giggling softly and her scurrying tread down the passageway.

"Strange they have arrived together..." Melissa said. "Is it a joint errand, do you think?"

"Highly unlikely... they are not that well acquainted." He sprang up and began pulling on his shirt from yesterday and searching for his trousers.

Trim and Jasper were conversing; Trim talking excitedly and Jasper murmuring obligingly, unable hardly to get a word in.

"How odd... you both arriving together..." he said, and Trim sprang up and dashed forward and gripped his arm. "Susan has had the baby..." he said, "... during the night!... a girl..."

"That is wonderful..." They gripped arms in a manner of comradeship, and then he glanced at Jasper. "He has told you, no doubt."

"Ah, yes..." Jasper said, with the tolerance of someone who had been forced to listen to the long-winded account of a long night in someone else's life.

"I wanted you to be the first to know... besides her father, of course, and my parents who obviously were aware..."

"Did Darnley deliver the infant?" Fairchild asked, seating himself opposite both men.

"No, no... he was on hand... with my father and me in the parlour the whole night... we played a few hands of cards to pass the time. His apprentice attended..."

"I see," said Fairchild.

"I was not allowed near... but Darnley went in occasionally."

"Of course you were not!" said Fairchild. "Delicacy has to be preserved."

"Ridiculous... I am the child's father and she is my wife."

He laughed. "Quite... but this is England, Timothy!"

Jasper was deliberating, his dark eyes serious. "Is apprentice the right word for the fellow?" he asked casually.

They stared at him and then rewound the conversation in their heads. "Probably not!" agreed Fairchild. "Junior physician is perhaps the term."

Trim ignored these corrections. "My mother was with her... and my youngest sister some of the time."

They watched Trim for a few moments as he rubbed his eyes and shook his head at the marvel of it, and they both thought of what it might be like to be new fathers, should the day come. "I am overjoyed." Trim said sheepishly, his modest nature to the fore. "Because, in truth, I was hoping for a daughter..."

"You did not tell me." Fairchild said and rang for Peggy to bring him an extra cup for coffee.

"No, no... one tends not to say that kind of thing, in case it upsets the..." he did not finish the sentence, and Jasper finished it for him. "The mother of the infant, if things are contrary."

"Yes, just so..." agreed Trim happily. "You will be godfather, so you must be among the first to know!"

"Wonderful..." concurred his friend in an ambiguous tone and Jasper laughed heartily.

"Where is Melissa?" Trim was animated again.

"She is still upstairs!"

Jasper replaced his cup saucer on the table and stood. "I sense a disturbance to your private devotions! So we should not linger."

"Not at all." lied Fairchild and Jasper erupted into more of his heartiest laughter. "Your unusually dishevelled appearance somehow gives it away..."

He flushed a little. "Well, 'tis quite early Saturday morning..." He stared at his feet while Jasper took out an envelope and handed it to him and said. "And also the reason I am here first thing."

"What is it?"

"A banker's draft."

He ripped open the envelope and pulled out the draft – it was for the amount Richard had embezzled. His jaw dropped. "But this is... how did you...? I did not think you could do it... get it back, I mean."

"*Oh ye of little faith!*" declared Jasper.

"But how did you obtain it?" He gazed at the draft as if it might ignite or dissolve in his hand.

"Ways and means..." Jasper said off-handedly, "a little coercion, a little pressure richly due..."

"I do not know what to say..."

"Perhaps begin with gratitude..." said Trimingham in an avuncular manner, sobering somewhat with this important information.

"Yes... yes... forgive me, Jasper... we are indebted to you... shall you stay to see Melissa..."

"If she is not too long in dressing." agreed Jasper and winked at Trimingham.

"I, however, must be away..." Trim stood. "I have a short list of people I must call on to give the news... would you ask Melissa to come and see us?... Susan has requested she visit."

"Of course... I shall bring her myself tomorrow... Susan will need to rest today, surely?... to sleep!"

Trim clapped his hand to his forehead. "Yes, indeed... you are quite right... she had very little sleep, of course!"

"Sleep is of the essence now. I do believe it will be in short supply for a while."

Trim nodded eagerly, as if this were something to look forward to. "Though my mother and sister have offered unlimited help..." He stared ahead unseeingly, envisioning the uncharted waters of parenthood, "but knowing Susan, she will want to do most of the nursing herself... she will not accept a nursemaid at this juncture."

"Naturally, this is Susan we are talking of." Fairchild laughed. "It is a wonder she did not insist on giving birth beneath a bush of some kind in the woods... just to be near certain roots or herbs or whatever!"

Trimingham laughed appreciatively and thought of the woman he loved who was now the mother of his child, and then he addressed Jasper. "We are living still at my family home... for the time being."

"Indeed... quite expedient under the circumstances..." Jasper said politely.

Fairchild was still examining the draft to be sure it was genuine. He had lost much to unscrupulous people in the past.

"Once more, my heartiest felicitations to you and your good lady..." Jasper was saying to Trim. "May this be the first of many."

"No... only three at most..." Trim said. "That is what we have agreed upon."

Jasper grinned. "*Many a slip twixt cup and mouth...*" he quoted jovially and Trim was overset by modesty and left the room with haste.

"Breakfast, I think..." Fairchild said. "Jasper, do you join us?"

"Perhaps just a slice of toast... and more coffee..." agreed Jasper who suddenly could spare more time than the allotted fifteen minutes.

* * *

In the dining room, they were talking of the returned money and Melissa was informed as she sat down, lost for words. She examined the banker's draft and then looked at Jasper. "How did you—"

He cut her off. "Lissy, do not worry... It is of no consequence. But I would take it to the bank without delay... lest it disappear again."

"Is it likely to?" she said.

"Hopefully not, but one never knows with these kind of people."

"We have hours before the bank closes." She said and her husband frowned. "No, we will go before noon... so hurry and finish eating."

She extended her hand and took Jasper's hand and he held it for a few moments. "Thank you, from the bottom of my heart." she told him.

"Nothing short of my duty, dearest cousin..." returned Jasper and then looked at her with his black brows knitted and his dark eyes intense. "But Melissa, take care in future where you leave your signature... you have little idea perhaps how entitled you are as a member of the family and its business..."

"I have told her this..." said her husband, "and to give her signature only to the dressmaker and the milliner and the trades people and so on... and only then when strictly necessary... otherwise to use cash."

"Yes... yes... yes." she intoned, sick of hearing this cautionary lecture. "It was you who took the sketch... and so I felt obliged to her."

"The sketch was not hers in the first place... she was owed nothing." he said testily.

"That is what people like Caroline Wentworth do..." Jasper helped himself to the rhubarb marmalade made by Honoria. "They prevail on other peoples' integrity and honesty. She is a seasoned fraudster..."

"Did she give up the money willingly?" Melissa enquired while thinking how to get a message to Melanie about the aborted mission which was unnecessary now.

Jasper savoured the taste of the marmalade "Of course not... I doubt she even knows about it... that is not her department."

*They did not employ a footman at Back Lane House and there was no one to instruct to take a note. Melanie would have to be left wondering for now.*

Then Peggy entered with a small basket, lined with felt and lidded, containing freshly boiled eggs, and the conversation was paused to let her deposit them.

"So now you will be able to look for a new house..." continued Jasper, "and employ more servants... so that visitors do not have to stand on the draughty porch for ten minutes until the door is opened."

She looked at her cousin and then at her husband. "Such hardship..." she intoned and helped herself to one of the eggs and cracked the top with her spoon, and thought of the advantage of having at least one footman to deliver letters at times like this.

"I believe your father knows of a place quite near the one you lost..." Jasper said.

"Did he tell you this?" she asked.

He hesitated, deciding whether to have more toast just to entitle him to more of Honoria's delicious marmalade. *He may as well sample her culinary delights as a compensation for losing her favours.* "No... he asked Eddy to look at it architecturally first... Damien overheard him... and could not resist gossiping."

She made a face and then said to her husband. "Take it with a pinch of salt then..."

"Yes, but Damien usually discloses the general drift even if the details are missing..." said Jasper.

She chirruped with laughter and Jasper took another slice of toast and prepared to wax comical. "He purposely did not grow as tall as the rest of us so he may move comfortably beneath everyone's elbows at gatherings and be overlooked as he collects information..."

This was music to her ears and she pushed the chair a little from the table and bent forward, unable to take in breath for giggling. "Stop it, Jaz! I will pass out."

"A noxious little windbag is cousin Damien..." Jasper swept his gaze to Fairchild to include him in the humorous family critique. "I recall when we were fifteen or so... my brother Justin and my cousins Lionel and Edmund and myself were all swatting for the end of term exams in the study at home one day... and Damien was over with grandmother who was left in charge..." Jasper paused and they watched him expectantly. "It was summer and beautiful weather so we climbed from the window and raced off to the river to swim for an hour... and Damien, who was considerably younger of course, told grandmama where we had gone... and not content with that, at the first opportunity he then told my mother when she arrived back."

Melissa gasped at the treachery, even though it was not surprising.

"The puffed up little bellwether does not know when to stop..."

"And what happened?" she enquired, not having heard this story previously.

"There was an unholy stink, naturally. So at High Lawns a few days later Justin and Eddy and I chased him all over the place... Eddy and Justin backed him eventually into the walled part of the orchard and I gave him a damned good hiding... but it still did not cure him." Jasper resumed his marmalade fest, the toast sagging beneath the mountain of rhubarb preserve. Her husband was grinning a little but with caution; he disliked name calling of this kind, especially within the family. It was not within his moral compass to find acceptable.

"Anthony likes him," she said, "So he may not endorse your humour."

"I neither like him nor dislike him..." he offered. "I am obliged to associate with him. He is harmless enough... if somewhat trying at times."

"He is not always harmless..." she amended. "He causes much trouble at times..."

"I would concur with that..." said her cousin. "In fact, not a year after the swimming escapade he attempted more unrest with the brother of a girl I was meeting with in secret!"

"And what happened then..."

Jasper looked vaguely at the wall. "Unfortunately nothing on that occasion... he obviously disappeared down a foxhole before I could lay hands on him..."

This was hilarious and she fell forward into her skirt to giggle.

Fairchild thought of his own boyhood and Lottie, and then remembered. "Oh yes, I am remiss... Trim was here to say that Susan has been delivered of the infant... a little girl... both are well."

"What? You are just now telling me?" She demanded, raising her head again.

He selected an egg from the basket. "... I have said we will go over to see them tomorrow... so we should buy something as a gift for the child... after the bank."

"We are to be the godparents!" she informed Jasper who had become serious once more, and was nodding politely in the same way he had to Trimingham's garrulous report of the previous night, and Fairchild peeled the shell from the egg. "The money returns in the nick of time, Jasper... I am godfather to so many it may well bankrupt me... Imagine if all the parents meet with demise in the space of two years!"

Melissa gaped at this statement but then recognised the satire. "How you do exaggerate!" she said lightly. "There can be no more than three, surely?"

"Five actually!" he amended

"Five?... Good God!... and you not even a father yourself yet." Jasper remarked and looked at Melissa.

"Please do not begin on the question of when we may have children, Jasper... 'Tis very tedious." she said.

"I would not dream of it!... who am I to talk? I am not even wed..." He was buttering more toast and heaping on more marmalade.

"And do not begin on the outlining of that campaign either..." she said gaily. "'Tis almost as wearying."

The rhubarb marmalade was nearly all gone and she tutted as she peered into the empty pot and raised her brows at Jasper.

"What?" he said in feigned innocence. "I have ridden on horseback in quite a high wind to get here... I need something with which to fortify myself."

But then this was a small price to pay for the return of the money, she put back her head and laughed.

"It will be Greg and Millie next, I suppose," offered Jasper, "tying the knot!"

"Yes, they are engaged... but say they will wait a while." she said.

"Unless she becomes expectant..." remarked her cousin.

Melissa gaped. "What, Millicent?"

"Indeed... unless they are careful..." Jasper scraped the marmalade pot clean. "Trust me... when he is not tinkling on the piano, he is tinkling on Millicent..."

She put the napkin to her mouth and began giggling again. Jasper had now swapped his business head for that of entertaining raconteur. He was well known for both. The comedy was thick in the air, like pollen. "Betimes, where is the delightful Honoria? Not avoiding me is she? I should like to compliment her on her marmalade..."

"She is with Isaac... he's home now." Fairchild told him.

Jasper hoisted the overloaded toast. "Is he here at the moment?"

"No, no, he is out with her." Melissa said.

"That's as well... I may have had to kill him!"

This amused her more and the giggling surfaced once more; the heady mix of Trim's news and the return of the money and Jasper's badinage, all at ten fifteen a.m.

"They have gone to Rupert's church..." her husband said and Jasper faked astonishment. "God-bothering too!... Is there no limit to the fellow's virtues?"

"They wish him to marry them in a few months."

"Of course! And I expect Rupert will be glad of the extra business..." Jasper rejoined with a harrowed face.

About to become serious, she sighed extravagantly and picked up her coffee – until Jasper offered more of his comedy genius. "I am beyond mortified!... you must forgive me if I need time to recover..." he looked anything but mortified but did not let it deter him. "Here am I, worshipping at her feet and adoring her... whereas he most likely wants her only for her marmalade... I may have to resort to Miss Van der whatnot from your office, Tony!"

She came up for air once more and stared at her spouse. "He has met her?"

"Unfortunately, yes... she winked at him."

"I would not go that way, Jasper." She cautioned. "She is an utter trollope."

"Not completely." defended Fairchild. "Only if she's been drinking..."

"He defends her because she works for him... and lusts after him."

"Ridiculous..." he said, "we have no time for all that..."

"So you say..." She scooped the remains of the egg onto the spoon. "But I have heard it from Susan who has it from Trim..."

"Really?" said Jasper with some greater interest. "She is a lustful trollope then?..." He made a statement in French to Fairchild who replied in the same tongue.

"And do not do that!" she cried, "'Tis so rude."

"What?" said Jasper.

"Speaking French when you are with someone who cannot."

Fairchild reacted. "You can speak French... I taught you, myself if, you recall."

Now the heady mix of irritation and humour vied within her for supremacy. "Well, you attempted to, I admit... but without much success, before you become full of your own importance."

He turned to Jasper. "You see the kind of scorn and contempt to which I was treated for my best efforts... and they wonder why I became a tyrant..."

Jasper raised his brows and left the silence, and she sprang to her feet and said. "So you admit it at last!... for the first time ever."

"I admit nothing..." he said.

"Too late... you just said it... *they wonder why I became a tyrant!'...* clear as day..."

"You perhaps misheard." he retorted off-handedly.

"I did not..." she leaned her hands on the table as she stood and glared. "You heard it, did you not Jasper? that admission of tyranny?"

Jasper had finished the last of the marmalade and dabbed his lips with the napkin. "My dear girl, I heard very little... your sudden flight into the air like a large raptor startled all memory from me..."

"You are lying too..." She seized her napkin and folded it lengthways and leaned forwards and flicked them both in turn around the head with it. Fairchild snatched it from her. "Melissa, you go too far in your present state of euphoria, no doubt resulting from all the good news!... we are at breakfast with a guest."

"Not far enough!... until you admit what you just said..."

"Please..." Jasper intervened. "Have the goodness to wait until I have departed before you begin on your infamous game..."

They spoke simultaneously.

*"Which game?" she said.*

*"There is no game." he said.*

And they subsided into their seats at the same time.

"I have to inform Melanie of this admission, you know." she told him, her decorum settling back with the rustle of her dress.

"I am quite afraid." His grin was swiftly controlling his entire face.

Jasper held his coffee cup aloft. "What a very colourful marriage you have."

"One way to describe it..." Fairchild said.

"Does Melanie join you in some sort of menage-a-trois?" Her cousin asked in throw away manner.

"Of course not," said Melissa. "Do not be vulgar."

"God forbid!" said Fairchild.

"Just with you bringing her into this conversation, I thought..."

"'Tis too long a back story and too tedious..." said Fairchild.

"I have been apprised of the synopsis..." Jasper replied airily.

"By whom?" she snapped. "No, don't tell me!... Damien!..."

"No, Geraldine!"

She scoffed roundly and fought her annoyance. "She is almost his equal where gossiping is concerned. She knows nothing... she too merely speculates then makes things up."

Husband and wife exchanged glances.

"Do not look at me..." he said. "'Tis not me who hurls tea around with historical allegations... 'Tis your best friend."

"Allegations you have just confirmed!... your life will never be the same, Anthony Frances Fairchild." Her satisfaction was undeniable.

Jasper watched them and saw the intense shroud of something unfathomable descend to unite them. It was all encompassing and left others in the dark. He cleared his throat and spoke into the void as a way of breaking the spell. "So about Miss Van der whatnot... do you suppose she is a soak?.. Or does she simply not understand the full effects of strong drink?"

"She is a slut and a trollope." confirmed Melissa. "Do not hear otherwise..."

"Well, Lissy..."  he replied cheerfully, "in truth, I admit to enjoying a nice slut or trollope now and then!"

Her high spirits returned and she laughed. "Besides, she lives under the protection of Jermain Ravond..." said Melissa cheerfully. "She is his muse and model..."

"This becomes more appealing..." Jasper scratched his forehead and dredged his memory. "Yes, I believe he played cards with my brother a few weeks ago and noticed Justin cheating... as usual. There was a fracas of some length. That is his pseudonym, of course... the artist, I mean... his actual name is Jeremy Stott... I saw it on the note he left to cover his losses..."

"He should use his real name... not the other pretentious appellation..." Fairchild commented.

"No, no..." she countered. "The pseudonym is better for his work. You have not enough imagination."

"And perhaps you have too much..." he said.

They glared at each other and the shroud of dark intimacy descended again. Jasper contemplated them for a few moments and then attempted to dispel it and bring attention back to himself. "Although, I may reconsider..." he said in lachrymose tone. "Or I may become helplessly besotted and she will up and marry the Stott fellow at the last minute... and I shall be left sampling only her marmalade..."

She made a face at him while her husband laughed and Jasper reverted to French and addressed another ribald remark to him.

"You are doing it again..." She leaned over to pick up Jasper's napkin this time, but he was too quick for her and grabbed it. She reached too far and lost her balance and slipped off the chair to the floor and rolled onto her side and continued giggling almost soundlessly.

"For God's Sake..." Fairchild told him." Look what you have caused... we shall not be at the bank in less than three hours now."

Jasper shrugged, pleased with himself. He took out his cigars, the same brand as her husband used. "We may as well smoke then, Tony."

"I expect we may..." he agreed and went to the fireplace for the matches.

And the mood was almost festive.

# END

www.ingramcontent.com/pod-product-compliance
Lightning Source LLC
Chambersburg PA
CBHW071233190726
48292CB00007B/2271